THE MIGHTY STORM

THE MIGHTY STORM

Samantha Towle

Text copyright © 2013 Samantha Towle

Published by Montlake Romance

PO Box 400818
Las Vegas, NV 89140

ISBN-13: 9781477805022
ISBN-10: 1477805028
Library of Congress Conrtol Number: 2012956357

This one is for Jenny Aspinall.
I couldn't have done it without you.
You rock like the stars.

CHAPTER ONE

I pick up my ringing phone just as I'm sitting down at my desk, taking a quick sip of my first coffee of the day.

"Trudy Bennett."

"Tru, it's Vicky...get your cute little butt in my office ASAP, I need a word."

"Okay, gimme five." I hang up the phone.

Vicky is my boss and the owner of the magazine I work for—*Etiquette*.

I'm a music journalist. *Etiquette* is...well, it's a fashion magazine.

So in essence, I'm a music journo that works for a fashion magazine.

It was the first and only writing job I could land after finishing university. I majored in popular music journalism. The two loves of my life always were, and still are, music and writing, in that order—so it was a no-brainer for me what I wanted to do when looking at university courses after I finished sixth form.

This job was meant to be a filler until I could get a writing job working for somewhere like *NME* or *Rolling Stone*, but six years later and I'm still here.

My job at *Etiquette* is to write up reviews on new album releases, talk about popular bands and singers, and also do the odd interview, that type of thing.

I'm a good writer and even better at music. I grew up with music, as my dad is a musician. He fed me it from the day I was born.

It's not my ideal job, working at a fashion mag, but I like Vicky a lot. We've become really good friends. At first, when I started here, I was just a column writer, but Vicky wanted me to keep working here, and, with that and my constant nagging, she let me take my column and make it a full feature page.

That was a happy day for me.

It's been running for a year now and has been well accepted by the readers.

The only downside of my job is that I have to keep the music mainstream, as that's what the readers of *Etiquette* are into.

I'm not so much into girlie music, well, except for Adele, I love her, but basically I'm more a rock, indie kind of girl. And all I want to talk about in my articles are rock bands, metal, indie, and brand-new bands; bands no one knows about that I've come across in clubs. Bands that deserve a shot at the big time.

The good thing, recently, is a lot of the major rock bands have mainstreamed a little from their early stuff, to pull them into the Top 40, and now the gals who read *Etiquette* are listening to them, so it gives me the opportunity to talk about these bands. But still, it's mainstream, and I want to talk a little off the beaten track.

So for now, I'm resigned to writing about easy listening.

But you never know, maybe one day.

I switch on my Mac; take another gulp of coffee, burning my tongue in the process; and set off for the short walk through the open-plan office, heading towards Vicky's office.

Her door is already open when I reach her office, and she's on the phone.

With a huge, white toothy smile, she indicates for me to come in. I sit down in the chair across from her desk.

Vicky is stunning. I would say she's midforties—although I've never been able to get her to confirm her actual age—and believe me, I've tried. But whatever her age is, she looks like she's in her thirties, and I can only hope I look as good as she does when I'm her age.

Vicky has blonde shoulder-length hair, trimmed neatly into a bob. A fantastic figure, and I'm not entirely sure everything on her is real. But I love her. She is no-nonsense. Tons of fun. And an amazing businesswoman and writer.

She used to be a journalist for a magazine when she first started out. Then she met her husband. He was a wealthy, older businessman. Very old school and didn't believe in women working—they were to stay at home with the children. Vicky loved him, so she gave up her career for him.

They married; then Vicky discovered she couldn't have children. They didn't have the happiest of marriages after that.

She was the trophy wife. He was the habitual cheater.

He died ten years ago of a heart attack, leaving Vicky a very rich woman. His business is still going; I don't know much about it, something to do with acquisitions, I think. I'm not sure, and I don't think Vicky is either. It has a board and a CEO that run it, so when he died, Vicky decided to stay well out of it, and instead took a chunk of the money he'd left her and went back to her first love, magazines, and that's when she started up *Etiquette*.

It's a small, low-priced magazine, a monthly, with a readership of 500k.

The magazine just about breaks even. Vicky doesn't make much on the magazine; she does it for the love of it and to keep busy.

She's determined to make it a success, and because she took a chance on me and gave me a job when no one else would, and also because I love her to bits, I'm determined to help her see that dream come true.

She's a brilliant, vibrant woman who was dealt a shit hand in life, and she deserves happiness. This magazine succeeding will make her happy.

And you never know, one day, if the magazine grows huge, she might let me spin off and create an insert music magazine.

Okay, well, I can dream, can't I?

Finishing off her call, she hangs up and grins at me, big hazel eyes alive, and I know straightaway she's up to something.

"What?" I ask, suspicious.

"Jake Wethers," she says, practically humming his name.

My heart sinks. I let out a light sigh.

Jake Wethers, one of the biggest rock stars in the world, lead singer of the hugely successful rock band, the Mighty Storm.

Who also, once upon a time, used to be my best friend.

We lived next door to each other growing up. We went to school together, did everything together, until he moved to America with his family when we were fourteen.

He was also the absolute love of my life, not that he ever knew that, of course, and I was devastated when he left.

I don't have a single childhood memory that doesn't have Jake in it.

When he left with his family to move thousands of miles away, we vowed to stay in contact. But that was twelve years ago, when there was no Internet or mobile phones for kids. Those were things solely reserved for adults, usually the ones with more money than Jake's family or mine had.

We wrote, had the odd phone call, then the calls from him stopped, and the letters dwindled until they became nonexistent.

I wrote to him for a while, but he never wrote back, so I gave up.

My heart broke for a long time over Jake Wethers. Well, if I'm being honest, I don't think it actually ever really healed.

And I didn't see or hear from Jake again. Well, until six years ago…

I was two years in at university, sharing a flat with my still, to this day, best friend Simone, and she was watching a Saturday music show that used to be on back then. I was nursing a hangover, like most days, and was coming back into the living room from the kitchen, with a coffee in hand, and there he was, Jake, on the TV, staring back at me.

He'd grown, obviously, looked a little different, yet exactly the same.

Covering my mouth with both my hands, I dropped my cup to the floor, coffee everywhere, but I didn't care. I stood there transfixed, watching him singing with his band.

I'd heard about this new fast-rising band, the Mighty Storm. I'd even heard their songs on the radio, but I'd never seen any pictures of the band members until that point.

Simone was obviously interested to know why I'd just dressed our living room in coffee, so I sat down and told her my history with Jake. Then we both immediately went to my room to Google him on my computer.

It made sense that Jake became a musician. He loved music as much as I did.

I knew he could hold a note vocally, but I never realised just how great a singer he actually was.

I've watched Jake's career over the years. Watched him rise to stratospheric levels.

And I've also watched his lows.

I still care for him, of course; he was my best friend for a huge portion of my life. We shared everything.

But I'm not in love with him anymore. That ended years ago. And really, what do you know about love when you're a teenager anyway?

One thing I don't do is tell people I knew Jake growing up.

I'm a private person generally, and I feel like telling people I knew him well would just sound a lot like bragging. And if my friends and colleagues knew I used to be so close to him, they'd want details, and there are things from Jake's past that I know he wouldn't want shared, so, for fear of a slipup, I pretend like I never knew him and that I'm just another TMS fan.

Outside of that, and I know I'm going to sound silly when I say this...but talking about Jake would be like sharing him.

The world has him now, and I don't want to share the Jake I had with anyone, because now, well...from what I see and read in the news, Jake's not so much like the Jake I knew back then anymore.

He's now the epitome of the rock star he is meant to be.

The only person I've ever told about Jake is Simone, and, of course, my mum and dad knew Jake too. Oh and…well, I also told Vicky, but that was in a complete, drunken error.

Last year I was ridiculously drunk at our work Christmas party, and for some unknown, alcohol-given reason, I made the fatal error of telling Vicky that I used to know Jake.

And when I say fatal, it's not because she has told anyone about my connection to him. Oh no, it's because ever since she found out that we were former buddies, she has been on my back for me to get in touch with him to do an exclusive interview for the magazine.

What Vicky fails to grasp is that I'm no longer friends with Jake, and haven't been for twelve years. It's not like I can just call him up to ask him for an interview.

She thinks I can. She thinks that Jake would be made up to hear from me. I know she's only saying that to try and urge me to get in touch.

But I won't ever get in touch with Jake. I think if he did want to see me again, then he would have been in touch himself by now.

Honestly, I think he's forgotten all about me. He's moved on to bigger and better things, and me rocking back up in his life, asking for an interview, would just be plain awkward and a lot weird, for him as well as me.

I've done my best trying to explain this to Vicky, but it's not sticking, so I'm now at the stage of dodging her whenever his name comes up.

"Earth to Tru, have you listened to a word I've just been saying?" Vicky clicks her fingers, instantly bringing my focus back to her, and I realise I'd zoned out.

My face flushes. "Um…no, sorry." I bite my bottom lip. "It's just the whole Jake thing…I know you want me to get in touch but I just can't—"

She holds up a perfectly manicured finger, halting my words.

"Well, if you'd been listening to me, my darling, you would have heard that I don't need your help getting an interview with Jake Wethers after all."

She's full-on grinning, like a kid who thinks they've just seen the real Santa Claus in Harrods.

Damn me and my zone out.

I sit up a little straighter in my seat. "Y-you got an interview with Jake?"

She nods proudly.

"How?" I breathe out, dumbstruck.

Jake's well known for not doing interviews. Another of the reasons Vicky was so desperate for me to try and grab one with him. An exclusive.

Jake's intensely private. He talks about his music when he has to for PR, of course. But he never talks about himself outside of that.

Which is funny, considering how he lives his life— very publicly in many ways—the drinking, the drugs…the women.

Vicky shifts uncomfortably in her seat and grimaces slightly. "Well, it doesn't matter how I got it—just that I did, and you're going to do the interview."

"What!" I almost reel backwards off my chair.

"Don't look so surprised. You're my best writer, Tru, and well…you're my only music writer. And you have this huge connection with Jake. You grew up together, for crying

8

out loud! He'll open up to you more than he would anyone else. You could land us an exclusive here."

"Oh no." I'm shaking my head rapidly. "I don't think this is a good idea."

I might be a journo, but I do have this thing called morals. I'm not going to spread Jake's guts all over the magazine in the name of news.

"It's an excellent idea, and we need this, Tru." Her normally smooth features furrow. "Sales are rubbish at the moment, and this exclusive with Jake Wethers will give us the boost we've been waiting for."

Ugh. She's right. It will be good for the magazine. No, scrap that, it will be amazing for the magazine.

All I need to do is get a great interview from Jake and keep my morals at the same time.

Holy fuck! Is this really happening? Am I really going to see Jake again after all this time?

A frisson of nervous energy passes through me.

He probably won't even remember me. It's been twelve years.

"Okay. I'm in."

"That's my girl." Vicky smiles, clapping her hands together.

"When and where?"

"Tomorrow, ten a.m., at the Dorchester."

"Tomorrow?" I feel another, much larger, shot of nerves rush through my blood.

"He's only here in the UK for a few days. This is the only window we've got."

"Okay…should I book Jim to go with me?" Jim is our photographer.

She shakes her head. "No pictures. We're to use old press photos. You're going in solo, gorgeous."

Crap. I was hoping for the backup.

I swallow down the nerves ramming up my throat and nod. "Okay."

"Don't look so nervous; you'll do great, Tru. Oh, and here's a review copy of the new album"—she picks up a CD case from her desk and peers down at it, reading—"*Creed...* ahh," she murmurs knowingly. "Anyway, have a listen before the interview, and it's not released yet, so remember..."

"Guard it with my life." I take the CD from her and start to walk away.

"I bet he'll be delighted to see you," she sings from behind me.

I look at her over my shoulder. Pulling a face at her, I stick out my tongue.

She laughs. "Well, maybe not with a face like that, he won't."

I grin, and then with my new Mighty Storm CD, and the heavy weight of the interview on my shoulders, I amble out of her office.

I slump down in my chair at my desk and look at the CD in my hand.

Okay, so tomorrow at 10:00 a.m., I'm going to see Jake for the first time in twelve years.

Jake Wethers, the man who used to be the boy I loved.

Jake Wethers, the biggest rock star and most wanted man in the world, tomorrow will be sitting before me giving me an interview, and I haven't got a bloody clue what I'm going to ask him.

I put Jake's album into the disc holder in my Mac, plug my headphones in, and start to listen as the music flows into my ears.

I pull the insert booklet out and start to read through the track listings. Then I flick to the back page to read the dedications.

There's one person I know, without doubt, who this album is dedicated to.

The person who cowrote the album, and who it's named after—Jonny Creed.

Jonny was Jake's best friend, the lead guitarist in TMS, and Jake's business partner, and he died in a car accident a little over a year ago.

Jonny's car crashed through a barrier then rolled down into a steep ravine not far from where he lived in LA.

I saw the pictures in the news the day after it happened. His car was totaled.

He never stood a chance.

There were no other cars involved in the accident, and after the autopsy was done, it was revealed that Jonny was way over the legal alcohol limit, and the level of drugs in his system was enough to take down a small horse, or so it had been reported.

The accident happened late at night, and the police said Jonny could have been swerving to avoid an animal in the road, or maybe, because of the alcohol and drugs, he could have fallen asleep at the wheel, though there's no evidence to prove either to be the case.

The press have speculated that it was a suicide. But the band's spokespeople have vehemently denied it, and there was no evidence to show that Jonny was depressed in any way at all.

His life was good. He was at the top of his game. He had everything to live for.

The band took his death badly. Jake even more so. And his pain was splashed all over the pages of the press for the world to see.

Jake upped his drinking and his drug use, and then fell in the worst possible way when onstage in Japan eight months after Jonny's death.

It was the band's first show since Jonny's death. Jake was wrecked. He could barely talk, let alone sing. When the crowd got antsy at the poor show, he berated them. When they heckled, he unbuttoned his jeans and urinated on the stage.

He was arrested for public indecency.

I saw the clips of the show after it happened. It burned my heart to watch.

He was so far from the Jake I had seen over the years in the press, and even further from the Jake I remembered and once loved.

He was lost to grief, trying to bury it with drugs and drink. And for that one moment he lost control.

It could have ruined his career.

Luckily for him it didn't. If anything, it only catapulted his status higher and the world's obsession with him further.

He is the ultimate bad boy of rock.

Jake was fined for his behaviour in Japan and thrown out of the country. Soon afterwards he went into rehab.

He spent four months in rehab and has been out for the last four weeks, and he's still maintaining a low profile.

But I know that's soon to change, hence the interview, as the band has the album, which Jake and Jonny wrote together, to release and promote.

For a while there was a worry amongst the fans that the band wouldn't go on when Jonny died, but from the press release that TMS put out a month ago, shortly after Jake got out of rehab, they said the band was Jonny's life and love, and that this album, his last and now his legacy, was his best to date. And also that if they didn't put out the album, Jonny would more than likely come back to kick their asses for quitting now.

And this is not me being cynical, I just understand the music business, and well…basically the band is what keeps the music label riding high, and you see Jake owns the label that TMS is signed to; if it's possible to sign the band you are in.

But basically, if the label falls because the band quits, then that's an awful lot of people out of work.

When TMS first started out they were signed to a small label, Rally Records, but as the band rapidly grew, becoming one of the fastest growing bands ever and breaking sales records worldwide, basically becoming a phenomenon, Jake grew too. And he and the guys soon outgrew the small label they were signed to.

It's well documented that Jake is a shrewd businessman for his young age, and a serious professional, barring his drug and alcohol addiction and the pissing-on-the-stage incident. It's also widely reported that he is notoriously difficult to work with.

Apparently, he was once quoted in the press as saying, "When you're the best like I am, and give only the best, why is it so wrong to expect the same in return?"

That, I can believe. Because that reminds me a lot of the Jake I knew. Never one to mince his words or hold back from sharing his thoughts.

So when the band felt they were too big for Rally anymore, they walked away from the label, buying themselves out of their contract.

The figure has never been reported. But I'm in no doubt they could have afforded it.

Jake is rumoured to be worth around $300 million and growing. They say he earned $90 million in the last year alone.

So when they left Rally, Jake and Jonny set up TMS Records together, put the band on the label, and have been signing other growing bands and musicians to the label ever since.

Well, until Jonny died, that is.

When Jonny died, his half of the label naturally went to his parents. It was reported that Jake bought them out, as per their wishes, because it was too painful for them to have any involvement with the label after losing Jonny.

So now Jake runs TMS alone. And he had maintained running it even in rehab, from what I've heard in the business news.

But even with Jake's combination of music and business talent, it is sadly not what he spends most of his time in the news for.

Pissing on the stage in Japan aside, Jake was already tabloid fodder for his drinking, partying, and women. He works hard and plays harder. He goes through women like most people go through loose change. He has dated some of the most beautiful women in the world. Actresses, models, singers…the list goes on and on.

More recently, he's been quiet on that front, obviously from being in rehab. But now he's back, clean and ready to reclaim his place in the news and on the charts.

Maybe that's how Vicky got the interview.

Jake will be keen to show he's back and means business. If anything, surprisingly, Jake's and TMS's popularity has increased since the Japan incident.

The fans love his outlandish behaviour. Men want to be him, woman want to screw him…most wanting to be the one to tame the untameable Jake Wethers.

All Jake did that night in Japan was immortalise himself as the rock god people always believed him capable to be, putting him among the ranks at the young age of twenty-six.

It's crazy—he left the UK when he was fourteen, and then four years later, the band was signed, and they were hitting the big time when he was twenty.

Such a fast rise. And I wonder, if he can achieve what he has in only eight years in the music industry, just imagine what he'll be able to do in twenty.

But all this aside, ignoring all the gloss and the money, all I see when I look at pictures of him is my old best friend, Jake Wethers. The guy I used to have movie-and-pizza night with. The guy who helped me bury Fudge, my pet rabbit, when he died. And sat with me holding my hand all day while I cried over his loss.

It's just been so long and we've been so far apart, our lives taking such different paths…what will we even have to say to each other? Anything at all? Will he even remember me?

My phone starts to ring, breaking my reverie. I pull my earphones out and answer it.

"Trudy Bennett."

"Hey, gorgeous."

My heart melts a little. It's my very lovely, very gorgeous, blond, blued-eyed, smart boyfriend, Will.

I've been with Will for two years. I first met him at university, but nothing ever happened between us, then after I graduated, I didn't see him again until two years ago when I bumped into him on a night out with Simone. We've been together ever since.

"Hey, yourself."

"We still on for dinner tonight?"

"We sure are." I smile.

"Wonderful, so I'll pick you up at your place at seven."

"See you then."

I end the call with Will and stare at my screen. I open Google and search for pictures of Jake.

I click on one, enlarging it on my screen. He's bare-chested, and he looks so incredibly beautiful.

Jake is lean but muscular, defined, with lovely slim hips. His hair is black, shaved close around the sides, longer on the top; he wears it high and messy. His hairstyle, on anyone else, would probably look silly, but not on him. On him it looks perfect. And in contrast to his black hair, his eyes are blue. Startlingly so, just like the colour of the ocean.

He's always had this cute little smattering of freckles over his nose ever since I can remember, but now, they somehow make his gorgeous bad-boy edge even more apparent.

Jake is also covered in tattoos. He's almost as famous for his tattoos as he is for his music and bad-boy antics.

Jake has a full tattoo sleeve on his right arm. Tattoos on his left forearm and "TMS" in script on its inner, but his most distinctive tattoo, for me anyway, is the one on his chest. It spans right across, sitting just below his collarbone, and says…

I wear my scars, they don't wear me

Sometimes I wonder just how true that statement is.

Looking back, I don't know at exactly what point I knew I was in love with Jake. I guess I just always was.

My mum used to say when we were toddlers I followed him around like a puppy dog.

Jake and I were best friends—as close as you could get. And I know it was all he would have, and ever did, see me as. He was always way out of my league.

I guess the sad thing for me, or maybe in hindsight the best thing, was just as I was realising the depth of my feelings for Jake, he was gone.

One thing I do find amusing is knowing how Jake is with women nowadays, basically a slut; when he was younger, he was never interested in girls.

Back then, we were all about the music. I guess it was what bound us together. Well that and the other stuff. The bad stuff in Jake's life.

Jake was always heavily into music, as was I, thanks to my dad.

My dad used to be a guitarist in a small-time rock band back in the eighties called the Rifts.

I was spoon-fed music. And my dad fed it to Jake too. I think to my dad, Jake was the son he never had.

My life was a little different than other kids'; when their parents were teaching them to sing "Twinkle, Twinkle Little Star," my dad was teaching me the lyrics to "(I Can't Get No) Satisfaction."

I was brought up listening to the likes of the Rolling Stones, Dire Straits, the Doors, Johnny Cash, Fleetwood Mac, and the Eagles, to name a few.

My mum tried to balance it out, bless her, but my dad lives and breathes music, and he is such a force in my life that she never stood a chance. I love my mum of course, but I absolutely adore my dad.

So because of my differences, and there were plenty of them, believe me, I never really fit in with any of the kids at school. And neither did Jake.

We were our own island, and when he left, I was left adrift for a long time.

My dad taught me how to play the piano. He tried with the guitar, but I could never get the hang of it. Jake, on the other hand, was an absolute natural on the guitar. My dad gave him his own first six-string when he was seven. He always did say Jake was a born musician, so I guess it's no surprise to him Jake is as successful as he is.

My dad is really proud of Jake's career.

He's always said I should get in touch with him, but I brushed it off, so there is no way I'm calling Dad to tell him I'm seeing Jake tomorrow. He'd probably try and come with me.

It's going to be surreal seeing Jake after all this time.

I click off the picture and open another, a close-up of his face. I stare at the picture, my eyes tracing the scar on his chin, the one that stretches along his jawline. It's not as noticeable as it used to be; maybe he covers it with makeup nowadays.

I know more about Jake than anyone. I know about a part of his past he's managed to keep hidden away from the rest of the world.

Then a thought sweeps my mind. Maybe he won't want to see me. Maybe he feels like he left behind the life he had here, and that's why he dropped contact with me.

Maybe me, home, reminds him of a time he'd rather forget.

Jake had a pretty rough time growing up, which led to his dad, Paul, going to prison when Jake was nine. Susie, Jake's mum, remarried a few years later to a lovely man called Dale. He was an architect brought over from the firm's office in New York to work on a long-term project in Manchester, where we lived. Then when Jake was fourteen, Dale was offered a promotion back in their New York office, and he took it.

Six weeks later Jake was gone. And my heart was left broken.

With a resigned sigh, I click off Google, and Jake disappears from my screen.

I force myself to open my Word document to get the questions compiled for tomorrow before I go to dinner with Will tonight.

I don't go to interviews unprepared. Especially if said interview is with my old best friend and onetime love of my life.

CHAPTER TWO

I arrive home from work, after somehow managing to compile a list of suitable questions for the interview with Jake tomorrow, drop my handbag on our coffee table, sling my jacket on the arm of the sofa, and kick off my shoes.

Simone is in the kitchen. We share a modest two-bedroom converted ground-floor flat in Camden, which we rent from Simone's cousin, who is a property developer. Our rent is really reasonable, as Marc and Simone are close. We would never have been able to afford it otherwise.

I wander in to the sound of the kettle boiling.

"Want one?" she asks, holding up the coffee jar.

"I'd love one, thanks."

I get the biscuits out of the cupboard, then Simone hands me my coffee, and with the biscuits under my arm, I follow her back through into our small living room.

I sit next to her on the sofa, putting the pack of biscuits between us.

"So how's your day been?" I ask as I munch on a biscuit.

This is my opener to telling her about Jake.

How's your day been, Simone? Mine, you ask? Well, tomorrow morning I'm going to be interviewing Jake Wethers.—Cue lots of screaming from Simone and maybe a little from me.

"Good." She beams, tucking her blonde hair behind her ear. "In fact, it was actually great." She turns to face me, tucking her legs under her bum. "We landed Penners."

"You did?"

"We did! And then afterwards Daniel took me into his office to tell me they're promoting me to senior ad exec!"

"Argghhh!" I scream.

"I know!" she screams back.

"That's brilliant, Simone! I'm so pleased for you! And mega proud!" I give her a one-armed hug, trying not to spill my coffee on her.

Simone works for an advertising agency. She's been working on landing Penners for ages, so I know how big a deal this is for her. She loves her job and, as proven, is very good at it.

With her lovely, swishy, long blonde hair, saucer-blue eyes, and skin the colour of cream, she's stunningly gorgeous and yet has no clue as to the actual effect she has on men.

She is sweet, kindhearted, and überwonderful, and I just love her to bits.

"We should celebrate tonight," I enthuse, getting more and more on board with the idea as I talk about it. "I was supposed to be having dinner with Will, but I'll cancel. We can get dressed up, have cocktails at Mandarin's…"

"No." She waves me off. "You can't cancel on Will."

"I can, and I will." I start to laugh at my own joke.

"You're a dork." She nudges my leg with her foot, chuckling.

"And you wouldn't have me any other way." I grin.

"That I wouldn't."

"Look, he'll understand. Will's a very understanding man." I take another bite of my biscuit and drop crumbs all over my T-shirt. I brush them off. "Tonight isn't a big deal, we were only having dinner. Seriously, you and I will go out and celebrate—I'll call Will now."

Honestly, I could do with the distraction of alcohol tonight because my nerves are fraught over the whole Jake interview thing, and Simone is my very best drinking partner.

"You're sure?"

"I'm definitely sure." I grin.

"Then you are definitely on."

Putting my coffee down, I lean over and retrieve my phone from my bag.

I have a text waiting from Vicky:

Good luck tomorrow, darling girl. Come straight to my office when you're done with Jake, I want ALL the details ;)

A winky smiley face. Christ, she's making it sound like a bloody date.

A white-hot thrill shoots through me at the very thought.

Jesus, Tru, sort yourself out.

A: Jake is way out of your league and always was.

B: It actually is just an interview.

And C: You have a very lovely boyfriend by the name of Will. The one whom you're about to cancel on.

I lean back on the sofa and speed dial Will's number.

"Hey, baby," he coos down the phone. "You okay?"

"I'm fine…I was just wondering, would you be majorly pissed if I cancelled tonight? It's just that Simone found out today she landed that big client she's been working on for months and also that they are promoting her to ad exec! So I thought I should take her out to celebrate."

"Of course I don't mind. Go out, enjoy yourself. And tell Simone congratulations from me. Rain check for tomorrow night, darling?"

"Definitely."

"Love you."

"You too."

I hang up, tossing my phone on the table.

"Get your best on," I say, grinning across at Simone. "Because tonight, you and I are celebrating."

I take a quick shower, washing my hair. I blow-dry it and run my straightener over, smoothing it out.

My hair is dark, thick, naturally curly…basically unruly. I wear it long to try and drag down the curl. I inherited my wild hair from my mum. She's Puerto Rican. My dad is English.

And no, before you ask, I don't look anything like J.Lo. I wish. Well, maybe except for my ass; it's about as big as hers.

My mum and dad met while he was touring America with the Rifts. My mum was in her first year of university. She'd moved to San Francisco from Puerto Rico to go to university. It was a big thing for her and her family; she was the first to ever go to university.

My dad was doing a gig at her university, and it was love at first sight. They spent the four days that my dad was in San Francisco together.

After my dad left to carry on with the tour, they kept in touch. Then six weeks later my mum found out she was pregnant with me.

She was only eighteen at the time, my dad twenty-three, with their whole future in front of them.

Dad went back to San Francisco, and they had a choice to make.

They said getting rid of me was never an option for either of them, so one of them had to give something up.

It was either my dad's music or my mum's university degree.

Mum gave up her degree.

She told my dad that being a mother was now the only important thing to her, as she'd lost her own mama when she was very young.

She broke the news to her dad, and he went ballistic. He gave her an ultimatum. It was either me and my dad, or her family back home.

She chose us.

He disowned her. Her whole family cut her off.

So she left San Francisco and her dream behind and went on tour with my dad and the band to follow his.

They tried to make it work on the road, but a baby on tour is just not possible, so eventually my dad made the decision to leave the band. They moved back to England, to Manchester where my dad is from, and got married.

For the first two years of my life, we all lived with my gran and granddad at their house, until Mum and Dad could afford their own house.

And that was when I moved next door to Jake.

Sometimes I feel like I ruined my dad's chances of hitting the big time and took away my mum's chance of a career. Neither of them has ever made me feel that way, not once, and I know they would be angry if they knew I even thought it. But mostly I feel that way about my dad. I just know how much he loves music and how hard it must have been for him to give it up.

I sweep some mascara over my lashes, dust on my gold eye shadow—it goes best with my brown eyes—and put some pale pink gloss onto my lips. Then I decide on my black maxi dress. I slip my feet into my silver heels and pick up my chain-mail handbag, putting my money and lip gloss in it.

I give myself one last look in the mirror. Not bad, Tru. Not perfect, but not bad.

I meet Simone out in the hall.

"You look gorgeous," I say. She's wearing a short, light blue puffball dress.

She wiggles her hips. "Right back at ya, sexy."

"And you call me a dork." I shake my head, laughing at her. "You got your keys?"

She dangles them in the air.

"Right, let's go then."

Simone locks up, and we walk out into the night air, heading for our local haunt, and most awesome cocktail bar, Mandarin's.

It's surprisingly packed for a Thursday night. We get a pitcher of margaritas and grab a free table.

I pour drinks into both our glasses.

Lifting mine, I say, "To my gorgeous and very smart friend, may you run the company one day."

Giggling, she clinks my glass.

I take a sip of my margarita. The alcohol runs down my throat, just the soother I needed.

"So how are things at the magazine?" Simone asks.

I snort out a laugh.

Okay, here goes…

"I'm, um…interviewing Jake Wethers tomorrow."

Her mouth opens in surprise, forming an O.

"Yep. Exactly." I nod.

Then she screams, attracting us quite a few stares.

"Sorry," she says, embarrassed.

I'm already laughing at her.

"Okay." She fans her face, calming down. "Any particular reason you're only just telling me this now?"

"Your promotion. We're celebrating that tonight. I didn't want talk of Jake overrunning it."

"Um…" She gives me a stupid look. "I'd rather be overrun by Jake Wethers than my promotion any day." She flashes her eyes at me.

I roll mine.

"So how did the interview come about? I'm guessing you didn't set it up."

"Vicky did."

"How in the hell did she manage to land an interview with Jake? Did she use your name to get it?"

Her words flitter through my mind.

I shake my head. "She wouldn't tell me how, but no, I don't think so. Using my name wouldn't have gotten her an interview with Jake anyway."

Simone pulls the face she always pulls whenever the subject of Jake comes up and I imply he has no care for me nowadays.

Not that I talk about him regularly or anything.

"I bet he's gonna be so made up to see you. Does he know it'll be you doing the interview?"

Does he?

"I'm not sure." I shrug. "His people will have my name, but I highly doubt he'll be bothered about who's interviewing him...and he won't be made up, Simone, we haven't seen each other in twelve years. He'll have forgotten all about me."

"Yeah, sure he will," she says, taking another drink of her cocktail. "Because you always forget your first love."

"I wasn't his first love!" I exclaim.

"You were the beautiful girl next door." She shrugs. "Of course you were his first love."

I shake my head despairingly at her.

"Come on," she says, smiling, topping up my drink, then her own. "Looks like we're celebrating two things tonight after all."

CHAPTER THREE

Oh God. What was I thinking getting drunk last night? Not my smartest plan. Not that I generally have many.

I was just so nervous at the thought of seeing Jake today. And the more I talked with Simone about it, the more I needed to drink.

When she pointed out that Jake probably won't be expecting me if rock stars aren't informed of who is interviewing them, and then when I walk in there it will be really uncomfortable and awkward…well, I kept on drinking more and more to dull the panic.

We practically drank Mandarin's dry. Sang Journey ("Don't Stop Believing") on karaoke like we were auditioning for a part on *Glee*, and then rolled home at 2:00 a.m.

I've had six hours' sleep; I'm seriously hungover and am currently travelling in on the Tube, feeling like I'm going to puke any second now.

One part hangover, two parts nerves.

When I finally get off the Tube at Hyde Park Corner, I grab a latte from Starbucks and guzzle it down, praying for it to clear my fuzzy head as I make my way on foot to the Dorchester, where Jake is staying.

The closer I get to the hotel, the more my nerves increase in intensity. My stomach keeps clenching in panic.

No, stop it, Tru. You are a serious journalist and it's just an interview. You've done loads of them. It doesn't matter who he is or that you used to love him.

Still do.

No, I don't.

Great, now I'm arguing with myself.

My phone beeps a text in my bag. It's from Simone; she'd already left for work this morning before I'd even rolled out of bed. I have no clue how she'd managed it.

I open up the text:

Breathe. It'll be fine. You'll be talking stories from when you were kids before you know it :) Call me when you're done. Love you x

I drop my phone back into my bag. Glancing up I see I've reached the Dorchester. I drop my empty cup in the nearest bin, take my thin jacket off, and shove it into my oversize bag.

I'm wearing my black skater skirt, loose-fitting grey T-shirt belted at the waist, and my favourite high-heeled, grey suede ankle boots. Not too flashy, not too casual, and I feel comfortable in them. They're me. And right now I just need to feel comfortable.

I stare up at the towering hotel.

Okay, I can do this.

I take a deep breath in and walk towards the door.

The concierge opens it for me, and I find myself in the plush foyer.

I instantly feel out of place. Maybe I should have dressed a little more conservatively.

But this is how I always dress for work and when I interview celebrities, but then I've never interviewed anyone as famous as Jake, and no one that I used to play kiss chase with when I was five, either.

Oh God. I am so totally shitting myself. And so totally out of my depth here.

I run my hands nervously down my skirt.

No, I can do this.

I lift my head high and walk towards the reception desk.

The woman on the reception desk is very attractive, in that groomed kind of way I'll never be able to achieve.

She looks up at me.

"Hi," I say, trying to exude confidence I am not feeling. "My name is Trudy Bennett. I'm here to see Jake Wethers."

She smiles. It's not real. "Of course you are. And I imagine he's expecting you too."

Ahh. Right, okay. She's being a bitch. She thinks I'm a groupie.

I reach into my bag and pull out my journalist ID badge and slap it on the counter.

"I'm a journalist. I work for *Etiquette* magazine, and I'm here to do an interview with Jake Wethers."

She glances at me again, eyes narrowed, then picks up the phone and dials a number.

"Good morning. There's a Trudy Bennett in reception to see Mr. Wethers…right…yes, of course."

She hangs up the phone.

"Please take the lift up to the roof suites, one of Mr. Wethers's staff will meet you up there."

I pick up my badge and walk away without thanking her. It kills my inbred manners to do so, but she was mean to me.

I just don't understand snotty bitches like that. Do I look like a groupie?

God, I hope not. I stop and glance at myself in the mirror on the way to the lifts.

My hair's frizzed up a bit with the humid morning air. I try to smooth it down with my hand as I run my eyes down myself in the mirror.

Well, I don't think I look like a groupie. I look like an überprofessional journalist, in my…um…skater skirt, which is actually quite short—has it always been this short or has my ass got bigger?

Oh, holy crap. I look exactly like a groupie.

I don't remember looking like this in the mirror this morning. Obviously, I still had my "Tru looks awesome in anything" margarita goggles on.

Fan-fucking-tastic. I haven't seen Jake in twelve years and I'm going to see him now, looking like some groupie chick in a desperately short skirt.

Good thinking, Tru. Get hammered the night before seeing Jake, then dress like you're here for a party.

Resigned to my groupie fate, I stand at the lifts and press the button.

In a few minutes I'm going to be face-to-face with him. I can't stop my hands from trembling a little.

The lift pings open.

It's empty, so I wander in and with my still-trembling hand, press the button for the top floor to take me up to the roof suites.

I stand there, foot jigging on the spot, fingers knotted together, counting the floors up. My stomach's popping, the higher the number on the counter gets.

The lift reaches the top floor, stopping smoothly, and the doors part.

There on the other side is a scarily huge guy. Closely shaved hair, and at least six and a half feet tall and about the same wide.

"Ms. Bennett?" he says in the deepest voice I've ever heard.

"Yes." My voice comes out in a squeak.

He smiles at me. I relax a little.

"I'm Dave, the head of Jake's security team. Please follow me."

Jake has a security team?

Duh! Of course he does.

I follow closely behind Dave. There doesn't seem to be any people around. The rooms must be huge, as we've passed by only one door on this hallway, and we've been walking a little while. I wonder if Jake has the full floor hired out for his people to stay in.

We reach the door facing us at the end of the hall. Dave knocks once, loudly, on the door and moves aside, standing by the door, leaning against the wall, leaving me standing in front of it on my own.

I'm instantly self-conscious. And my face is burning up with worry and nerves.

What if Jake really doesn't remember me, and then it just becomes embarrassing and horrid.

Right here and now I'm making the decision not to say anything about our childhood or even acknowledge I remember him. I'll just wait for him to say something first, and then I'll act all cool and nonchalant about it. And if he doesn't say anything because he doesn't remember me, then it's cool, as I won't look like an idiot explaining who I am.

Or not.

Whatever.

I'm just not saying anything first.

The door opens, and standing before me is a sharply dressed man in a designer suit and the shiniest shoes I have ever seen. And holy hell he is beautiful.

"Ms. Bennett, hello, I'm Stuart, Jake's PA. It is so lovely to meet you." He gives me a warm smile and reaches out his hand to shake mine.

My cheeks flush red. Gorgeous and friendly. Personal assistants are usually not so nice to journalists, or this good-looking.

I take hold of his hand and give my most professional "I'm a serious journalist" handshake. I just hope he doesn't notice how badly my hand is shaking.

He gives me another smile, his eyes crinkling up at the corners.

Yep, he felt the shake and knows how nervous I am.

"Jake is in the living room, waiting for you. Please follow me," he says, gesturing.

I follow Stuart down the hall, the door magically closing behind me—Dave, I'm guessing.

Stuart rounds the corner, I follow behind, and then I find myself in a huge living room, and standing across the room from me is Jake.

My heart lurches out of my chest, jumps across the room, and whams straight into him.

I feel lost.

My eyes meet his, and I see it...the instant recognition.

He remembers me.

I feel absolute relief amongst my jittery nerves. Like little monkeys are swinging from trees across my nerve endings.

He's wearing fitted black jeans and a black V-neck T-shirt, and his hair is in its trademark style.

And he just looks so painstakingly beautiful.

Stuart moves aside, and I walk a little farther into the room on seriously wobbly legs. I wish I'd worn flats now.

Jake's eyes stay trained on mine. I think he looks a little stunned, and I'm not quite sure in this moment if that is a good thing or not.

"Tru?" His voice. It sounds the same, just deeper, manly, and more American than British now, of course, but still the same. I've heard him talk on the TV, but hearing him, here, now, talking to me—it's just Jake—the Jake I knew.

"Trudy Bennett?" he repeats. "My Trudy Bennett?"

His Trudy Bennett?

My heart goes haywire as it returns safely to my chest. Thank God he can't hear it.

He takes a step forward. "Shit, it really is you."

I nod. "Yes. It's really me." I sound like his echo, but I don't really know what else to say.

Before, I wasn't exactly sure why I was so terrified and nervous about seeing him. I just figured it was because of who he is now, his stature. But looking at him here, in person, I know why I was so scared.

I was afraid that seeing him again after all this time would cause my old feelings to resurface.

And seeing Jake, looking like this, I just know that I am so completely and totally fucked.

Because I'm now fourteen-year-old Trudy all over again.

CHAPTER FOUR

H oly shit," Jake exclaims, his lips shaping into a heart-breaking smile as he takes another step closer to me. "When Stuart said the name of the interviewer was Trudy Bennett, I just thought—there can't be that many Trudy Bennetts here in the UK, can there?—I mean there probably is but…" He laughs. Surprising to me, he sounds a little nervous.

"But then I just thought it would be too much of a coincidence for it to be you…and shit…here you are."

"Here I am." Still echoing, sounding like some lame fucking parrot.

He comes over to me. Each stride closer he takes, my heart whams against my ribcage.

Then he stops in front of me, only inches away.

Holy crap, he's even more beautiful close up. And he's so much taller now than I remember, but then he was fourteen the last time I saw him in the flesh. He looks even better than he does on TV.

Wow, he really has grown up.

He's smells like of a mixture of cigarettes, aftershave, and mint. It's a surprisingly alluring smell, and it's doing all kinds of funny things to me.

"It's been, what, eleven years?" he says, his voice quieter now.

"Twelve." I swallow.

"Twelve. Christ, yeah, right." He runs his hand through his hair. "You look different...but the same...you know." He shrugs.

"I know." I smile. "You look different too." I gesture to the tattoos on his arms.

He grins down at them, then back at me.

"But still the same." I point my finger to the freckles on his nose.

Surprised by how much my fingers are itching to touch him, I draw my hand back.

He rubs his hand over his nose. "Yeah, no getting rid of them."

"I always liked them."

"Yeah, but you liked the Care Bears, Tru."

I flush. I can't believe he remembers that.

It's crazy that he, Jake Wethers, rock god extraordinaire, remembers that I liked the Care Bears when I was little.

"You remember that, huh?" I murmur, cheeks flaming.

"I remember a lot." He grins devilishly. "Come on, let's sit down."

He grabs hold of my hand. A jolt of electricity fires up my arm, searing into me. His hand is so rough, his fingers calloused. Must come from his years of playing the guitar.

Jake leads me over to the plush sofa and sits down, letting go of my hand. My hand feels instantly cold.

I clutch my bag and sit down beside him.

He turns his body towards me, resting his foot up on his thigh. It's only then I realise his feet are bare.

Seriously, what is it about men in jeans and bare feet that is so totally hot?

I take my bag off my shoulder and put it on the floor.

"Do you want something to drink?" he asks.

I shift my legs towards him, turning my body slightly to face him. His eyes are already on my face.

I flush under his stare. "Water would be great, thanks."

I could actually do with a neat vodka right now to calm my nerves, my hangover suddenly disappearing. But it's 10:00 a.m., and Jake is a recovering alcoholic.

"Water? You sure you don't want orange juice or something?"

I shake my head. "Water's fine."

"Stuart!" Jake yells, making me jump a little.

Stuart appears a few seconds later through a door to the right of us.

Was he standing by the door, waiting or something? Actually it's only now I realise I didn't even see him leaving before. The guy's pretty stealthy.

"Can you get Tru a glass of water, and I'll have an orange juice, please," Jake says to him.

Tru.

I love how his voice sounds when he says my name. It's giving me the warm and fuzzies.

Stuart nods, smiling at me, then disappears off again.

I can see Jake's leg jigging in my eyeline. I have the urge to reach over and put my hand on his leg, settling him, but I don't, obviously.

"So this is a little crazy, huh?" he murmurs.

"Hmm. A little." I press my lips together in a small smile.

Actually, I was thinking more like…surreal, off the charts.

A silence falls between us.

Wow, twelve years apart and I'm just full of conversation, aren't I?

It's weird but I just can't seem to find a thing to say to him, and I had all yesterday to prepare. I've thrust myself upon him, and he's doing just fine in the talking department.

But then he was better with people than I was. Hence his success, I guess. Well, that and his ability to sing, and of course his looks. His gorgeous, lovely face, and his toned, tight body…

"So how have you been?" he asks me.

"Good. Great. I'm a music journalist now, obviously…" I trail off.

"You always were a good writer," he says.

"I was?"

I didn't even know he thought that.

"Yeah, those stories you used to make up when we were little, and then you used to make me sit and listen while you read them back to me." He chuckles, eyes shining with the memory.

I feel my face go bright red. "Oh God," I groan, embarrassed. "I was so lame."

He laughs again, louder this time. "You were five, Tru. I think we can forgive the lame." He drags his fingers through his hair. "And, of course, you always loved music, so it makes sense the two went together," he adds.

My heart suddenly feels all warm and squishy. He remembers so much more than I thought he would.

"You still play the piano?" he asks.

"No. I stopped…"

I stopped playing after you left.

"I just, um, haven't played in a long time. I fell out of it, you know. Well obviously you don't know." I gesture to the guitar propped up against the far wall.

He smiles. Stuart reappears with our drinks.

"Thank you," I say as Stuart hands me my glass of water.

"Anything else?" Stuart asks Jake.

Jake looks at me. I shake my head.

"No, we're good, thanks."

Stuart closes the door when he leaves. Leaving Jake and me alone again.

I sneak a look at him as he has a drink of his juice. It's so weird, he's Jake but not *Jake*.

And I don't know why, but I feel so completely uncomfortable and so completely at home in his presence. It's one of the most confusing feelings I've ever had.

I take a sip of my water. It's ice cold and welcomingly refreshing.

"So I'd ask how you're doing but…" I gesture around at the plush hotel room as I put my glass down on the table in front of us.

"Yeah." He laughs. It sounds a little forced. He rubs his hand over the scar on his chin, I notice. "I'm great." He shrugs, smiling, and leans forward, putting his juice on the table. I watch the muscles in his arm stretch and tense with his movement.

He doesn't sit back; he stays sitting forward, arms resting on his thighs, looking straight ahead.

He seems a little uncomfortable now, and I instantly regret my words.

How stupid could I be?

He's not long out of rehab. His best friend died a little over a year ago. Of course he's not okay. I don't think all the money and nice hotel rooms in the world could make that okay.

I couldn't have been more insensitive if I'd tried. I bet he thinks I'm a complete idiot now.

"I've followed your music career," I say in a bright but too-loud voice, just for want of a better thing to say.

"You have?" He turns his head to look at me, surprised.

"Of course I have." I smile. "Music is my job." His face falls and instantly I know I've done it again. "But that's not the only reason," I hastily add. "I wanted to see how you were doing. And you've just achieved so much. I was really proud watching you on TV and reading the articles about your music, and when you set up your own label—I was like, 'Wow'...and I've bought all your albums, of course. And they're really brilliant." I'm babbling. Someone stop me, please.

He's staring at me again, but there's something different in his eyes this time.

"Why didn't you get in touch with me, Tru?"

His question throws me. I stare at him, confused.

Why didn't I get in touch with him? He was the one who stopped calling me. Stopped writing. Ignored my letters.

And I didn't know where he was until he became famous, and then it's not like I could get anywhere near him even if I'd wanted to.

I mean, of course I wanted to, but I just couldn't.

"Um..." My mouth's gone dry. "You're not exactly easy to get in touch with, Mr. Famous Rock Star." I try to come off as lighthearted, but even I can hear the edge to my voice.

"Yeah, that's me. One of the most accessible, inaccessible people on the planet." His stare is hard on me.

Have I pissed him off or something?

And now I just feel totally uncomfortable, because if anyone should be pissed off it's me. He stopped contact with me.

I feel a sudden rush of unexplained anger towards him and have the urge to yell at him. I want to ask why he never got in touch with me. He could have found me so easily.

He was the one who stopped the contact, not me, so he should have been the one to get in touch.

I want to know why he just disappeared off the face of the planet and didn't rock back up until he was sitting in my TV.

But I don't ask any of those things. Fear is keeping my mouth shut. I have half an hour max with him, and the last thing I want to do is waste it arguing about things that happened twelve years ago or fuck this interview up—it's way too important to Vicky, and the magazine as a whole.

He pulls a pack of cigarettes from his jeans pocket and gets one out. He puts it between his lips, holding a lighter up; then he pauses.

"Do you smoke?" he asks, cigarette still perched between his lips.

"No."

"Good," he replies.

Hypocrite, I think.

"You mind if I do?"

"No."

He lights his cigarette, dropping the pack and lighter onto the table, and takes a long drag.

I watch the smoke trickle out of his mouth and billow up into the air.

He really does have nice lips.

My phone starts to sing a text in my bag. Shit, I forgot to turn it off. It's unprofessional of me to have it on in an interview.

Jake's eyes follow mine down to my bag.

"Sorry," I mumble. I get my phone, silencing it. "It might be my boss."

It's not. It's Will asking how my day is going and saying that he misses me and is looking forward to seeing me tonight. He really is sweet.

"Adele?" Jake grins, referring to the tune just playing on my phone.

"I like her," I respond defensively.

"Oh, me too." He nods. "She's a nice girl. I just figured from what I remember of you, I'd have been hearing the Stones playing on your phone."

"Yeah, well, I've changed a lot since you knew me." That actually came out a lot sharper than I meant.

Avoiding his eyes, I turn my phone off, drop it in my bag, and pull out my notebook and pen, ready to get this interview started.

I have got my Dictaphone with me. But right now, I need something to concentrate on, something to do with my hands, and writing seems as good a thing as any, and my questions are all in here anyway.

When I look up, Jake's eyes are on my notepad. They lift to meet mine. For a moment, I think I see disappointment there.

"So, I should get started with the interview—I'm sure you're really busy and I don't want to keep you for longer than necessary."

"You're not keeping me." His tone is dry. He takes a long drag of his cigarette. "And I'm not busy today. My schedule is clear."

"Oh. You haven't got any other interviews after mine?"

A smile flickers over his face. "Well I did have…consider them cancelled."

"No! Don't do that on my account." My voice shoots out.

I know how hard it must have been for those journalists to get this interview with him. It seems to have cost Vicky dearly from the reaction I got yesterday when I probed her about it. But I do like the fact he would do that for me.

I like it a lot.

His face darkens, prompting me to add, "I don't mean I'm not happy to see you, of course I am, and would love to talk old times with you, but I don't want others to miss out on a great opportunity because of me."

"A great opportunity?" He smirks.

I shrug. "Oh, you know what I mean."

"Look, Tru." He turns his body towards me. "I haven't seen you in twelve years. The last thing I want to do right now is talk business with you, or anyone else for that matter. I want to know all about you—what you've been doing since I last saw you." He looks at me curiously, his blue eyes piercing mine intrusively.

A shiver runs through me.

"Not much." I shrug, looking down.

"I'm sure you've done a lot more than 'not much.'" His tone is surprisingly firm.

He seems so much more forceful than he used to be. But then, of course, he was a teenager back then. He's a man now.

A very rich and very famous man.

And I instantly feel intimidated in a whole other way.

"What did I do after you left Manchester?" I shrug, looking up at him. "I lived my life, I finished school." My voice suddenly sounds a little bitter; it surprises even me.

"How was it?" His face stays impassive, eyes trained on me.

"School? It was school. A little lonely after you left, but I got through it."

That was a dig meant to hurt him. But if it does, it doesn't show on his face.

His just continues to stare impassively at me, and I'm starting to squirm under his heavy gaze.

"You still see anyone from school?"

I tuck my hair behind my ear. "No, I'm friends with a couple of people on Facebook, but that's about it. What about you?" I ask.

I've always wondered if he kept in touch with anyone else; not that he had many other friends aside from me, after he binned me off that was.

He laughs. "No. Then what did you do after school?"

"Moved here to go to uni. I got my degree in journalism. Then I landed a job at *Etiquette*, the magazine I work for, and I've worked there ever since."

"Cool." Another drag of his cigarette. "You're not married." His words come out with the smoke, and I see his eyes flicker to my left hand.

"No."

"Boyfriend?" He takes another drag, then leans over and stubs his cigarette out in the waiting ashtray.

My heart halts. I don't know why, but I have the sudden urge to not tell him about Will.

"Yes," I say slowly.

"Live together?"

"No." This seems a little personal and a lot grilling. Why is he so interested? "I live with my flatmate, Simone, in Camden."

His face stays impassive. "How long have you been with the boyfriend?"

"His name is Will, and we've been together for two years."

"And what does Will do for a living?"

Why is he so interested in Will?

"He's an investment banker."

"Smart guy." I can't actually tell if he's being sarcastic or not.

"He is." I nod. "He's very smart…top of his class at uni, and he's climbing the ladder at work very quickly."

I don't know why, but I suddenly feel the urge to needle him with Will and how great he is.

Seeing as though Jake is a rich megastar, I don't want to seem so left behind, I guess, even though all I can sell myself with is Will.

Jake gets another cigarette out of his pack and lights it up.

Wow, he smokes a lot.

I curl my fingers around the edge of my notebook.

The atmosphere has shifted, and I'm not entirely sure where to. And I suddenly just want to get out of here. I want to get this interview done, so I can leave.

He's not the Jake I remember. Or the Jake from the papers. I'm not actually sure who this Jake is that's sitting before me.

I unclip my pen from my notebook and open to the page where my prepared questions are.

"It's been really nice catching up with you, Jake, but I really should get to the interview—especially if I want to keep my job." I try to keep my tone professional and add a smile for good measure.

Not that Vicky would ever fire me—well, I hope she wouldn't—but he doesn't need to know that.

"You won't get fired."

"You sound pretty confident of that." I force a little laugh out.

"I am."

He takes another long drag of his cigarette, eyes fixed on mine.

Looking away, I shift nervously in my seat.

"You okay?" he asks. "You seem a little uncomfortable."

Still as direct as ever. That hasn't changed.

"Of course I'm not uncomfortable."

Yes, I am. I'm a little intimidated by you and confused by your questions and flustered and ready to leave, to be honest.

"I just need to—"

"Do your job." He finishes for me. "Okay, go ahead, ask me anything. I'm all yours, Tru, for the next thirty minutes." He glances at his expensive watch, then leans back against the sofa, putting one arm to rest on the back, and smiles at me. It's a smile with something behind it. A cheeky kind of smile.

And it doesn't relax me at all. Not one single bit. If anything, it makes me even more nervous.

Putting the end of my pen in my mouth, I glance down at my first question, but now it just seems so lame, and I feel embarrassed. I've done so many interviews in my time, but I can honestly say this is my hardest to date. Maybe it's because I know…knew…him so well.

I know his eyes are still on me, I can feel them, and a heat is fast rising up my neck.

I get my water from the table, have a drink of it, put it down, and without looking at him, say, "It's been said in the past that you're a perfectionist when it comes to your work—your music—and because of that you can be…at times…difficult to work with. Do you agree with that? Do you consider yourself a perfectionist?"

The question was actually fourth on my list, but I decide to go straight in with the question that may possibly piss him off first. I'm just in that kind of mood now.

I look over at him, and I can see the tiniest hint of a smile on his lips. He actually looks impressed. And for a moment, I wonder what he was expecting me to ask him.

"People don't work *with* me, Tru, they work *for* me. And the guys in my band, the ones who matter, don't seem to have a problem with the way I run things."

Wow, arrogant much? And kind of hot.

Crap.

"But to answer your question," he continues. "I want my music and my label to be the best they can be. Currently they are, and I intend to keep it that way, so if I have to bust a few balls and have myself labelled as a complete shit to work for, or a 'perfectionist'"—he air quotes—"to keep me, my band, and my label at the top of our game, then yeah, call me a perfectionist. I've been called worse." He grins.

And it travels all the way through me. I have to press my knees together to stop my legs from trembling.

I scribble down the last of his answer quickly and clear my throat. "The general feeling, and what people are saying, is that *Creed* is your most chart-friendly album to date. Do you agree with that?"

"Do you?"

Eh?

"Me?"

"Yes. I'm assuming you've listened to the album."

He's testing me.

"Of course I have…and…yes, I agree with the general consensus. I think that a lot of the songs are holding a softer tone than your previous albums. Especially 'Damned' and 'Sooner.'"

Ha, suck on that!

"Good. Then then the point of the album is being received." He smiles, and I feel a little lost.

What?

Okay, recover yourself, Tru.

"So tell me, what would you be doing right now if you weren't talking to me?"

"I'd be catching up with an old friend."

Oh.

"Um…" I stumble, caught totally off guard, yet again. "Okay…it's been a while since you toured, are you looking forward to getting back on the road and playing live again?"

He sits forward, closer to me. I have the urge to lean back, but I don't. Instead I cross my legs in front of me, feeling like they can somehow protect me from whatever answer, or quite possibly question, he has ready to throw at me.

He was always smart when we were kids, and so quick, but this grown-up Jake is like a snake in a stallion's clothing.

He most certainly does not come across as the womanising, drinking, drug-addicted Jake the press claims him to be. Or even like a man who just got out of rehab a little over four weeks ago.

He seems in control. Or maybe this is just what sober Jake is like.

His eyes flicker down to my bare legs, quickly travelling up them and back up to my face.

And there's the womaniser in him.

"Playing live is what I love to do, it's what I live to do… and I have a feeling this tour is going to be a very interesting one—probably my most interesting to date."

"Oh yeah, and why's that?"

I'm curious now. If anything, I thought this tour would be hard for him with Jonny gone. Especially considering what happened in Japan.

He runs his hand through his hair. "I've just had a recent addition to my team, and I know for sure she'll make things different, interesting…better."

She?

Maybe he's got a girlfriend nowadays. But then he did say his team—I'm sure he doesn't screw the staff. Actually, he probably does.

"And this new addition, I'm taking it she's not new a band member?"

He shakes his head, lips pressed together.

"So she's part of the team putting the tour together?"

"I put the tour together."

"Right. So she's…?"

"Let's say she does…PR."

Okay…I decide to move on from there, seeing as though he's not keen to expand on the mystery woman who's going to make his tour his most successful to date.

"So tell me about your personal favorites on the album and where the inspiration for them came from."

Then I see the spark in his eye, and I know I've caught him with his music, the one thing he truly loves, and I'm reminded of that boy I loved all those years ago.

It makes my heart ache a little.

Forcing myself to focus, not wanting to miss a word he says, I start to write quickly, trying to catch up as his enthusiastic words spill out.

And that's how it is for the next thirty minutes. Question after question, I listen to him come more and more to life as he talks about his music; just like the old Jake I knew in so many ways.

It makes me miss him, in the oddest way, even though he's sitting right here before me.

I keep all the questions music based. I don't ask any of the questions I had lined up about Jonny Creed's death and how it affected him or about his time in rehab or about his personal life. It just wouldn't feel in line with the whole vibe of the interview, and I don't want to spoil the obvious pickup in his mood. And I've got a feeling he wouldn't answer them anyway.

To be honest I'm surprised I wasn't vetted by Stuart on what I could and couldn't ask Jake when I first arrived. That's how it usually works with celebrities. Especially ones as high profile as Jake.

But then I get the distinct impression that Jake doesn't play by the rule book in anything, and that any vetting to be done he does himself.

I finish shorthand-scribbling down his last answer and then close my notepad and put it back in my bag.

"Thank you," I say.

"It's been really good to see you, Tru."

"You too."

I feel a sudden lump in my throat, and I realise, even though half an hour ago I felt like bolting, now, I don't want to leave him. The thought of not seeing him again is constricting my heart in the weirdest kind of way.

Crazy, I know.

I reach down, pick up my bag, and stand. Jake follows suit, standing beside me.

I'm not really sure what to do now.

Do I shake his hand or hug him or what?

"Did you bring a coat?" he asks.

"It's in my bag." I turn to him. He looks down at me with his crystal-clear blue eyes. "Thank you again for the interview. It was great."

"You don't have to thank me; I'd do an interview for you anytime."

"I might hold you to that." I laugh.

"Do," he says. Not a trace of humour in his voice.

I suddenly feel unsteady. I put my bag strap onto my shoulder, holding my bag to me for support. "Thanks again for your time." I smile and start to walk towards the door, my legs feeling like lead.

"So you're heading back to work now?" Jake asks, following behind me.

"Yes."

"Do you need a ride? I can get Stuart to drive you."

I feel a smart of disappointment. I actually thought he was going to offer to drive me back for a moment there. But then I guess Jake going out in a car is an awful lot of hassle to go to, just to drop off little old me. He'd probably need his full security team with him.

Not that I've seen many of them around. Just Dave.

"It's okay, thank you, I'll walk. It's not far."

"You're sure?"

"I'm sure."

He reaches for the handle to open the door for me, and stops. "Do you have plans tonight? Because I was wondering if you would have dinner with me."

My heart stops. Literally, stops.

Then goes *kaboom* in my chest.

I'm supposed to be going out for dinner with Will tonight. Will, my lovely boyfriend. Whom I can't cancel on again.

Can I?

If I say no to Jake, I might not get the chance to see him again.

Yes. No. No. Yes.

I'm speaking before I even realise I'm doing it.

"No, I don't have plans, I'm free. Completely free."

He smiles widely. "Great. Cool. So we can catch up properly without the threat of an interview hanging over us." He gives me a small smile, a cheeky glint in his eyes.

Holy shit. Dinner with Jake.

My heart is doing somersaults in my chest.

It's not a date. It's not a date. It's not a date.

"Yes." My voice goes a little squeaky. I clear my throat. "Sounds like plan."

He smiles again; it reaches all the way to his beautiful eyes. "Eight o'clock okay?"

Now would be fine with me. Yesterday, whenever, I'm easy.

"Eight o'clock is great."

"Write down your address and I'll come pick you up."

I pull my notepad back out of my bag, quickly scribble down my address, tear the page out, and hand it to him.

My fingers touch his in the exchange, and my skin hums. I feel my face start to heat up again.

Jake glances at the paper in his hand, then folds it up and puts it in his back pocket.

He opens the door for me and stands aside to let me through.

We walk to the front door in silence. Stuart and Dave are nowhere to be seen.

When we reach the door, we stop for a moment facing one another.

I have no idea why, but I just feel sad again saying good-bye to him. Like I'm never going to see him again. Which is stupid because I'm going to see him tonight.

I'm seeing Jake tonight. A thrill shoots through me.

He reaches his hand up to my face and tucks my hair behind my ear. I almost swoon, my legs trembling, tummy butterflying.

Then he leans down and kisses my cheek.

The feel of his lips on my skin, his hot breath, momentarily halts every moving particle of me, paralysing me to the spot, nearly sending me into convulsions.

As he moves back, he smiles warmly at me. "So I'll see you tonight then." He opens the door for me.

"Yes, tonight. At eight." Oh God, I sound like a complete idiot.

I stumble through the door, legs failing me. I grip hold of my bag like it's my life support.

"Bye, Jake," I say, lingering.

"Bye, Trudy Bennett."

I force myself to turn and walk down the hall.

When I reach the end of the hall, I turn, looking back, but the door is already closed.

I reach the lift and the doors instantly ping open.

I wobble into the lift, press for ground, and fall back against the mirrored wall.

I'm going out for dinner tonight with Jake.

Holy shit.

CHAPTER FIVE

It's going to be okay.

No it's so totally not.

How the hell am I going to explain to Will that I'm cancelling on him for the second night in a row, this time to go out for dinner with Jake Wethers, who I forget to mention I knew very well when I was younger and have just interviewed today, which he also didn't know as I neglected to tell him that too.

Okay, deep, calming breaths, Tru. It's not a big deal. Will is cool, he's understanding. And really there is no issue to have. It's just two old friends having dinner. One of them just happens to be the world's biggest rock star.

Oh crap.

The concierge opens the door, freeing me from the Dorchester, and I step onto the busy street. The warm air on my face does little to help me. Right now I need a blast of the cool.

Looking at my watch, I see it's 11:15. Digging my phone out of my bag, I decide to call Will at work and see if he's free to have lunch with me so I can tell him about tonight.

"Will Chambers."

Oh, I love his work voice. All deep and professional. So cute.

"Hey, it's me."

"Hey, baby." He sounds happy to hear from me. He won't be happy when I tell him I'm cancelling tonight.

"I was calling to see if you fancied meeting me for lunch?"

"Sure. What time?"

"Whenever you're free. I'm already out of the office; I just finished up on an interview." *With Jake Wethers, whose album you were listening to the other day.*

"How does half an hour sound? I'll meet you at Callo's?"

"Brilliant. See you soon."

I head straight to Callo's, which is a little upmarket café. I take a window seat and order a latte.

Then I ring Vicky.

"Trudy, my superstar! How did it go with the gorgeous rocker?"

"Good. Great." The memory of his lips on my cheek flashes through my mind, and I feel myself heating up. "I got plenty for the article. I've just stopped off to have an early lunch with Will, and then I'll be heading back to write it up."

"So he remembers you then?" There's a teasing tone in her voice.

"Yes." I can't help the smile on my lips. "He...um...well he actually asked me out to dinner tonight to catch up on old times."

She actually squeals down the phone. She doesn't act like my boss at times, or the owner of a magazine.

"You're going, aren't you? Please tell me you said yes?"

"I said yes."

Another squeal.

Jeez, has she been drinking or something?

I look up and see Will coming in through the door.

"Look, I'll have to go, Will just arrived."

"My office when you get back. I want *all* the gory details."

"There are no gory details." I laugh but keep my voice quieter so Will doesn't hear in his approach.

"Sure, there aren't. See you soon," she sings.

I hang the call up and Will leans down and kisses me on the cheek. On the same spot as where Jake kissed me. I feel this odd territorial feeling and a flash of anger towards Will. Annoyed that he's just erased Jake's kiss. Which is completely crazy, even by my standards.

Will sits down across from me and the waiter comes over. Will orders himself a white coffee and me another latte.

"What would you like to eat?" he asks me.

"I'll have a ham-and-cheese panini," I say to the waiter.

"BLT on brown for me," Will says, handing him back the menu.

Will reaches over and takes hold of my hand. I notice how soft his hands are compared to Jake's rough ones.

"I missed you last night," he murmurs.

"I missed you too." I smile.

"So how was it? You have fun with Simone?"

"I did. We got quite drunk though."

"Don't you two always?" He smiles. "Great news about her promotion."

"It is." I fidget nervously with my free hand. Taking a deep breath, it's now or never, I say, "So, I have some news."

His eyes flicker to mine with interest.

I'm not actually sure where to start first. Maybe just at the beginning.

"Well, I never told you this, not because it's a big deal or anything, just because it was never really relevant, and I don't really tell anyone, but growing up, I lived next door to Jake Wethers."

I see confusion that suddenly clicks into understanding in his eyes.

"Jake Wethers...as in...the Mighty Storm, Jake Wethers?"

"The one and only." I give him a tight smile.

"Wow!" he says, clearly impressed. "Wow. Okay. So did you know him in passing or quite well?"

"He was my best friend."

"Oh."

"We lost touch when his family moved to America, when we were fourteen, and well, we recently just got back in touch."

His brow furrows. "When?"

"Well, today. This morning."

"Oh," he says again. His voice is tight now.

"That's who I was just interviewing. Vicky managed to land an interview with him, and she sent me, knowing I knew him."

"So Vicky knows you knew him?"

Crap.

Why is he so quick? He's clearly hurt by it.

"Yes...I...um..." I tuck my hair behind my ear. "I told her when I was drunk last Christmas, purely accidental and not a big deal."

The waiter appears with our drinks and food, forcing Will to let go of my hand and giving me a momentary and welcomed reprieve.

"So you did the interview this morning…how was it seeing him after all this time?" he seems a little easier now.

Good.

"Um…it was little surreal, I guess." I shrug. "I knew him when he was younger. He's a lot different now."

"He most certainly is." Will's tone is sharp. It surprises me.

How can he make that statement when he doesn't even know Jake? I suddenly feel very protective over him.

"So, anyway," I say mildly, hiding my annoyance. "Because I was interviewing him, we didn't really get to chat much—you know, catch up on old times—and well, he asked me to join him for dinner tonight."

He puts down the sandwich that he'd just picked up.

"Jake Wethers has asked my girlfriend out for dinner." He suddenly sounds all territorial. Not like Will at all.

"It's not a date, silly. It's just two old friends catching up."

"Yes, and one half of those old friends happens to be my very beautiful girlfriend, and the other, the man-whore of the rock world."

"Will!" I exclaim, shocked. "That's a little unfair. You don't even know him."

"Clearly you do."

Hang on. When did this turn into an argument?

It must be the expression on my face that prompts him to say, "Look, I'm sorry. I've just had a crap morning at work, and I was looking forward to seeing you, and I guess my green-eyed monster is raising his head a little. You can't blame me for that—I mean look at you." He reaches his hand over, cupping my cheek, sinking his fingers into my hair.

"You have nothing to be jealous of."

"He's a rich, good-looking rock star. I'd have to be a little stupid not to be jealous."

"That he may be." I take hold of his hand and kiss his palm. "But he's not you. And I love you."

That seems to appease him, as his face relaxes a little.

I release his hand, allowing him to pick up his sandwich.

"How long is he in town for?"

"A few days."

That seems to please him further.

"I guess it will be nice for you to catch up, seeing as though you were childhood friends."

And I loved him.

Covering my thoughts with a smile, I omit that thought and say, "So, as I've let you down two nights in a row for my friends now, I'm going to do something special tomorrow night to make it up to you."

His brows rise. "I'm intrigued. Go on."

"I'll leave it to your imagination, and then tomorrow night you can tell me if I fulfilled it." I grin at him.

"You never fail to make me happy, Tru, and I can't see that changing anytime soon, so I'm sure whatever you have planned will live up to my already high standard of you."

That is so sweet. And now I feel kind of crap for having no clue what I'm going to do to make it up to him tomorrow night. I'm going to have to come up with something awesome.

I pick my panini up and take a bite.

Will walks me back to my office building, giving me a long, lingering kiss before leaving me.

I head through the lobby and take the stairs up. Our office is only on the second floor, and the exercise is good for me.

Going bright red at the whistles from my colleagues, I'm guessing Vicky's already told them about my interview with Jake. I quickly drop my bag at my desk and head straight to her office.

She's deep in concentration, reading something on her computer screen, when I knock on her open door.

Her eyes brighten when she sees me, and she smiles. "Sit down and tell me all about the dirty boy of rock."

I frown at her. I know Jake's got a reputation, but I don't like her calling him that.

"He's not so much a boy, Vicky."

She raises a perfectly plucked eyebrow. "And what does that mean—pray tell?"

I feel like I'm about to have a chat with one of my girl-friends over cocktails about a guy I just went on a date with. Not about an interview I just did with a celebrity.

I love that I have this kind of relationship with Vicky.

I drop myself into her chair across from her desk. "It means that people seriously underestimate him, Vicky. Yes, he's a singer in a band and he sleeps with lots of women…"

"Did he say that?" She looks at me hopefully. Another exclusive in mind.

"No." I laugh. "That's just it…he's very careful, circum-spect about what he does say. He seems to ask questions more than answer them—don't worry I got plenty off him,"

I add at her worried expression. "It's just..." I pause, searching for the right words. The ones that have been evading me ever since I was with him. "I guess he just...might act the dirty rock boy, out there." I gesture. "But I feel that behind the scenes, he's very much the *man*—the one who is very much in charge of what happens—as it's been said before by the few people who have interviewed him."

"So you think the women, the partying, it's all an act?"

I shake my head. "No. I just think there are two sides to Jake. The young guy who is very much living the lifestyle he is privilege to, but then there's the business Jake, the one who runs his label and his band exactly the way he wants to and is very good at it."

"So the incident in Japan..."

"Expected, I'd say. His best friend and business partner had just died. Add that on top of the quick rise to fame he had, the money he has—my guess is it just all got a little too much, and unfortunately his fall was in front of thousands of people."

Wow, I'm actually sounding smart here. A first for me.

"Hmm." Vicky leans back in her chair. "So is he as hot in the flesh as he looks on the TV?" She grins and I know the serious, journalistic aspect of our conversation is gone for now.

"He's...a little good-looking, sure," I downplay.

"A little good-looking," she scoffs. "Yeah, I'm sure that's all he is." She purses her lips, like something has just occurred to her. "And he's asked you out for dinner tonight?"

I was wondering when she was going to mention that. Nothing slips by her. Ever the journalist.

"He did. Just a catch-up." I shuffle forward in my seat, getting ready to make an exit.

"I bet he's after a *thorough* catch-up with you."

"Vicky!" I screech, then cover my mouth with my hand, realising how loud that was. "I can't believe you just said that," I add in a quieter voice, peeling my hand off my mouth.

"What?" she laughs. "Look at you—you have a face and an ass to die for. And him? Well, good grief. He's so delicious I could serve him up on toast and eat him…and he is well known for his *antics.*"

"Yeah, well I'm not, and I do have a boyfriend, remember?" I'm a little snippy, but it doesn't seem to faze her.

"Yes, well, we're all as clean as whistles, my darling, until men like him come along and dirty us right up."

She winks at me, grinning, relieving the tension I'm feeling.

"You're incurable." I shake my head humorously at her, rolling my eyes. "And I don't see him that way."

She presses her lips together and narrows her heavily lined eyes suspiciously at me. "Yeah, sure you don't. And how did the lovely William take the news of dinner with Jake? You did tell him, didn't you?" I sometimes get the impression Vicky doesn't like Will.

"Of course I did." I sound defensive; I've no clue why.

"And?"

"Nothing. He was fine with it." *After a while.*

She lets out a little laugh. "He was fine with you going out to dinner with the most beautiful, prolifically womanising rock star in the world?"

I press my lips together and let out my breath through my nose. "He was fine with it because there's nothing in it. It's just two old friends having dinner and nothing more."

"If you say so, my darling." She brushes her hand through her hair.

"It is," I chirp. "Now, if you're finished grilling me, I'm going to do the work you pay me to do. I'll type up a draft of the interview and have it ready for you to look over by the end of the day."

"That would be fabulous, thank you." She leans back in her chair and brushes her hair off her face.

Giving her a light smile, I turn and sashay my way out of her office, away from her quizzical stare, because she's a little closer to the truth on everything then I would care to admit. Jake, my reaction to seeing him after all these years, and Will's reaction to the news that I'm seeing him tonight. But mostly, how I feel about seeing Jake tonight. And the only word I can think to describe it is…exhilarated.

CHAPTER SIX

Okay. I'm having dinner with Jake.

Jake Wethers.

But he's still just Jake…the same Jake I knew.

No he's not—he's now rock-god Jake.

Oh crap.

I've been ready for the past half an hour and have been pacing around my flat ever since. I've had a large glass of wine already and am starting on my second, trying to calm my nerves.

And Simone's not here to help either. She was so gutted when I told her Jake was coming to the flat to pick me up. She's working late on a project for this new client of hers and couldn't get out of it.

Maybe it's best she's not here; I'm freaking out as it is. Simone is a big Mighty Storm fan, so she'd be freaking too, making me worse.

What on earth am I going to talk to him about tonight?

I know, I've known Jake a long time, but I knew him back then. Not now.

Now he's a megarich superstar. And I'm just a lowly journalist working for a small, up-and-coming magazine, with enough money to pay the bills and fill the cupboard with food and wine to get me through the week.

He probably earns in an hour what I do in a year.

I've stayed in exactly the same place, and Jake has sky-rocketed to the stars.

We live in two very different worlds. I don't know anything about his life now, except what I've read in the papers.

I wonder if he still likes the same things he did when I knew him.

Of course he doesn't. Do I still like the same things I did when I was fourteen? Nope. Well, except for kids' cereal. Coco Pops are awesome.

I'm just wondering, once the step back in time has dried up, what on earth we will talk about. We are so worlds apart now. Our childhood aside, what else is there?

I'm just hoping the childhood stories will somehow stretch us through the night.

I gulp down another mouthful of wine.

The doorbell rings. It's a minute after eight. If nothing else, he's punctual. And here was me expecting him to be rock star late.

Putting down my glass, I pick up my handbag, get my keys, and wobble on nervous legs to the door.

When I open it, he's standing there looking all kinds of gorgeous, wearing dark blue fitted jeans, Converse trainers, and a pale blue shirt with its sleeves rolled up, top buttons open, his tattoos on show.

And once again, I suddenly feel totally of out of my depth.

"Hi," I say.

"Wow. You look great."

I flush. "Thanks, you too."

I'm doing a little minidance inside.

This dress was totally worth it—okay, so I might have popped to my favourite clothes shop, Dixie's, after work and bought the dress I've been eyeing in the window for the last few weeks. The dress I couldn't really afford at the moment—so thank you, Visa.

It's not to impress Jake or anything. I mean, it's not like we're going on a date. But he's rich and I wanted to look nice. And the dress is so damn cute.

It's a black shift dress with silver embellishment all over it, and so totally me. I've teamed it with my black heels and silver clutch bag, and I left my hair down and curly and kept my makeup minimal, how I always wear it.

I step through the door, deciding against inviting him in for a drink. He probably lives in a mansion. I don't want him looking around my tiny flat.

I lock up and follow him down the path.

"Nice place." He nods back at the house that hosts my flat.

"Thanks…wow, is this yours?" I ask as he approaches a silver Aston Martin DBS.

He grins and unlocks it. "Loaner, but I do have one back home."

Loaner? I'd be lucky if I'd be able to borrow a scooter.

And once again, I'm reminded of how very different our lives are.

"Isn't this James Bond's car?" I ask as I slide into the supple leather seat, putting my seat belt on.

"Well, not this specific one, no—but I have driven his."

I slide him a look. "Show-off." I smile.

"Oh, you have no idea." He winks at me, leaving my stomach to free-fall off into the next galaxy.

We pull away, roaring off down my small street, in his very flashy car.

"So where are we going?" I ask, still trying to recover myself from his earlier comment.

"It's a surprise."

"A surprise?" I turn to look at him.

He slides me a look, a smile playing on his lips. "Yeah, a surprise, you remember those? They usually happen on birthdays, that kind of thing."

"But it's not my birthday."

"Yeah, well, I've missed twelve of them, so I've got quite a few surprises to make up for."

I really don't know what to say to that, so for once, I keep quiet.

I look out the window and notice a black Land Rover that is driving pretty close to the back of the car.

Turning my head, I look over my shoulder at the car. It's tinted and I can't see in the window. I hope it's not paparazzi following him. Don't they usually drive big smog chuggers like that?

"That car's pretty close behind," I say, tilting my head back in its direction, trying to alert him.

Jake's eyes flick to his rearview and then back to me.

"It's Dave, my security guy."

"Oh. Does he go everywhere with you?"

"Yeah…well, everywhere except the bathroom." He slides his grinning eyes in my direction.

"Why is he riding back there and not in the car with us?"

"Because I wanted to be alone with you."

"Oh."

Oh.

My nerves have instantly gone haywire. I could really do with another glass of wine.

Actually, I feel the need to drink every time he looks at me. I have a feeling I'm going to get very drunk tonight.

I look out the window again, watching the buildings of London, thinking how surreal this is. Last night I was out getting drunk in Mandarin's with Simone, nerves ragged over interviewing Jake, wondering if he would remember me, and now I'm here in his fancy James Bond car, and he's driving me to my surprise night out.

Jake Wethers, my old best friend, onetime love of my life, biggest rock star and most sought-after man in the world, and he is sitting inches away from me. I could reach my hand out and touch him.

I won't though, 'cause that would be pretty weird.

Actually, things don't get much weirder than this.

We're in Convent Garden when Jake pulls the car up and parks it on the main road just outside a Pizza Hut. His security guy pulls up behind.

"I don't think you can park here," I say, looking around at the No Parking signs.

"Don't worry, come on." He climbs out of the car. I guess when you're him you can do whatever you want.

I climb out of the car and notice there's a guy standing outside the entrance to the Pizza Hut, staring at us. My first thought is he must recognise Jake, but then I realise it's Stuart, Jake's PA.

"Hey," Jake says to him. "All ready?"

"Yep." Stuart nods.

Jake tosses the car keys to him. "I'll call you when we're done."

"No worries, have a good night...hello again, Trudy," Stuart says as he walks past us.

"Hi," I say, offering him a smile.

Stuart hops in the James Bond car and promptly drives away.

"Come on," Jake says, taking hold of my hand.

My skin tingles at his touch again. He's so much more tactile than he used to be, I notice.

He walks me to the entrance of the Pizza Hut.

I stop and look up at the sign, then back to Jake.

"We're going to Pizza Hut?" I grin.

He remembers.

That was what he meant in the car with the comment about my birthdays.

Every birthday we would come here; it was kind of a tradition with us—and who doesn't love Pizza Hut, right?

I can't believe he remembers. I feel all warm and squishy inside and a little overdressed.

He smiles back at me; it reaches all the way to his beautiful blue eyes. "Like I said, I've got twelve birthdays to make up for. I know it's not the one we used to go to in Manchester, but I figured you wouldn't want to drive all the way up there, so this was the next-best thing. After you..." He gestures for me to pass him.

My heart is buzzing around my chest at his thoughtfulness. I walk past him and make my way down the stairs.

Jake is the only guy I know who would pick me up in an Aston Martin DBS, then bring me to Pizza Hut. And that's why I love him.

I mean, of course, I don't love him, love him. I just used to love him when I was younger.

Anyway, the Covent Garden one is a little smarter than the usual Pizza Huts. Especially the one we used to go to in Manchester, at least from the outside. For starters, it's underground, and you have to take the stairs to reach it, but once you get inside, it's just a regular Pizza Hut and I love it.

I'm greeted at the bottom of the stairs by a waiter. The instant he sees Jake, nerves and awe light up his eyes.

I feel sorry for him, as it must be a shock when the biggest rock star in the world turns up unannounced in your place of work. I mean, Pizza Hut is not where you'd usually expect to see Jake Wethers.

It'd be pretty hard not to be overawed, but I think he does okay overall. He doesn't ask for Jake's autograph, which is a good start, because I totally would have.

As I glance around, I see the restaurant is empty.

Surprising, but lucky, as I'm pretty sure Jake would have got hassled nonstop for autographs in here. Hopefully, it will stay quiet while we're here.

The waiter shows us over to a booth table. I slide into my seat, Jake sits opposite me.

His legs are long under the table. I bump his leg with my foot.

"Sorry."

He smiles at me.

It squirms its way through me. I feel like I'm a teenager all over again.

"Can I get you some drinks?" the waiter asks, handing us our menus.

Jake looks at me.

"Beer," I say.

"Two Buds," Jake orders.

The waiter disappears to get our drinks while I stare at Jake, surprised.

"What?" he asks, seeing my staring.

"Um...nothing." My face flames.

"No, go on," he urges, leaning forward. He rests his arms on the table.

"Well, I just thought you didn't drink anymore—you know—*rehab*." I say the word quietly, like it's a really inappropriate word to be saying.

He lets out a laugh. "Drinking was never the problem, Tru."

"Oh."

He leans back in his seat. "That's the press for you. But still, everything in moderation for me nowadays. Except drugs—they're completely off the menu, of course, but my cigarettes have increased."

"When did you start smoking?" I ask, wondering if it was after he got clean, as a replacement for the drugs, as he never was interested in smoking when we were teenagers.

He scrunches up his face in thought. "When I started in the band."

Awhile then.

"Bad habit."

"It is," he agrees. "But not as bad as being an addict."

I instantly tense.

He smiles. "Relax, Tru. It's not the worst thing in the world I've ever said, and my drug counsellor says I'm supposed to be open about these things."

Okay...

"Was it horrible?"

"What? Rehab?"

"No—but I can't imagine that was a great place to be. I meant being an addict."

How can he be so together and so successful but have been a drug addict? It doesn't feel like the two should go together. But somehow in him, they did. I guess everyone has a weakness.

He starts to drum his fingers on the table. "When it was good, it was great, and when it was bad…it was really fuckin' bad. I reached the point when all the highs, which were basically every day for me, were all bad. And that was when it was time to get clean."

"I'm glad you're clean," I say.

"Me too." He smiles.

The waiter comes over with our beers.

"Are you both ready to order, or do you need more time?"

"Oh, sorry, I haven't even looked at my menu, yet," I say, opening it up.

"Give us another five minutes, man."

"So what were you thinking?" I ask, looking down at the menu.

"Pizza."

I glance up at his smiling face.

"Ha, ha, funny. They do serve pasta and salad here as well, you know." I stick my tongue out at him.

"I remember."

I get the impression he remembers so much more than I could have hoped.

"Do you want to share?" I ask.

"Are you still greedy?"

"I was never greedy!" I say, feigning outrage.

"You ate like a guy." He laughs.

"Are you saying I was fat, Jake Wethers?" I quirk my eyebrow at him.

"No. You were always a skinny little thing. I could never actually figure out where it all went."

"My ass. It still does."

"From what I remember of your ass, it was always nice. I'll have to check it out later—I'll let you know what I think."

"So you didn't already check it out coming down the stairs?"

I can't believe I just said that!

It's him; he seems to bring out a newfound flirty, naughty side of me.

He grins at me; it's a sexy smile. My cheeks heat, and so do other parts of my anatomy.

"So are we sharing or not?" I ask, looking back down at my menu.

"We're sharing."

Why do I always feel like there's an undertone to everything he's saying to me?

But he is a renowned womaniser, so flirting is probably just part of his genetic makeup nowadays.

"Okay, so we have the exotic choice of—Posh Pizzas, the Hut Classics, or Make Our Own," I say as I pore over the menu.

"I was thinking we could have our old favourite…"

"Oh my God." I look up at him, laughing. "The Blazin'…"

"Inferno," he finishes.

"I haven't had that pizza in years!" I'm still laughing.

"Me either." He laughs. "So that's what we're having?"

"Definitely." I beam.

I close my menu and that's when I realise he'd never actually opened his.

He remembered the pizza without even seeing it on the menu.

I take a swig of my beer.

Jake signals to the waiter, who has been loitering by the doorway for the last few minutes, and orders our pizza.

He picks up his beer and has a drink.

It's still dead in here. Not one single person has turned up for a pizza.

"It's good that it's quiet in here tonight," I say, echoing my earlier thoughts. "No fans to hassle you."

He smiles. "I paid for it to be quiet."

"Huh?"

"I bought the place for the evening."

"You bought Pizza Hut?"

"Not Pizza Hut as a whole, Tru." He grins. "Just this one, rented, for the evening."

"Why?"

"So we wouldn't be interrupted."

"Oh."

I can't believe he rented out the whole of Pizza Hut so we could have dinner together here, because it was, once upon a time long ago, our place.

I know he can afford it, easily, but still, it's crazy sweet.

"Where did Stuart take the car to?" I ask, just thinking of it now, and actually why he was waiting outside to take it.

"He just took it back to the hotel. He'll bring it back when we need it."

"And your security guy?"

"He'll be at the top of the stairs."

"Oh."

"Hey, do you remember those matching friendship bracelets you made us with that kit your mom bought you that one Christmas?" he says, putting down his beer.

I wonder what made him think of that.

"Oh God, I really was lame." I cover my face with my hands, my cheeks burning.

"I thought they were sweet."

I stare at him, surprised.

"Do you still have yours?" he asks.

I do. But if I tell him I always kept mine because it was just one of the many things that reminded me of him and I could never part with it, it might sound as lame as it actually is.

"I still have mine," he says as if reading my thoughts.

"You do?" Now I'm surprised.

"Yes."

"Where is it?" I look at his wrist.

"In LA at my house. So do you still have yours?"

"Yes." My voice is lower.

"Where is it?"

"Here, in the UK, in my tiny flat."

He laughs. "You'll have to show it to me later." His expression suddenly turns serious.

He wants to come in my flat? My stomach starts doing somersaults across the room.

"Okay." I cough nervously, my face flaming.

"How are your mom and dad?" he asks.

"Good," I say, smiling. "They still live in Manchester, in the same house."

"You're kidding?" He grins.

I shake my head no. "And my dad's teaching music now to underprivileged kids."

"He always was a good man. Is it a charity-based organisation he works for?"

"Yeah."

"What's it called?"

"Why?"

"Because I want to donate some money to it. If it wasn't for your dad, I would never have picked up a guitar let alone learned how to play one, and I wouldn't be where I am right now. I owe him a lot."

I fill with pride for my dad. He is the best.

"It's called Tuners for Youths."

"Cool," he says. "I'll make the arrangements tomorrow."

"My dad will be made up when I tell him."

"You don't need to tell him the donation was from me."

I knit my eyebrows in confusion at him.

"I don't want him thinking I'm being a flashy bastard."

"He wouldn't think that; he's really proud of you."

He looks up, surprised. "He is?"

I nod. "He follows your career, like I do. Probably more so—you know how he is about music."

"I bet he wasn't proud of the drugs...and women." His lips turn down at the corners.

I have the urge to reach out and smooth my finger across them, but I don't. Instead I reach out and put my hand on his arm.

I see his eyes go to it, then he lifts them back to mine.

"He was worried about you, like I was. But he's really proud of everything you've achieved. And to be honest,

I think he was quite impressed with all the models and actresses you've been pictured with." I laugh, trying to come off as lighthearted, but if anything, my own words sting me.

Moving my arm away, I pick up my drink. "I bet your mum's real proud of you." I take a swig of my beer.

He shrugs. Glancing down at his beer, he starts to pick at the label. "She's proud...sure, she just worries a lot—you know."

"I know, but she's your mum and it's to be expected," I say.

I know Susie feels like she let Jake down over the years. That she should have forced his dad out of their lives. Then what happened to Jake never would've happened.

I overheard Susie talking to my mum one day. I never told Jake though.

He shrugs again, and I get the feeling there's something more, but I don't press it, and then the waiter appears with our pizza.

After that we just fall into conversation like we've never been apart.

We talk school and childhood memories.

He tells me stuff about the band and his label, which bands he has signed to it.

I tell him about my time at university, living with Simone, and my job as a music journalist at the magazine.

But mainly we just talk music, like we used to. Recent and old stuff. And Jake's music.

I haven't spoken to anyone about music in the way I'm speaking to Jake now. Not in all my time at university while studying it, and not even in all the time I've worked at the magazine.

It's how we used to talk about it, with real passion. And to me Jake was and is music, it's what glued us together, and now it's like a dam is opening back up and everything Jake is just flowing out of me.

One thing I don't talk about is Will. And he doesn't ask.

I also notice he doesn't mention Jonny. It must still be so raw for him to talk about.

I also notice he's only had the one beer all night. I'm glad because he's driving. I like that he's being responsible. Because the Jake I'm used to seeing in the news never appears responsible, despite all his success.

But the more time I spend with him, the more I feel like there are two Jakes.

The one the world sees, and the one I'm getting to see here. The one I used to know.

I've kept light on the drink too. Funny, because earlier I thought I would need it to get me through the night. But not at all.

This is one of the best nights I have had in a long time.

We talk for hours, and when we're finished, Jake calls Stuart to let him know he needs him to bring the car, then he pays the bill.

"Let me pay my half," I press as we walk to the exit.

He laughs. "No, Tru. Just call it birthday present number one of twelve."

"I owe you twelve birthday presents too, remember?"

"Oh, I haven't forgotten. I'll start collecting on them soon."

And there it is, that flirty undertone again.

No wonder women are always throwing themselves at him. I'm having a pretty difficult time myself not doing just that.

Jake gestures for me to go first up the stairs.

"You still eat like a dude," he says from behind me. "But your ass is definitely all woman."

I gasp.

Pausing, I turn and look at him, agape.

"What?" he feigns innocence, stopping behind me, but I can see the look in his eyes, and he's close, so very close to me. "I told you I'd let you know what I thought of your ass, and I'm telling you it's perfect. Even better than I remember."

Eyes back front and I'm up those stairs quick march. My insides turning over with embarrassment and want.

Okay, there, I've said it. I want Jake.

He's beautiful and sexy, and flirty. And he's a rock star. And he was my boy next door. But of course nothing is ever going to happen.

Because he's Jake Wethers…and I'm just Trudy Bennett.

And also I have a boyfriend, which is actually reason number one.

Stuart is there, waiting with the James Bond car, just like Jake said he would be. Dave is in his car behind, ready to follow us.

We are a lot quieter on the ride back to my place than we were in the restaurant.

I'm not really sure why for him. But for me it's because I feel sad that the night is over, more than likely I won't ever see him again. Well, apart from on the TV, that is.

He pulls up outside my place way too quickly for my liking.

"Thanks for dinner," I say, taking off my seat belt, turning in my seat. "I had a great time."

"Me too." His voice sounds deeper, huskier in the dark. It does funny things to me.

I don't want to get out of the car, I have that same feeling of loss I had when I was leaving him at the hotel, but at least then I knew I was seeing him tonight. But now the night's over and I don't have any reason to see him again.

"So, I guess I'll go in. Thanks again for the pizza and beer."

I reach for the handle, just clicking open the door, when he says, "I'll walk you to your door. Too many weirdos about in London. I want to make sure you get in okay."

Pushing open the door, I smile to myself as I exit the car. Jake gets out at the same time. My front door is only thirty feet away; I hardly think anything is going to happen to me in thirty feet.

Jake walks me up my path, and I get that feeling of being a teenager again. Butterflies and giddiness. The way I would feel when I was crazy about him back then and he would look at me and my insides would just go nuts.

I reach my door and fish my keys out of my bag.

Should I invite him in? I guess it would be rude not to. Even though Simone will die of heart failure when she sees him.

"Do you want to come in for a coffee?" I gesture.

He looks at my door, then at my face. "I've got an early start tomorrow. I really should get back to the hotel."

A no then.

"Oh, okay, sure." I try not to sound as disappointed as I feel.

Not very rock star sounding to need his sleep…oh God…I was just blown out, wasn't I?

I'm so slow.

But it's fine because I wasn't inviting him in for anything other than coffee anyway.

Obviously he doesn't think I'm attractive. He didn't fancy me when we were younger, so why should it be any different now?

Because I'm not fourteen anymore. And I'm a little prettier than I used to be back then!

I suddenly feel like stamping my teenage foot and asking him just what's wrong with me that I'm not good enough for him now, and why I wasn't back then.

But I won't, obviously, because that would be way too weird and majorly embarrassing.

"Well, it was really great seeing you again. Surreal, but great."

Did I just say "surreal"? Oh God.

He smiles at me, humour clear in his eyes. "Can I have your number? I don't want to lose contact again."

"Yes, of course!" My voice has gone way squeaky, totally giving me away. Traitor voice. And my heart is pounding at my ribs, threatening a break very soon.

Jake pulls his phone out of his pocket, and I recite my phone number to him, watching as he types it in.

Adele starts to sing in my bag. As I look down, he lifts his phone, gesturing. "And now you have mine."

I have Jake's number!

I'm tapping out a happy number inside my head right now.

He suddenly leans close to me, lifting his hand, tucking my hair behind my ear, fingers tipping my jaw, he kisses my cheek.

I close my eyes, absorbing the feel and smell of him. Cigarettes, beer, and aftershave.

"Seeing you again was way better than I ever thought it could be," he murmurs.

What?

By the time my eyes are open, he's already retreating down the path, heading to his car.

He stops near the bottom and turns back as if remembering something. "Oh, Tru, when I said earlier that you looked great, what I actually should have said was that you look beautiful." He smiles. "I'll call you soon."

And then he's back in his car, pulling away.

I let myself in my flat and fall back against the door, heart still pounding up a storm.

Then the very next thing I do is get my phone out and save Jake's number to my contacts.

CHAPTER SEVEN

"W hat did you do to that boy last night?"
Vicky is already advancing through the office towards me, and I haven't even sat down yet.

"Because whatever it was, just keep on doing it, please." She grins.

"Eh?"

I'm still trying to recover from last night. It took me hours to get to sleep after my night with Jake, so I overslept. This morning was a rush and the interrogation from Simone prevented me from even grabbing a coffee. I'm also still coming down off my Jake cloud and dealing with the probability of never seeing him again.

I'll call you soon.

He won't call. Why would he? And even though I have his number, I'm not calling him. Well, not yet, anyway.

"I just got off the phone with him."

"Who?"

"Jake Wethers!" she screams like a teenager. Not like the owner of a successful magazine.

"Jake?" I'm confused. "Why's he calling you? No offence," I add when I see the disappointed look on her face.

"Because you, my darling, are a skinful of magic, and delicious to boot!"

I hate it when she starts talking in riddles.

"Vicky, I'm a little lost here—help me out, will you?" I chuckle so as not to offend her.

"Did he not speak to you about it last night? No—wow, okay, well, Jake Wethers just called me and has asked the magazine to host his official bio! Arrghhh!" she screams.

It's way too early for Vicky's hysterical screaming. But wow, that is so totally cool.

"He called you himself? Don't they usually have their PAs do this stuff?"

"Yes!" she screams again. "I know, I could not believe it!"

"Wow. That is awesome, Vicky! Really awesome! I'm so pleased for you—for us—for the magazine!"

And I might get a chance to see Jake again, maybe.

I feel a little frisson of excitement buzz inside me at the thought.

"So, who is his biographer?" I ask, taking my jacket off and hanging it on the back of my chair. I wonder if it's anyone I know. I'm going to probably have to work with them for the spreads...that is, if Vicky is putting me on it. God, I hope she is.

She cocks her eyebrow at me in confusion. "Jake really hasn't spoken with you about any of this? He never mentioned anything at dinner?"

"No. Mentioned what?"

"Well, my darling girl, I'm happy to tell you that Jake's official biographer is...well...you."

What? What!

All I can do is stare at her, dumbfounded. And then my mobile starts to ring on my desk.

But I can't move. I'm frozen to the spot.

He's hired me? Jake's hired me to write his bio without even asking me. Is that even legal?

Vicky walks over to my desk, peering over at my phone. She picks it up and holds it out to me.

"You might want to take this call. It's Jake."

All I can do is stare down at it like it's a bomb about to go off.

Why would he do this?

I mean, of course it's awesome and very flattering that he thinks I could do it, but I've never written a book before. I write articles. Little ones that fit on the page of a magazine.

I don't think I can write a book.

Oh God.

I just don't understand why he's done this and why he never talked to me about it. He had ample opportunity last night.

All the air has been sucked out of the room. I think I'm having a panic attack or something. I'm going to pass out.

"Take the call," Vicky urges, pushing the phone closer to me. "You can't pass up this opportunity. The magazine can't pass up this opportunity, Tru." She looks at me wistfully.

But I just can't move my hand to take the phone.

"An opportunity Jake didn't even offer me himself." My voice comes out croaky.

My phone stops ringing.

We both look down at it.

Vicky retreats her hand, taking my bomb of a phone with it.

"Maybe Jake just wanted to speak to me first. You know, with me being your employer. He probably wanted to check it wouldn't cause any problems with your permanent job here first before offering you the job."

"Did he say that to you?" I look at her suspiciously.

"Yes, of course he did," she answers brightly.

She's so lying. He never asked her. I can't imagine Jake ever asking anyone for anything.

All he's done by calling Vicky first is put me in a position where I can't say no.

Did he know that would be the case? And if so, then why would he do that?

"Call him back," Vicky urges.

I shake my head, swallowing down my dry throat. "I don't think I can. I don't think I can do this. I can't write a book, Vicky. I'm a journalist. A music journalist, not a novelist."

"You can. You are a wonderful writer, my darling."

I look up at her, mild panic in my eyes. I know what she's worried about. She's worried Jake will pull the bio from the magazine if I don't write it.

But he wouldn't do that.

"Jake will still have the magazine do the feature, even if I don't take the job, Vicky. He wouldn't pull it. I know him."

She shrugs. "I don't know, honey, I did sort of get the distinct impression you are part of the deal."

"Did he say that?"

"Not exactly."

Yes he did.

Crap.

"Why would he do this?" I say my thoughts out loud.

She smiles. "Maybe he just doesn't want to let you go this time."

"So he forces me to write his bio? No, that doesn't make any sense. I'm his friend. You don't force people to be your friend. I'd be his friend without this."

I'm so confused. I need to sit down. I slump back into my chair.

Vicky moves round and leans against my desk. "Maybe he doesn't just want to be your friend," she says softly. "And if that is the case, then this way he gets to ensure he sees a lot more of you, for a long while."

My eyes flash up to hers. "No." I shake my head. "It's not that."

He had the chance to make a move on me last night, and if I'm being truthful, I probably would have kissed him back if he had kissed me, but he didn't. And that's how I know that's not the reason.

I just have no clue what his motive is.

Maybe it's a genuine one. Maybe he thinks I'm a really good writer.

I scoff at the very thought.

"Well, for whatever reason he is doing it," Vicky says, "this is a huge opportunity for you and the magazine as a whole. It can only be a good thing, Tru. And maybe Jake recognises that. He'll know what this will do for your career. Maybe he just wants to help you. He did say to me that he's been considering doing a bio for a long while now, and with this tour it's the right time. It was obviously just good fortune that you met back up with him; it could be someone else getting to hop on that tour bus."

Shit. I'm going to have to go on tour with them. Of course.

I'm so screwed.

This morning I was worried I was never going to see him again, and now I'm going to be spending a huge amount of time with him, following him around, watching him, learning all about him, while we tour around some pretty cool parts of the world.

Yes, I am so completely and utterly screwed.

"Call him," Vicky urges one last time, placing my phone on my desk, tapping her nail on the screen before leaving me to it.

I stare at my phone and then with shaky fingers I pick it up and press redial on his number.

He answers on the first ring.

"Tru," his voice comes deep and sexy down the line.

"Hi, Jake."

Silence.

"So…," I say, not really knowing what to say.

"I'm taking it your boss beat me to it?" he states rather than asks.

"She did."

"And?"

"And what?"

"Will you do it—the bio?"

"Do I have a choice?"

There's a really long pause. I can practically feel his tension radiating down the line.

"There's always a choice, Tru." He sounds a little pissed off.

"Sorry," I say, recovering. "That sounded a little shitty. It's just a lot of information to process this early in the morning. Especially when I haven't even had a chance to have a coffee yet."

"You haven't?"

"No, and I don't function without coffee," I say in a Spanish accent. I'm actually fluent in Spanish, something my mum insisted on, and it does comes in handy at times—mainly holidays in Spanish-speaking countries. And my crap Spanish accent always used to make Jake laugh when we were kids, so I'm aiming for just that again.

He chuckles, deep and throaty down the line. It does incredible things to me. "I see you're still an idiot."

"I am, and it still takes one to know one."

"That it does...so you'll do it?"

I get the distinct feeling he's not asking me. And really in what world would I ever say no?

"I'll do it." I smile.

I can practically feel his grin.

"Okay, so as your new boss—well, one of them—I order you to go get some coffee, as I can't have you talking in that cute Spanish accent of yours all day. You'll drive me nuts."

I'll drive him nuts? In a good or bad way...

"I'm seeing you today?"

"Of course. Go get that coffee and I'll call you back soon."

He hangs up, and I sit staring at the phone in my hand, feeling a little dumbfounded.

And somehow a little played. I just haven't figured out as to how yet.

I'm also feeling a little excited—okay, a lot excited. I'm going on tour with the Mighty Storm...with Jake.

Shit. And double shit. I'm going to have to tell Will.

Well, that thought quickly dilutes my good mood.

I don't go and get a coffee straightaway; I go to Vicky's office.

"You called him?" She looks up at me hopefully.

"I called him."

"And?

"And of course I'm doing it."

"Oh, thank God! You had me worried for a moment there. Oh, Trudy, you are my superstar!" She gets up from her desk and hugs me in a cloud of perfume and perfectness. "I knew from the second you stepped into the interview for a job here that hiring you would be the best thing I would ever do."

She holds me back by my shoulders, smiling her gorgeous smile at me. "You, my girl, are going to lift this magazine off the bottom shelf and put it in its rightful place amongst those glossies on the middle shelf."

"You really think this exclusive with Jake will do that?" I know it will lift sales, but I don't want her to pin all her hopes on this.

"I do." She nods emphatically. "This boy is unattainable. Getting a concise straight answer out of him is bad enough, but full-blown insight into his life? Hell, all those women out there who sit listening to his album, watching him on TV, dreaming of Jake Wethers in their beds will wet their panties over this."

I can't help but laugh.

"And they are also going to love the fact that you guys grew up together and have just reunited to do this story. Women will envy you and love you for bringing that man into their houses."

"Um." I tuck my hair behind my ear. "I was thinking maybe we should keep that part under wraps."

I've been thinking about this, and I don't want all the attention it will bring me if people find out Jake and I grew up together. And there could be the chance that when the press is delving into Jake's and my history together, someone from our former years might just tell the story of what his dad did to him and his mum. I shudder to think. Somehow Jake's managed to keep that part of his life out of the press; I don't want to be the reason it comes out.

Obviously I'm not going to say any of that to Vicky. I've already quickly planned out what I'm going to say.

"I just think it will seem even better if they don't know of my history with Jake. It might take the focus off the bio when they realise Jake and I have history, and I don't want that to be the running feature. I want it to be about Jake and *Etiquette*."

She grins at me. "Good thinking. Always the journalist. Have I told you lately how much I love you?"

"No." I grin.

"Well, I do, lots and lots."

"So the tour...Jake said he's going to see me again today—I assume to talk about the tour. But can you give me a heads-up now?"

"You're seeing him again—today?" She grins, sitting back down.

She's like a teenager at times.

"Yes, about business. Brief me about the tour, please, boss?"

She leans back in her chair. "Seven weeks. Touring Europe for the first three, then America and Canada for the last four."

"And I can come home in between the dates?"

"There are a lot of dates on the tour. It's pretty intensive—ten dates in Europe and thirteen in the US and Canada. There is a two-week break between Europe and the US, and I can't imagine you'll be needed all the time—but check with Jake."

"What about my column?"

"I was going to get Jane to cover what you couldn't manage?"

"Sure. Sounds like a plan."

I get out of my chair. "What did you think of the piece of the interview with Jake that I sent you?"

"Really good. I e-mailed back a few possible changes, have a look—let me know what your thoughts are. But there's no rush on finishing it as I think we're going to use it as the precursor for the bio."

I start to leave her office, then stop at the door. "Why do you think Jake never mentioned the bio to me last night?"

She shrugs. "You said last night was a catch-up on old times, so maybe he didn't want to talk business with you at that point."

"Hmm, maybe…he could have called me first thing this morning…but I guess it doesn't matter."

She leans forward, resting her elbows on her desk. "You want my honest opinion? I think he asked you out to dinner because he wanted to see you again. I think he hired you for the bio because you're fabulous at your job—and also because he wants to have sex with you."

"Vicky!" I screech, eyes wide.

I can't believe she just said that.

"What?" she says innocently. "I'm merely pointing out the conclusive facts."

"Which conclusive facts?"

"That Jake wants to have sex with you."

"Will you stop saying that!" My face is flushing bright red. "And Jake could have sex with anyone he wants, and trust me he wouldn't want to have it with me."

I think of the little brush-off at my door last night. I don't tell her, of course.

She frowns at me and shakes her head. "Sometimes I don't think you realise how gorgeous you are, Tru."

I pull a face at her compliment.

"And yes, you are right. Jake could bed any women he wants to…but currently I think he wants to bed you."

I frown at her. "It'd be an awful lot of trouble for him to go through just to get laid, when he can have it so easily accessible elsewhere."

"Easily accessible can get boring, my darling. And you are right; it certainly would be a lot of trouble to go to." She raises her eyebrow. "So I guess that shows the worth of the person as to the level of trouble he's willing to go to."

"Or just the new challenge."

"That too." She leans back in her chair. "Just be careful, when mixing business and pleasure. Things can get awful messy sometimes."

"I don't intend on mixing anything. I'm with Will, remember?"

"You are."

"And I don't think Jake is like that. Contrary to popular belief, I think he's professional in business; I don't think he screws the staff—just everyone else."

"Of course. I can imagine Jake Wethers to be the utmost professional."

She's being snarky.

"He was actually a real gent at dinner last night."

"He was?" She smiles, a real genuine smile. "Good. I'm glad."

I ignore the little nag of disappointment, tugging away inside of me, that Jake Wethers, who is well known for sleeping around, had no interest in me whatsoever last night.

Of course it stings. I would never have slept with him, because of Will. But I might have kissed him.

But then kissing is cheating too.

Ugh, my head is all gooey right now. I need a coffee.

I'm being irrational and silly that my pride is hurt, I know, but I'm a girl and it's my prerogative to be just so.

"You want a coffee?" I ask Vicky as I'm leaving her office. "I'm making."

"I'm fine, my darling, thank you."

I'm just heading past my desk, on my way to the kitchen to fire up the kettle, when my mobile starts to ring.

I lean over my desk and grab my phone. It's Jake. Little butterflies set flight in my tummy.

I'm going to have to knock this off if I'm going to be working with him.

People don't work with me, Tru. They work for me.

Okay, so working for him—whatever. I hope he's not as bad a person to work for as it's claimed he can be.

"You had that coffee yet?" he says before I get a chance to speak.

"*No, debido a las interrupciones constantes.*"

95

"Tru, I haven't got a fuckin' clue what you just said, but I'll take the 'no' I caught out of that, as you haven't."

"No, I haven't," I say, laughing.

"Okay, well, I'm not calling back again, so listen up. I'm picking you up for lunch because I want to go over with you what will happen on the tour."

Do I get a choice?

"Shouldn't that be your assistant's job to talk to me about that stuff?" I question.

"If I wanted my assistant to have lunch with you, then yeah, it would be, but I don't, so you're getting me—okay?"

"What if I already have plans?"

"Do you?"

"Yes?"

Silence.

"With?"

Do I detect a hint of jealously there, Jake?

"Starbucks. I meet him every day at one for a coffee and a blueberry muffin."

I hear him exhale down the line.

"Would you consider ditching him for me?" His voice has gone all seductive and flirty again.

"I don't know…it's a pretty serious thing me and Starbucks have going on."

"I'll make it worth your while."

"Go on?"

"I'm talking cake, Tru, lots and lots of cake."

"Starbucks who?" I giggle.

"Cool, be outside your building at one."

"*Sí, señor.*"

I hear him laugh before I hang up.

I feel absolutely full of glee. Jake is being lovely and flirty, and I'm seeing him again in just a few hours.

But no, I need to calm myself down. I'm going to be working for Jake, so I need to keep myself professional.

He might be an old friend, an incredibly flirty old friend. But that's Jake. That's his MO.

And I need to remember that and not confuse this into something it's not.

The black Land Rover that Dave was following us around in last night is already parked outside my building when I go down at one.

Dave gets out of the car and walks around, opening the back passenger door for me.

"Hello again," he says.

"Hi," I whisper shyly.

I climb in the back and Jake is there waiting for me. Looking his gorgeous rock star self in light blue ripped jeans, a faded black Stone Roses "I Wanna Be Adored" T-shirt, and the same Converses he wore last night.

"Hey," he says, his voice all rough, and smooth like honey, as Dave closes the door behind me.

"Hey yourself." I smile.

I can smell Jake's scent across the car. Cigarettes and aftershave. It makes my tummy flutter.

Dave climbs back in the driver's seat and pulls us away into the heavy lunchtime traffic.

"So how's your morning been?" Jake asks me.

"Oh, you know, long."

"Much happen?"

I slide a look at him. "Apart from a famous rock star who also used to be my next-door neighbour growing up calling me and offering me a job to write his bio on his upcoming tour? No, not much at all." I shake my head, grinning.

"Is that all I was—your next-door neighbour? I thought I earned the title best friend back then."

His words make my tummy feel funny. Suddenly empty.

"You did…and we were best friends."

"Were?"

"Well it's been a while, Jake. You don't just get that status back after one dinner." I smile again, trying to alleviate whatever this is.

"I guess I'm going to have to work a little harder then to claim my title back." His voice is low with meaning. He smiles at me, and my heart lurches out of my chest and whams straight into him once again.

"So am I allowed to know where we're going for lunch today, or is that a surprise too?" I give him a lighthearted look, trying to straighten out my erratic heart and shaky emotions.

"Just back to the hotel. I hope that's okay?"

"Sure it is."

I'd eat fish and chips in the backseat of a car if it meant being with you.

"It's just less hassle, means we won't get bothered," he adds, as though he has to explain why he's taking me back to his suite.

"Jake, it's okay, I understand." I touch his arm.

He looks down at my hand on his tattooed arm, then up at my face.

Something passes in the air between us.

I withdraw my hand, swallowing down, and shift in my seat.

"You should have told me we were just staying at the hotel. I would've come over. It's not too far of a walk."

He gives me a stupid but firm look. "I was picking you up, Tru."

"Okay, Mr. Bossy...I hope you're not gonna be like this for the tour."

"What—bossy?"

"Yes."

"Well, when I know what I want I say it...or take it." He tilts his head to the side, staring at me for a long moment.

My legs start to tremble.

I press my knees together.

I flicker a nervous glance at Dave, but his eyes are focussed ahead on the road.

I keep mine ahead too.

And we travel in silence for the rest of the short ride to the hotel. I'm at a complete loss for words after that little exchange.

Dave pulls the car into the hotel's parking lot, and then I follow him and Jake through the lot into the hotel and to the lifts.

I ride up with them both in silence, and leaving Dave out in the hall, I follow Jake into his suite.

I can't believe it was only yesterday that I was here to interview him, and now I'm going to be working for him. It's crazy.

As I follow him I see Stuart at the far side of the living room, sitting on the sofa, reading a magazine. He closes the magazine, dropping it onto the coffee table, and stands at our arrival.

"Hi," I say, feeling a little shy.

I wonder if he knows I'm going to be working for Jake. I'm sure he does; he's Jake's PA. He'll know everything about him.

Probably some things I don't want to know.

"Hello again." He smiles at me.

"Is everything ready?" Jake asks him.

"Yes."

"Thanks," he says to Stuart.

Stuart gives him a brief nod and then heads out of the room, leaving us alone

"Come on," Jake says to me, taking hold of my hand, giving me a fire in my belly again. He leads me across the living room and out onto the terraced balcony.

The air is refreshing on my skin, not chilly at all, and as I step through the door and out from behind Jake, I see there's a table set up, with two chairs, and it is filled with tiers of little mini cakes. So many different varieties—cupcakes, cream buns, éclairs, cheesecakes, and, oh my God, cream-filled muffins, and some I can't even identify.

I know he said there'd be cake, but I never expected anything like this. And there is also fresh coffee waiting.

In this moment I just love him. Not love him, love him—but love him. Oh, you know what I mean.

Jake turns, seeing my openmouthed expression, and says, "Well, you gave up a date with Starbucks for me, it was the least I could do."

"This is a little better than Starbucks though," I say, my voice a little hoarse. "Is this birthday present number two?"

He squeezes my hand ever so slightly and smiles, a mysterious smile, and leads me over to the table to sit down.

In the last two days, Jake has done more thoughtful things for me than anyone has ever done in my whole entire life.

He pulls out my chair for me.

"Why, thank you, kind sir," I say with a giggle.

He sits down across from me.

I feel all fuzzy and up in the clouds here on this penthouse balcony.

And I also feel like I'm on a date. Which of course I'm not, this is a business lunch, just with lots and lots of yummy, scrummy cakes.

I let my eyes roam over the cakes. They look fresh and delicious, and I literally don't know which one to try first. I just want to take a bite of each one.

Jake laughs at my staring. "You look like a kid in a candy store. You always did have a sweet tooth."

"There's just so many to choose from, and they are just so damn cute. Where did you get them from?" I ask.

"Just a little place I know."

Unable to resist anymore, I nick a bit of cream from the cream-filled muffin closest to me, and lick it off my finger.

"Oh my God," I groan. "This is gorgeous. I think I may have died and gone to cream heaven."

"So does this win me back my best-friend status?"

"I think I might be proposing marriage to you soon, if you keep this up."

It just slipped out. And I can't take it back.

I know my face is bright red.

Jake grins at me, obviously enjoying my discomfort.

"Shall I pour?" I say, gesturing to the coffee. Anything to change the subject.

"I got it," he says, taking hold of the pot.

Jake pours me a coffee. He looks so funny, sitting there in rock star clothes, covered in tattoos, pouring me coffee, while we have afternoon tea together.

"You know, Jake, afternoon tea isn't very rock and roll. You're kind of killing your rock star image."

"Ssh." He puts his finger to his lips, doing a comical glance around. "We'll just have to keep it our little secret." He grins and hands me over my coffee. "And shouldn't it be afternoon coffee?" he adds.

I furrow my brow in thought. "Is there such a thing?"

He shrugs, smiling. "If not, then there is now."

"Jake and Tru's afternoon coffee, rock star style."

"Abso-fucking-lutely!" he laughs.

Laughing, I pick up the milk and add some to my coffee, and then help myself to the cream-filled muffin I've already started on.

I pick it up and take a bite.

"Holy creaming Jesus," I mumble with my mouth full. "This is amazing."

If I thought that little taste of cream was heaven, I was sorely mistaken, because the whole thing—sponge and chocolate chips and cream—together is bliss. If I die today, then I will die a very happy lady indeed.

"Seriously, Jake, you have to give me the name of this place because I'm going to have to set up a credit account with them."

He smiles at me, but I detect a hint of nervousness. I'm instantly curious. "Delivery might be a bit of a problem."

"Why?" I say taking another bite.

"Because the delicatessen is in Paris."

I pause midbite, staring at him.

"I had them flown in this morning," he adds.

"Oh." I put down the cake.

"It's one of my favourite places, I always go there whenever I'm in Paris, and I knew you'd love them so…"

"Wow, Jake…um…wow, that is so nice and incredibly thoughtful of you, but you didn't have to go to any trouble for me."

"I didn't. I pay other people to go to the trouble for me, Tru."

"Oh."

Shit, I am so way out of my league here.

He pulls his cigarettes out. "You mind if I smoke?"

I shake my head and watch as he lights up a cigarette.

I can't exactly complain about his smoking around the food, when he's just had said food flown in on an aeroplane. From Paris.

Jesus Christ. This is me getting a little glimpse into just how much pull Jake Wethers actually has.

But he's just so erratic.

He takes me for a simple dinner to Pizza Hut—well maybe not simple, as he did hire the place out—but still, it was Pizza Hut. And now today, he's flown in mini cakes from Paris.

I feel like my head is spinning from just being around him. I don't remember him being this confusing when we were younger.

Straight talking, yes. Confusing, no.

"So what does your boyfriend think of you coming on the tour?" he asks out of the blue, taking a sip of his coffee.

And there's the straight talking.

"Um…I…um…he doesn't think anything yet, because I haven't had a chance to tell him."

That's a lie. I've had all morning to ring Will and tell him, but I'm not sure how he'll take it, so I'm putting it off until tonight when I've fed him and seduced him. Then I'll tell him.

Suddenly the idea of seducing Will, while here with Jake, doesn't feel alluring at all. It actually makes me feel quite unwell.

"I'm going to tell him tonight when I see him," I add.

He puts down his coffee and takes a drag of his cigarette. Then reaches down and picks up an ashtray from off the floor beside his chair, and placing it on his thigh, he taps the ash into it.

"Are you doing anything nice?"

"When?"

"Tonight."

"Oh, um, no, Will's just coming round to my flat to have some dinner."

He's staring at my face, his own impassive.

"How did you meet him?"

"I knew him from uni, and we bumped into each other on a night out a few years ago. He asked me out, and we've been together since."

"But you don't live together."

"No."

"Do you think you'll marry him?"

What? Personal much?

I shift uncomfortably in my seat. I hate it when he starts being direct like this.

I feel like I'm up for a job interview, I'm just not actually sure of the job. Unless he has another one lined up for me that he's also not told me about.

For want of something to do with my fidgety hands, I dip my finger in the cream of my half-eaten bun again and pop it in my mouth.

I notice Jake staring at my mouth.

I quickly pull my finger out and dry it on a napkin. "Well I was proposing marriage to you a few minutes ago." I laugh. He doesn't.

"I don't know." I shrug, turning serious. "It's not something I've thought about. I guess I don't really see myself ever getting married."

He has another drag of his cigarette and slowly blows the smoke out from between his lips, tapping his ash into the ashtray.

"Why?"

I shrug again, looking down.

I'm not going to tell him that I don't think any guy would ever ask me.

"I always figured you'd end up with a musician," he says, in a low voice.

I look up at him, surprised.

Surprised that he even considered that about me.

"So how long are you in the UK for?" I ask, for want of a subject change.

"I'm flying back to LA first thing in the morning."

"Oh," I say, disappointed he's leaving so soon. "Do you have a private jet?" I ask, being nosey.

"Yeah. It's the label's."

"You mean the label that you own."

"Mmm."

Bloody hell, he's got his own private jet.

"So the next time I see you will be at the tour."

"Yes."

I feel quite sad that I'm not going to see him for two weeks.

"Some best friend you are," I pout jokingly. "You do remember that the contract for being my best friend has a beck-and-call clause in it, don't you? I mean, what if I need...I don't know...chocolates from Belgium? Who's gonna get them while you're off in LA? I don't know, Jake, I might have to seriously consider trading you in," I tell him with a grin.

He chuckles, amused. "Don't worry, I'll make sure you don't miss me."

"I never said I'd miss you."

"You never said you wouldn't."

God, he's so bloody quick. I'm getting whiplash just sitting here with him.

"I just want you for your cupcakes," I jest. "And talking of cakes, will you help me eat some of them before I scoff them all and get seriously fat...and while you're at it, tell me about the tour too?"

"I can't ever imagine you'd get fat, Tru...but your wish is my command."

And he grins in that sexy way he does; the one where I definitely know there's something going on behind it, I'm just not entirely sure what, as he leans forward and picks up one of the cakes.

CHAPTER EIGHT

Will's at the door with a bottle of wine in his hand, looking as handsome as always.

"Hey," he says, pulling me into his arms. He kisses me firmly on the mouth.

"Hey, yourself." I smile up at him.

He releases me and I walk back down the hall and into our living room. Simone's out with her work colleagues tonight, so it's just Will and me, and I have big plans of seduction and then to tell him about working for Jake and the tour.

"Are you ready to eat now? Dinner's ready."

"Definitely, I'm starving .What are we having?"

"Lasagne," I answer, heading for the kitchen.

Will follows me into the kitchen and sets about opening the wine, while I dish up the lasagne.

I carry both our plates through to the living room, putting them down on the coffee table, while Will brings through the wine.

I sit down on the floor, and Will sits opposite me.

I take a sip of my wine, watching Will as he tucks into the lasagne.

"This is good," he says. "You make the best lasagne ever."

"Thank you, baby."

Seeing as though he's happy with my culinary skills, I decide to tell him about the tour now.

I spoke to Will this afternoon on the phone; he'd called when I was out at lunch, so I called him back. For some reason I didn't tell him I'd had lunch with Jake. I think mainly it was because I would have had to tell him about the tour, and I wanted to do that tonight. He did quiz me about my night with Jake though, naturally, which I also downplayed quite a lot.

He scoffed when I said we'd been to Pizza Hut. It really annoyed me, to be honest; he can be such a snob at times, so I didn't even bother to explain the relevance of it to Jake and me.

"So I was...um...offered this amazing opportunity at work today."

"Oh yes?" he says, forking lasagne into his mouth.

"Well...Jake...Wethers has asked the magazine to cover his official biography...and well...he's asked me to write the bio."

"Really? That's wonderful news," he says.

"Yes, it is. But...um...the other thing is that to do so, I'll have to go on tour with the band, you know to follow Jake around, write about the tour and the band. Especially as it's their first tour without Jonny."

Will's brows knit together. "So you're going on tour with Jake Wethers?"

"Yes, and the rest of the band."

"So my girlfriend—my very beautiful girlfriend—is going on tour with a bunch of musicians, one of whom is Jake Wethers, the notorious womaniser."

"Yes," I say, mildly. "But what Jake is or isn't, is of no relevance to me."

"Even though you used to be best friends growing up."

"Which was twelve years ago."

Though it doesn't feel like Jake and I have been apart at all, we've fallen back in line with each other with such ease. I omit that though.

"And if I said I didn't want you to go..."

"Well, I kind of hoped you wouldn't want me to go, but..."

"You'd still go anyway."

"Yes. It's an amazing opportunity for me, Will."

"Hmm." He nods. "So, how long would you be gone?"

"The tour's for seven weeks in total, with a two week break after the first three in Europe. Then it's four weeks in the US and Canada, then done."

"So you'll be gone for three weeks to start with." He sounds unhappy.

I nod. "But I will do my best to get home if I can."

"And you've already said you'll definitely do it?"

"Yes. The magazine really needs this. And this is a published book I'm talking about here, writing a book on a band like the Mighty Storm will be huge for my career. It could open up all kinds of doors for me."

"But why ask you? You've never written a book before."

Wow, thanks for the support.

"No, but I have been writing for a long time, and there is a first time for everything, Will. You know maybe Jake actually thinks my writing is good, and he's a good friend so he thought he'd help me out by giving this opportunity to me.

You know, supporting me in my career—which was what I was kind of hoping you would do." I drop my fork onto my plate with a clatter.

"Sorry," he says, backtracking. "I am supportive, and I'm pleased for you, it's just a little out of the blue, and I'm sad that I'm going to have to be without you for such a long time."

Sighing, I get up and walk around to him and sit in his lap. He puts his fork down on his plate and wraps his arms around me.

"The time will fly by, baby," I say, kissing his cheek. "And then I'll be back home and everything will be back to normal. Except I'll be writing a book." I can't help the smile that spreads across my face.

Will touches my face, brushing back my hair. "I am really pleased for you, darling. I'm just going to miss you so much."

"I'll miss you too."

He leans in and presses his lips to mine. He tastes of red wine and lasagne.

I wrap my arms around his neck, kissing him back. I part my lips and his tongue moves in my mouth.

I turn in his lap so I'm straddling him, kissing him still. He groans in my mouth.

Normally when Will makes that sound it really turns me on, but for some reason I don't feel as turned on.

I push myself closer to him, trying to ignite a fire in my belly.

I feel Will get hard beneath me. He puts his hands on my ass, and pulls me hard onto him.

But still nothing is happening for me.

I'm probably just tired and overwhelmed with everything that's happened over the last few days. I'll get turned on any second now, I'm sure of it.

But I don't feel any different when he's leading me into my bedroom and undressing me and making love to me. And I can't for the life of me figure out why not.

It's half ten when Adele starts singing, telling me I have a text. I must change my ringtone.

Will is already asleep. He fell asleep pretty much right after we made love, but I've lain here for ages unable to sleep, watching the TV in my room with the sound low.

I whip my phone up off my nightstand, silencing it. Then I see the text is from Jake. My heart jumps in my chest.

With nervous fingers, I open up the text:

So I'm sitting here bored shitless and I was thinking about that time when we blew off school, when it was that mad heat wave that one summer, and we took the train to Hebden Bridge so we could go swimming in Lumb Falls... do you remember?

Smiling at the memory, I climb out of bed, pulling my dressing gown on, and I go into the kitchen, taking my phone with me. I put the kettle on to make a tea. While it's boiling, I type a text back:

Of course I do! That was such a fun day, well until you dared me to jump off the high rocks, and I did and when I resurfaced I'd lost my bikini top and you had to go diving for it!

Laughing to myself, I press Send. I put my phone on vibrate so as not to disturb Will, then get a cup out of the cupboard and drop a teabag in it. My phone vibrates in my hand:

That's what I was remembering ;)

My face flushes red. Is he flirting with me? I instantly type back:

Perv! I was only thirteen!

My phone vibrates immediately:

So was I. x

He put a kiss at the end. I grab the milk out of the fridge and type back a reply.

You're still a perv ;) Seriously though, I did just want to say thank you again for lunch. I've never quite had a lunch like it before.

I hover my finger over the Send button. Then I go back and add a few kisses, then press Send.

Me either. I'll miss u while I'm gone. Be good. x

He'll miss me? And he's telling me to be good. When am I never good? I hold the phone to my chest, contemplating texting him back.

Unable not to, I quickly tap out a text:

I'll miss u 2. And fyi, I'm always good. It's you that needs to learn the meaning of the word. x

It's a minute before he replies:

I'm starting to. x

I stare at my phone for a while, confused, until the kettle boils, bringing me round.

I make myself a cup of tea and take it back to bed with me. I climb in bed beside Will. He groans and rolls over in his sleep, facing me.

I look at him and sip my tea, then it hits me why I didn't feel turned on before with Will.

Because of Jake. Because I can't stop thinking about him.

CHAPTER NINE

I'm in a taxi on my way to Heathrow airport to fly out to Sweden for the first leg of the tour.

I'm mega-excited about this tour, and I'm also really looking forward to seeing Jake again.

I might not have seen Jake for two weeks, but we've been in regular contact; I've spoken to him every day. Well, not actually spoken, but we've been e-mailing and texting every day since he texted me that first night.

It's like we've never been away from each other, the last twelve years dissolving into irrelevance.

Some of the e-mails and texts have been a little flirty, mostly on his part, but I've made sure not to cross any line. I don't want to blur things and give Jake the wrong impression.

I'm not up for being another notch on his incredibly long belt, even if he is gorgeous and lovely and so very sweet to me. It's not worth losing Will over.

And Will...well things have been amazing these last few weeks. It's been like it was when we first got together. Hot sex everywhere.

It seems that lag I had, which I'm totally putting down to Jake's huge bang back into my life, vanished with his going back to LA.

We were in bed together last night when Will did the sweetest thing…

"So I bought you something," Will said, climbing out of bed, leaving me feeling cold without him.

"You did?" I sat up, feeling a little frisson of excitement.

Will always buys me the best presents. He knows what I like. He knows me so well.

He retrieved something from the pocket of his pants, which were slung over the chair at my dressing table, while I admired his hot, tight body and cute bum from behind.

He's so gorgeous and lovely. I love that he's mine.

He came over and sat down on the bed beside me. "I bought this for you because I want you to have something to remember me by while you're gone." He held out a black velvet jewellery box.

"Jewellery." I smiled. My itchy fingers reached out to touch the soft black velvet.

Will looked a little nervous as I opened it.

"Oh my God! Will, it's beautiful!" I touched my fingers to the platinum chain-mail bracelet feeling completely overwhelmed by his thoughtfulness.

"You like?" He looked at me hopefully.

"I love!" I leaned forward and kissed him firmly on the lips.

He held my face in his hands, prolonging the kiss. When he finally released me, he removed the bracelet from the box, and I held my arm out, allowing him to put it on.

"It looks perfect," he said, staring down at it. My own eyes fixed on it too. "I want you to wear it all the time you're away from me, so you have a permanent reminder of me and our life together." Will's voice was deep and low.

My heart started to hurt in my chest at the thought of the length of time I'm actually going to be away from him. The enormity of it finally hit me.

I felt tears start to prick the backs of my eyes.

"Like I would ever forget about you," I said gently. I touched my hand to his face, feeling the starter of his rough stubble under my fingertips.

Will took hold of my hand, kissing my palm. He started to kiss a path down my arm slowly, making my tummy tingle, as his lips moved over my shoulder and up my neck, until he reached my mouth.

He took my face in his hands, fingers buried deep in my hair. "I love you so much," he said.

"Show me how much." I grinned, biting down on my lip.

Will's eyes came alive with instant lust, and then he set about showing me just how much he actually does love me for the rest of the night.

Leaving Will in the morning was really hard. I cried a bunch. He wanted to drive me to the airport but he had an early meeting that he couldn't get out of, so we said our good-byes at my flat, and I promised to call him as soon as I landed in Stockholm.

I was sad to leave Simone too. We were both a little teary as I was getting in my taxi. Thank God for Optrex eye drops and Touche Éclat; otherwise, I'd look a puffy mess right now.

Simone and I have not been apart since university. Any holidays we go on, we go together, so it'll be weird being away without her, doing all the fun stuff I imagine I'll be doing.

She's promised to come and visit me on tour, and I don't doubt she will as she's desperate to meet Jake and the other guys in the band.

I'm really looking forward to meeting them too. Obviously, I've seen pictures of Tom and Denny, and have read interviews they've done, but it'll be real nice to meet the guys behind those images and words.

I called my mum and dad to tell them the news of the tour the day after I found out. My dad was ecstatic, to put it mildly. Actually he freaked out. He's like a big kid at times!

He was also really happy to hear I was back in touch with Jake. My mum seemed a little bit reserved about the whole thing. I know it's just because she worries about me.

It was in that call that Dad told me about this huge donation they'd received at Tuners for Youths, by an anonymous benefactor, and they were freaking out as the donation was sizeable—huge in fact…£1 million.

One freaking million pounds!

I nearly choked when he told me. The charity is only small, so the difference that kind of money will make to them is immense.

Jake's generosity seemingly knows no bounds. I knew he would make the donation, but a million pounds—he's just amazing.

I was so proud of Jake in that moment. Not that I haven't been so over the years, but this was different.

My eyes filled with tears as I listened to my dad telling me all about what they would do with the money. And when I told him it was Jake who had made the donation, I know he was floored. He was silent for a long time.

I gave my dad Jake's phone number so he could call him to thank him.

I'm guessing he has, but neither Jake nor my dad has mentioned it to me, and I don't want to pry.

I really hope they are back in touch properly, and hopefully they'll get a chance to actually see each other again, as I'm going to talk to Stuart to see if I can get my folks some tickets to come out and see one of the shows on the tour. I know Stuart deals with all that kind of stuff.

I know my dad will just love it.

I'm going to buy the travel and hotel as presents for them, and I'm particularly hoping for the gig in Spain, as it's on a weekend—a Saturday night—so it's perfect, as they would both be off work, and then I could spend the weekend with them. I haven't spent enough time with them recently.

I haven't said anything to them yet. I thought I would wait to make sure I could get the tickets for the gig first.

I'm feeling a little daunted by the whole tour thing, to be honest. I mean, it's a huge deal, and the closer I get to the airport, the tighter the knots in my stomach become.

The only person I'll know on the tour is Jake, and of course he'll be busy a lot. So when I'm not following him around doing my job, I'm going to be at a loose end, and it could get a little lonely for me. I intend to do plenty of sightseeing in those amazing cities I'll be going to. First stop, Stockholm.

I've never been and I'm stoked to see the place for the first time. And I've already got myself guidebooks for all the places I'm going to and they are downloaded and ready on my Kindle.

Geeky, yes. Practical, very.

The taxi pulls up at Heathrow, and the driver kindly lugs my huge suitcase out of the boot for me.

Slinging my carry-on over my shoulder, I wheel my suitcase into the busy airport.

I'm a little nervous about flying alone. I've never done it before, but thankfully it's a short flight, and I've got my Kindle and my iPod to keep me company.

I reach the check-in desk. Parking up my case, I take my passport and travel details out of my bag.

Stuart had booked the plane ticket for me and as it was an online booking, he e-mailed me paperwork to bring with me. He also said one of Jake's drivers would be there to pick me up. I hope it's Dave; a familiar face would be good when landing in a strange city. I get the impression that Jake's drivers are also his security guys—makes sense if you ask me—and I'm yet to meet the others. As Dave is the head of Jake's security, there's bound to be others. I just get the impression Jake always has Dave with him; he seems to trust him implicitly.

I hand my passport and papers over to the woman behind the desk.

"Can you put your case on the scales, please?"

I lift it on, praying to God I'm not over my allowance. I don't pack light; I get it from my mum.

Phew, I just skim in my allowance.

"Okay so you're in first class," she's saying, "so that gives you access to the first-class lounge…"

"Sorry, what?"

She looks at me like I'm slightly slow.

"You're travelling first-class, so that entitles you to use the first-class lounge. Just show them your boarding pass and passport at the reception, and that will grant you access."

Jake.

I can't believe he's done this. Actually, yes I can.

"Okay. Thank you," I say, feeling a little breathless, taking back my passport and boarding card from her.

Stuart had sent me the travel details, but I didn't see anywhere on there that I would be travelling first-class when I read over them.

I've never had first-class anything in my life. I'm not really a first-class girl. I'm more likely to be found in the standard airport bar getting pissed before the flight, then staggering around duty-free buying more booze for the holiday.

And I just don't want Jake spending his money on me like this, even though it's totally generous and I don't mean to sound ungrateful…it's just…well, I bet he doesn't have all his staff travelling first-class. I don't want to be a special case. I don't want him making allowances because of our history. And as it stands now, I'm part of his staff and should be treated as such.

I'll have to make sure he doesn't do it again. But I'll make sure to say it in a very nice way.

I make my way up to the first-class lounge and get myself a drink. Alcoholic, of course, white wine; I know it's early but I'm on vacation, kind of, and well I've just had a bit of a shock with this whole first-class thing, and the wine is just too insanely delicious to turn down.

And the lounge is amazing, sumptuous; it's better than my whole flat.

Seeing as though I'm here, I may as well make myself at home, so I get myself well acquainted with the lounge and pick a window seat, one of the most comfortable seats I have ever rested my derrière in, and I can sit and watch the planes taking off from here.

I retrieve my Kindle from my bag, to read a book while I wait for my flight.

I try to read, but I just can't focus, as my mind keeps flickering back to Jake and the whole first-class thing.

Despite my feelings about it, I really should thank him. I get my phone out of my bag and type out a text:

So I'm sitting in the first class lounge, in the most comfortable seat my ass has ever graced, sipping on the best glass of wine I've ever tasted, courtesy of this amazingly generous guy who paid for my ticket. You don't happen to know who he is, do you? x

I get a text back a minute later:

Nope not a clue. ps. I wish I was the chair ;) x

I reply:

Thank you. Not necessary…but so totally awesome!… and behave! :) x

I get a text immediately back:

This is me behaving ;) And I couldn't have my best friend flying coach, could I :) I'm already in Stockholm so I'll see u in a few hours. x

I get a frisson of energy rushing through me about the tour and about seeing Jake.

I might be nervous about the whole tour and bio thing, but I'm also totally excited too. It's a huge opportunity to be touring with the Mighty Storm.

Smiling to myself, I reply:

Cool. Have I mentioned I'm excited about the tour? It's gonna be so totally epic! x

His reply comes a couple of minutes later:

A few times ;) And sure it is, it's a TMS tour...with the added bonus of u. x

He can be so sweet at times. I'm getting the warm and fuzzies again, and getting more and more keen to see him as the time nears.

The announcement of my flight boarding comes over the tannoy. I quickly tap out a reply to him:

Boarding now. See u on the other side. x

I drop my phone in my bag and make my way to the gate. While I'm in the queue, I get my phone out again to see if he's replied. He has:

Can't wait. x

Butterflies take flight in my stomach.

Me either. And I'm really going now. x

While I have my phone out, I quickly type out a text to Will, letting him know I'm boarding and that I'll call him when I land. Then a quick one to Simone, saying pretty much the same.

I switch my phone off, drop it in my bag, hand my boarding pass to the guy waiting, and make my way onto the plane and to my first-class seat.

Okay, so I am totally flying first-class all the time. It is just awesome, and you get so well looked after. I had two glasses of champagne on the plane and they give you them for free!

I'm currently feeling a little fizzy happy.

I'm off the plane and just going through customs, and glad I wore one of my loose-fitting skater skirts to travel in, as it's boiling here in Stockholm.

The skirt I'm wearing is blue with a gold chain print on it and longer than the black one I wore to Jake's interview. It's respectably long—serious writer long—a few inches above the knee, but still very smart, and I'm wearing my three-quarter-length-sleeved sweatshirt, but the material is thin so it's not too bad in this heat. Also, I'm wearing my gold ballet shoes.

Flats, I don't wear them often, but they're ideal for travelling in.

I wanted to look nice, as it's the first time I'm seeing Jake in two weeks, and quite possibly meeting the other guys in the band.

I get a fizz of excitement running through my bloodstream at the very thought.

I'm through customs pretty quickly, and then on to retrieve my suitcase.

While I'm waiting for my suitcase, I get my phone out and switch on roaming, then call Will.

"Hey, baby." He sounds all deep and lovely. "You got there okay?"

"I did. I'm just waiting for my case now."

"So how is Sweden so far?"

"Hot."

He laughs. "I miss you already."

"Miss you too."

"You still wearing your bracelet?"

I touch my wrist. "Of course."

"Good."

I spot my suitcase making its way around the conveyor. "My case is coming so I'm gonna go. I'll call you later. Love you."

"Okay, baby. Love you too."

I hang my phone up and catch my suitcase just in time, before it sets off to make the journey back around.

Then I head towards arrivals. I spot Dave immediately and am so relieved it's him waiting for me.

"Hi," I say.

"Good flight?" he asks in his super-deep voice, taking my suitcase from me.

"It was awesome." I beam.

He looks at me a little puzzled. My cheeks flush. He's probably used to the whole first-class thing, working for Jake.

"The car's just outside."

I follow Dave through the airport and over to a brand-new black Mercedes SLK, presumably a hire, parked up in one of the drop-off and pickup bays.

The windows on the car are heavily tinted. I guess they have to be for when Jake's travelling in it.

Dave parks my suitcase at the side of the car and gets my door for me.

"Thank you," I say, climbing in, and then my heart nearly leaps out of my chest.

Jake is sitting in the backseat of the car, waiting for me, a huge smile on his face.

"Hey!" I beam at him. The door shuts with a clunk behind me, and then without thinking, I throw my arms around his neck, hugging him tight.

His arms go around me, hugging me back, just as tight, I notice.

And for this brief, momentary hug, all I can do is breathe him in. His scent soothes me, and I feel like I'm home.

I didn't realise just how much I was missing him until this very moment. Or maybe I just didn't allow myself to feel it for fear of how I would feel, like how I do, right now, here in his arms.

Just so completely overwhelmed by the emotion and level of feelings I have for this man.

"I can't believe you came to pick me up!" I say, still beaming a smile, releasing myself from him.

Jake lets me go but keeps me close, taking hold of my hand.

And once again my skin simmers under his hand. I wonder if I'll ever stop feeling like this from his touch.

A big part of me hopes not.

"Well, I'm glad I did now, if it meant getting a welcome like that." He grins. He's being all flirty again.

"I was just hanging around the hotel, so I thought I'd come...sorry I couldn't come in the airport to meet you... you know." He shrugs.

"I know." He'd have probably been recognised and mobbed in ten seconds flat.

It must be pretty hard being a prisoner of your own success. Never able to go anywhere alone.

A simple thing like walking through an airport alone would probably mean the world to him if he was able to do it.

Dave gets in the driver's seat, turns on the engine, and the radio comes to life.

I pull my seat belt on, using one hand, as Jake doesn't seem willing to let go of my other hand.

"How was your flight?" Jake asks as we start moving out of the airport.

"It was awesome thanks to you—did you know you get free champagne in first class? Of course you know..." I peter off at his amused expression.

"You make me laugh." He squeezes my hand, rubbing his thumb over my skin, continuously leaving a delicious trail wherever it goes.

"In a good way, I hope?"

"Always in a good way." He turns his head to the side, directing a fixed look at me. I shiver inside, looking away.

We're quiet for a moment, before Jake says anything more.

"So I spoke to your dad last week."

"You did!" My face nearly cracks with the smile on it.

His lips quirk up at the corner. "Yeah, he called to thank me for the donation..." He lifts an eyebrow.

"What?" I say innocently. "You never said it was a secret. You just said you didn't want him thinking you were a flashy bastard—and he didn't." I push my lips out into a pout.

He shakes his head, laughing at my expression.

"So you talked?" I probe.

"We did. It was good to talk to him after all these years. He's still just the same."

"You talk music?"

"Of course." He slides me an amused look. "So I brought something for you," he says, changing tack.

He reaches into his jeans pocket, pulling something back out. I recognise it instantly. It's the friendship bracelet I made him all those years ago. It's a little frayed, the white, black, and blue fabric faded slightly.

"I can't believe you actually kept it." My words come out with my breath.

"You thought I was lying?" He screws up his face.

"No! I'm just surprised...hang on." I let go of his hand and reach forward into my bag in the foot-well, unzipping the inside pocket to get what I'm looking for.

My friendship bracelet.

I brought mine with me too. I put it in my carry-on; I didn't want it in my suitcase in case it got lost in transit. This bracelet is irreplaceable, so I wanted it safe.

I don't know why I brought it; we hadn't arranged to. I guess I just hoped he would have his with him too.

And he has…I can't believe it.

"I brought mine too," I say, holding out my hand, showing it to him.

Mine is exactly the same as his—in my geekdom, I made us matching ones.

He stares down at it, then lifting his eyes to mine, smiles and says, "Great minds."

My heart is flopping around in my chest like a fish out of water.

"How old were we when you made these?"

"Ten."

"So they're, like…sixteen years old."

"Practically antiques," I say, smiling.

Jake takes hold of my hand and pushes the platinum chain-mail bracelet that Will bought me farther up my arm.

He removes my friendship bracelet from my hand, placing it on his leg. Then I watch as he takes his own friendship bracelet and slips it on over my hand and tightens it to fit around my wrist.

Then he picks mine up, loosens it, and puts it on his own arm.

I let out the breath I didn't realise I was holding.

"Don't ever take it off," he says, voice deep with meaning.

"Not even to shower?" I swallow down.

"Not even to shower."

"And you'll keep yours on?"

"Always." He takes hold of my hand again.

And my heart leaps out of my chest, then thuds its way back in.

I rest back in the seat. I'm going to have to be so careful. Jake is a naturally tactile person, incredibly sweet, and obviously happy to have me back in his life as his friend again.

I'm going to have to be very careful not to confuse this with him having any feelings for me, in that way. And to make sure I don't let my own feelings get confused too.

We talk all the way back to the hotel, and Jake points things out to me, important buildings and sites, as we drive through this amazing city.

Dave parks the car in the hotel lot; we're staying at the Grand Hotel Stockholm. And grand is most certainly how it looks from the outside.

When we arrive, there is a guy waiting for us in the parking lot, seemingly expecting our arrival.

Jake introduces him to me as Ben. He's one of Jake's other security guys. He works under Dave.

Security seems a little tighter for Jake here. Maybe it's because of the hype of the tour, which brings the crazies out.

Ben, I'd guess, is in his early thirties and attractive in a Jason Statham kind of way.

I follow along with the three men, Ben wheeling my suitcase for me.

We all ride in silence up in the lift, getting out on the top floor.

I follow Jake down the hall, Dave and Ben behind us.

Jake stops outside a door and produces a key card from his back pocket.

"This is your room for the next few days."

He opens the door and I step through. I actually gasp.

This isn't a room. It's a bloody suite. And a huge one at that.

"Thanks," Jake says to Ben and Dave. "I got it from here."

Ben parks up my suitcase just inside the room and closes the door behind him.

I slowly turn around to face Jake.

"Jake this is awesome…but it's too much."

"All the suites on the floor are the same size." He shrugs.

"But I'm just one person, I don't need all this room." I wave my arms around.

"So am I, and I'm staying in one exactly the same as this." He seems a little irked by my statement.

"I just…" I can't seem to find the right words. I run my fingers through my hair. "Are all your staff staying in suites like this?"

"Some."

"Who?"

He meets my eyes. "Tom, Denny, Stuart, Smith, and Dave."

"And the rest?"

"On the floors below."

"In normal-size rooms…rooms that are just that—one room and a bathroom."

He nods, slowly, not moving his eyes from mine.

"I should be in one of those rooms, Jake."

He looks a little annoyed now, and a little hurt.

"I'm not trying to sound ungrateful, Jake, but the first class at the airport, and now this…I don't want you spending money on me like this."

He folds his arms. "It's my money; I can do what I want."

"I know, but…" I'm at a loss to find a plausible and strong enough argument against him. "I just don't want to piss your other staff off when they find out I'm staying in such a lovely suite."

His face lightens. "Tru, you won't piss anyone off, it's not in you to be able to do so, and anyway you're important. You're writing my bio, so I have to keep you sweet so you write nice things about me."

"Ahh, so that's what all this niceness has been about." I kink my eyebrow.

He grins. "Not at all, but if it gets you to stay in this room with no complaint, then I'm sticking with it."

"Suite…not room," I correct.

"Whatever." He waves me off. "So you wanna unpack first, or do you wanna meet the guys now?"

I glance at my suitcase.

Hmm, let me think…unpack or meet rock stars…

"Meet the guys," I say, beaming.

"Don't get too excited." He frowns. "They're uglier in real life than they look in their pictures."

"Are you jealous, Jake Wethers?" I tease.

"Me—jealous? Never. Come on." He opens the door. "I left those idiots in my room draining my minibar when I came to get you. Knowing those greedy bastards, they'll still be there, saving their own for later."

I can hear the male voices laughing and joking as we approach Jake's door. I get a little ball of nervous energy in my tummy the closer we get.

I am, in a few seconds, about to be standing in a room with some of the best musicians the world currently has to offer.

I'm going to be in a room with the Mighty Storm!

I'd have to be crazy not to be a little excited.

Jake opens his door, allowing me through first, putting me immediately in the living room, and I see the guys all sitting around the dining table, playing cards, drinking beer.

"Tru, this is Denny." Jake stands behind me. He places his hand on my lower back and points over my shoulder at a dark-haired guy, who is very cute, and who I instantly recognise.

Even distracted by Denny, I still tense under Jake's touch.

"Denny—this is Tru, my old friend from Manchester and biographer for the tour."

"Hey, Tru, it's great to finally meet you." Denny smiles at me, running his hand through his short hair.

Finally meet me? So Jake's already told him about me?

Of course he has, dopey, you are their biographer.

"Hi." I smile nervously at him.

"And this is Smith, our session guitarist, who is playing lead for us on the tour." Jake points at the only person in the room I don't recognise.

And sweet baby Jesus, he is gorgeous. Long, messy blond hair and dark green eyes. He looks like a surfer.

"Hey," Smith says in a Southern drawl, giving me a nod.

"He's married," Jake whispers in my ear. I feel his fingers tense against my back.

What?

I look up at Jake, wanting to ask him what the hell he meant by that with a look, but he's not looking at me.

"And not forgetting, Tom," Jake says, pulling my eyes away from him and back across the room.

Tom has his back to me, but of course I instantly recognise him the second he turns around in his seat to us.

Tom has light brown hair, shaved close, and he is covered in tattoos, just like Jake. He is really good-looking, though not my type; his face is a little too round for my liking. I like my men a little more chiselled, but I can certainly see the allure for the women who love him.

"Hel-lo, gorgeous." Tom gets up from his chair.

"No," Jake says sternly, pointing a finger at him, stopping him in his tracks.

"What?" Tom says innocently, holding up his hands in surrender. "I was just coming over to say hello to the gorgeous Trudy, and to greet her in my genuine Tom style... and also to find out where he's been hiding you," he says directly to me, conspiratorially winking.

I actually blush.

What am I—sixteen?

"Yeah, and your style usually involves tongues and groping. Tru has had a long flight and can do without you pawing her—and also she has a boyfriend, so hands off." Jakes sounds so protective, like he's my big brother or something. Maybe that's how he views me, in a sisterlike fashion.

The thought depresses me a little. Well, quite a lot actually.

"Jeez, down boy—I get it." Tom rolls his eyes at Jake. Laughing, he sits back down in his chair and takes a swig of his beer.

"You want something to drink?" Jake asks me as he starts to move away.

I suddenly feel a little bereft without his touch. And still a little saddened by the brotherly protectiveness.

"No, I'm fine, thanks...you know, I think I will go and unpack my suitcase, leave you guys to finish your game." I gesture to the ongoing card game being played at the table.

Jake stops, turning to look at me. "You sure?" he asks.

"Yeah, I'm sure." I smile. "I'll see you all later." I wave in the guys' direction. "It was nice to meet you all."

I turn and leave the room, acutely aware of the fact that Jake's eyes are on me the whole time I'm walking away.

Chapter Ten

It's my second day in Stockholm and tonight is TMS's first show.

I'm at the stadium with the band. The opening show is at the Ericsson Globe. It's the strangest and most cool building I have ever seen. It's shaped like a large white ball. It's also quite a small venue for the guys; it takes only about sixteen thousand people. There's the Stockholm Stadium, which hosts double that, but I think the guys wanted to kick off the tour with a small venue.

I'm sitting out in the seats watching them rehearse for tonight, while the roadies get everything set up for the show.

It's the first time I've ever seen Jake up on stage in person and not watching him through a TV screen.

He looks at ease up there, but I can tell he's a little on edge. I can see it in his eyes. That little lost look he gets. He exudes calm control to everyone, but I can tell. He was the same when we were kids.

Other people probably miss it, but I see it. I've always seen it in him.

I'm guessing he's on edge because it's his first show since Japan. I think he struggles onstage without Jonny by his side. It must be hard for all of them, and for Smith too, having to fill the stage where such a big presence once stood.

I spent yesterday in the hotel with Jake and the guys. After I'd finished unpacking and calling my dad, Will, and Simone, Jake came knocking to see if I wanted any food. The guys were ordering up room service. Surprisingly, they weren't going out partying.

Maybe they were being good boys with the first show being the next day.

So I went and hung out with them, ate, drank beer, and played cards.

I wasn't technically working yesterday but just being with them all gave me a good initial insight into the dynamics among them, especially with the new addition of Smith for the tour.

It's funny, because even though Jake's the "boss," it didn't come across that way with them. They all seem to have a great relationship. Watching them together, it was just like watching a bunch of guys in college. Even with Smith, there's no weirdness with him there, the way they act towards him, it seems like he's always been there.

But it did make me wonder what it was like when Jonny was still here.

It's clear that Denny is the sensible one, so I get the impression he's the one Jake can rely on for work. Tom's not unreliable, but he's the definite player, I'd say. The one always cracking jokes, the partier, and clearly a womaniser.

Tom's eyes spent a lot of time on my boobs while I was there with them. It didn't bother me, but I got the clear impression it was bothering Jake. Mainly because he kept asking me if I was cold, and did I need to put a sweater on over my vest top.

Yeah sure, Jake, it's a hundred degrees in here, of course I want to wear a sweater!

His behaviour, if anything, just highlighted the big brother vibe I got earlier, when he made the comment about Smith being married.

Tom is well known, like Jake, for enjoying the female "perks" of his profession.

I can imagine Tom is that kind of player who would work the room, flirting his way around. I think Jake is the kind of guy who waits for women to come to him. He doesn't work for it. Then again, he doesn't need to.

Not that I've seen any of this in action yet, but I'm sure I will very soon. And honestly, I'm not looking forward to seeing Jake with other women. The thought turns my stomach.

I didn't do any of the sightseeing I had intended to on my first day in Stockholm, and I probably won't today either, as I'm here with Jake and the guys at the stadium, and then it's the show tonight, then we leave first thing in the morning to go to Germany.

I get a feeling this is how things might be for the whole of the tour.

It's lunchtime. Jake's called a break from rehearsal and I'm in one of the large dressing rooms with him and the guys, and a few other people from the tour, eating lunch.

I'm sitting on the sofa, my notepad rested on the arm, and I'm writing up some things, pulling together some of my notes from the rehearsals.

"Did you get anything good from this morning's rehearsal for the book?" Jake asks, slumping down into the empty space next to me, indicating my notebook.

He sits so close, a nervous energy suddenly takes rein under my skin.

"A few things." I turn my head, smiling at him. "It was great watching you up there onstage."

"The show tonight will be even better." He smiles confidently back at me.

He can be such an arrogant sod at times, but it's so alluring.

"I'm sure it will be." Then a thought pops into my head, and I remember something he said to me back when I interviewed him, about that woman he'd hired for the tour, who was going to make it amazing. He hasn't mentioned her since, and I haven't been introduced to many women on this tour. Jake seems to have a lot of men working for him; I feel quite outnumbered. It's a good job I get on better with men. Men, especially those who are into music, I can get on with no problem. Bitchy groupies looking to hook up with Jake, maybe not so much.

I wonder if that's a deliberate thing on his part, keeping it mainly to a male-orientated tour, keeping the temptation from wanting to screw any of his staff away from him. Fucking the staff wouldn't make for a good working environment, I'd imagine.

"So when do I get to meet the mystery woman on this tour?" I ask, crossing my legs.

Jake looks at me, confused. "What do you mean?"

I turn my body towards him slightly. "When I interviewed you, you said you'd hired some woman who was going to make this tour your most successful to date."

He laughs. "You're wearing her shoes, Tru." He glances down at my dangling foot.

I follow his stare, lifting my high-heeled black studded ankle boot up a little higher.

"Eh?"

He leans close, and his hot breath brushes over the skin on my neck, tickling me, as he says, "I was talking about you, Tru."

What?

I stay stock-still as he leans back, assessing my face.

"But you didn't offer me this job until the next day," I utter, finding my voice.

He grins. "I know."

"So how did you know I'd take the job?"

"Because women never say no to me." With a wink, he gets up and wanders over to the food table.

God, he's such a cocky, arrogant bastard at times. And I totally fancy him.

No, I don't.

Yes, I do.

No. I. Don't.

Ah fuck.

I'm at the side of the stage, standing in the right wing with Stuart. The support band finished a while ago, and now TMS are about to take the stage.

Jake walks slowly onto the stage, coming in from the left, with a confidence that only he can carry, his guitar slung across his back.

He looks across at me, his eyes move over my clothes, my body, then they meet with mine and he grins.

I feel a blush rise in my cheeks. I'm glad it's a little darker here where we're standing, so Stuart can't see what a girl I'm being.

When Jake reaches the mike, he leans close, but then pauses, leaning back as he surveys the crowd. Jake has this way of looking around at everyone in the room but making you feel like the only person he's actually looking at is you. That you are the object of his desire. You're the one he's taking home tonight. He can undress a woman with one look alone. And when his eyes meet and fix onto mine, I suddenly feel it and more, and it strips me naked to the core. My legs start to tremble.

Then his eyes drift away from mine.

"So I see we have Stockholm's finest in here tonight. Ladies, you look beautiful tonight…and guys, well, hang on tight to your girls is all I'm sayin'." He releases a slow chuckle. Moving back slightly, he looks at me, gives me a wink and a secret smile, then launches into one of their early hits. "Undress You."

And boy do I feel undressed.

And I stand here basking in the Jake Wethers experience in full 3D, HD glory, feeling exposed and naked, and good lord it's amazing.

I feel high.

On him.

His voice is like hands moving over my skin, touching me. His hands. Touching me.

I want that now.

No I don't.

I mean, it's just a reflex reaction to the rock star lover in me. The dream of wanting to be the one to tame him.

Of course it's not real.

Halfway through the show, Jake slows things down to a stop.

He swings his guitar to rest behind him and lifts his hand to his head, running his fingers through his hair. "I just wanted to pause for a minute to talk about Jonny…"

A few fans cry out from the crowd, "Jonny, we fuckin' love you!"

I feel the hairs on my arms prickle. I can see how hard this is for Jake. I get the sudden urge to hold him, run my fingers through his hair, kiss him, and tell him everything will be okay.

Jake bows his head, resting it against the mike.

My throat tightens, tears biting my eyes, as I worry that he's losing it again, here on stage.

Denny's over his drum kit, jumping it in one swift move, and he's at Jake's side instantly. He puts his hand on Jake's shoulder and rests his forehead against Jake's head, speaking into his ear. Tom is there now too. I notice Smith take his leave to the side of the stage.

The venue is at a standstill.

There is a golf ball the size of Africa in my throat. Tears well in my eyes as I watch these three men whom I know, one of whom I care for very much, still grieving over the loss of their best friend.

I glance at Stuart beside me. His eyes look glazed. It must have been hard on him too, losing Jonny. I know he works for Jake, but he would have known him too.

Feeling overcome with emotion, I press my lips together and wrap my arms around myself, then look back out to the stage. Back to Jake.

Jake lifts his head and clears his throat. "I met Jonny at high school. I'd just moved to the States from England. I was the new awkward British kid—a little lost and a lot lonely, and there he was. He took me under his wing and taught me to be his level of cool." He pulls in a deep breath. "We formed TMS, with just the two of us. Then at college we met Denny through one of Jonny's many girlfriends, and Denny introduced us to Tom, and that's when TMS was properly born." Another deep breath. Jake glances at Denny, then Tom. "Jonny wasn't just our band member," he says, looking straight ahead. "And he wasn't just our best friend...or our wingman. He was the mighty in our storm. The man was a fuckin' musical genius, and he was taken from us too soon. And we miss him every single fuckin' day."

Jake pulls his mike out from the stand and walks to the front of the stage, Tom and Denny following, as a runner hands him up three bottles of Jack.

He hands one each to Tom and Denny.

"So I want you all to raise your drinks for Jonny Creed—the best guy this world ever had the good fortune to know." Jake raises his bottle and looks up the sky. "Jonny, man, we love you, and we miss you every day, and I know for sure that you're looking down right now with a bottle in your hand, a cigarette in the other, saying, 'Quit being a set of pussies and give these good people the show they fuckin' paid to see!'"

I see Tom and Denny smiling at Jake's words, nodding their agreement.

Jake chinks bottles with them both, and the three of them, at the same time, throw the whiskey back.

The crowd is screaming out Jonny's name.

Men and women are openly crying in the audience. And I can't help the tear that runs from my eye.

I quickly wipe it away.

Jake returns back to the mike stand with his much lighter whiskey bottle. He fits his mike in the stand. Denny climbs back into his drum kit, Tom wandering back to his place on Jake's right-hand side.

And for this moment, all three of them look a little lost, together.

It makes my heart ache with feelings for Jake.

Jake leans down and puts his whiskey bottle by the mike stand.

I see Smith quietly reappear onstage to Jake's left.

"This song we're playing next is one Jonny and I wrote in the early days. It was the one Jonny was most proud of… his favourite, and I know how much it meant to him when we released it and you guys loved it too, when you took a chance on us. It's one I'm sure you'll all be familiar with, so I want you to stretch your lungs out and sing this one with me—for Jonny."

Jake swings his guitar around to the front, bows his head, and looks down at his guitar as he strums a few chords, then Denny kicks the beat in and Jake lifts his head and starts to sing one of their early biggest hits, "Hush, Baby."

I get goose bumps all over my skin, listening as the crowd goes wild. And I stand here, transfixed, singing along with the words, watching Jake. I can see how hard it is for him to get through this song, and I know he's thinking of Jonny the whole time.

I wish I had been there for him when Jonny died. I wasn't then, but I want to be every day from now on.

Jake and I will always be friends. No matter what. I'm never losing him again.

I'm at the after-show party, which is being held at this upmarket club called the Spy Bar. It's packed to the rafters with showbiz people from Sweden and everyone who works on the tour.

I'm glad I dressed nicely for tonight, as most of the women here are glamorous and classy. I went for something a little different though. Well, I always wear different, but I bought this matching navy-blue pinstripe V-neck fitted waistcoat and straight-leg cropped trousers suit just before I left for the tour. It was love at first sight, and I just had to have it. I've teamed it with my skyscraper patent black heels. I know most of the woman here are in dresses, but I like to be a little different, and technically I am working, so it's like I'm wearing work clothes.

I'm at the bar with a couple of the roadies, Pete and Gary, who I was chatting to earlier, drinking a margarita.

I haven't seen Jake since the show. He had some interviews to do straight after, so when he exited the stage, he was swept off by Stuart.

I was going to hang around and wait for him, but Pete came over and said they were heading straight for the party, and did I want to catch a ride with them; normally the roadies have to stay on and pack up after the show, but Jake, being the good boss he is, lets them pack up in the morning so they can enjoy the party with everyone else. So of course I accepted; better than hanging around the stadium like a spare part.

"So how long have you worked for Jake?" I ask Pete. Gary is busily chatting to one of the other roadies, Jared I think his name is.

Pete's a cute guy, short dark hair, about six foot, quite muscular—must be from all the heavy lifting he does on tour.

"Five years on and off," he replies in his strong American accent, leaning back against the bar, resting his elbows on it.

A lot of bands have crews for abroad when they tour, but Jake has a set group of guys he trusts that tour everywhere with him.

"You must have seen a lot of the world."

"A few places." He grins. "It's a good gig working for these guys. So how did you land up here?" he asks.

"Oh, I er…" I'm just about to reply, when I see Pete's eyes flick up, and I instantly feel Jake's presence behind me.

Turning, I almost come face-to-face with him, he's that close.

"Hey," I say, beaming.

"Hey, beautiful." He kisses my cheek and rests his hand on my waist and stares across at Pete.

I feel a little heady under his touch.

"You want a drink, Jake?" Pete asks.

"Beer," he replies. His tone is stony.

Pete turns to the bar to order Jake's drink for him.

Sliding out of Jake's arm, I retrieve my margarita from the bar, feeling a little annoyed by his big brother attitude again.

"You shouldn't leave your drink unattended like that," he comments. "Anyone could slip something in it."

I glance down at my drink, then back up at him. "You saying your staff are untrustworthy?" I grin over my glass at him, as I take a sip.

He shakes his head slowly at me, eyes gripping mine.

"You forget your shirt tonight?" He gestures at my bare arms and waistcoat.

"Funny." I roll my eyes at him. Then pouting, I say, "You don't like my outfit?"

He moistens his lips with his tongue. "No, I do, it's really nice." His eyes flicker to my boobs, then back to my face. I don't miss that. "I just happen to know every other guy in this place is gonna think so too, and I'm gonna spend most of tonight kicking their asses."

Sighing, I shake my head. "You can quit with the big brother act, Jake. We're not kids anymore. I can take care of myself."

He presses his lips together, grinning. "Big brother act?"

"Yeah, the whole 'hands off Tru, she's got a boyfriend' thing you keep doing. I'm pretty much the only girl on tour here, and if you scare off every guy who talks to me, I'll only be left with you to talk with."

"Suits me."

"Jake!" I exclaim, feeling quick to exasperation. "I'm not a bed hopper, you know. I'm not going to sleep with all these guys just because I talk to them. I'm not going to cheat on Will. It'd just be nice to have people to talk to when you're not around."

And it's kind of annoying, and hurtful, that he thinks I am, to be honest.

His brow furrows. "I know you're not a bed hopper, Tru. I'm just taking care of my best friend. It's written in the rules, if I remember correctly."

"Your version of them or mine?" I grin. I can't stay mad with him for long.

He presses his lips together again, supressing his own grin. "Mine."

Pete hands Jake his beer.

"Thanks," he says, taking the beer from him but not taking his eyes off mine.

"Come and sit with me," Jake says, holding out his hand for me to take.

I stare into his eyes for a long moment. "Okay." I take his hand. "See you guys later," I say to Pete and Gary.

Jake leads me over to a booth already filled with Tom, Denny, Smith, Stuart. I can see a group of girls hanging nearby, and I feel the hard stares I earn from them because Jake is holding my hand.

It makes me feel a little uncomfortable.

Jake ushers me into the booth first, next to Denny, and sits beside me, trapping me in. I put my drink down on the table and my bag on the floor beside my feet.

"You enjoy the show?" Denny asks me.

"I did." I smile. "It was amazing."

"You're looking very beautiful tonight, Tru." Tom smiles across the table at me.

"Thank you." I flush, feeling a little shy.

I don't know what it is about Tom, but he has this ability to make me feel like I'm a sixteen-year-old girl. I think he has that effect on most women. And I don't even fancy him. It's so totally weird. Maybe it's his patter that does it. It always feels like there's a hidden agenda behind what he's saying.

A lot like Jake in that respect. But I get the impression Tom's hidden meaning when directed at me is a lot dirtier than Jake's.

Jake shifts around in his seat, pressing his leg up against mine, and puts his arm around the back of the seat behind me.

I see Tom's eyes flicker in his direction, and he grins.

Big brother Jake is back, and I get the distinct feeling that Tom is enjoying winding him up with me.

"Well, you assholes are boring the shit out of me, barring you of course, Tru." Tom flashes a toothy smile at me again as he climbs out of the booth, stepping over Smith, jumping to the floor. "I'm off to go pick a skirt up for the night."

"Is there ever a time when you're not horny?" Stuart asks him.

Tom looks at him like this is the most ridiculous question he's ever been asked.

"Nope." He grins. "I'm like a horny tomcat, always on the prowl for new pussy."

Jake splutters out a laugh. I have to hold one back myself.

"Did you actually just refer to yourself as a tomcat?" Jake asks, still laughing.

"Hell, yeah! And don't you go all prim on me, ass-face, because I know for a fact you've referred to your dick as a snake on many an occasion."

Stuarts snorts his drink up his nose and starts choking.

I feel Jake tense beside me. I can't even look at him.

"A python, if I remember right." Tom grins, obviously enjoying getting under his skin.

"More like a fuckin' cobra, from what I hear!" Denny chips in.

Smith starts laughing too, obviously in on this whole Jake the Snake joke.

"Hey, I can't help it if I was blessed with a big dick, unlike you douche bags," Jake says, picking up his beer, quickly getting back in the game.

"Fuck off!" Tom says, grabbing his crotch. "I'm well packed here, primed and ready to go."

It's a good job I'm not prudish in any way sitting here with these lot. Though talking about Jake and his *snake* is making me feel a little light-headed. I wonder how big it actually is? I'm tempted to cast my gaze downwards at his crotch, but I hold off the urge, pinning my eyes up front and ahead.

"Hey, thinking about this," Toms adds, leaning his groin up against our table. "I'm feeling a theme coming on here. We've got, of course, me—hunky fuckin' Tomcat, Jake the Snake there...now we just need to figure something up for you three fuckers." He gestures to Denny, Stuart, and Smith.

Denny lifts his head. "No fuckin' way, man, leave me out of your weird animal fantasies."

"Ah shut up, you miserable fucker! Denny? What rhymes with Denny?" he muses. "Ah, man, your name is shit! Nothing rhymes with it. We're gonna have to change it."

Denny climbs up over Stuart, then Smith, and jumps lithely to the floor. "Remind me why I'm friends with you again?" he asks Tom, patting his shoulder.

"Because I'm fuckin' awesome, and I can get chicks to play with your dick."

I can't help but snort a laugh out at that one.

Jake slides me an amused glance. But all it manages to do is tighten my stomach into knots, and then I have the sudden urge to want to touch him.

"I'm off to piss." Denny laughs, shaking his head at Tom. He wanders off in the direction of the men's room

"You coming to pick up some skirts, dickhead?" Tom says, directing a look at Jake, already sounding like it's a given he'll go.

I instantly tense. I don't want Jake going to pick up girls. The thought is curdling my insides.

Jake shakes his head, taking a drink of his beer. "No, I'm good here."

Tom looks at him like he's grown another head. Even Stuart gives him a surprised stare.

I relax in my seat.

"Did they amputate your dick while you were in rehab? Or has Stuart finally managed to turn you?" Tom asks, laughing.

Turn him? Is Stuart gay?

It must be the expression on my face that causes Stuart to lean over to me and say, "I'm gay, honey."

"Ah, right." I nod.

Makes sense. He's ridiculously beautiful and has the best taste in clothes.

Jake laughs. Reaching forward, he puts down his beer. "No, and no," he says, answering Tom. "I've told you, I don't fuck the staff."

I'm "the staff." So he won't be fucking me, then.

Thank God, of course, that he won't be trying it on with me. I know he wouldn't anyway because he doesn't see me that way, but it's just good to know Jake doesn't have sex with the few women who work for him. Just everyone else, of course.

Stuart snorts loudly.

Jake leans forward, looking at him with interest.

"Chloe?" Stuart raises his eyebrow.

Jake screws up his face in thought, quickly shifting to remembrance. "Ah yeah, okay...so I don't fuck the staff anymore."

Okay, so he did used to screw the staff.

I suddenly feel uncomfortable and a little sick listening to this conversation.

This is the Jake I read about in the papers. I don't want to hear about this Jake.

"Can you let me out?" I say to him.

"Sure. Where you off to?" he asks, sliding out of the booth, letting me out onto my wobbly legs.

"Bathroom," I answer, keeping my tone even.

I walk away, heading for the ladies', trying to ignore the stares from his waiting groupies and from Jake himself.

CHAPTER ELEVEN

We're in Barcelona. The show is tomorrow night at the Estadi Olímpic Lluís Companys.

My folks are arriving first thing in the morning. I'm so excited to see them.

Jake was all for it when I mentioned getting them tickets for coming over here to see the show. I think he's looking forward to seeing my dad again.

I've been touring with TMS for almost two weeks now, and the time has just absolutely flown by. I've barely had time to think, let alone miss anyone. I'm with Jake pretty much all the time, but it will be so good to see my folks tomorrow.

And I'm looking forward to seeing Will in a week. I've spent time away from him before, of course, but I think with my folks coming tomorrow, it's made me a little sick for home. For him.

I lift my bracelet up, looking at it, dangling it in the light. Picking up my phone, I decide to call him.

"Hey, gorgeous," he murmurs down the phone.

"What you up to?" I ask.

"Working."

"At this time? It's…eight forty-five there, baby."

"I know. It's that big acquisition I told you about. Well, some shit kicked off with it, and there's an emergency meeting first thing in the morning, so I have to prepare a load of stuff for it. Good thing is it's keeping me busy, stopping me dwelling on how much I'm missing you."

"I miss you too," I murmur.

"You do?"

"Of course I do, silly."

"So you're at work…" I say, putting on a sultry tone.

"Mmm."

"And you're in your suit?" I love Will in his suits. He looks really hot wearing them.

"I am."

"Are you in the office alone?"

"No, Mark's working late too."

"Oh," I say, feeling a little deflated. I was up for some dirty phone talk. Not like me at all, but I'm feeling pretty horny at the moment.

"Where are you?" he asks.

"Lying on my bed."

"Really?"

"Yep. Shame you're not alone, I was gonna…maybe… uh, talk dirty things with you."

"I'll call you when I'm home." His breathing suddenly sounds short.

"How long?"

"Couple of hours."

"I'll be waiting…and naked," I add, grinning to myself, feeling all confident.

"Two hours," he confirms, voice husky.

"Not a minute more. I love you," I add.

"You too."

I hang up the phone with Will, feeling restless, and now have two hours to kill before I can talk dirty with my boyfriend.

Not exactly sex, but the closest thing I'm going to get to it with him for another week.

Realising I haven't eaten dinner yet, I decide to go see Jake, see if he wants to have dinner with me. I hope he hasn't already eaten. I hate eating alone.

I knock at his suite door, and Stuart answers a few moments later.

He looks all dressed up to the nines. Stuart always looks smart, but tonight, he looks foxy. Like he's dressed for a date.

"Well look at you," I say suggestively. "Someone got a date by any chance?"

"Dinner with an old friend, chica." He winks. "Jake's in the living room." He passes me heading out the door.

"Have a good night." I grin.

"Oh, I will," he says, walking backwards, grinning. He turns and strides off down the hall.

Looks like someone's getting laid tonight.

I sigh.

Closing the door behind me, into the silence of the suite, I hear Jake strumming lightly on his guitar.

The sound makes the hairs on my arms prickle. I stand for a moment listening as Jake starts to sing Chris Isaak's "Wicked Game."

He sounds stunning.

On quiet feet, I walk down the hall. Rounding the corner, I pause, leaning against it, watching him.

His eyes are closed. He's lost in the song. And he looks beautiful.

My hands are suddenly desperate to touch him. I want to smooth my fingers over his lips, his face, up into his hair.

I want to kiss him so very badly in this moment.

I have a flashback to young Jake, sitting in my parents' living room, playing the guitar for me. I remember how my tummy used to feel funny when I listened to him play, even back then. I had no concept of those feelings, what they meant.

Love. It was love for him.

And I'm getting that very same feeling in my stomach again. But more intense now.

Jake's eyes open, meeting straight with mine. His gaze burns into me, and I feel naked to him. Like he can read my thoughts in this moment.

He doesn't break from a note singing.

Keeping my eyes locked on his I walk towards him, my body erupting with trembles, ricocheting from the inside out, as Jake sings to me.

Sitting down on the edge of the coffee table just across from him, I'm entranced.

And in this moment I want him.

I know it's just because I haven't had sex for a while, and talking to Will on the phone just got me all horny.

And I know this is what Jake does. He has this amazing ability to draw you into him the instant he opens his mouth and starts to sing. His voice is so insanely beautiful. It's all just so natural to him.

That's why he's so adored, loved by the world. And why women want him.

This song is stunning, and not easy to sing at all, but Jake does, and effortlessly.

In this moment I realise how lucky I am to be sitting here with him, listening to him sing like this. Most people would sell their soul to be where I am right now.

Finishing the last note, Jake smiles at me.

I feel like my whole body is on fire, and my brain too.

"That was amazing," I say, feeling a little out of breath.

He shrugs lightly and puts down his guitar. I hate it when he dismisses himself like that.

"So your folks get here in the morning?" he asks.

"They do." I beam.

"What time does their flight land?"

"Eight a.m."

"You want me to get Dave to pick them up?"

"No." I shake my head. "I want to meet them at the airport."

"Do you want me to drive you?"

"Can you do that?"

"Drive a car? Surprisingly, yes." He chuckles.

"Shut up, idiot." I giggle. "You know what I mean."

"I do, and of course I can." He gives me an earnest look. "I'll have to stay in the car while you go into the airport though."

"Of course." I run my fingertip over the table. "And yes, I would love you to drive me to the airport. Thank you."

Looking up, I meet his eye. We stare at one another for a long moment. My mouth dries.

Running my tongue around my mouth, I say, "So I, uh, came to see if you haven't had dinner already, did you want to eat with me?"

"I haven't eaten."

"Cool. So what do you fancy—in or out?"

His eyes linger on mine again. A shiver erupts deep inside me.

"In," he finally says. His voice sounds a little gruff, I notice. "We can order up room service and watch TV."

"Sounds perfect." I smile as Jake reaches for the TV remote, handing it to me. He picks up the room service menu, and I climb onto the sofa beside him.

It's 7:00 a.m. and I'm in the car with Jake going to the airport to collect my folks. I'm practically bouncing around in my seat with excitement. It's been nearly two months since I last saw them.

"You look like you've got ants in your pants." Jake chuckles.

"Sorry! I'm just really looking forward to seeing them." I smile broadly. "And my dad is gonna be so stoked to see that you've come to pick them up with me."

"He won't be." He slides me an amused glance.

"Yes he will. He always thought of you as the son he never had, and I know he's looking forward to seeing you again."

Stopping at the lights, Jake looks across at me. This look is intense, meaningful. "Billy didn't need a son, Tru. He got everything in you."

I gulp down.

"But he was the closest thing I ever had to a dad," he adds.

Without thinking, I reach over and caress his cheek lovingly.

Jake looks at me surprised, instantly tensing under my touch.

Coming to, I take my hand back, my cheeks heating. I sit face forward. My heart is pumping hard in my chest.

I can't believe I just did that.

We're silent for a moment. And I'm sitting here squirming in my seat at the act of intimacy I just showed to Jake.

"Tru...," he begins, voice soft.

A horn beeps behind us, making me jump, and I look up to see the light is on green. Jake shifts the car into drive, never finishing his sentence.

Jake pulls the car up into a waiting bay outside the airport, and I climb out to go and meet my folks.

Walking into the airport, I check the board for arrivals. Seeing their flight has already landed, I head straight over to the arrivals gate.

I'm waiting only five minutes when I see the familiar faces of my mum and dad.

"Daddy!" I cry out, jogging over to him. I launch myself into his arms.

"Hey, baby girl." He squeezes me tightly.

I feel a sudden lump in my throat and tears in my eyes.

"Mama." I smile, hugging her.

"My beautiful girl." Taking my face into her hands, she kisses my cheek. "You look well...happy."

"I am happy, because you both are here." I put my arm through hers; resting my head against her shoulder, we start to walk, following my dad, pulling their case along.

"The car is just over there, Dad." I point to the left at Jake's rented Mercedes.

My dad turns back, eyebrow raised. "You're driving a Merc?"

"Not me, silly." I laugh. "I got a ride here."

I was going to tell them Jake was in the car, but I think it will be a nice surprise for my dad when he sees him.

We approach the car, and I pop the boot. My dad lifts the suitcase into it.

My dad goes for the backseat door, but I say, "Sit up front. I'll sit in the back with Mama."

Giving me a funny look, he opens the door and climbs in, and I get in the backseat with my mum.

"Hey, Billy," Jake says to him.

"Jake, my boy!" my dad exclaims, and pulls Jake in for a manly hug.

Jake looks a little taken aback, but really he shouldn't be surprised; my dad has always been a huggy kind of guy.

Jake looks back at us. "Hi, Eva," he says to my mum. He sounds nervous.

"Hi, Jake." She nods, smiling lightly.

I can tell he's wary with my mum.

She's a no-nonsense kind of person, says it how she sees it, and I know he's worried what she will think of his antics over the years.

Funny, he's this rich, famous man, but my mum can make him feel like a misbehaving teenager again.

As we travel back, my dad talks away in the front with Jake, of course about the show tonight, and I talk with my mum about what I've been doing since I came on the tour.

When we get back to the hotel, Jake has to go, as he needs to head over to the stadium to prepare for tonight's show. So I get my mum and dad settled in their suite.

They're staying in Stuart's suite, and he's moved into Jake's for the two days that they are here.

The hotel didn't have any other available suites, and Jake wouldn't have my mum and dad staying in just any old room, which was sweet. I offered to give mine up for them, but he wouldn't have that, either. Then Stuart said he would crash in Jake's suite, as it's got two bedrooms anyway, and he'd let my parents stay in his suite, which Jake agreed to.

Once they're all settled, we head down to have breakfast together in the hotel. While we're eating, Jake calls me on my phone and asks if my dad would like to go down to the stadium to watch rehearsals.

My dad's face nearly splits in two when I relay it to him.

One glance at my mum and she nods her assent, so my dad heartily agrees. He will be in his absolute element there with the guys.

Jake tells me he's going to send Dave to come and pick Dad up in thirty minutes, so we finish up our breakfast, and Dave turns up as expected for my dad.

Kissing both me and Mum, Dad heads off to the stadium.

"So what do you want to do today, Mama?" I ask. "Go to the beach or shopping?"

"Shopping." She smiles.

We get our bags from our suites, then head out into Barcelona for the day.

I love shopping with my mum. She has really eclectic taste in clothes; that's where I get my fashion sense from.

We stumble across this little boutique that sells the most amazing clothes and shoes. And I instantly zone on these black block high-heeled, strappy sandals with white and orange bars going across the toe area.

I buy them, and a black-and-orange two-in-one waisted prom dress with asymmetric straps to go with my beautiful new shoes.

I decide not to wear them tonight, as it's really hot in Barcelona today, and it will be even hotter at the stadium tonight, so I buy a cute little strappy, black-and-white feather-print playsuit. It has this gorgeous pink fabric belt, which will go perfectly with my pink heels I have back at the hotel.

My mum buys quite a few items as well and insists on paying for my things too. I protest, but not for too long, as I am squeezing a lot on the old Visa nowadays.

We are out most of the day shopping and arrive back loaded with bags. I leave my mum at her suite and head to mine to call Will, as I haven't spoke to him all day.

I'm just finishing up on the phone with him, when there's a knock at my door.

I answer it to a happy-looking Jake.

"Hey, beautiful," he says, kissing my cheek. He walks into my room.

"Hey, yourself," I say, closing the door, still coming down from his kiss. "You had a good day?"

He nods, smiling, sitting on the arm of the sofa. "Yep, your dad came up with these ideas for tonight's show, some riffs…ah they work perfect, Tru. I forgot how fuckin' awesome that man is with a guitar in his hands."

"He's kind of awesome all the time," I say, smiling at his enthusiasm, sitting on the seat opposite him. I tuck my legs under my bum.

"You had a good day?" He indicates my pile of shopping bags.

"Yep, Mama took me shopping." I grin.

"Any sexy underwear in there?" He lifts his chin in the direction of my bags.

I shake my head, rolling my eyes at him. "Big brother one minute, pervert the next." I chuckle.

He laughs, getting to his feet. "Okay, well I just came to tell you we're going out for an early dinner tonight with your folks, so you've got half an hour to get ready."

"We are?" I say, getting to my feet and following him to the door. "And whose idea was that?"

"Mine, of course." Smiling, he gives me another swift kiss on the cheek, and then he's gone.

I get a quick shower, not washing my hair. I decide to tie it up off my neck because of the heat, so I put it up into a loose chignon, leaving some loose strands around my face. I put my new playsuit on with my little heels, a spritz of Chanel, and I'm out the door, heading to my mum and dad's suite.

Jake's already there when I arrive, so we all head out to dinner, with Dave driving us.

Jake's reserved a table at a swanky restaurant called Arola, which is situated on the second floor of the equally swanky Hotel Arts.

The waiter shows us to a table out on the terrace. The restaurant is beautiful, very modern and very expensive looking. It has these billowing sail-like shades, fitted out above each table, to shade the fading Spanish sun.

Dinner is awesome; my dad is in top form, talking away about the rehearsals today and how awesome a musician Jake is. Jake is naturally embarrassed and waves his compliments off.

But my dad is having none of it. He is totally in his element talking music. I love seeing my dad like this.

After dinner is done, Jake and my dad argue about who will pay the bill. Jake wins of course on the press that they are there as his guests. Dave drives us straight to the stadium for the show.

Leaving Jake backstage, we head out to our seats up front.

The show is, as expected, amazing, and I have the best time here with my mum and dad. It's so great being here with them, watching Jake. It makes me feel a little nostalgic.

After the show is done, we three head backstage to meet back up with Jake. There's no big after-show party tonight; the guys have just hired out the VIP area in Barcelona's most exclusive club, Elephant. There is just the band, some of the roadie staff, and me and my mum and dad here. Stuart hasn't come tonight—he said he had some work to tend to after the show, so he headed straight back to the hotel.

Jake's hardly left my side since we arrived. And I know it's a weird thing to say, but it almost feels like we're a couple tonight, the way he's being so attentive to me, even though we are clearly not and never will be. I know Jake doesn't see me that way, his reaction to me touching his face, amongst other things, proved that to me. And of course I'm with Will.

Jake leaves our table to go to the bathroom, leaving me and Mum alone. My dad is over at the bar, talking to Smith and Denny.

"That boy has got feelings for you," my mum says, nodding in the direction of Jake's retreating back.

"*No, él no tiene. No seas tonto, Mama,*" I say, speaking in Spanish to her.

I said, "No, he hasn't. Don't be silly, Mama."

I'm talking in Spanish to her, as I don't want this conversation to be aired in English.

Speaking back in Spanish, she says, "He has. I've been watching him, watching you all night. Jake has barely taken his eyes off you. He clearly has feelings for you, but then he did when he was younger."

"No, he didn't." I brush her off. "And he hasn't now."

I don't mention the fact that Jake inadvertently knocked me back in London when I invited him into my flat for coffee that time.

"Whatever you say, sweetheart. But I know what I see, and I see that boy wants you. Men like Jake can be very hard to say no to. I married your father, remember." She smiles, winking at me. "You love Will, yes?"

"Very much."

"So promise me you'll be careful with Jake. You have a gentle heart, my darling, and I don't want you to get hurt."

"Okay, Mama, I promise." I sigh, picking up my drink and taking a sip.

Jake returns to our table a few minutes later, but I feel on edge around him now after what my mum just said.

I don't think she is right about Jake's wanting me, but all she has done is remind me of my own growing feelings for him. Or as I should say, reignited ones.

We don't stay too late at the club, and leave at midnight, my mum and dad being tired after their plane journey and long day.

Dave takes us back to the hotel, and Jake decides to come too, leaving the rest of them at the club.

I kiss my mum and dad good night at their door, agreeing to meet at nine for breakfast.

Jake walks me to my suite.

"Do you wanna come in and have a drink?" I ask him, getting my key card out of my bag.

"Sure," he says. "Actually, come to mine. We can sit out on the balcony. Stuart will be in bed by now."

Jake's suite is the only one with a terraced balcony.

Agreeing, I follow Jake to his suite.

He pauses outside his door. Turning to face me, he tucks a few stray strands of hair behind my ear.

"I had a great day today, but an even better night with you. This whole tour has been amazing so far…having you here, Tru. It's…just like old times."

My heart starts to beat rapidly in my chest, and my face heats under his unwavering gaze.

Forcing a clumsy smile onto my lips, I say, "It has. I'm really enjoying it."

He stares at me for a moment longer. Trembles erupt deep in my belly. And for a stupid moment, I actually wonder if he's going to kiss me.

"Let's get that drink." He breaks our gaze and pushes his key card into the slot, opening the door.

All the lights are still on inside, and we find Stuart watching TV in the living room.

"You're still up," Jake says to Stuart. His tone is surprisingly frosty.

Stuart's eyes flicker between Jake and me, and I read clearly in them what he thinks I'm here for.

"I didn't think you'd be back until later." Stuart switches the TV off and gets to his feet. "I was heading to bed in a minute anyway."

"I just came back for a drink," I pipe up. God that sounds even worse now I've said it. Like I'm covering something up, which blatantly wasn't going to happen. "Stay, have a drink with us."

Stuart's eyes flicker to Jake, then back to me. "No, I'm fine. I'm just gonna hit the sack." He steps back.

"Come on…" I coax, smiling.

He looks at Jake again, then says, "Okay. Just one drink."

I ignore Jake's obvious sigh from beside me.

What's his problem all of a sudden? He gets on really well with Stuart, so why doesn't he want him here for a drink?

Because Mama was right, says a little voice in my head.

No, of course she wasn't. I brush the thought to the back of my mind.

Jake's just being a snarky bastard for whatever reason.

Stuart grabs a handful of the mini spirits out of the little fridge. I love these tiny bottles. Helping, I get some cans of mixers and three glasses.

Jake is already out on the terrace, having a smoke, when we get out there.

Stuart and I put our little drink collection down on the table.

I opt for a vodka and soda. Stuart has the same as me, and I pour out Jake a neat whiskey.

Jake takes the seat on my left. His knee bumps with mine under the table, but he doesn't say anything.

He seems a little irked to be honest, and I can't figure out what happened to make him change from the sweet Jake just outside the door of the suite, to grumpy Jake now.

He picks his whiskey up and takes a drink, then puts it down and taps his fingers on the metal table.

The atmosphere feels a little uncomfortable.

I'm racking my brain trying to think of something to talk about, but I'm coming up dry, so I almost heave out a sigh of relief when Stuart asks me, "So where is that beautiful mother of yours originally from, Tru?"

"Puerto Rico," I answer.

"So can you speak Spanish?" Stuart inquires.

"I can." I nod.

"So you know Spanish swearwords." An impish grin crosses Stuart's lovely face.

"I do." I smile.

"Ooh, teach me some." He leans close to me, eager.

"How old are you?" Jake snips.

"Old enough to kick your ass, you miserable bastard." Stuart winks at me. "Go on, Tru, say 'asshole' in Spanish."

"*Gilipollas.*" I grin.

"*Gilipollas,*" Stuart tries to imitate.

Jake throws his drink back and pours himself another.

"Okay, how do you say 'fuck'?"

Jake shifts in his seat, then picks up his cigarettes, lighting one.

"*Joder.*" I take a sip of my drink, soothing my dry mouth.

"*Joder,*" Stuart copies. He's doing quite well with the accent for a beginner.

"So how would you say, 'Fuck off, asshole'?"

"*Vete a la mierda, gilipollas.*"

Jake takes a long drag of his cigarette, and the smoke billows past me.

I let out a light cough.

"Fuck, that's a hard one!" Stuart laughs. "Say it again."

"*Vete…a la…mierda…gilipollas,*" I say slower.

Jake stubs his half-smoked cigarette out in the ashtray and abruptly gets to his feet. "I'm off to bed. I'll see you tomorrow." He strides away into the suite.

I look across at Stuart, confused. He lifts his eyebrows at me, shrugging.

I stay with Stuart for another ten minutes, finishing my drink, teaching him how to swear in Spanish, then I make an excuse about being tired and head to my own suite.

I'm not tired at all, just confused as to Jake's bad mood, unable to shake the feeling that for some reason, it's me that he's angry with.

Chapter Twelve

I'm sitting in the small audience at a TV studio in Copenhagen.

TMS is doing an unplugged show for a division of MTV that will be aired worldwide in a few days.

Everyone in the audience is a competition winner. The competition was put out by the station a few weeks back, so to win a ticket to see them perform like this is a big deal.

I'm lucky enough to be here because I know the band. Because I know Jake. And I'm also here to work too. But that aside, I don't discount how very fortunate I am to be here.

The set is an hour long, and the guys are half an hour in, playing acoustic mainly. Denny is off the drums and is playing keyboard tonight. I didn't even know he could play until now.

Jake is sitting on a stool, microphone in front of him, playing acoustic guitar, and Tom is playing rhythm. Smith's not playing this show tonight.

Jake finishes up singing "Microscopic," another song off the *Creed* album. The audience claps.

Jake pauses, lightly strumming his fingers over the strings. He breathes into the mike.

"Okay, so I'm going back to a song from our first-ever album now. A good friend of mine told me that it's her favourite of all the songs I've ever written, so tonight, I'm dedicating it to her." He looks straight at me. "Trudy Bennett, this one's for you."

I gulp down.

Me? He's singing a song for me.

Shit.

I suddenly feel a little breathless. Then when he starts to sing "Through It All," those hauntingly beautiful lyrics he wrote, strumming his guitar. My heart starts to drum pure feeling in my chest.

And I feel a heavy mixture of emotions stream through me.

It is pin-drop silent in here, and I am spellbound to him.

I'm not the only one. Everyone in this room is eyes on Jake, and it's in this exact moment, I truly see just to the level of power he has over people.

Mostly, over me.

I'm so totally mesmerised by him.

And so totally in lust with him.

And so totally screwed.

I have my notebook with me in my hand, ready to make notes, but I can't move. I can't do anything except breathe.

Even when he finishes up the song, I'm still immobile.

And for the next half hour of the show, all I can do is watch Jake sing.

Watching as he makes every single woman in this room feel like he's singing to her, that tonight she is the one he is taking home. She's the one he's going to share his bed with tonight.

And right now, all I want, more than anything, is to be the one he chooses.

We stay backstage after the show and have some drinks with the staff. The talk is business, mostly about when the recording of the show will go out and how they felt it went. The general consensus is everyone is really happy, but in all honesty, I'm barely listening.

Jake is entrancing tonight, more so than normal. And I'm struggling to keep my eyes off him. Something has changed since the show. There's an almost physical charge there, flowing out of me and heat seeking onto him like a bloody missile.

So evident and tangible I'm sure people must be able to see it. I'm kind of worried he can.

I don't know, maybe it's always been there, but now, it's heightened somehow for some unknown reason. So I'm keeping my distance from him, staying in the safe zone for as long as I can, until this thing, whatever it is, goes away or dies down at the very least.

Because right now I want Jake.

I just need to keep repeating my Will mantra.

I love Will. I love Will. I love Will.

Jake's still on a high from the show, all the guys are, for that matter. Maybe it's something about smaller, intimate shows and the live recording for TV that buzzes them, but they are happy, buoyant, and everyone's feeling it, including me.

But I've noticed that Jake seems even more pumped than the rest, and he is not ready to go back to the hotel.

I'm also feeling wired from my Jake hormones, which are currently on heat, but mainly because of the serenade Jake did to me—I wonder if that's what set me off. Oh, and also the accompanying two glasses of wine I've had, all contributing to a horny Tru.

Horny Tru, who wants in Jake's pants.

All in all, not great.

Well, it would be great I imagine, but it's not going to happen.

Jake doesn't see me like that. I know he screws any woman he deems sexy enough—but to him I'm just Tru Bennett whom he used to live next door to once upon a time. His newly reacquainted best friend.

Best friends, that's what Jake and I are.

I know we have the innocent flirty banter thing going on, but that's all it is, innocent.

And of course I'm with Will.

Will, my boyfriend. Whom I love very much.

And even though my feet are killing me from my shoes—note to self, break in expensive pretty shoes before wearing for a night out—I still hear myself agreeing to go clubbing with the guys.

With Jake.

Deep down, I know I'm just not ready to be away from him yet. Dangerous, but also very true.

So now we're in the car on our way to an exclusive club here in Copenhagen.

Ben is in the car behind, driving Denny and Smith. And Dave is driving me, Tom, and Jake.

Tom is in the front, and I'm in the back with Jake. I'm hyperaware of his nearness. Of every single move he makes.

And even though this car has a roomy backseat, Jake is sitting close to me.

Close enough for me to feel his heat in this air-conditioned car. I know he doesn't realise or mean to, but he's not helping my current attraction to him subside at all.

If I didn't know better, I'd think he's doing it on purpose.

Dave pulls the car up outside the club. It looks fancy and expensive, and there is a queue of people waiting to go in.

Dave tells us to wait in the car, and I watch as he goes over to the three burly doormen and speaks to one of them, who looks to be in charge. These guys are big but they have nothing on Dave, and he seems to have such an air of authority over these doormen as he speaks to them.

The head doorman looks over Dave's shoulder in the direction of our car, then nods his head.

Dave hands the car keys to one of the other doormen, who then follows him towards our car.

Dave opens Jake's door, then Tom's, as the doorman climbs into the driver's seat of our car.

Jake climbs out and then, waiting for me, takes my hand, helping me out of the car. He doesn't let go when I'm out of the car and no longer needing his help, and my body flames under his touch.

The music is pumping out of the club, and the level of chatter from the people in the queue increases exponentially at the arrival of the TMS boys.

I feel proud in this moment to be here with them.

Denny and Smith join us, leaving Ben to park their car, and then we all walk towards the club entrance, Dave sticking close by Jake, who is keeping me close to him, and the doormen make a clear path for us into the club.

Once inside, a guy introducing himself as the manager of the club guides us straight up to the VIP section.

I know Jake hates VIP sections in clubs. He never has them at the after-show parties. When I asked him why, he said, "What's the point of throwing a party and then just sitting on the outside watching everyone else have all the fuckin' fun?"

His words, not mine.

But he also knows it's not always viable for him to go to a club and sit in the cheap seats, so to say; well, not unless he's after a good groping and a night of signing autographs and posing for pictures. Actually, knowing Jake, the groping probably wouldn't bother him too much.

And I guess he and the guys being up in the VIP section makes Dave and Ben's job a lot easier.

Me, personally, as I've recently discovered, am also not a huge fan of the VIP sections either, except for maybe at airports—those are my newfound love.

I just find VIPs in clubs to be a little pretentious, and I'm talking about the people in them. Not Jake and the guys, though. We're all pretty much cut from the same cloth in that respect.

Jake and me especially.

The fun is happening downstairs in the main part of the club, not in this stuffy area, but it's not like I can just off and hop downstairs to mingle. It would be rude of me.

So I'm here in the VIP section, trying not to talk to Jake too much.

Right now I'm sitting in a booth, talking to Denny.

I like Denny, and even more so, the more time I spend with him. He's the kind of guy, if you were lucky enough to have a brother and got to pick who it would be, then Denny would be your first choice.

He's funny, quick, and laid back, really easy to talk to. And why the guy is single is beyond me. Or maybe it's a choice, the way he wants his life to be at the moment. It's known he was in a serious relationship for a long while, and they split not long after Jonny died.

So I've been sitting with Denny for the last hour drinking bottled beer while he's been regaling me with stories of all of their time together at college, before they left to focus on the band, and also when they first started out gigging, things they got up to, that kind of thing.

He's kept the stories pretty clean—I'm guessing for my benefit. And one thing I have noticed is he's staying light on the stories about Jake. I can imagine there are a lot of stories to be told about Jake in college and even more on the road with the band, so I wonder why Denny's holding back on them.

We've also been having a real giggle over Tom and his prowling on the ladies.

The man is unstoppable.

Some of these girls just don't stand a chance. But then I don't think they want to—I think they are more than willing to be Tom's girl for the night.

And it seems he's picked his girl out for the night, seemingly settled on a pretty blonde.

Occasionally, I've cast a quick glance in Jake's direction just to see what he's up to. Currently he's leaning up against the bar, elbows rested back on it, drinking beer and talking to Smith.

He's giving off an unapproachable air. And he's showing absolutely no interest in any of the women who are trying to drown him in looks.

Actually, now I think about it, since I've been on this tour, Jake hasn't been living up to the womanising ways he's so famous for. Right now he's talking to Smith. The only married guy here. He's not with Tom, the one who is always on the lookout for a skirt or some pussy, as he puts it.

I wonder if it's because I'm here. Not that I'm vain enough to think it's because he wants me. I just mean, I wonder if he's trying to keep things respectable for my sake.

I hope not. I'd hate for him to feel uncomfortable and not be able to be himself because of me. But I am also glad I don't have to watch him mauling women.

Maybe I should talk to him about it. Hmm...I'm not sure how I would broach that subject though. One to file for later, I think.

Jake glances over, catching my eye. I smile at him, then focus back onto what Denny is saying.

The next thing I know, Jake is standing over me. "Tru, come and dance with me."

Picking up my bottle of beer, I glance up at him and shake my head. "No, I can't be bothered, and my feet are killing me."

These goddamn shoes, I really should have broken them in first.

"But I want to dance," he says. There's a real insistence to his tone. It surprises me.

"So go dance," I say, giving him a look. "I'm talking to Denny right now."

"But I don't want to dance on my own." He pouts, and I know he's trying a different line of attack. He reminds me of young Jake here.

I let out a laugh. "Jake, there are plenty of willing victims for you to dance with." I waft my hand around at the women, some who aren't even pretending not to stare at him right now.

"But I don't want to dance with them, I want to dance with you." He sets his mouth into a hard line.

I'm getting the impression this is more because for some reason he doesn't want me here talking to Denny anymore, and not that he actually does want to dance with me.

"Just dance with him and get it over with, Tru." Denny chuckles. "He won't let up until he gets his own way."

Denny gives Jake an amused look as he takes a swig of his beer, and I feel like I'm missing out on the something that passes between them.

"Fine," I sigh loudly, putting my beer down on the table. "But if I can't walk later because these heels have shredded my feet, then you're carrying me back to the hotel."

"Deal." He smiles a winning smile. It irks me some. Quite a bit, actually.

Denny shuffles out of the booth we're sitting in, letting me out. The instant I stand up, my feet start to hurt in these goddamn shoes.

Jake takes hold of my hand and starts to lead me off, but it's hurting to walk.

"Actually, hang on," I say to Jake, stopping. Keeping steady on his hand, I pull my shoes off with the other.

I toss them onto the seat beside Denny. "Look after these for me."

As I turn back, Jake's looking at me like he doesn't actually know what to do with me right now. Like he's never seen a woman take off her shoes in a club before.

I bet women have taken off more than just their shoes in a club for him; actually maybe their shoes were the one thing that did stay on, maybe that's what's freaking him out.

And with that thought in mind, I walk past him, barefoot, a smirk on my face. "You coming or what?"

"These floors are gross, you know," he says, falling into step beside me. "Beer, gum, puke…"

"You want me to dance with you, this is how you're getting me."

"With puke-covered feet?"

"Uh-huh." I glance up at him, a grin in my eyes.

"Whatever way I can get you, Tru," he murmurs.

I don't look at him…can't look at him.

I'm not sure whether he meant me to hear that comment in the noise of the music or not, so for now I'm pretending I didn't.

He takes hold of my hand again and veers off, leading me away from the tiny VIP dance floor and down the stairs, leading us straight towards the main dance floor.

This is more like it.

I look over my shoulder and see Dave shaking his head, looking exasperated, following quickly in our wake. I'm guessing Jake pulls this stuff on a regular basis. It must frustrate Dave that Jake doesn't count his personal safety as something high on his list. Makes Dave's job a lot harder.

And in this moment Jake reminds me of the rebellious teenager he used to be. The rebellious teenagers we used to be together.

Before he left me behind.

I tread carefully down the stairs behind Jake, regretting leaving my shoes now, in case of broken glass or getting my toes trodden on. But as we move downwards, heading into the masses, Jake doesn't have to push his way through the people crowding the stairs. They just seem to automatically move for him, like he's commanding them to with his sheer presence alone.

It's a lot weird, and also a little awesome.

And at least there is also no danger of anyone getting close enough to tread on my feet.

"You're short without your heels on," he says, turning to me, as he hits the bottom step, leaving us a little closer to eye level.

"Yeah, and you're a selfish prick."

Whoa! Where the hell did that come from, Tru?

"What?" He looks taken aback and pissed off.

Can't say I blame him, really.

But if I'm being honest, I know where that came from. I'm a little angry with him. I've felt it simmering away under the surface all night. It started back at the show at the serenade.

The moment he started singing to me, I felt a huge, heady mixture of lust and anger, and it lanced through me and straight in his direction.

Okay, so if I'm going with total honesty here...I'm pissed at him because he's made me want him tonight.

And I don't just mean I want in his pants. I mean I want him—*want* him. I want him to be mine.

I know it's stupid and irrational, and I'm with Will, but I can't help the way I feel.

He's Jake.

I've loved him for a long time. But this, here now, what I feel inside for him…it's like a fire is burning inside me, and I don't foresee a way to put it out anytime soon.

And I'm not exactly in a position to be able to douse that fire named Jake.

I'm also currently in a position where I have to spend an inordinate amount of time with him. A position he put me in.

It's the worst kind of torture.

So yeah, I'm feeling a little pissed at him, and for some reason it's decided to make an appearance now, here on the steps of this club, surrounded by hundreds of people.

It's just…he serenaded me, for God's sake! How the hell am I supposed to recover from that?

"You heard," I say, standing tall. "You serenaded, and outed, me in front of two hundred people."

"Outed you?" he gives an amused look, but I can tell behind the façade, he's still a little pissed off.

Of course it only manages to annoy further.

"You told everyone my name, and I like my anonymity, Jake, and not to become the subject of your groupies' hate chat."

"Okay…"

"And you sang a song like 'Through It All' to me."

He looks at me, puzzled. "But I thought you liked the song. You said it's your favourite out of all the songs I've ever written."

"It is, and I do love it. But that's not the point. It's an inappropriate song to sing to me—I have a boyfriend."

He steps back a little, and a tiny frown sets on his face. "It's not like I was dry humping you onstage, Tru."

"I know but…"

"Of course, it can be arranged if you want. I'll be only more than happy to dry hump you onstage, or in private, you know, whatever suits, just let me know."

And there he is. It's like a bloody affliction with him.

"Arrghh! Stop with the constant flirting!" I put my hand to my head, frustrated.

He frowns for real now. "The flirting bothers you?"

"Yes!"

"I thought you liked it."

"No. I don't."

"Okay." He scrunches his brow up. "Look, song and flirting aside." He steps closer to me. It muggies up my thoughts. "Have I done something else to upset you, Tru?"

Yes, you've made it almost impossible for me not to want you. And now I'm confused and wanting you, and worried if I dance with you that I might do something stupid, like make a move on you, and ruin our friendship when you reject me, and I'll also quite possibly screw things up with Will.

"No."

"So why the theatrics?"

It's my turn to frown. "I'm not being dramatic! I just didn't want to dance with you because my feet are hurting from my shoes, and you wouldn't listen to me, and you all but forced me into it!"

He looks confused now. To be honest, I'm a little confused as to where I'm going with this myself.

It's like I'm desperately throwing mud at him, waiting for some to stick.

I want him to fight with me. But he just won't.

"Okay, I'm sorry. We won't dance." He lifts his hands in surrender, looking all wounded, and moves to walk back up the stairs past me.

Oh God! Now I feel all bad for projecting my own feelings onto him and blaming him for just being himself.

I'm such a bitch.

I catch hold of his hand as he's passing, bringing him to a stop beside me. "I'm sorry," I say.

He stares at me, saying nothing, and I feel compelled to keep talking, to explain my behaviour.

"I'm just tired and ratty, and I shouldn't have said those things. I didn't mean them. I'm just being a bitch. Forgive me?"

His eyes soften. "You're forgiven. Like I could ever stay mad at you." He cups my chin with his other hand and kisses my cheek. "Look, if you're tired we can go back to the hotel and go to bed?" he says into my ear, his hot breath tickling the skin on my neck, and other far-off, unreachable places.

Go to bed? Okay, as inviting at that is, it's probably not the best idea, because my belly is pooling warm with the way you feel on my skin right now.

"No, we'll dance. I mean my feet are already covered in nightclub crap…puke." I smile. "Come on."

He smiles back at me, and it's beautiful. He looks so very beautiful. And all kinds of wrong.

My heart climbs out of my chest and sneaks into his, nestling in for the night.

Beyoncé's "Sweet Dreams" starts to pump out of the speakers, and I know I'm in trouble, but even still, it doesn't stop me from leading him onto the dance floor.

All eyes are on Jake and me. This is how it always is around him. And to be honest, I like it.

I like that every woman in this club is wishing she were me right now.

Jake grabs my hips and pulls me close to him. Staring down into my eyes, he starts to move me in time with him, and the people around us just melt away.

All I can do is stare up at him, trapped in his thrall, completely helpless as he moves my body with his.

Jake can dance. And I mean really dance. Sexy, sensual... every move he makes with me, for me, is like he's caressing me, heightening my senses to him.

If he can move like this on the dance floor, then I can only imagine how good he is in bed.

An image of me in bed with Jake flickers through my mind. So vivid that I feel lost in it. Lost in him. To him. Consumed and totally intoxicated.

I feel reckless. Heedless. Like I could do anything... want to do anything, with him, right here and now.

"Where did you learn to dance like this?" I ask, forcing my voice to work, as I try to focus my mind on anything but the feel of his body pressed up against mine, as Beyoncé's vocals continue to aid my mental and physical assault over my need for Jake.

"The bedroom."

Bedroom. Bed. Jake in my bed. Naked.

Focus, Tru, focus.

"Is that a dance school?"

I really couldn't imagine Jake going to dance class; it doesn't really fit with him.

"No, Tru." He stares down at me, blue eyes piercing. "In. The. Bedroom."

"Oh."

Oh crap.

I gulp down.

"There's no real difference between having sex and dancing." He runs his hand up my arm, slowly, deliberately, until it's cupping my shoulder. He starts to rub his thumb over my skin. It hums wherever he touches.

"N-no?" I stammer.

I mean, what else can I say? I'm kind of having a pretty hard time concentrating right now.

"No." He presses his delicious lips together and slowly shakes his head. He hasn't taken his eyes off mine yet. And I suddenly feel naked, so very naked.

"It's just unfortunate you have to keep your clothes on for one of them."

"Um...well, naked dancing here might attract some stares, Jake," I manage out.

I'm trying to remain calm, but my heart has exited on me, my legs are trembling, and every sense in me has headed somewhere south.

Jake leans in close, cupping the back of my neck with his hand, his lips brush over my ear as he whispers, "And that's why I prefer to dance in the bedroom."

Holy shit.

He leans back and stares down at me, and then I suddenly see it there in his eyes, unconcealed.

The lust. The want. He wants me. He's trying to seduce me.

I'm so completely fucked.

And now I'm left wondering how I never saw it before.

I've obviously been missing it all along. The flirting—not so innocent after all. The electrical charge I felt for him earlier—maybe not so one-sided. The serenade. Sitting close to me in the car. The lack, or actual nonexistence of other women in Jake's life since I've been back in it.

It's like all of my lights have turned on at once.

My head compounds, and my stomach tightens into a thousand tight, but very delicious knots.

And I'm here gazing back at him like a rabbit mesmerised by a beautiful cobra, and any minute he's going to strike and I'm done for.

Jake lets his hands drift back down to my hips, then he takes hold of my hand and spins me around, putting my back flush with his chest.

His large hands span my waist, holding me firm against him.

And I'm trying to pretend I don't feel him getting hard against my ass.

It's not going so well. I'm starting to lose any rationality I may have had.

I want him. I want him so badly. I've never wanted someone as much as I do him, now.

So much so, that I'm actually trying to figure out some way to have sex with Jake without it actually counting as cheating on Will.

Currently I've come up with the different time zone theory.

Okay, so I never said it was a good theory.

Then before I know I'm doing it, I'm moving slowly down his body, bending my knees, keeping my back flush with him, my hands feeling their way down his sides. Then I'm very slowly moving back up again.

I'm putting it down to the alcohol that I suddenly think I'm sexy and could ever pull off a move like this.

When I'm back to height, I rest my head against his chest, sliding my hands around him, holding him to me, pressing my ass against him.

I can feel his heart hammering in his chest. It makes me feel heady and like I'm suddenly in control here. I feel like I have control over Jake. It's an insanely good feeling. Maybe sexy Tru knows what's she's doing after all.

Jake suddenly grasps hold of my shoulders, spinning me around to face him.

His eyes are smouldering. His look is dark and inviting.

I want him to kiss me.

No, I don't. Yes, I do.

One hand goes to the small of my back, the other around the nape of my neck, his thumb resting lightly against my throat. And we are close. Dangerously close. Our faces inches apart, as he moves us both to the music again.

My breathing has hitched up, and so has his.

Jake—a sweet dream? Or a beautiful nightmare?

Which one, Tru?

A beautiful nightmare. This is Jake. This is what he does with women. It's his MO.

Don't screw things up with Will for one night with Jake.

Finally sense grabs hold of me. I step back from him, freeing myself from his thrall.

He stares at me, wanting, confused, disappointed.

"Toilet," I say, breathless. "I need the toilet." Then I turn on my bare heel and swiftly move through the parting crowd, heading straight for the ladies'.

I lock myself in the cubicle and sit down on the toilet.

What the hell am I doing? I was so ready to kiss him then. Kiss Jake and more.

Shit.

I don't know what I'm doing. I think I've just had way too much to drink tonight, and I was letting myself fall into something that felt altogether too good but is so very wrong.

Jake's…Jake. He's a rock star and as hot as hell—smoking, in fact.

But he's also a womaniser. This is what he does.

I can't lose my sense around him again. I can't let myself become just another name in his long list of conquests.

I have too much to lose if I do.

I use the toilet, wash my hands, cool my face with the water. Then, with a clear, straight head, I make my way back to our table in the VIP lounge.

Jake is already there, sitting with the guys, and also the girl Tom has acquired for the night.

He looks up at my approach and the second my eyes meet with his, whatever sense I had just talked myself into packs its bags and fucks off, leaving me to the mercy of my hormones.

The booth is full. Jake shuffles over, giving me a sliver of room to sit on and also forcing me to sit next to him.

He puts his arm around the back of the seat, behind me. My thigh is pressed up tight against his.

"All right?" he asks me quietly.

I nod yes, briefly meeting his eye.

He passes me a fresh beer. My fingers touch his and a charge flies through my hand and up my arm.

"I thought we could have one more, then head back to the hotel," Jake says quietly to me.

"Ahum." Nodding, I take a mouthful of my beer.

He moves his hand down, and then I feel his thumb start to gently stroke the bare skin on my back.

It feels intimate. So totally intimate, and that's because it is.

I chug harder on my beer, ironically wishing I was sober so I could think clearer in this situation and see how exactly to extract myself from it.

No, I'll rephrase that—figure out how *to want* to extract myself from it.

My head and heart are not matching at the moment, and my hormones are raging a war all on their own.

Continuing to sip on my beer, I listen to the guys talk, but I really can't concentrate. All I can focus on is Jake's thumb, gently stroking that one small part of my body.

It's like everything has honed in on this one small area. I'm heated. My skin is humming, buzzing under his touch.

I put my beer down on the table and bind my hands together in my lap.

Focus. I just need to focus.

Then Jake puts his hand under the table. He pushes his fingers between my palms, forcing my hands apart, and takes hold of my hand.

Jake often holds my hand, that's nothing new, but this time it's different. There's a different meaning there. Or was it there all the other times too?

I don't know, but what I do know now is that this feels like he's staking a claim on me.

And I like the feeling. I want to be his.

He slides his fingers between mine, entwining our hands like lovers would, and rests our bound hands on his hard thigh.

I could try to pretend his touch on my back was nothing. But not this.

I look across at him.

He stares back at me steadily, for a long moment before looking away, but I read his eyes clearly.

He wants me tonight.

And from what my eyes were saying back to him, I think I just said yes.

CHAPTER THIRTEEN

We finish up our drinks and leave the club, heading straight into the waiting cars.

I managed to untangle my hand from Jake's on the way out of the club, so I make a quick dash for Ben's waiting car, which Denny and Smith are just climbing into. Denny looks a little surprised to see me in their car, but he says nothing.

I could feel Jake's eyes on me as I climbed into their car, leaving him with Tom and his girl for the night, but I don't care. I just need to put some distance between us right now.

If I can just get to the hotel first and back to my room alone, then tonight will be without incident.

If not…then I really don't know what will happen.

But even as I think it, I don't really believe it. I know exactly what will happen.

If Jake wants me tonight, then me travelling back in a separate car will not make the least bit of difference. Because I want him too, and I don't think I can find the will to say no.

When we reach the hotel, Ben pulls up first and I clamber out of the car. My feet are still bare and my shoes are in my hand, along with my handbag.

I'm vaguely aware of the other car pulling up, but I'm too distracted by how cold this floor is outside the hotel.

"Jesus Christ! This floor is freakin' freezing!" I cry out, hopping from one foot to the other on the tiled floor. The night air isn't cold, but it's like there is air-con blasting out across the tiles, deep freezing them.

Smith chuckles at me as I start to tread on my tiptoes carefully across the frozen tiles. "You okay there, girlie? You need a hand?" He holds out his hand for me to take, but I don't get a chance to respond, because the next thing I know, Jake is scooping me up in his arms.

"Arggh! Put me down, you idiot!"

Jake says nothing and just strides through the door and into the hotel lobby with purpose, and me in his arms.

Everyone is staring at us, and Smith, Denny, Tom, and his girl—whose name I still haven't gotten—are all finding this highly amusing.

"You can put me down now," I say, a little clearer and a little firmer, as we reach the carpeted floor in the hotel outside the lifts.

He stares straight into my eyes. "I know, but I'm not going to. I start a job, I finish it."

My heart takes a clear blast in my chest, and I gulp down.

The doors ping open, and Jake strides into the lift with me still in his arms.

Not even waiting for the others, he presses the button for our floor.

"We look silly like this," I say quietly.

"And since when have you cared about how we look?"

What can I say to that?

And truth be told, I don't want him to put me down; I like the feel of being in his arms.

Jake makes me feel like a girl. Like a woman. It's not something Will's ever truly managed to do. Not that Will's not manly, of course he is, but Jake is in a whole other league. He's alpha to the extreme.

And yes, I'm independent and strong, but sometimes… just sometimes, it's nice to be taken care of. It's nice to be made to feel like a lady.

The lift quickly reaches our floor; the top floor, of course, and Jake exits, taking a left, heading towards my suite.

My suite is next to his, so I'm praying he just drops me at my door and goes to his. Actually thinking on it, my suite's always next to Jake's, whichever hotel we stay in. Hmm…

Okay, so the rational side of me—what small part of it there is left—is praying that Jake will just leave me outside my room. But I know he won't.

"Key," he says, stopping outside my door.

I rummage in my handbag and pull out my key card. Reaching down, I put it into the slot and push the handle down, as Jake shoves my door open with his leg.

He carries me through the darkened living room of my suite, letting the door swing shut behind us. I drop my shoes to the floor and toss my handbag onto the sofa as he passes by it.

"Fuck!" he curses, walking into the coffee table.

"You okay?" I stifle a giggle.

"No," he grumbles. "It hurts like a motherfucker."

"I'll rub it better for you."

"Is that a promise?" His tone is serious. He's staring down at me, his eyes impenetrable in the darkness of my suite.

Looking away, I say nothing.

We reach the bedroom and Jake gently deposits me down on the bed.

"Why, thank you, kind sir," I say, putting on a really bad Southern accent like Smith's, except his is actually cool. "Your work here is done."

"Not yet, it's not." He pulls his boots off and climbs onto the bed, lying down beside me.

"Are you staying?" I ask, nervous.

"Of course I am. I'm not leaving my girl drunk and alone. You might be sick and choke on your own vomit."

His girl? And also, worst excuse ever for climbing into my bed, Jake, seriously.

But then I'm not exactly fighting him out of here either.

"I'm not drunk!" I laugh. "And just trust me, I've taken care of myself in worse states than this."

"Yeah? Well you shouldn't have had to."

What's that supposed to mean? Was that a dig at Will?

He turns on his side and faces me in the darkness. "Do you want me to go?" he murmurs, and his voice suddenly sounds all deep and intense.

Shivers envelop me. My heart rate increases, and my breathing hitches.

"No, it's fine, stay. But I need to pee," I say, voice pitchy, as I climb off the bed.

I cross the bedroom on seriously wobbly legs, which has nothing to do with the alcohol in my system and everything to do with Jake in my bed over there, and grab my pyjamas—a vest and short set—and stumble into the bathroom, closing the door behind me.

I pee, brush my teeth, take my makeup off, and climb in the shower.

After I finish my shower, I put my pyjamas on, towel dry my newly clean hair, and tie it damp into a messy knot.

I'm hoping I've been gone long enough that Jake has fallen asleep, because I've got a feeling if he hasn't, I'm soon going to be making the mistake I really want to make with him tonight.

I turn the light off before opening the bathroom door, then I quietly let myself back into the bedroom and pad my way across the carpeted floor.

As I'm nearing the bed, Jake utters, "Well that was the longest pee in history. What the fuck were you doing in there?"

So he is still awake. Crap.

"I took a shower, just like you should."

"You saying I smell?" He chuckles.

I pull the duvet back and climb into bed.

"That's exactly what I'm saying, but if you're too lazy to take a shower, can you at least take your stinky-ass clothes off and get your own blanket out of the wardrobe?"

Lying on my back, I tuck the duvet safely around me.

Like that will stop Jake getting near me if he wants to. The man could undress a woman with one look alone.

"Yes, ma'am."

He clambers up off the bed and I watch in the dark as he pulls his T-shirt off over his head and removes his jeans, leaving him in just his boxer shorts. His sexy, tight black boxer shorts.

"Fuck, I do stink," he says, sniffing his T-shirt, then his armpit. He tosses his shirt to the floor next to his jeans. "I'll take a quick shower."

He disappears off into the bathroom, leaving the door ajar and the light flooding into the bedroom.

I lie there, my heart beating up a storm in my chest. My whole body is on fire as I listen to the running water, desperate to go climb back in that shower with Jake and do things with him I shouldn't want to do.

I hear the water go off, then he reemerges a few minutes later wearing only a towel around his waist, his hair all damp and mussed up.

I'm so done for.

He leaves the bathroom door ajar again, a splay of light in the room illuminating his nearly naked form, his tattoos looking intricate in the low light. He looks beautiful, and I wonder if he's done it on purpose, leaving the light on him, giving me a full view.

Maybe he left the door open while he was getting a shower on purpose too.

Maybe it was an invitation.

He saunters over and drops back onto the bed, wearing only the towel.

This is not good. Well, it is good, great in fact…but not good for so many reasons.

He rolls onto his side facing me. "Do you remember when we used to sleep together like this when we were kids?"

"I do." I smile at the memory.

In the early days—the bad days when Jake's dad was still around—he started staying over at my house regularly to get away from him, and even after his dad was gone, Jake still carried on staying over. By that point it had just become our thing.

"My dad put a stop to that when we were about eleven though, if I remember rightly," I add.

"He always was a smart guy. I wouldn't have left me alone in bed with you if you were my daughter, either."

"Even when you were eleven?" I laugh.

"Even when I was eleven." His voice is suddenly thick with inclination.

I feel a shiver deep inside my stomach, which quickly heads downwards, settling between my legs.

I turn onto my side so we're facing each other. "How old were you when you lost your virginity?"

I know that's a really intrusive question, but I'm little drunk and I don't care, because I want to know if he ever slept with anyone back home before he left for America. I always thought I knew everything about Jake back then, but after he left and he cut me off, I started to think maybe not, because the Jake I thought I knew would never have left me like that.

He stares at me for a long moment. I wish I knew what was going through his mind.

"Sixteen," he finally answers.

Even though I got the answer I wanted, I still feel a sharp stab of jealously.

"Who was she?"

"No one...someone who should have been you."

Whoa!

He reaches his hand up and runs his fingertips along my jaw. My skin hums under his touch.

"I had such a crush on you when we were kids," he murmurs.

He did? Holy fuck.

"You're a bit late telling me now." I smile weakly.

I'm nervous. So very nervous.

"Am I?"

I knew this moment would happen when I danced with him at the club. The moment he climbed into my bed.

Maybe even subconsciously, I knew it would happen the very first moment I saw him standing there in that hotel suite for the interview.

I'm trying to remain calm, but my insides are going nuts. My heart is pounding in my chest.

"No," I whisper. "You're not too late."

He traces his thumb over my lower lip. I gasp at the feeling.

"I'm calling in one of my birthday presents, Tru," he says softly. His eyes look opaque, heavy with desire.

"What do you want?" My voice is quiet, trembling.

Propping himself up on his elbow, I tilt my head back as he looks down at me.

He pulls my hair free from its knot, running his fingers through it.

"You." He moves his face close to mine, staying a breath away, waiting for his invitation.

"Happy birthday," I whisper.

He pulls in a breath, then very slowly, not taking his eyes from mine, leans in and kisses me.

My body and mind explode with sensation and feeling. I've never felt anything like it before.

I'm lost to him.

All these years of wanting him and wondering, and he is so much more than I could ever have imagined.

My fingers snake into his damp hair, holding him to me.

"Oh God, Tru," he groans in my mouth. "I've wanted you for so long." There's such a ragged need in his voice, it makes me tremble all the way down to my sex.

"Me too," I breathe.

With a moan, he continues his gentle assault of my mouth with his tongue.

He tastes and feels even better than I ever dreamed he would. It's like waiting years and years for the present you have always wanted, longed for, then unwrapping it and finding it's so much more than you ever imagined it could be.

Will is far, far from my mind, and I couldn't stop this even if I wanted to. And I don't want to.

We're tangled up in each other, kissing, deep and passionate, and for this moment, in this darkness, there is only me and him in the whole entire world.

Jake pushes the duvet off me, rolls me onto my back, lying on top of me, resting up on one arm so as not to crush me.

I run my hands up his tattooed arms and over onto his bare chest, tracing his skin with my fingers.

He breaks from our kiss and stares down at me for a long moment. Then he places his hand on my chest, over my heart, and very slowly, moves it down, his fingers tracing over my breasts.

My heart is thumping.

His fingertips skim my stomach, moving around the hem of my vest.

Nervous, but wanting him so badly, I reach down and lift my vest up, inclining slightly, I pull it off over my head, tossing it to the floor, I lie back down. I'm not wearing a bra, and I'm obviously feeling really brave thanks to the alcohol in my system.

Jake's eyes roam me, devouring me.

"You are so beautiful," he says in a low voice.

Beautiful? He thinks I'm beautiful.

He leans down and kisses me again, hard and deep, almost like his life depends on it. He puts his hand on my breast, gently tracing his thumb around my nipple. It hardens instantly under his expert touch.

He definitely knows how to touch a woman. But then he's had a lot of practise.

I shove the thought aside

Jake gently pushes my leg to the side. I part them farther, allowing him closer.

I can feel his erection digging into my thigh. I'm so turned on, my whole body is trembling.

I'm nervous. I've never been this nervous with a guy before, not that I've been with many. Three, to be exact.

But Jake's different. He's always been different.

And he's slept with so many women. What if I don't measure up? What if I'm a disappointment for him?

I'm also trying not to think about the fact that even though I promised myself earlier I wouldn't become another number in Jake's very long list, I'm well on my way to letting that happen, with no care or inclination to stop.

His hand moves from my breast down my body. Lifting up, he kneels between my legs, and it's at that point I see he's lost his towel.

Holy fuck, he is huge. And I mean *huge.*

I gulp down, worrying how the hell he's going to actually fit inside me.

Jake sees me staring and grins.

I bite my lip to stop from passing comment, knowing I'll probably come out with some lame shit and kill the moment.

His fingers hook into the top of my pyjama shorts and he starts to pull them down. I lift my bum, allowing them free, then put my leg to the side, so he can remove them fully.

I can't take my eyes off him. I'm entranced, and I'm his completely.

As I'm moving my leg back around him, he grabs hold of it and kisses my leg, ever so lightly running his tongue over my skin, upwards. He travels higher and higher, teasing my skin with his tongue and light kisses until he reaches the apex of my thigh.

I feel heady with desire. All I want is him, now.

Lifting his head, he stares up at me. My mouth goes dry from that one look alone. I moisten my lips with my tongue.

His eyes flicker and flame. Without taking his eyes from mine, he slides his fingers between my panties and skin, then very gently he pushes his finger inside me. I almost come on the spot.

Rubbing his thumb over my sex, he starts to kiss a path up my stomach, to my neck, my jaw, my mouth, all the while, his fingers working their magic on me.

"Ahh," I moan, closing my eyes.

"Is that good?" he asks, his voice rough.

"So good," I breathe.

Needing to feel him, I reach my hand down and wrap my fingers around his hardness. Taking a firm hold, I start to move my hand, up and down.

He makes a low guttural sound in his throat, then pulls his finger out of me so quickly that I gasp.

Then he's ripping my panties off. And when I say ripping, I mean he actually tears them off, shredding them. No one has ever done that to me before, and it's insanely hot.

Leaving me wanting, he reaches down to the floor, picking his jeans up. I hear rustling and then he's returning with a condom in his hand and a question in his eyes.

He's asking for my permission. He wants me to say yes.

I want to say yes. More than I've ever wanted anything before.

With trembling fingers, I take the condom from his hand and tear the foil open with my teeth.

His eyes are wide and flaming. His breath's heavy.

He kneels before me.

I reach over and, with shaky fingers, put the condom on him. I can feel his body trembling under my hands.

It does extraordinary things to me. I'm literally panting with desire.

He moves between my legs, resting up on his arms, hovering over me. He starts to kiss me hard on the mouth again.

I grab hold of his backside, pulling him closer to me. I just want him inside me. I want him so much. I'm aching to feel him. Years and years of wanting him, coursing through me.

He pauses, breathing heavily, and lifts himself up on his arms, away from me, parting our bodies. "You've been drinking, Tru. Maybe we shouldn't do this now, maybe we should wait."

What? Is he joking?

I look up at him. No, he isn't.

He waits until we're this close to pause. To think.

I don't want to wait. I don't want to think. And I'm the one who really should be thinking right now out of the two of us.

My body is screaming for him. I need him to relieve the ache I have for him. The one that has been trapped in me for well over a decade.

I lift my hips, meeting back with him, pressing against him. "I've waited long enough," I breathe.

Whatever control he was trying to maintain instantly vanishes.

Then he's back on me, pressing me into the bed, fisting my hair, kissing me deeply, holding me in place.

I kiss him back, equally as passionate, my hands on his back, gripping him to me.

I want him so badly, but now I'm also feeling a little nervous about his size.

Jake must sense this, because he whispers, "Don't worry, I'll take it slow."

He slides his hand under my lower back, lifting me up. He very gently and very slowly eases himself into me.

I gasp, all but convulsing on the spot. He is filling me and more.

"Are you okay?" he asks, voice soft, lifting his head to look at me.

"I'm better than okay." I reach up and pull his mouth back down to mine.

He moves his hand out from under me, but I leave my hips lifted, meeting him, as he slowly pulls out and then rocks back into me, going in a little farther, a little deeper.

I moan in line with the feeling.

"Jesus, Tru," he groans, gently biting down on my lip. "You feel amazing."

I try not to think of how many women he's said the very same thing to.

Then as if reading my mind, he stops moving inside me.

Holding my face with his hand, fingers buried deep in my hair, he stares down at me in the darkness.

"It's always been you, Tru. Always."

And suddenly it doesn't just feel like we're having sex anymore. It feels intense, meaningful.

It feels like he's making love to me.

I know it's stupid, because Jake doesn't do love.

But I want to believe it. I want to believe his words. I want to believe that it's always been me.

Because if I'm throwing everything I have with Will away for this moment, then I need to believe it's worth it.

Jake takes hold of my hand, entwining our fingers. He rests them beside my head on the pillow, his other hand cupping my face. He kisses me, his pace picking up, moving farther inside me, and now I'm used to his size, I let him, needing this and more.

"Fuck," he groans. "This is…Tru…you feel…*fuccckk.*"

I move my mouth from his, kissing his jaw, nipping his skin with my teeth. Knowing that I'm doing this to him, making him feel this way, makes me feel hot, sexy, and uninhibited.

So totally unlike me.

And I surprise myself when I hear the words escaping my husky-sounding mouth: "Sit up, Jake."

A brief pause while he meets my eyes.

Understanding what I want, Jake puts his arm under my back, lifting me with him, staying inside me, he sits back onto his heels with me straddling him.

With my hair damp and flowing down my back, I place my hands on his shoulders. Very slowly, I start to move up and down on his length. In this position I can have as much or as little of Jake as I want, and I want all of him.

His hands are on my hips, moving with me. Then they're on my breasts, then upwards tangling into my hair, and he's pulling my face to his, kissing me again.

It's like he doesn't know which part of me he wants to touch the most.

And I like that he's this out of control over me.

I start to move faster and faster, and before I know it I feel the build inside me, so soon and so intense, I couldn't hold off even if I wanted to.

"Oh, Jake," I groan as I come forcefully, like I've never come before, exploding all around him.

While I'm coming, Jake drives me back into the bed, and starts to fuck me hard, then he's tensing, rigid, calling out my name.

We lie, panting breathless for minutes after, both coming down from our high.

Jake moves off me, lying beside me, he takes his condom off, tying a knot in the end, he drops it to the floor and pulls me into his arms.

"That was amazing," he murmurs, kissing my hair. "I wish we'd done this years ago."

I can't find the words to speak.

Because he's right, we should have done this years ago, before he left. Pre-Will.

Guilt washes over me like a tidal wave, taking everything with it.

But then if we'd had sex all those years ago, he would have ruined me, because I would never have recovered from it. I would never have recovered from him.

Because I know unequivocally I'll never recover from this, from what we've just done.

Chapter Fourteen

Where the hell is that music coming from?

Adele. Crap, my phone's ringing, and it's in my bag in the living room.

I untangle myself from a very naked Jake and make a dash for my bag.

Grabbing it off the sofa I rip it open, retrieve my phone, and answer without looking at the caller display.

"Hello," I say, breathless.

"Why are you out of breath?"

Vicky.

"Because I was in bed and my phone was in the living room."

"And were you in bed with Jake?"

What?

"What?"

"Jake—is it true?" she asks with a conspiratorial tone to her voice.

I look around the room suspiciously. I'm half expecting her to jump out on me any second now.

"Is what true about Jake?" My voice trembles slightly, and I curse it.

"Tru, stop evading—is it, or is it not true that you and Jake are sleeping together?"

My heart stops in my chest. No beating, no nothing. I think I may actually be dead right now. And it would so serve me right if I was.

"No!" I exclaim, coming back to life. "Why would you ask that?" I try to keep my voice steady, but it did wobble a little again, I'm just hoping she didn't notice.

"You so are!"

"No. I'm not." I put my best "I'm not fucking kidding" voice on.

I hear Jake move in bed. I spin on the spot, looking at him through the open door.

Guilt stains all over me in this moment, as I look on at the very evidence of my betrayal of Will, before me.

So not only do I cheat, I also lie about cheating.

I hate to lie to Vicky, but I can't exactly tell her the truth. Will has to be the one to be told first. And honestly, I haven't even had a chance to sort it all through in my own mind quite yet as to how that's going to unfold.

Then I look down at myself and realise I'm completely naked.

"Tru? Are you still there?" Vicky sounds a little concerned.

"Um…yeah. Just give me a sec," I mutter.

Removing my phone from my ear, I keep it in my hand and tiptoe back into the bedroom. I pick up the first item of clothing I find, which happens to be Jake's stinky T-shirt from last night, and pull it on.

But it doesn't smell so stinky anymore. It just smells of Jake. It pains and pleases me at the same time.

Silently, I walk back through to the living room, closing the door quietly behind me. I sit down on the edge of the coffee table facing the closed bedroom door.

"Okay, I'm back," I say.

"All okay?" Vicky asks. She still sounds concerned. And I feel sick.

"Yeah, I just needed a drink of water, was feeling a little dry...so why on earth do you think I'm sleeping with Jake?"

"Because it's splashed all over the Internet, my darling," she says softly. "Pictures of you dancing up close and personal in a club with Jake, then there's shots of him carrying you into a hotel."

Oh, fuck.

We were followed here by the paps.

Her words are thudding around my head, chasing on the tails of many, many other questions and fears I have.

How did I not even notice we were being photographed in the club or at the hotel?

Because I was too wrapped up in Jake.

Why would they be so interested in Jake with me? It's not unusual for Jake to be seen with a woman.

"They know who you are, my darling," she continues as if reading my mind. "That you're doing his bio. Your name is in the article."

Okay, so maybe there's my answer why they're so interested. Jake is sleeping with his biographer. That's going to pique a little interest for the dirt-dishers.

"What else does it say?" I ask in a small voice.

"That Jake serenaded you at the show they were recording last night."

"Oh," I sigh.

"So that's true?"

"Ahum."

"Which song?"

"'Through It All.'"

"Oh," she says.

Yes, oh, indeed.

"Okay, it also says here that he said you are the love of his life right before he serenaded you."

"He never said that!" I cry.

I cover my hand with my mouth, realising how loud I was. I don't want to wake Jake.

"He never said that I'm the love of his life," I repeat in a quieter voice.

Goddamn tabloid journos.

"You know how they like to make things up, honey."

"What else does it say?" I ask, cringing on the question. "Do they know Jake and I grew up together?"

"Hmm…" I can just imagine her eyes scanning the text in that way she does. And then I'm suddenly hit with stinging tears at the back of my eyes, and I just want to tell her everything. She's one of my closest friends, and right now I really need a friend.

But deep down I know I can't tell her. I've betrayed Will enough already as it is.

"No," she concludes. "It just goes on about you being his biographer…oh, and the magazine is mentioned!" she squeals. "Um…well it just says you work here," she quickly adds, recovering herself. "Okay, there's the dancing together in the club…that Jake's eyes were on you all night and no one else according to onlookers…" *They were?* "That he seemed really into you…" *He did?* "Showed absolutely no interest in anyone else whatsoever, and that you left the club together and went back to the hotel, and it finishes saying that maybe you're the one to finally tame Jake."

The one? They think I'm the one to tame Jake?

Not bloody likely. I don't think Jake is tameable.

Then his words from last night play in my ears, *"It's always been you, Tru. Always."*

"Tru, are you still there?"

"Um...yes, sorry, I'm here."

"Look, this is fine," Vicky impresses. "No press is bad press, remember, my darling. The media interest in you will quickly die down, and then you can get back to concentrating on the bio. If anything, it will be good for the story."

"What, that people think Jake's screwing his biographer?" I come off as short and terse. It's because I am.

And because it's the truth. Jake has screwed his biographer. His nonsingle, in-a-relationship-with-Will biographer.

"I'm just trying to look at the positives here, Tru."

"I know. I'm sorry." I run my hand through my tangled hair. Hair that Jake tangled up. When he was in bed with me.

Inside me.

Shit. I've so totally and monumentally fucked everything up.

And even though the shit has totally hit the fan, I still get a shiver at the memory of his hands on me...of him inside me.

"I'm sorry, it's just all a lot to take in with a hangover and a few hours' sleep." I blow out a breath. "I'm going to have to call Will, aren't I?"

"He probably won't have seen the news yet. He's more likely to read the *Times* than the *Sun*, right? And it's not like you've done anything wrong, my darling, so don't let that boy give you a hard time about this."

I feel sick. I wish I was in the bathroom right now because I'm pretty sure I'm going to throw up any minute.

"I won't," I say. "And thanks for calling to give me the heads-up. You're too good to me."

"Of course I'd call. I would always call. I love you, darling girl. You'll call me later?"

"Of course I will."

I end the call with Vicky and stare down at my phone in my trembling hand.

I quickly go online on my phone and straight to Google and search Jake's name under recent news.

And there they are, the pictures.

Crap.

They do not look good at all. They look incriminating.

Which they are, were…kind of.

Fuck.

With shaky fingers, I close the Internet down, and speed dial Will's number.

"Hey, beautiful," he coos down the phone. "I was just thinking about you."

At the sound of his lovely voice, I almost break down.

And by his tone, I'm guessing he hasn't seen the news yet. I don't know if that's a good thing or not.

"All good I hope?"

"That's all my thoughts of you ever are. I miss you," he breathes down the line.

I'm wicked and evil, and I'm going to hell.

"I miss you too…um, Will…I just wanted to give you a heads-up…because well, there's a story in the tabloids about Jake…and me. And it suggests that we are…um…sleeping together. Which obviously we're not."

Why did I say that?

Because you're a coward.

No, I just can't tell him this over the phone.

Will hasn't said anything, and the silence is stretching.

"Are you still there?" I ask.

"Yes." His tone is as stale as last week's bread. "Why do the tabloids think you're sleeping with him, exactly?"

"You know journos." I cringe as I say the words. "Jake sang this song at his show for me, and they stupidly interpret it as he's serenading me. And they've said that Jake said some stuff which he most definitely did not. Then I danced with him in the club, as I did some of the other guys in the band." *A total lie.* "And then my feet were cut and hurting from my new shoes, so Jake carried me into the hotel…and that's all," I add lamely at the end.

Silence again. I can hear him breathing down the line.

I hold my breath, nervously fingering the hem of my T-shirt.

Jake's T-shirt.

I'm the worst kind of person.

"And there's definitely nothing for me to be worried about?" he finally asks, his voice tentative, wary.

"No, of course there isn't, baby."

I'm evil, pure evil.

I hear him exhale. "Then it doesn't matter. Don't worry yourself with it, darling."

"Well, I'm just worried about you…that it will cause you some problems. You know, stick from the guys at work."

"It's not your fault, Tru." His voice is soft. "You haven't done anything wrong, so who cares what the papers say, or the dickheads I work with. They'll soon get bored and move on to something else when they realise there's nothing in it."

The bedroom door opens and I glance up to see Jake standing here in all his glory, before me.

Crap.

"*Will,*" I mouth to him, pointing my finger to the phone, which is now pressed firmly up against my ear.

His happy face drops, and he turns and goes back into the bedroom, closing the door behind him.

And I feel sicker from that one look on his face than I have from anything I have heard and said since I woke.

"So we're okay?" I murmur to Will.

"We're more than okay. I'm sorry, darling, but I have to go, I've got a meeting and they're calling me in now."

"Of course. Go. I'll call you later."

"Love you," he says.

"Love you too."

I hang up the phone and drop my head into my hands.

Then taking a deep breath, I get up and go to see Jake, with absolutely no clue what I'm going to say to him.

He's sitting cross-legged on the bed, wearing his boxer shorts, and the TV is on. One quick glance tells me it's the Entertainment Channel.

"So we made the news," he says, gesturing to the TV with the remote. His eyebrow is raised, but I can see the wary in his glance. "Was that what the phone call was about?"

He says this like it's a normal thing. But then I guess to him it is.

"Yes," I answer, sitting down on the edge of the bed beside him. "Vicky called to tell me about the story, and I thought I should call Will—you know."

"So…um…did you tell him about us?" His voice is soft from beside me.

"No! Of course not!" I turn, looking at him horrified.

His face hardens, and I instantly see how bad that sounded.

"I didn't realise the thought of me and you together was so bad," he bites back.

Shit, he's hurt.

"No, that's not what I meant—I just…it's complicated." I sigh.

He brushes my hair back over my shoulder, his finger-tips skimming over the skin on my neck. "Are you ever going to tell him what happened between us?"

I lift my eyes to his. "Yes…no…I don't know," I shake my head, disconsolately. Staring down at my toes, I curl them into the carpet.

We sit in silence for a long moment.

I turn to face Jake, but he's not looking at me, his eyes are staring blankly at the TV.

"I just…I don't even know what's going on between you and me, Jake. I don't know what this is." I point my finger between the both of us.

He drags his eyes from the TV to mine, and he does not look happy in the least. "You don't know what this is? Sorry, was I alone in that bed last night?" His eyes flick to the very spot where we had sex only hours ago.

"No, of course not. But this is your MO, Jake. This is just what you do." I signal to the very same spot.

He climbs up off the bed, leaving me feeling a little bereft.

"Yeah, I always sleep with my best friends just for the hell of it. I fuck Denny and Tom all the time."

Okay so that's pissed me off.

"Well how the hell am I supposed to know what you do and don't do, Jake? What your guidelines to sex are? You generally screw anything in a skirt!" My voice is raised, and I'm on my feet now facing him, the bed between us.

He gives me a long, hard stare. "Nice, Tru. Real nice."

"Well, it's the truth!"

"Yeah, well, that may be, but you're not just any girl. You're my girl."

"What do you mean—I'm your girl?"

"You know exactly what I mean." His gaze fixes onto mine.

I lose my breath and my stomach tightens.

"And at least I was always straight with those girls. They knew the score. I fucked them, showed them the time of their lives. They went home and I never saw them again— end of."

"God, you're such an arrogant prick!" I yell. "And wait— hang on—what? You're saying I wasn't straight with you?"

"That's exactly what I'm saying."

I drag my fingers through my hair. "I never said I was going to leave Will, and you never asked me too."

"Un-fucking-believable!" He picks his jeans up off the floor and starts pulling them on.

My heart is pumping hard in my chest.

"Jesus Christ, Jake, just what exactly do you want from me? You want me to leave Will so I can become your fuck buddy—*your girl*," I air quote. "While writing your bio, and you get to carry on living your rock star lifestyle, screwing anything that moves!"

He pauses buttoning up his jeans, and he stares across at me. The stormy look in his eyes makes everything in me come to an abrupt halt.

"I haven't been near anyone since you came back into my life, Tru." He runs his hand through his hair, hanging it off the back of his neck. He exhales loudly.

All I can do is stare at him, my blood heating, goose bumps racing across my skin.

"You ask what I want from you?" His eyes move to my lips, then my eyes. "I want you, Tru. I just want *you*. All day, every day."

His words are so simple, so easy.

My heart stutters.

I'm stunned. I literally don't know what to say.

He wants me? I wasn't just another lay to him.

I have waited more than a decade to hear Jake say he wants me, and now, here, at quite possibly the worst time in my life he could say it…and he's saying it, and I have no clue how to respond.

"What?" is the best I can muster up.

"I get it, Tru, it was a one-time thing for you, it's fine—you want to stay with Will. Why would you want me?" he mutters, backing up, turning for the door.

It's clearly not fine. And he clearly doesn't get it. I'm not entirely sure I do.

One thing I do know is everything has just got so much more complicated than I could have ever imagined. But a very big part of me doesn't care. Because he doesn't just want one night. Jake wants more. He wants me.

"No. Wait." I rush forward, grabbing hold of his arm, stopping him. "You've got it wrong. I thought this was just a one-off for you. I didn't know this…us…that you wanted an…us."

He stares down at me with his blue, blue eyes. "It's all I want."

My heart sighs and scatters across the floor.

I look up into his eyes. "I've wanted you for the last decade, Jake. I want to be with you."

He stares down at me, hope evident in his eyes. "And Will?"

Will.

"I'll talk to him." I swallow. "When I go back home for the tour break. I'll talk to him then."

He frowns.

"I can't do it over the phone, Jake. He deserves more than that from me, and it's only five days away."

He nods, but I can see the reluctance in his agreement.

Then he takes my face in his hands and leans his mouth down to mine and kisses me. A long, slow, delicious kiss.

My whole body responds to him.

"So you're mine?" he murmurs.

"Yes," I breathe, barely believing I'm saying the words, that this is even happening.

"You're wearing my T-shirt." His traces his finger over the fabric on my breast and my nipple instantly hardens. "I like you in my clothes…but I also like you out of them." He takes hold of the hem of his T-shirt, his fingers skimming my skin as he lifts it over my head, dropping it to the floor. "But

I like being inside you even more," he whispers, pulling me up tight against his firm body.

He starts to kiss my neck as he backs me up towards the bed. "You didn't have any plans for today, did you?" he murmurs against my skin.

"Um…no." Even if I did they would have been cancelled for sure.

"Good. Because you're not leaving this room today, and neither am I."

He picks me up and puts me on the bed. He pulls his jeans and boxer shorts off in one and climbs on top of me, ready for round two.

And once again, Will and my life back in the UK disappear off into the ether.

CHAPTER FIFTEEN

We stayed one more night in Denmark for the gig at the Parken Stadium, and now we're in Paris for the last show of the European tour, at the Stade de France, tomorrow night.

And the whole time Jake and I have been sleeping together, and when I say sleeping, we've not done much actual sleeping.

Behind closed doors we're acting like we're a couple, and in front of others pretending like nothing is different between us.

I've been putting on a façade, acting like everything is okay to Will when I speak to him on the phone, when clearly it's not.

I know that I'm the worst kind of person, but currently I just can't see past Jake.

All I see is him.

I'm so completely in love, and lust, with him.

Fortunately, the media interest in Jake and me quickly died down when Stuart put out a press release stating there was no story.

The release was firm on the point that Jake and I have a purely professional relationship.

Jake had Stuart put the statement out, and he did that only for me. If Jake had his way, the whole world would know about us.

For obvious reasons that can't happen.

But I'll be going home in a few days, after the show, and I'm going to tell Will then.

I think.

Well, that's what I've promised Jake I'll do. And I know I have to tell Will the truth, I just feel absolutely sick every single time the thought passes through my mind about telling him. So I'm trying not to think about it.

Instead I'm just immersing myself in Jake, as much and as often as I can.

We haven't spent a night apart since that night in Copenhagen, and honestly, I can't imagine spending a night apart from him ever again.

Every night though I have the same internal battle.

I go and call Will before bed as scheduled.

I feel sick with guilt after the call.

Jake is jealous and antsy with me when I return to him.

A part of me wants to leave Jake because of the guilt I feel over Will; the other part, the bigger part, wants to stay because of the way I feel about him.

We fight a little, sometimes a lot.

Then we spend the rest of the night making up.

Tonight, we're in my suite. The guys have all gone out.

Jake and I both made some lame excuse up for not going out so we could spend the night together.

We ordered room service, ate our fill, and are now snuggled up on the sofa. I'm nestled between Jake's legs, head on his chest, and we're watching *Armageddon*.

There wasn't much on the hotel's movie listing, and I like *Armageddon*, it's a sweet film.

Jake has been stroking my hair for the last ten minutes, and I'm starting to feel sleepy and content.

I must have fallen asleep on Jake, because the next thing I know, he is lifting me up off the sofa and into his arms, and the room is in darkness.

"What are you doing?" I mumble, sleepy.

"Putting you to bed."

"And where are you sleeping?"

"With you, of course."

I don't argue tonight. I'm too tired. And I wouldn't argue anyway. There's no guilt, because I haven't called Will.

Crap.

Well, I'm not going to call him now. I'll just call him in the morning, tell him I fell asleep.

That's at least the truth.

And the fact is, I love sleeping with Jake.

I know it's wrong. Everything about this is wrong.

But it also feels so very right. And I don't have the energy to care about right and wrong now.

Jake lays me down in bed and pulls the duvet over me.

I hear him moving around the room, undressing, and then the bed dips as he climbs in beside me.

I feel his hand reach out in the dark, and he takes hold of mine. He pulls my hand over and holds it against his warm, hard chest. I can feel his heart beating under my palm.

"I love being in bed with you," he whispers.

"And I love having you in my bed."

"Are you still tired?" he asks.

"Not so much now." I stifle a yawn. "Why, what did you have in mind?"

"A few things."

"Go on?" I coax, smiling.

He shifts closer to me and runs his hand up my leg. I part my legs as his hand moves higher.

"Say something in Spanish to me," he murmurs.

"Why?"

"Because you sound so sexy when you do." He runs his tongue over the skin on my neck, and I shiver inside.

"I do? I always thought I sounded dorky."

He lifts his head, staring at me in the darkness. "Dorky—are you kidding?"

"Well, you laughed every time I did the accent when we were kids."

"I laughed to try and kill my hard-ons."

"And I did it to make you laugh." I giggle.

"Tease."

"Perv." I grin. "So you really like it." I push my fingers into his thick hair.

"I *really* like it." His voice is dark and sexy. "I spent most of my early adolescence with a hard-on because of you—I still do now. I can't watch a Penelope Cruz film without getting a hard-on—it doesn't bode well at premieres, you know. I associate all things Puerto Rican and Spanish with hard-ons, and it's totally your fault."

I giggle again.

"When you were teaching Stuart Spanish swearwords the other day, fuck, Tru…"

"*Joder,*" I whisper.

"Christ," he groans. He grabs my hair, kissing me hard on the mouth.

I like this seeming sense of power I have over him.

"Shit, Tru, what are doing to me? It took everything in me the other night not to bend you over the table and take you right there and then in front of Stuart."

"Is that why you were so moody?"

"I was frustrated," he growls.

I grin in the darkness, shivers ricocheting through me.

"You should have taken me then."

"Don't think I won't," he says, tone serious and really hot. "The next time you speak to me in Spanish I'm going to do some seriously dirty things to you and I won't care where we are."

I press my legs together and moisten my dry lips. "*Hazme el amor*," I say, trying to sound seductive.

He groans, biting down on my bottom lip, tugging it into his mouth. "What did you say?"

"Make love to me."

"That, I can do." He yanks my shorts and panties down and pushes his finger deep inside me.

I gasp, gripping the sheets with my hands.

"I'll never tire of doing this with you," he breathes.

"I'm sure one day you will."

He has me flat on my back and is on top of me, pinning my arms above my head before I get chance to blink.

"Never," he reaffirms. Then he starts to kiss my neck, working his way downwards, hands cupping my breasts, touching me in just the right way, like he's been doing this to me always.

And once again, I lose myself in him, basking in his glory, and the feelings only he can create in me.

Jake and I are lying facing one another in the darkness, the shine of the moonlight coming in through the huge hotel window as we stare at each other.

"Do you still dip your fries in your milkshake?" he asks.

We're talking food. We've been talking nonsense for the last hour, my tiredness faded long ago with the sex, and I'm loving it. I'm loving him.

"Of course." I grin.

"You still know that's gross, don't you?"

"Yep, but I don't care because I love it."

"You always were a weird case."

"Ditto." I pull my tongue out at him.

"Yeah, but I always pulled off the weird in me way better than you did. I made it appear cool to others."

"Ahh, so I guess I should get some tips from you then on how to be the bomb."

"Most definitely. And I've got plenty of *tips* I can give to you that will raise your cool points in no time." He runs his fingertip down the length of my nose. A finger that has just been doing all manner of naughty things to me not short of an hour ago.

It makes me shiver inside.

"Hmm, I just bet you have."

A question is buzzing around in my head. The one I've wanted to ask him since I first saw him in that hotel room for the interview.

I take a deep breath in. "Why did you stop calling and writing?"

He stares at me for a long moment.

"I was young and selfish and stupid, and I hated how much I actually missed you once I'd left. I didn't know it was possible to miss someone as much as I did you, then. And every time I spoke to you on the phone or got a letter from you, it hurt just that bit more. Then I met Jonny and we started up the band, and my old life—you—all just seemed so very far away. I still missed you, but the ache had started to dull, and I knew if I kept in touch it would just rake all those bad feelings up, so I decided to stay away."

I run my fingertips along his jaw. He takes hold of my hand and kisses my fingers.

"Why didn't you ever get in touch with me once the band got big?"

I sigh. "For that very reason. You'd stopped calling and writing to me, and it had been so long, I didn't want you to think I was only getting in touch because you were famous."

"I wanted you to. I thought about you often. Wondering what you were doing."

"So why didn't you find me then? It's not like you couldn't have. You've sure got the resources."

I feel a wave of anger. If he'd got in touch years ago, we'd have got together then, and I would never have met Will. And I wouldn't be in the mess I'm currently in.

He presses his lips together. "I was afraid to."

Those four words send shivers spiralling through me.

"Why?"

He sighs. "In the beginning I was too absorbed in the band to care about anyone or anything. And I was mostly high—not the best person to be around at times." He pulls in a breath. "Then we hit the big time and things were pretty wild. Then Jonny died, and…" He pauses as if gathering composure. I can see how much it still hurts him, even now.

"Everything just fell apart. Denny and Tom were a mess, and they were looking to me to somehow fix it for them. And I just didn't know how to. For a while back then, I didn't think the band would make it. Especially when I went fuckin' AWOL in Japan."

He grimaces at the memory.

"Yeah, pissing on the stage. Not your finest hour but completely understandable."

"That was one of my lower points, Tru. And then I realised that Jonny had been my glue, and then it hit me just how much he reminded me of you...you and he were similar in so many ways. And I'd relied on him, like I had you for all those years, to keep things straight for me."

"When I moved to the States, the very first thing I did, without realising, was go looking for another version of you. It just happened to be Jonny." He shrugs.

"And through all the grieving for him, all I could think about was you. But we'd been apart for eleven years, and I didn't know how to get in touch. I wanted to, so badly, but I just kept thinking you'd moved on, and what if you didn't want to see me...I just couldn't bear the thought of losing you all over again, so I bottled it. And when you walked in that hotel room, I just..."

He runs his fingers through my long hair, brushing it over my shoulder.

"I just couldn't believe my luck that it was you. Stuart had given me the list with the interviewers' names on that morning, and there was yours, right at the top. I spent the next hour pacing the floor, hoping it would be you, and then there you were, standing before me, looking the most beautiful you ever had, and I knew with absolute certainty I was never letting you go again."

I push my lips together, scrunching my brow. "So that's why I'm doing the bio?"

"Partly." He half smiles. "But mainly because you are a fan-fucking-tastic writer."

"Good save." I smile and lean close to him, kissing him gently on his lips.

He grabs my face, keeping me there. "Don't ever leave me, Tru. I can't lose you again." There's a quiet desperation in his voice. It makes my insides tremble.

"You won't ever lose me. I promise."

I'll always be in Jake's life, one way or another. I know that for sure.

His kiss deepens to intense, his tongue invading my mouth, crashing with mine, pulling me farther into him.

We are all lips, hot tangled emotions and sensation.

The way he holds me, kisses me, it's with such a wretched need, an intensity of the likes I've never felt before. It's blindsiding. And I feel like I'm getting a glimpse of what I may mean to him.

After a while, Jake slows down his kiss and moves his lips from mine, chasing kisses down my neck. He pulls me close to his chest, holding me tight.

"Jonny would have loved you," he murmurs, stroking his fingers down my spine.

"You think?" I tilt my head back to look at him.

"Definitely." He kisses the tip of my nose. "I'd talked to him about you in the beginning quite a lot, so he kind of already knew you fairly well." He looks at me, shy.

I like the look.

I smile at the thought of Jake talking to Jonny about me. I wish I had gotten the chance to know Jonny. He seemed like such an awesome guy in his interviews, and he was incredibly important to Jake.

"I'd have had a fight on my hands with him for you though. You were just his type."

"I was?"

"Yep, exotic, smart…beautiful."

Exotic?

"Charmer."

"Damn straight."

"Jonny was gorgeous…" I grin.

"Hey!" he chastises, slapping my behind through the covers.

"But not as gorgeous as you, of course!" I squeal.

"That's more like it."

I like that he's talking about Jonny with me, with such ease now and no sadness.

He presses his forehead against mine and closes his eyes. I bask in his contentment, feeling it like it's my own, as I breathe him in.

"Who was your first girlfriend?" I ask, tracing my finger over the tattoo on his chest.

I know he never had one back in the UK. So she was definitely an American.

I hate that I don't know this stuff about him.

"Aside from you?"

"I was never your girlfriend."

"You should have been." He opens his eyes and stares into mine. I'm surprised at the intensity of his gaze. "But to answer your question, little Miss Interviewer…" He grins, moving back. "I've never had one."

"You've never had a girlfriend?"

"Nope. Never."

"You're shitting me."

"I'm not shitting you. I'm being completely serious." His eyes are steady on mine.

"Sorry, I just find it a little hard to believe—Jake Wethers has never had a girlfriend. What about all the models and actresses?"

"And did you see any pictures of me with them for any longer than a week?"

I rake through my memories, cringing at the images that flash through my mind of Jake with other women.

I shake my head no.

Wanting to change the subject, I say, "Okay, seeing as though I'm in interviewer mode, I want to ask—if you, Jake Wethers, had to pick one song as your title song to describe yourself, what would it be—and it can't be one of your own," I quickly add.

"'Hurt,'" he answers without hesitation.

It makes *me* hurt inside he picked that song.

"Why?"

He lets out a light sigh. "Some people said Reznor was writing a lyrical suicide note. Others said he was writing about finding a reason to live. I think it's both…it just depends on which side you're looking at it from."

"And which side are you looking at it from?"

He stares at me for a long moment. My heart is hammering in my chest.

"Now? A reason to live."

My insides start to tremble.

"Reznor's version or Johnny Cash's?" I ask quietly, trying to conceal the pain from my voice.

"Johnny Cash."

"Why?"

He closes his eyes briefly. And in this moment I just want to magic up all the power in the world to soothe his pains away.

"Because I have a few things in common with him," he answers, opening his eyes.

"Like?"

"The drugs...the women...hanging out for the girl of my dreams."

I take a sharp breath in. Tears instantly prick the backs of my eyes.

He touches my face, his thumb smoothing over my lips. "You're my June, Tru."

Holy shit.

"Except I can't sing," I say, trying to make light of the moment.

"Well, yeah, there is that, but you can play a mean tune on the piano."

I tilt my head to the side, forcing a smile I don't really feel.

"So what's yours?" he asks.

"Oh, without a doubt, 'I Can't Get No Satisfaction.'" I push the smile into a grin, trying to take us back to moments ago.

"Do I detect a hint of sarcasm there, Bennett?"

"Mmm." I press my lips together.

"Well, I'll just have to see what I can do about that." Then he's flipping me over onto my back and kissing my neck.

"Jake?" I say after a moment.

"Hmm," he murmurs, running his tongue over my skin.

"Why have you never settled with anyone for longer than a week?"

He lifts his head and stares down at me with such an intensity it makes my insides ache.

"Because I was waiting for you." He tucks my hair behind my ear and kisses me gently on the lips.

"I just wondered if it was because of your past...you know—your dad?" I ask tentatively. "Why you're afraid to have a relationship."

I feel him stiffen under my hands, and I know I've said the wrong thing.

"I'm not afraid of having a relationship." He sits up abruptly, leaving me cold. "I'm *trying* to have a relationship with you, but you seem to be having a pretty fuckin' hard time letting go of your current one. You asked before if I've ever had a girlfriend—no. But you don't ask if I want one. Because I do—you. I want you in my life all the time. I want to be able to go out with you in public and tell everyone that you're my girl, without hiding here in these fuckin' hotel rooms, while you decide if you want me or him."

Whoa! What the hell?! How did we get here?

"I've told you I want to be with you."

"But you haven't told Will, and therein lies the problem, Tru. Because really, I don't think you do know what you want."

"I do."

I sit up and take his face in my hands, forcing him to look at me. "I want you. I want to be with you."

And I mean those words. I do want Jake. But I know I love Will too, and honestly, I don't know how I'm going to feel when I see him again.

The truth is, being here with Jake, like this, it's easy because I just feel so far away from Will. Far away from my life with him.

Like he and I was a different lifetime ago.

But when he steps back into it…I guess I just don't know.

Still, no matter how I feel, I will do the right thing. I will tell Will about me and Jake. I just have to find the right moment.

I move my mouth close to Jake's, but instead of kissing his lips, I dip my head and kiss the scar on his chin, pressing my lips gently to it.

He sharps in a breath.

I run my tongue over his rough stubble, upwards, until my mouth finds his.

He grabs a handful of my hair, holding me to him.

"You're mine, Tru. I'm not sharing you with him anymore."

"I'm yours," I murmur into his mouth.

I just feel so utterly intoxicated by him, and in this moment I am his, completely.

Jake pushes me back onto the bed, grabs a condom from the nightstand, and has it on in moments.

He slides himself inside me, no hesitation. I groan as I feel him fill me completely, like only he can.

He kisses me hard on the mouth, and then rolls onto his back, taking me with him, putting me on top.

I start to move slowly, up and down, my hands placed on his toned stomach.

"Fuck, Tru," he groans, his fingers digging into my hips as he lifts his, meeting me, pushing himself deeper inside.

"I want to," I breathe, meeting his eyes, biting down on my lip.

Jake has me on my back again, in one swift move, taking my breath with it.

And then things get urgent and heated, and hard.

I'm hips up, meeting his thrusts, hands splayed on his back, fingers digging into his muscle, gripping him, while Jake fucks me like I want him to.

"Oh God, Jake," I moan. "Harder. I want it harder."

"You'll tell him about us tomorrow." He slams into me, his teeth gritted. He's not asking.

"I'll tell him." I'd say anything right now if it means he'll keep doing this with me—to me.

"I won't share you anymore," he repeats, as he continues driving into me over and over again. "You belong to me."

"Yes," I cry out.

When we find our release together, Jake holds me tight to him, his face buried in my neck. Almost like it's the last time he's going to hold me.

And I lie here, confused, trembling on the inside from the intensity of it all. Of the intensity of his feelings for me.

I hadn't realised they were so deep. Or that Jake was quite so possessive.

CHAPTER SIXTEEN

I wake to the sound of knocking on my hotel door. A glance at the clock tells me it's 9:15 a.m.

I wonder who the hell that is.

Jake is wrapped around me like a sheet. I disentangle myself from him. He groans and rolls over in his sleep.

I pull on my robe and pad my way towards the main door. I peer through the peephole, and my heart stops in my chest.

It's Will.

Will is standing outside my door, and Simone is with him, and Jake is in my bed—holy fuck!

Holy fucking fuckety shit!

For a moment, I literally don't know what to do.

Then Will knocks at the door again. A little louder this time.

I take a couple of quiet steps back, then turning, I run into the bedroom.

"Jake," I whisper, shaking him. "Wake up."

He blinks open heavy eyes.

"Will is here, outside the door! Here now!" I hiss.

He blinks again as my words register. Then very slowly, he sits up.

He doesn't look panicked in the least. Me, I'm absolutely shitting myself, but Jake seems quite leisurely about it.

"You have to hide." I pull on his arm, glancing around the room, my eye catching sight of the bathroom door.

"What?"

"Hide. You need to hide in the bathroom. Will is here outside the door."

I run around, gathering up his clothes. I shove them in his arms and try to pull him off the bed. He's reluctance is apparent.

"You want me to hide in the fuckin' bathroom?" His tone is less than encouraging.

"Ssh, keep your voice down, he'll hear you."

"I don't give a fuck," he says, audible.

Oh no.

"Please, Jake. I can't let him find out this way. Not when he's come all this way to see me. I will tell him, soon. But not like this. *Please*." I try to urge him off towards the bathroom again.

Another knock. Louder, more insistent this time.

Jake glances in the direction of the knocking, then looks back at me, giving me a hard, unforgiving stare.

I stare back with pleading eyes.

He gets to his feet and storms into the bathroom, shutting the door firmly behind him.

My head is an absolute mess.

I quickly make my way towards the door. Smoothing my hair down, I take a deep breath, then swing open the door.

"Surprise!" Will and Simone sing in unison.

"Arghh!" I cry out in Oscar-worthy fake surprise.

Will throws his arms around me, enveloping me in a big hug.

His scent washes over me, musky and minty, and I almost break down crying on the spot.

"God, I've missed you," he says, holding me tight.

"I missed you too," I murmur. I can't stop the tears that fill my eyes.

Guilty tears.

"You took your time answering the door." He holds me back, looking at me like he's drinking me in.

He looks so happy.

Oh God.

"Sorry, I was sleeping." I somehow manage to get the words out of my clotted throat.

"A late one, huh?"

"Mmm."

Simone pushes her way in, hugging me. I wrap my arms around her.

I'm so glad she's here.

Will moves past us, wheeling their little suitcases into my suite.

"Hey, gorgeous," she says. "The flat has been so quiet, and so clean, without you."

I hug her tighter.

"Hey, you okay?" She holds me back, appraising me.

"I'm just happy to see you." I hug her again.

Releasing her, I follow Will into the living room, Simone behind me.

Okay, so Jake is trapped in the bathroom, and I somehow have to get them out of here for a little while so he can get out of there and back to his own suite.

"Holy shit!" Simone exclaims from behind me. "This place is huge."

I shrug, smiling through tight lips.

My eyes keep flickering in the direction of the bathroom door.

Jake is in there. In the bathroom. Wearing just his boxer shorts. I hope he's dressed into his clothes.

Not that it will make the slightest bit of difference if Will finds him trapped in my bathroom. It'll be pretty clear what he's doing in there.

Fuck. Fuck. Fuckety-fuck.

What am I going to do?

After setting down the suitcases, Will comes back over to me and wraps his arms around my waist and plants a kiss firmly on my lips.

I squirm a little.

I wonder if he'll be able to smell Jake on me? Freeing myself from his kiss, I lean back away slightly.

He stares down at my face. "Are you okay, darling?"

"Of course." My voice is a little strangled, and I'm dying under his gaze. I feel like I'm going to crack any minute.

"This is okay, isn't it? Simone and I turning up to surprise you?"

"Of course it is!"

Simone is wandering around, checking out the place.

"This bedroom is massive!" she exclaims, poking her head through the door.

Don't go in there. Please don't go in there.

She's gone in.

Crap.

I can see her over Will's shoulder moving around, checking things out, looking at the view through the window, which is right next to the bathroom door.

Don't go in the bathroom. Don't go in the bathroom.

I see her hand reaching for the door handle.

Fuck.

What am I going to do? I'm trying to think quickly, but I'm frozen. Nothing's working. Every function in me is failing right when I need it most.

Then everything slips into slow motion, and I freeze solid in Will's arms as I watch in absolute horror as Simone pulls open the bathroom door.

"ARGHH!" she screams.

Fuck.

Shit.

Bollocks.

"Simone, are you okay?" Will asks, concerned, turning in my arms.

I keep a firm hold of him.

This is it. This is the exact moment that everything is over.

If I'd have known this was going to be the last time I held Will, then I'd have held him with a lot more conviction. I'd have taken in everything about him. Because when he finds out Jake is in there, he's never going to forgive me. He'll never look at me the same again.

Simone is silent for what seems like forever. I tentatively hold my breath, waiting for her response, feeling like my head may explode any second.

"I'm fine!" she hollers, but her voice sounds a little strangled.

Then I hear the bathroom door close.

I exhale.

"It was just a spider. A massive spider in the bath. Frightened the shit out of me," she says, coming back into the living room.

"Do you want me to get rid of it?" Will asks, turning in my arms.

"No!" both Simone and I say in unison.

Will looks between the two of us, puzzled.

"I like spiders," I say quickly.

"You do?" Will focuses his inquisitive stare on me.

I instantly heat under his gaze.

"It's gone. It bolted when I screamed at it," Simone tells him, saving me from his quizzical stare.

I meet her eyes briefly. One slow blink, thanking her.

She nods gently and sits down on the arm of the sofa.

"So how did you know what room I was in?" I ask, releasing myself from Will's hold, but he keeps his arm around my waist, keeping me close.

Will answers, "Well, we wanted it to be a surprise, and we figured you'd be up on the top floor, so we asked the security guy who was out by the main door guarding it, I'm guessing Jake's security people—who looked none too pleased to see us up here might I add. But then we told him we were looking for you, that we'd come to surprise you, and he showed us to your room."

It worked. I was surprised. And so completely screwed. Literally and figuratively.

"Good thinking." I force a smile. "So when did you decide on this?" My voice is wobbling all over the place.

I need to get them out of here, just long enough so I can get Jake out of the bathroom. It's the only current working thought in my mind.

"A few days ago." Will leaves my side and sits down on the sofa.

Crap, he's getting comfortable.

I stay where I am. I can't seem to stand still. I'm practically hopping from one foot to the other.

I wrap my arms across my chest.

Simone keeps flickering glances my way, but I can't bring myself to look at her. The shame is burning up my face.

"I knew you were stressed about the whole Jake affair article," Will says.

I nearly choke on my own spit, quickly turning it into a cough. I cover my traitorous mouth with my hand.

Will doesn't seem to notice and continues on regardless, "And I know today is the last day of the tour, so I thought I would come out and watch the gig—if that's okay with Jake and the guys, obviously."

"I-I'm sure it will be." My voice is so squeaky.

This is just getting worse and worse.

"So, well, I called up Simone to see if she fancied coming too, and here we are."

He was being thoughtful. And I was sleeping with Jake.

I'm going to hell. Straight to hell.

"I got us seats on the same flight back as yours tomorrow night so we can all fly home together," he adds, smiling.

"Sounds wonderful." I force a smile. "So I bet you guys must be starving." My voice lifts. "Why don't you go downstairs and get some breakfast; the food here is amazing. I'll just get dressed and I'll meet you down there in ten."

"Yeah, I could do with something," Will says, putting his hand to his stomach. "But we'll wait for you, darling…go get changed." He tips his head in the direction of the bedroom door.

"I need to shower."

"It's fine we'll wait."

I flick a "help me" glance at Simone.

"We'll be waiting bloody ages, Will, you know what's she's like, and I'm starving. Let's go down now and get a table, and Tru can join us once she's ready."

"Okay," Will says hesitantly.

He gets to his feet and comes over to me. Tipping my chin up with his thumb and forefinger, he plants a kiss firmly on my lips.

"We'll see you down there, and don't be long. I've been away from you too much already."

"I'll be ten minutes max."

Simone squeezes my hand on the way past. I almost break down on the spot.

I wait until I hear the door close behind them before I move.

I go into the bedroom and slowly open the bathroom door.

Jake is sitting on the edge of the bath, dressed in his clothes, and he doesn't look happy. But then I didn't expect he would be.

"I'm so sorry…," I start, but he cuts me off.

"Did you know he was coming?"

"No." I look at him, surprised.

He gives me a look of disbelief.

"Seriously, as if I'd have you here in my bed if I knew he was coming."

He stares at me for a long moment. My stomach is knotted and my body wired. I can't stop fidgeting.

I go over to him, kneeling down between his legs. "I am so very sorry."

"Why did you make me hide in here?"

I give him a puzzled look. "Because I didn't want him to walk in and find you in my bed."

He narrows his gaze at me. I feel hot and uncomfortable under it.

"So you're not going to tell him about us?"

"What? Yes, of course I am."

I think. Maybe. I don't know.

"So go tell him." He gestures towards the door with his hand. "You know where he is. Go tell him now. I'll wait here for you."

"Jake…" I get up off the floor, sitting on the toilet. "He's flown all this way to see me. I can't just go and tell him about you and me ten minutes after he's arrived."

"You promised me last night that you would tell him. He's here now, so what better opportunity is there? You didn't want to tell him on the phone—well, now you don't have to."

I run my hands through my hair and blow out a breath. "Be reasonable, Jake."

"I think I've been pretty reasonable overall, and patient. So very fuckin' patient, but it's wearing thin."

I look down at my toes.

He sighs loudly, then gets up and storms out of the bathroom.

I'm quick to my feet, following after him.

"Jake, wait," I call.

He stops just shy of the bedroom door and turns back to face me. "Will you tell him today or not?"

I let out a light breath, wrapping my arms around myself. "I will tell him, but I can't today." I shake my head. "Not today. Please try to understand."

Moving forward, I reach for him, but he shakes his head no.

The rejection from him hurts more than I ever realised it could.

He walks out of the bedroom, heading for the main door.

"Don't leave like this, please," I say, desperation in my voice, catching hold of his hand from behind.

He stares down at my hand in his. The look on his face makes me let go.

"I'm not the other guy, Tru."

"I know, and I will tell him, I promise you."

He looks down at the floor. "Are you going to bring him to the show?"

I press my lips together. "I can't go to it and leave him and Simone here."

"No. I guess you can't." His tone is sardonic.

"Do you not want me to come to the show? I can make up some excuse why—"

"No. Bring him to the fuckin' show. I don't care."

Then it's like an invisible force field settles down between us.

"I'll do whatever's easiest for you, Jake."

"No you won't. Telling him the truth is what would be easiest for me." He gives me a firm stare.

I look away, ashamed that he's right. Right that I won't tell Will.

"Just do whatever you want, Tru. I don't give a shit anymore."

Then he's gone and the door is slamming behind him, and I'm left alone, knowing I have to pull myself together and go downstairs to face Will. To act like everything is okay, when it couldn't be any further from okay.

I glance down at the two bracelets on my wrist from the two men I love.

Now I just have to figure out which one I'm going to take off.

CHAPTER SEVENTEEN

The show is insanely good.

Jake, Denny, and Tom are on top form—Jake most of all. It's the last show of the European tour, and he is making sure they finish on a high.

I haven't seen Jake since this morning. He's avoiding me for obvious reasons.

I know it's hurting him, Will being here, and I hate it. I can't stand the thought of Jake being in pain in general, but when it's because of me, it's a thousand times worse.

I wish I could make it better for him. But right now I feel like I'm caught between a rock—Jake—and a hard place—Will.

For a change, I'm out front watching the show with Will and Simone. I thought it would be better than stageside for obvious reasons, and Stuart very kindly sorted me out some fantastic seats for the three of us.

We're seated close to the stage with a clear view of the guys, but maybe saying "seated" is wrong because Simone and I haven't sat down since the show started.

It's hard not to fall into the pull of the show, because Jake and the guys are on fire.

I'm just glad I wore my floral print cami top and blue denim skirt, as it's crazy hot in here tonight.

And I don't think the heat is helping with my wrecking ball nerves, but then I've been this way all day.

I'm trying to keep thoughts of what happened this morning out of my head and to focus on Will, but it's difficult, especially here now looking at Jake, so beautiful up on the stage.

Jake finishes up singing one of the new hits, "Pure Thing," and slows things down to an easy stop.

The stage darkens. The lights are killed.

There're some whistles from the audience, but it's so silent that you could hear the beating heart of a mouse.

I find myself holding my breath along with everyone else.

Then the spotlight hits Jake.

He looks like a god up there. So beautiful, with the world at his feet.

Eighty thousand people and not a single sound to be heard. The stadium waiting, breath bated, to hear what will come out of Jake's mouth.

A man with the adoration of the world at his feet, and I can't exactly figure why he wants me.

Jake steps back from the mike and pulls his cigarettes from out of his back pocket, puts one between his lips, and lights it up.

Blowing the smoke from his mouth, he reaches down and grabs his beer from the side of his mike stand, taking a long swig from the bottle.

The crowd cheers, encouraging him to down the bottle—even Tom is egging him on—so Jake, being Jake, downs the bottle and tosses it to the ground in front of the stage as the crowd cheers.

I can tell he's already been drinking a lot; that's apparent enough.

He takes another drag of his cigarette and steps up to the mike.

The whole stadium is silent, once again, in anticipation of what Jake will say next.

He exhales his smoke as he leans into the mike, and starts to speak. "Okay." He runs his hand through his hair, looking contemplative. "I know the guys are going to kill me for this...but I'm thinking of maybe mixing things up a bit, doing something a little different." Jake leans back from his mike, looking at Tom with a question on his face, covering his mike with his smoking hand.

Tom wanders over to him, bass in hand. Jake says something in his ear. Tom looks up, surprised, then nods once, at Jake.

Tom heads back to Denny, climbing up, leaning over the drum kit, he says something to him. I see Denny look over at Jake, a puzzled look on his face. Jake lifts his shoulders, grinning.

The room is abuzz, the crowd wondering just what's going on.

Tom jumps down from the kit and goes over and speaks to Smith.

Smith looks across at Jake and gives him a quick nod.

Tom walks back past Jake, putting his hand on his shoulder, he speaks briefly in his ear. I see Jake laugh as Tom walks away.

Jake looks back out at the crowd. "Okay, folks, sorry about that." His beautiful voice echoes around the stadium. "We're going for a song change, but one I think you guys will dig. We're doing something a little different—it's not one of ours. This song was out around the time that we were breaking into the music scene, and these were guys we admired—still do. It's a personal favourite of mine."

He takes another drag of his cigarette.

"So all you ladies out there…no, actually, guys too, how many of you have had your heart broken?"

Every hand in the whole place goes up.

"I've had my heart broken too, believe it or not, quite recently in fact," he says.

Oh God.

"I'll mend it for you, Jake!" cries a female voice from the audience.

Jake chuckles into the mike. "I might have to take you up on that, honey."

"Say when and where, and I'll be there, baby!" yells the woman.

Then a collection of female voices all start screaming, vying for Jake's attention.

My throat is starting to get tight. I'm nervous and on edge, to know where he's going with this. I know he can be unpredictable at times, especially when he's been drinking.

"Okay." He lifts his hand, quietening the crowd. "So tell me, out of all those broken hearts, how many of them was because your guy or girl cheated on you?"

Holy shit.

Some of the hands go down.

"Bad shit, huh?" he says into the mike.

"Okay…" He takes another drag of his cigarette and drops it to the floor, putting it out with his boot. "How many of these hands up have ever, in their time, been…a cheater too?"

My heart drops through the floor. I can't believe he's doing this in front of eighty thousand people.

A huge majority of the hands go down. I bind mine together in front of me.

I sneak a glance at Will, but he's watching the show.

I can't even look at Simone. I haven't really had a chance to talk to her about Jake. I gave her a brief overview while Will was in the toilet, but catching Jake in the bathroom attached to my bedroom told her all she needed to know.

She's not judging, and I love her for that, but she did say I need to make a decision. And she's right, I do.

I'm just not fully sure on which decision to make.

"Okay, well this song is for all of you who have been cheated on," Jake continues. "And also for the ones they cheated with. The ones of you who were used and abused, filled with a shitload of promises, then left hanging dry. This one is for you guys…"

Denny hits the cymbals twice, Smith kicks in with the guitar, and Jake leans into the mike and starts to sing.

My whole body freezes cold, as he lullabies the lyrics to the Killers' "Mr. Brightside."

Holy fuck.

So he's not only just talked about adultery in front of eighty thousand people, he's now singing about it.

Singing about a guy who believes his girlfriend is having an affair.

He's trying to tell Will. He's trying to get Will thinking.

And in this moment, I'm filled with absolute anger towards Jake.

Then, as if reading my thoughts, he tilts his head to the side, staring straight in my direction, I didn't realise he even knew where I was sitting.

I thought I at least had some anonymity.

Apparently not.

Now I'm standing here, open wide to whatever he chooses to throw at me. And I can't move, I'm paralysed, as he openly sings in my direction.

Anger burns through me, turning to rage and fear.

He's no right to do this. It's up to me to tell Will, in my own time. It's just cruel playing shitty games like this.

I'm just praying on the fact that Will doesn't get music like we do. He doesn't read the messages in lyrics.

I want to look at Will, I need to know if he's seeing this or I'm right, like I'm praying, and he doesn't.

But I can't move because I'm trapped in Jake's stare. Like a rabbit in the headlights of a very beautiful truck, careening its way towards me.

I'm so very afraid at the game he's playing, and I get a distinct feeling this is just the start of tonight's games.

And when Jake does finally release me from his gaze, singing back to his adoring fans, I steal a glance at Will and find he's just watching the stage, completely oblivious as to what has just transpired up there.

Then I feel Simone's hand take hold of mine.

I turn my head to look at her. She gives me a sad smile, then rests her head against my shoulder, as the song finally comes to an end, Jake finishing my first torture of the night.

And I keep hold of her hand for the rest of the show.

After the show, I head straight to the after-show party with Will and Simone. Ben had kindly offered to drive us, so we ride through the streets of Paris in his safe hands. He drops us off out front, with the offer to pick us up later, but I wave his kind gesture off and tell him to get back to the hotel and chill out for the night.

Showing my pass to the security, we're waved in.

We quickly grab a table, and I ensure it's one with a good view of the door, so I can see when Jake arrives.

Will goes to the bar to get us some drinks. The party is buzzing already. But all I can think about is Jake. When is he going to get here? And what kind of mood will he be in when he does arrive?

"So the show was great," Simone enthuses. "A little crazy in parts." She raises her eyebrow and I know exactly what she's getting at.

"No kidding," I mutter.

"Is Jake always that...intense?"

"Not generally, but with me, recently...yes."

"God, when he started talking about all the cheating stuff, then he started singing 'Mr. Brightside,' I nearly died for you."

"I think I did die." I give her a weak smile.

"He's definitely got it bad for you, sweetie."

"I don't know about that." I lift my shoulders. "I think maybe it's just because currently, I'm the one thing he can't have."

She shakes her head. "No, it's more than that. He wouldn't put himself out there on the line like that if it was just for a conquest. I'm pretty sure there are others things out there for Jake to conquest if he wanted."

Yeah, and mostly that's what I'm worried about.

I see movement in the door, distracting me.

Denny walks in with Stuart. But no sign of Jake or Tom.

Where is he? Wouldn't they come together? They usually do, but then I've been with them on those occasions.

Odd though because Stuart is always with Jake. I wonder why he's sent him on with Denny.

People stop Denny, congratulating him on the show. Stuart spies me and comes over to our table.

"Hello, my gorgeous chica." He kisses me on the cheek. "Oh, and another gorgeous." He kisses Simone. She flushes scarlet.

"Are all you Brit chicks gorgeous, or just the ones Tru knows?"

"All British girls are hot—especially the half–Puerto Rican and foxy blonde ones." I grin at him.

"Well, if the men are anything near as good-looking as your hot boyfriend, then I'm flying over now," he says to us, grinning, setting both Simone and me laughing.

Even though I'm laughing, all I want to do is ask Stuart where Jake is. But I can't. It might look too obvious.

Denny finally makes it to our table and drops down into the seat next to Simone. I see her instantly tense up.

"Hey, Tru." He smiles.

"Denny, this is my best friend and roommate, Simone," I introduce.

"Great to meet you." Denny turns, looking at Simone for the first time, and I see his eyes widen the instant he looks at her.

I'm not surprised; she is absolutely gorgeous.

I see her eyes are already lit up like a Christmas tree over Denny. You'd have to be blind not to notice the obvious, instant attraction.

Oh, I have a good feeling about this.

I smile to myself as Denny starts to talk to Simone; happy that at least out of the two of us, one of us is currently happy.

Will comes back with our drinks. A margarita for me. He knows me so well.

I take a sip, the fresh alcohol kick is perfect. My drinks from the gig were starting to wear off.

"Sorry guys, I didn't realise you were here; otherwise, I'd have got you some drinks in," Will says to Stuart and Denny.

"Hey, no problem, man," Denny says, waving him off.

"Oh, Denny, this is my boyfriend, Will."

I don't know why but it suddenly feels odd referring to Will as my boyfriend to Denny.

"Nice to meet you, man." Denny shakes Will's hand.

"You too," Will says politely. "Great show."

"Thanks."

"I'll go to the bar," Stuart starts to get to his feet, but Denny gets up. "Sit down, man, I'll get these—beer?" he asks Stuart.

"Beer's good," Stuart replies, sitting back down.

Denny heads over to the bar, and Stuart starts talking to Will about the show.

I lean across the table to Simone. "So, Denny…" I raise my eyebrows at her.

She flushes red. It's so cute to see. I haven't seen her like this about a guy for a long while.

"He's even better looking in the flesh," she whispers, shyly.

"He is," I agree. "And he's a really great guy. He was in a long-term relationship, but they broke up about a year ago and he's been single ever since."

"So basically he's not a womaniser like the other two?"

It's my turn to flush. "Um…yes."

She grimaces. "Sorry that sounded—"

I flash my eyes in Will's direction, cutting her off.

She presses her lips together, apologising with her eyes.

I sit back in my chair and give her a light, forgiving smile. But it feels heavy on my face and I can't hold it for long.

Denny comes back with his and Stuart's drinks, taking Simone's attention again. And I'm glad because I just can't seem to muster up any conversation with anyone. My mind is far too busy working overtime, wondering where Jake is, what he's up too and who with.

If he was with Denny, I wouldn't be worried. But he's with Tom, and Tom's…well, he's exactly the same as Jake, when it comes to women. A complete slag.

And the fact that Denny is here without them, meaning he left them to whatever they were doing so he could come to the party, as he isn't into the whole shagging thousands of women thing, isn't looking good right now.

What if Jake is with some groupie who managed to scam her way backstage? Or even worse…with some gorgeous French model or actress who was a VIP at the show?

Jake's blatantly angry with me because Will is here, so maybe he's decided to forget all about me with the help of someone else.

I start to feel sick, so I pick up my margarita and get chugging on it, trying to kill all thoughts of Jake.

We've been here an hour, the drink is not soothing me, and I'm getting antsy, because Jake and Tom are still no-shows.

Simone and Denny are getting on a treat, which is awesome. I've picked up my conversational skills with Will and Stuart some, but not by much; I'm more pretending to listen than actually listening.

My eyes are surreptitiously trained on the door, and person after person, I'm met with disappointment that it's not Jake walking through those doors.

I don't even know if he'll speak to me when he does arrive. Or maybe he won't come because I'm here with Will.

No, it's the after-show party for the final leg of the European tour, a big deal, and there are a lot of important people here. Jake's a businessman as well as a musician; he'll show.

I'm getting the urge to want to call him. I keep considering it over and over, whether or not to go to the bathroom and call him.

I'm on my second margarita, and trying to pace myself for the night, as I feel it will more than likely be a long one. And counting the drinks I had at the show, I'm three glasses of wine and two margaritas in already.

Denny has gone to the bar, Simone accompanying under the pretence of helping him carry the drinks back. She just wanted to get him alone, and I can't say I blame her.

Stuart and Will are talking cars now, so I open up my handbag on the table and check my phone for the tenth time to see if Jake has called or texted me, but there's nothing but a blank screen staring back at me.

I'm turning into a crazy person over him. Is he doing this to me on purpose? Knowing him, yes, quite probably.

But I have to know whether he's coming tonight or not.

I decide to go to the bathroom to call him, and I'm just about to get up from my seat, when I hear the noise that always accompanies Jake, as he comes into the party with Tom. Dave and Ben are obviously with them, and there's a group of people I don't recognise also.

Rapturous applause breaks out, the masses encroaching on Jake. And in this moment I feel incredibly proud of him as all eyes in the room are focussed solely on him.

I'm so relieved to see him that I think the huge smile on my face might split my cheeks in half.

But my relief doesn't last long, and I see as the crowd shifts, standing beside Jake is a very beautiful girl, with long, thick red hair, huge cleavage, and legs that go on forever, wearing a dress that shows them off to their max. She looks like model.

And Jake is holding her hand.

My gut empties hollow, the smile quickly falling from my face, as it starts to prickle.

And therein I instantly get my answer as to where, and with whom, he's been for the last hour.

A thousand thoughts and emotions stream through me.

None of them good.

I feel sick and stupid, dizzy, and my heart is physically hurting in my chest.

My legs are itching to take me up from this chair and running for the door and out of here, and far, far away.

But I don't move. I just sit here, rooted with pain, as I watch Jake with this girl.

I see his eyes scan the room. They lock on to mine. I freeze for a long moment while his eyes burn me.

I look away. It's too hard to look at him for another moment longer, as thoughts whip through my mind as to what he's been doing with her.

I wonder if that is what it's like for him when I'm with Will.

Maybe that's why he's with her, to hurt me. Well, if it is, it's working, and well.

I'm raw with jealousy. I didn't know I had it in me to feel it to this level.

With my trembling hand, I finger the stem of my glass; picking it up, I tip my head back and let the margarita run down my throat.

As I move my eyes downwards, resting my glass back on the table, I'm met with Jake. He's standing at our table, directly in front of me, his redhead in tow.

He's not holding her hand anymore, I notice. Even still, it doesn't make me feel any better.

I just feel angry with him, and jealous. So very jealous.

And for a second, I wish I was sitting next to Will and not Stuart, so I could hurt Jake like he's hurting me. But then it would be a little strange if I leaned over Stuart to get to Will.

More like obvious, and childish, I'd say.

I force composure on myself.

"Where's Denny?" Jake asks Stuart.

He's ignoring me. It hurts.

"The bar." Stuart points in Denny's direction.

Seeing Denny with Simone, Jake grins and nods his head in approval.

"Hi, I'm Will," Will says to Jake, getting to his feet. "Tru's boyfriend. We haven't had a chance to meet yet." Will holds his hand out to Jake.

Jake glances down at his hand like he's not sure what to do with it.

And for that long second everything seems to hang in the air, precariously balancing.

Then Jake takes his hand and shakes it. "Good to finally meet you. Tru's told me a lot about you."

Jake casts a glance in my direction. It tears right through me.

"All good, I hope?"

"Of course." Jake lightly shrugs his shoulders, taking his hand back.

I let the breath out I was holding.

"The show was amazing," Will continues, sitting back down. "And I thought your version of 'Mr. Brightside' was bloody brilliant—better than the original."

I nearly crack into pieces on the spot.

Jake's eyes flicker in my direction again, and he smirks. "Thanks."

"Jake, are we getting a drink?" Redhead pulls on his arm. Her voice is sweet, laced with a heavy French accent, and she pronounces Jake, *Zzhake*, rolling his name around her tongue.

It sounds as sexy as she looks. I hate her.

Why do the French always sound sexy? So much sexier than my Spanish accent, the one that turns Jake on.

Fine, he wants to play games, well I'm up for that.

"Yeah, in a minute," Jake answers her, sounding irritated.

"Aren't you going to introduce us to your new friend, Jake?" Stuart asks.

Jake narrows a gaze at Stuart, who seems unfazed by the darts he's shooting him down with.

I don't think I want to know her name. It somehow makes her even more real if she has a name.

Jake glances back at the redhead. "Um…yeah, this is… um."

She rolls her eyes at him. "I'm Juliette." She presses her small hand to her large chest.

Zzhuliette.

So not only is she beautiful, she has a beautiful name. Which, Jake either couldn't remember or hadn't even bothered to find out.

I don't even know if that should make me feel better or not.

"*Zzhuliette,*" I hear myself saying in a really bad French accent.

Jake's eyes flicker to mine. Zzhuliette stares at me too.

Oh God.

"It's a really pretty name." I somehow recover. And I don't know if it's the booze or a mild hysteria setting in, but I say, in bad French again, "*Zzhake* and *Zzhuliette.* Has quiet a ring to it. Don't you agree?" I stare at Jake.

He shifts on his feet, looking at me like I've just grown another head.

I know Will's staring at me too, but in this moment I don't care.

Jake laughs, getting his cool composure back. "What have you been drinking, Tru?"

"Oh, just a few margaritas." I stare at him steady, shrugging, forcing the best smile I can muster up. "I'm just feeling happy. Looking on the *Brightside*, you know. Will and Simone are here, it's all good, I'm happy, happy, happy!"

His eyes harden, burning into mine. "So what did *you* think of the show, Tru?"

Is he asking my professional opinion or asking me in my current state of anger with him? Honestly, I don't even know why he is asking. And hearing him say my name, it's like I'm hearing it for the first time.

How can this be the same man who made love to me all through the night? Told me how much he missed me for the years we'd been apart. The man who pleaded with me to never leave him.

"Trooo?" Zzhuliette looks at me puzzled, with bitch in her eyes. "Your name is Trooo?"

I've never wanted to slap someone as much as I do her now.

Take my guy—fine. Don't dis my name. Even though I just did yours a few moments ago—kind of.

"Trudy," I explain. "My friends call me Tru for short." I emphasise the "u."

"Ahh, I zee." She runs her fingernails through her hair, seemingly bored now.

Obviously she has the attention span of a gnat.

Ugh, I'm turning into one of those bitchy women. Good.

I pick up my margarita and take a mouthful for courage.

"And to answer your question, Jake," I start to speak in my Spanish accent, because I know how much it affects him, and I want to be a bitch.

Jake's eyes widen and fire, and I know I'm playing a dangerous game. I dare not even look at Will.

"In my professional opinion, the show was brilliant, one of your best to date." I smile sweetly up at him, desperately trying to hold the pieces of me together.

His flaming eyes soften, slightly. I see him shift uncomfortably in his pants.

He's squirming.

Good.

Or maybe I've just turned him on and am about to send him off with his redheaded groupie.

Smart, Tru, real smart.

"Glad you think so. Plenty for the bio?" he asks.

Work. He really wants to talk work with me. Fine.

"Yes, plenty of stuff."

Barring the "I'm having an affair with you" part of the show, which you are now clearly past, as you have a shiny new French toy to play with.

I bite my lip until it hurts.

Tom comes swaggering over, a couple of girls in tow.

"Where the fuck is Denny? Are we getting this party started or what?" he says loudly, clearly already drunk, slapping Jake on the back.

"Yeah, I'm coming now," Jake answers him, without moving his eyes from mine.

Jake casts his eyes around the table, landing back on me lastly, and says, "Have a good night."

Then he's walking away, over to the bar, with his long-legged French redheaded beauty, Zzhuliette.

Leaving little ordinary English Trudy to watch him from the sideline, like everyone else in this room.

Chapter Eighteen

I've been surreptitiously watching Jake since he walked away from me thirty minutes ago.

I'm aware of every single move he makes, my eyes tracking him around the room, watching him greet people who are clearly here just to see him, as I force an interest in what Will has to say.

I know I'm not being fair to Will. But I just can't seem to get my focus straight anymore.

Jealousy and anger are in my driving seat.

Jake hasn't looked in my direction once in all that time. And now he's seated at his table, in the smoking area of this place, with Tom and Smith, and hordes of groupies are hanging around them, and of course the leggy Zzhuliette.

I had thought at one point, while he was working the room, he'd binned her off, as she was nowhere to be seen, but the second he sat down, she was there again. And my temporary sense of relief was gone.

While Will is talking to Stuart, I sneak another peek across the room, just in time to watch as Zzhuliette leans across the table, her cleavage well on show for all to see, mainly Jake, with an unlit cigarette perched between her glossy pink lips.

Jake pulls his lighter from his pocket. Sparking it, he holds it up to her cigarette.

She puts her hand on his wrist, touching his friendship bracelet, my bracelet, holding his hand in place, and bats her eyelashes seductively at him as she puffs her cigarette lit.

I'm angry that he let her touch my bracelet. I know that sounds stupid, but I'm not exactly feeling rational right now.

She moves back into her seat in a cloud of smoke, pushing her chest out, crossing her long legs suggestively at him.

She's the kind of sexy that I could only dream to be.

She is beautiful and I feel suitably inadequate. She is Jake's type for sure. His equal.

I really don't know what it is he sees in me. Or maybe I'm just a conquest like I said to Simone, because of our history. And the unobtainable, because of Will.

Maybe that's why he wants me so much.

Or maybe not so much now, as the case may be.

As I'm staring, I see Jake's eyes flicker past Zzhuliette and straight in my direction. I quickly look away, staring down at my drink.

I can't do this. I need a breather.

Getting up from my seat, I say to Will, "I'm just going to the ladies'."

I grab my bag and as I'm walking past, Will catches my hand.

"Are you okay, darling?" he asks in a quiet voice, looking up at me.

"I'm fine." I smile.

"You just seem a bit quiet, not your usual self."

He's noticed. I really am not being fair to him at all. He flew all this way to see me, and I'm just visually chasing Jake around this room.

I'm going to go to the bathroom to sort myself out, and come back and focus all my attention on Will, just like he deserves.

"I'm fine, baby, honestly." I touch his face with my hand. "I just think maybe all this travelling with the tour has finally caught up with me. I'm not used to it."

"Well, you'll be home tomorrow night for a few weeks' break, so you can relax then. And I'll be there to take care of you."

I feel sick at his kind words. I'm the lowest of the low. How could I cheat on this wonderful man?

Because you love Jake.

I push the thought to the back of my mind.

"Sounds wonderful," I say.

He kisses my hand, then releases it and turns back to Stuart, resuming their conversation.

I cross the huge room on unsteady legs, feeling like they might give out on me any moment now. Forcing a calm I don't own, I hold my head up high and carry on forward.

I see Simone is still at the bar with Denny, deep in conversation. Catching her eye, I give her a mini thumbs-up. She grins happily at me.

I'm just opening the bathroom door when someone grabs me from behind and drives me into the empty bathroom.

As I turn, surprised, I see it's Jake.

He locks the door behind him and leans back against it. His eyes look like they are on fire.

Something in my stomach drops, then coils lower. My legs start to tremble.

I'm ecstatic he's followed me here, and angry too.

Then my whole body catches up with my legs, and the tremble runs from my head, back down to my toes, tightening me up in those special places. The places only Jake can somehow magically touch with one single look alone.

"What are you doing here?" I say, going with my anger. "Someone might have seen you come in."

"No one saw me." He sounds confident, assured. Like always.

I don't know how true that statement is. Eyes are always on Jake wherever he goes.

"Great performance tonight. 'Mr. Brightside'—really, Jake? Why not just spell it out to the whole world?" I say bitingly.

He shrugs, grinning.

"What do you want?" I ask, rattled by his calm demeanour.

He lifts his eyebrow. "You." He starts to move slowly towards me like a tiger stalking its prey.

"Jake, no...not here, not now. Someone could come."

"Dave's outside the door, and it's locked. No one will bother us."

So Dave knows I'm sleeping with Jake? Brilliant.

"No, Jake. *Please*," I beg as he moves closer.

I'm begging because I don't know if I have the ability to say no to him. I haven't so far.

When I see he's got no intention of listening to my pleas, I start to back up and quickly find myself up against the sinks, with nowhere left to go.

My whole body is rushed with adrenaline, want, and fear. It's a heady combination.

When he reaches me, I put my trembling hand out, pressing it flat against his hard chest, stopping him at arm's length.

"You look beautiful tonight," he whispers intensely, eyes fixed on mine.

The exhilaration of being in here with him, him taking control like this, is doing crazy things to me.

He pushes hard against my hand, and I'm weakened to stop him, and truthfully, I don't want to.

The second I saw him with that girl, I hated it, and I wanted to reclaim him as mine.

So when he grabs hold of my hair, fisting his hand into it, and crushes his mouth to mine, I don't stop him.

What is it about him that makes me lose all reason and sense? What is it about Jake that turns me into a person I don't want to be, don't even like at times, yet makes me feel so completely and utterly alive?

His tongue invades my mouth, claiming me. I wind my fingers into his hair.

He tastes of sweat and whiskey and cigarettes...everything Jake.

With his hands cupped around my backside, he picks me up and sits me on the edge of the sink. I wrap my legs around his, holding him to me.

"I want you so bad," he groans into my mouth.

My hands go under his T-shirt. He stops kissing me and pulls it off over his head.

I drink him in. All I want is him. I don't care about anything else right now but having Jake.

He grabs my hair again, pulling my head back, looking into my eyes. "Tell me you want me." His tone is commanding, possessive.

"I want you," I breathe, my voice trembling.

He grins, then covers my mouth with his, pushing his hips firmly against me.

He's hard already. The feel of him, like this, sends waves of intense sensation rushing through my body.

Jake drags his hand from my hair, down over my breast. He breaks from kissing me to pull my cami off over my head, leaving me in my bra. That's gone a few seconds later.

He bends, putting his mouth around my nipple, sucking hard.

I groan at the feeling. I reach forward and undo his jeans, freeing him. I wrap my hand around him, working him up further.

He moans over my skin, moving his mouth to my other breast, kissing every part.

Jake grabs hold of my thigh, lifting my leg to the side, his hand moves to my skirt. He drives it up, then his hand continues, higher, his mouth clamped on mine, kissing me harder and harder.

My legs are still trembling from the lust and the danger of it all. Anyone could catch us in here.

Jake hooks his fingers under my panties and pushes his finger inside me, then without hesitation, another.

I arch my back, pushing into his hand, my head falling back.

"Ahh," I moan as his fingers move inside me.

In this moment, I'm his completely, whatever he wants me to do, I will.

"I want you now," he growls.

"Yes, now."

Then before I realise, he's tearing my panties in two, putting a condom on, and pushing himself inside me.

I'm so accustomed to his size, that when he slides his hand under my thigh, pulling me closer, lifting my leg higher, hooking it on his hip, giving him full access, I move willingly.

"Oh God, Jake," I moan.

"That's it, baby," he breathes, briefly closing his eyes. "Feel me inside you. I'm hard like this for you only."

I curl my fingers around the edge of the sink, holding on as Jake takes me here on it.

"I need you," he groans into my ear. "I fuckin' need you so much."

I hold my legs tighter around him, bringing him even deeper inside me.

And I realise in this exact moment, just how much I love this man. Completely.

I'm addicted to him. And he's an addiction I don't think I'll ever be able to give up.

He's grabbing at my flesh, driving into me, making love to me, and I'm so turned on, so close to coming, that when he groans, "Come for me, baby." I instantly do.

He follows, and we climax together.

I'm all sensation as Jake kisses me deeply, his tongue invading my mouth, my body tightening all around him.

For a few long seconds, we stay locked together, Jake's arms around me.

Then I come down from my Jake high with a hard bang.

Will.

What have I done?

I push him aside, sliding down off the sink onto my wobbly legs. I retrieve my bra and cami off the floor, quickly putting them on, seeing my torn panties on the floor.

Fuck!

How the hell am I going to explain to Will why I'm not wearing any underwear?

Angry with Jake, I pick them up off the floor and throw them at him.

He catches them. Holding them up in his hand, he stares at me.

"What the fuck were you thinking?" I hiss. "Ripping my panties off—Jesus Christ, Jake! What the hell am I going to tell Will?"

He removes his condom, binning it, zips up his pants, bends down, and retrieves his T-shirt, pulling it back on. Then he stares back at me with narrowed eyes.

"What was I thinking? I was thinking about wanting you. I don't really give a shit what you tell Will."

"Jesus Christ!" I repeat, putting my hands to my head, trying to sort through my tangled thoughts.

No, it'll be okay, I'll just tell Will that I came out without any panties on. Not that I've ever done it in the past, but I can make out it was a sexy thing for him.

The very thought makes me feel sick.

How can I be thinking sexy stuff with Will when I've just had sex with Jake?

This is so very screwed up.

I stare at him, my underwear still in his hand. "Give them to me," I say, holding my hand out.

He smirks at me. "No."

"Give them back." I keep my voice low but my tone firm.

Jake pushes my torn panties deep into his pocket. "Come and get them." He tilts his head to the side, challenging me.

I don't have time for this. I have to get back out there to Will; he'll be wondering where I am.

"Keep them," I say, turning for the door. "I haven't got time for your games."

Jake catches hold of my hand from behind. "Where are you going?" There's a quiet desperation to his voice.

"Where do think I'm going?"

I'm angry with him for coming in here, disgusted with myself for being unable to say no. Angry for what I've just done here, in this bathroom, with him.

But what's worse is I feel angry at myself because I wanted it. I wanted him more than I can ever begin to explain.

He steps closer, taking my face in his hands. I try to move. I don't want to look at him right now, because it will mean having to face what I've done, but he forces my face to his.

"Look at me," he says firmly.

I pull my eyes to his.

"Don't go to him, Tru, *please.*"

I sigh. "I'm sorry...I have to."

He rubs his thumb gently over my skin. I'm lost to his touch again. I close my eyes, revelling in the feel of his skin on mine.

"You don't have to. Just go out there and tell him the truth, baby," he says, voice low, soft. "Tell him you're with me now...then we can get out of here. Just you and me. We can go anywhere in the world you want."

I flick open my eyes. "Don't be ridiculous! I can't just tell him right here and now that I've been screwing you—that I've just screwed you in here, and then just bugger off with you! It doesn't work like that, Jake! Not everything in life is as easy as you seem to think it is! I can't do that to him. He deserves better than that from me."

"And I don't?" He drags his hand through my hair, pulling my head back so I'm forced to look up into his eyes. "And that's what we're doing here, Tru—just screwing? I thought it was a lot more than that." He sounds hurt, angry, bitter.

He's every right to be.

But I've been drinking and I just can't see straight at the moment. I'm so confused. My head is just an absolute clusterfuck of a mess.

"Currently, screwing is all that seems to be on your mind. This isn't about me. I don't think it ever has been... and all this, in here, was just because your ego was hurt, so you came in here looking for a quick fuck to make yourself feel better. To get one over on Will."

He looks like I've just slapped him. He drops his hand from my hair and steps back.

"I didn't hear you saying no."

"No, but I should have. Can't you see what we've just done in here was wrong—what we've been doing is wrong?"

"You regret me?" He looks hurt.

It hurts me to see his pain.

"No!" I rub my face, pulling in a deep breath. "No, I don't regret you, I just...I don't know." I shake my head, frustrated.

"Well seeing as though you don't know, why don't I just make this easy for you?" He turns to leave.

"No, Jake, please." I grab his arm, looking into his face despairingly. "I'm just so confused."

"I'm not. I know what I want—*you*. I want to be out there, with you, as mine."

"You seem to be doing just fine with Juliette keeping you company. She looked to be soothing your pain right away from what I saw."

It just slipped out.

I know I have no right to be jealous, my current situation pending, and I hate to show my hand to him, but it was out before I could stop it.

"You're jealous? Seriously, Tru?" I see the smirk in his eyes, and that just fuels my anger right back up.

"Just fuck off back to your tart!"

"I don't want to fuckin' go back to her. I want you."

Then suddenly I just want to hurt him.

"Well you can't have me. Not tonight. Not for a while. I'm going home tomorrow, remember." I let go of his arm.

I see the pain flicker over his beautiful face, and I feel sick. And all I want to do is take the words back.

"I'm sorry," I start talking quickly. "I didn't mean that— I just—I will tell him, Jake, soon. It's just difficult, and the constant pressure from you is driving me crazy. I feel like I can't breathe. You just need to give me space and let me do this in my own time."

But I can tell I've already lost him.

"You want space—you've got it. Shitloads of it." He turns from me again and stalks away, heading for the door, then stops just before it, turns and marches back until he's close to my face.

"I'm not the other guy, Tru. It doesn't fit with me—who I am. I'm *the* guy. And if you're saying you can't give me that now, then…" He leaves his words hanging.

"Then what?" My voice is trembling.

Saying nothing more, he turns from me and walks away.

"Answer me!" I cry after him. "Then what, Jake? You're done? What?"

I can feel panic rising in me. I'm losing him completely.

He stops and turns marginally, his lips pressed together in a tight line. "Interpret it whichever way you want. I don't give a shit anymore."

He unlocks the door and stalks out of the bathroom, slamming the door behind him.

I look at myself in the mirror. Right now, I hate myself.

Gripping hold of the sink, I try to control the shakes convulsing through me.

Then I throw up.

CHAPTER NINETEEN

Y ou were gone ages," Will says.

I smooth down my skirt as I sit in my seat, acutely aware of the fact that I have no panties on.

"Sorry. The queue for the toilet was really long, and when I was in there, I felt a little sick."

"Are you okay?" His brow furrows with concern.

Concern I really do not deserve.

"Yes, I'm fine. I just felt a little hot, a little queasy, but I'm fine now."

I'm not fine. I'm miserable, disgusted with myself, and so very screwed up.

Here I was promising myself I'd be better for Will, and then I go and have sex with Jake in a bathroom. And now I'm an even bigger mess than I was before.

I pick up my margarita.

"Is it a good idea to drink that if you feel sick, darling? I can go to the bar and get you some water if you want."

"No, I'm fine—honestly," I add at Will's worried expression.

What I need right now is alcohol and lots of it. I take a deep gulp of my margarita.

Stuart catches my eye and gives me a knowing look, lifting his eyebrow.

He knows I'm sleeping with Jake.

Of course he does. Dave knows, so it makes sense he does.

I've spent the last five days holed up with Jake. And Stuart is his PA. He knows Jake's itinerary, his every movement. It's his job to.

I bet he thinks I'm a complete slut.

My cheeks burn with shame.

I glance across the room, past Stuart, and see Jake is with Zzhuliette again.

I get a twisted feeling in my stomach.

She's sitting in his lap and they're sharing a cigarette. She puts it in his mouth, holding it to his lips while he takes a drag. Touching his lips with her fingers.

Lips that were on mine minutes before. Kissing me, everywhere.

She transfers the cigarette to her own lips and takes a long, sultry drag. Leaning close, she blows the smoke into Jake's mouth.

I feel a flash of white-hot jealously streak through me, as I see that his hand is on her thigh, his other stroking her arm, intimately.

I have a flash of memory, his hands on me, touching me.

Then I watch as Jake releases the used smoke from his mouth and leans in and whispers something in her ear. She throws her head back and laughs.

How can he do this when he was just in there with me? How can he move on so quickly?

He's sitting there with her in his lap and my torn panties in his pocket.

I feel sick.

He catches my eye.

Don't kiss her. Please don't kiss her.

Then with clear defiance on his face, he grabs hold of the back of her head and plants his mouth on hers.

I almost vomit into my drink.

How could he do this? He was having sex with me less than ten minutes ago, and now he's out here kissing another woman.

I know I'm no angel in this, but I would never have come back out here, after being with him in there, and stuck my tongue down Will's throat.

Hot tears burn the backs of my eyes. I have the urge to run.

But where to? And it's not like I can just run off anyway. Will would wonder what the hell was wrong with me.

I'm trapped here, doomed to watch, while Jake kisses another woman, minutes after having sex with me.

Deep breaths, Tru. It's okay. It's all going to be okay.

Closing my eyes, shutting them out, I pick up my margarita and drain the glass.

But I have to look again. It's torture, but I can't help myself.

I open my eyes to see Jake's no longer kissing her; he's talking to Tom, who also has a groupie hanging off him. But Zzhuliette is still in Jake's lap. Her hands are on him.

I hate her, and I hate him.

No I don't, I love him. But I want to hate him. In this moment, it's all I want. It would make all of this so much easier if I did.

Because this is Jake. This is what he does. It's what he's famous for.

He never gave a shit about being with me. I'm just a challenge to him. Something to conquer. He would have got bored with me the instant he took me off Will and would have tossed me aside like all the rest of them.

Jake can have his pick of women. There's not one single reason why he would have wanted me as his forever.

And I'm seeing the evidence clear, now, before me.

"Another drink, darling?" Will's already on his feet, gesturing to my empty glass.

He's so attentive. I don't deserve him.

I do love him.

But I love Jake. More. I think. I don't know.

Crap.

"Shots!" I blurt out.

Will gives me a puzzled look.

"Ooh, I'm down for shots," Stuart chips in, grinning, tapping his fingers on the table.

I think I've just found my drinking soul mate for the evening, seeing as though Simone has abandoned me for the gorgeous, sweet Denny.

Why can't Jake be more like Denny?

"A round of tequila shots please, baby...oh, and a beer chaser and another margarita—Stuart?" I look at him with a question.

He looks back at me, impressed.

Well, if I have to spend the night watching Jake maul a leggy redhead not long after having sex with me, then I'm going to do it drunk.

Stuart looks up at Will and says, "I'll have what the lovely Tru is having. Oh, and make sure to put it on Jake's tab."

He winks at me.

"Okay. Good. I'll be back in a minute," Will mutters, still looking slightly perplexed.

I know he thinks I've lost it. He probably thinks I'm spending too much time around musicians. He's right, I am. But not in the way he thinks. My problem is I've been spending way too much time with one musician in particular—in the very blackest sense of the word.

But right now, I don't care. It's either get drunk or go ass-over-backwards crazy.

I opt for drunk.

And I'm kind of loving Stuart right now for supporting me in my alcohol binge and for spending Jake's money in the process of helping me do it.

I watch Will go over to the bar. Anything to keep my wandering eyes off Jake and Zzhuliette.

I see Simone is still perched at the bar, she and Denny deep in conversation, totally engrossed with each other.

I'm glad for her. Denny is a cool guy.

"You hanging in there, gorgeous?" Stuart asks me, bringing my attention around to him. "Or do you want me to go kick his ass."

"Who?" I'm confused.

"Jake." He raises his eyebrows at me.

"Oh." I lean my head into my hand and glance over at him. "Am I that transparent?"

"No. But he is." He tilts his head back in Jake's direction.

"Please don't say anything to anyone...Will."

He gives me an "as if I would" look.

"Thank you," I utter quietly.

"Tru, I don't like to stick my nose in other people's business...but look, gorgeous, Jake's not only my boss, he's my friend, and I've known him a long time—I live with the guy.

And basically, the idiot is crazy about you. I have never seen him, with anyone, the way he is with you."

I look at him, surprised by his words.

"Except for when he's sticking his tongue down the throat of a leggy redhead," I add, trying to muster up a smile.

It doesn't work.

"Don't let that bother you, honey. That's just Jake trying to prove a point to you and himself. Trying to prove you don't matter to him as much as he knows you do. It's not going so well, as you can see. He doesn't do hurt well, so he's trying to hurt you to make himself feel better. He's all about the pain, that one."

He leans closer to me.

"He's not used to this, gorgeous. Women don't play with Jake. He plays with them. He uses them as he sees fit and then tosses them aside when he's had enough. It's what he's done since I've been with him, and long before that, I imagine. It's all he knows how to do. I can't even begin to tell you how many women I've driven home, consoled, fielded calls from, had to arrange restraining orders against...anyway, I digress," he says at my pained expression. "Basically, since you arrived back in his life, he's changed."

"He hasn't." I shake my head.

He touches my arm briefly. "He has, chica. He was living in his own world, floating along in his overly large, Jake bubble, screwing every hot girl available to him—which was a *lot*, and then you came back into his life and I saw the instant change in him. From that day in the hotel, when he saw you, he's been different. No screwing around. He's like a freakin' Catholic priest—minus the boys." He chuckles.

"He can't screw around, because he finds himself not wanting to, because he can't get you out of his head. It's an alien concept for him, sweetheart. He's ten shades of crazy about you, which I'm pretty sure he's already realised. Add in to that you have a boyfriend you won't give up for him… and this is the result." He waves his hand over his shoulder in Jake's general direction, leaning back in his chair. "He's met his equal in you, that's for sure."

"I don't know about that, and it's not that I won't give Will up," I whisper. "There's just…"

"Never a right time, honey, I know. There never is when it comes to breaking someone's heart. But you will have to break one of those boys' hearts, and I'd say sooner rather than later. But I figure you already know that. And Jake, well he'll regret whatever continuing performance he puts on tonight—tomorrow. Remember, honey, he's a man, and with men you just have to treat them like the children they are."

I raise my brow at him. "You're a man."

"Yes, but I'm the best kind of man, my gorgeous one. I'm Venus *and* Mars." He winks at me.

I can't help but laugh, even though inside I'm in complete and utter agony.

Then one of my favourite dance songs comes on.

"You wanna dance?" I ask Stuart, getting to my feet, holding my hand out to him.

I refuse to sit here wallowing for a moment longer. I want to forget, and dancing will make me forget.

"You're asking a gay guy if he wants to dance? Is the pope celibate? Actually, no, don't answer that." He gets to his feet and takes hold of my hand. "It will be my absolute pleasure to grind on that dance floor with the hottest chica here tonight."

"Ah, now you're definitely just being Mars."

"Damn." He grins.

I catch Will's eye at the bar and indicate to him that Stuart and I are hitting the dance floor. He gives me a brief nod.

Stuart leads me onto the dance floor by the hand. I instantly start to relax.

I leave all thoughts of Jake and Will and complicated relationships at the edge of this dance floor and lose myself in my one true love: music.

And hell, I thought Jake could move—Stuart would knock him on his ass in a dance-off, and Jake being knocked on his ass is something I would take great pleasure in watching right now.

Stuart is moving around the floor like a pro, and I actually look like I know what I'm doing, thanks to his awesomeness. Not that I'm a bad dancer, but Stuart is dynamite.

I wonder if he ever used to dance professionally.

We are starting to attract quite a few stares. And I can see Jake watching us from his table. Zzhuliette is off his lap for the time being, thank God. She's probably plumping up her cleavage in the toilet.

The toilet I had sex with Jake in.

I feel sick.

Then I catch Jake's eye, and for that brief moment, my heart stops its beat.

He doesn't look happy. He looks angry.

I look away.

He can't be annoyed that I'm dancing with Stuart, surely? One—Stuart's gay. And two—he's just had his tongue stuck down another woman's throat.

The thought turns my stomach. I shut the image out of my mind.

You know what? I hope it is pissing him off. Right now I want to hurt him, and I'm going to do just that.

I throw my arms around Stuart's neck, and moving close to his body, I dance into him.

As we move around, I see Tom look at me, then lean across and say something in Jake's ear.

Jake nods his head without taking his eyes off me.

My cheeks start to burn. It's awful knowing I'm being talked about but have no clue as to what's being said.

Does Tom know about us? Seems like everyone else does, so why not Tom too. He is one of Jake's closest friends after all, he and Denny both.

Jake pulls a cigarette out of his pack and lights up. Then throws back his glass of whiskey and refills it from the bottle on the table.

"A girl who can dance—finally!" Stuart cheers, pulling my attention back to him, grabbing hold of my hips. "I've found my Ginger! Tru, seriously, if you had less tits and more cock, I'd be proposing marriage to you right now!" He spins me around.

"It can always be arranged." I laugh. "Marry me?" I hold out my hand dramatically to him.

He grabs it and yanks me back to his chest. "Vegas tomorrow, baby. I'll be the one in white at the Elvis chapel."

"I'll be there." I wink at him.

We both start laughing as he starts to move me around the floor again.

I like Stuart. He's so much fun and so uncomplicated and as hot as hell. He could give Jake a run for his money in those stakes.

Why isn't he straight?

Actually no, my life is complicated enough as it is without trying to add another guy into the picture.

"Our favourite rock star is not happy that I'm grinding with you on the dance floor," he whispers in my ear.

"Right now, I'm having way too much fun to care whatever Jake is."

"Atta girl!" He smacks my behind with his hand, and I squeal with laughter as he spins me around and presses his chest up against my back.

Bending his knees into mine, he takes me down slowly with him and then back up.

Dancing with me just like Jake did in the club.

The first night we slept together.

"Uh-oh, here comes the trouble now," Stuart whispers in my ear.

I flicker my eyes in Jake's direction and see he is on his feet, stubbing his cigarette out in the ashtray. He has a seriously pissed-off look on his face, eyes fixed on me and Stuart, and is now heading straight for us.

My stomach flips over.

Maybe I've pushed it too far? No, he was just giving mouth-to-mouth to his little groupie before. I'm doing nothing wrong.

But what if he causes a scene in front of Will?

"Don't worry, gorgeous, I can handle Jake, it's my job—remember?" Stuart whispers, seeing my worried expression. "He won't cause a scene, I promise you."

I want to believe that, but Jake can be irrational.

When he reaches us, his face is stony. I think he's going to chew me out here and now, but ignoring me, he turns to Stuart.

He leans in and whispers something in Stuart's ear, while I stand here like a spare part.

Stuart puts his hand on Jake's shoulder, saying something back to him. I wish I could hear their exchange.

Jake's expression tightens. Whatever Stuart said, Jake didn't like it.

Stuart turns to me, giving me a warm smile. "I gotta go work for a little while, gorgeous. Always on the clock." He winks at me. "We'll finish this dance later?"

"Definitely." I smile.

I start to walk away, going the opposite direction to Stuart, heading back to our table, but Jake catches hold of my hand, pulling me back. "Where are you going?"

I yank my hand free. "Well you just got rid of my dance partner, so now I'm going to drink myself into next week."

"Can I come with you?"

I press my lips together and stare at him.

"Dance with me." He holds out his hand.

"Yeah, because that worked out so well for me the last time I did. And where's your redhead anyway? Won't she want to dance with you?"

Withdrawing his hand, he stares down at me. "She's not mine, I told you. There's only one girl I want to be mine."

My skin aches on my suddenly tired bones.

"You seem to have staked a fairly certain claim on her earlier." I'm trying to come off as nonchalant, but the truth is, it's hurting like a bitch.

I want to call him out for kissing her after having sex with me, but now certainly is not the time or the place.

The previous song fades and No Doubt's "Don't Speak" starts to pump out through the speakers.

Jake looks up like Gwen Stefani is here and speaking to him right now. And really the song couldn't be more apt for him and me.

I wonder if he's thinking the same.

He looks down at me, a sudden darkness in his light eyes. "Well, the woman I want is here with another man... so what's a guy to do?" he says, the words slow, deliberate.

Honestly, right now, I have no clue. But all I do know is we're ripping each other to pieces. And this song is killing me.

I make to leave, but he's not letting me go anywhere, and the next thing I know, he's up against my back, arms holding me there, dancing with me, moving me with him.

"Stay with me tonight," he whispers in my ear. "I don't want to sleep without you. I need you."

It makes my heart ache.

"No you don't." I turn, brushing against his chest. "You made that pretty clear earlier."

"You sure about that?" He stares down, looking deep into my eyes.

"Have you still got my panties in your pocket?"

He grins.

"Can I have them back?"

"What do you think?"

He spins me out, then pulls me back, hard into his chest.

My heart is beating out of mine.

"Why did you stop Stuart from dancing with me?"

"Because he has work to do." He pulls me even closer, his hand on my lower back.

I raise my eyebrow sceptically at him.

"Fine." He exhales loudly. "Watching him dancing with you was driving me crazy."

"He's gay!" I exclaim.

"I don't care if he's a fuckin' monk. I hated seeing his hands all over you. If he wasn't so good at his job, I'd fire his ass," he mutters.

"You'd fire Stuart for dancing with me?"

"Yes."

"I didn't know you were so jealous."

"Neither did I."

I stare at him for a long moment. "For your information, I asked Stuart to dance with me, and he only agreed to, to help distract me from your sexploits with your groupie."

"You told him about us?" He looks surprised.

I shake my head no. "He guessed, he's not stupid."

"Shame your boyfriend is."

I give him a sharp look. "Don't," I warn him. "I'm not fighting with you again about this."

"Why not? I think we're pretty good at it. Even better at the making up. You felt amazing before, Tru," he whispers close. "You always feel amazing, and I want to spend the rest of my life with you, making you feel as good as you do me."

My skin hums.

He's so close. I can feel his heat all over me.

"You're mine, Tru."

"I thought you were done with me?" I say, making sure my voice is steady, even though my insides are trembling. "And after watching you with her, I'm feeling pretty done myself."

I don't mean it, but I'm hurting badly.

He stares down at me for a long moment. I see such a multitude of emotions pass over his face, it's hard to pin down an exact one.

Jake opens his mouth to speak, when I hear Will's voice come from behind him.

"Mind if I dance with my girl?"

I was so lost in Jake, I didn't register Will's approach.

I feel Jake's body stiffen under my hands. He looks down at me, myriad emotions flickering through his eyes. Then he releases me and steps away.

"She's all yours."

There's more meaning in those three words than there has been in anything he's said to me all night.

Panic rips through me. And all I can do is watch weakly as Jake makes his way through the crowd, all eyes on him, as he heads straight to the bar.

Will pulls me into his arms.

I'm numb. Completely devoid.

"You looked amazing out here dancing with Stuart and Jake," Will murmurs in my ear. "I was starting to get a little jealous."

"It's only Jake," I downplay, even though inside I feel like I'm dying. "And you do realise Stuart's gay, don't you?"

"Ah right." I see the realisation fire up in his eyes.

Will moves me around on the dance floor, and I catch sight of Jake. He's doing tequila shots at the bar. He's not looking anywhere in my direction. And he's got company again.

Zzhuliette is back and hanging off him like a cheap suit.

Then I watch, with distasteful horror, as she dips her finger in Jake's tequila glass, draws a wet line across her huge chest, and pours the salt across it.

It's like a car crash that I can't take my eyes off, even though watching it is making me feel sick to the pit of my stomach.

And Jake, with Tom cheering him on, leans down and licks the salt off her chest, slowly. Then he grabs his shot and throws it back.

I feel a burning shot of jealously and rage so intense that I just want to go over there and kick her ass. And Jake's too.

I turn away, burying my head in Will's neck, forcing back tears.

He holds me tighter. "I've missed you so much, darling," he murmurs, running his fingers through my long hair and down my back.

I lift my head, looking at him. "Me too."

And I realise in this moment, I have missed him. So much. My lovely, sweet Will.

He would never hurt me. He would never lick salt off the chests of long-legged redheads.

I'm safe with Will. I'll always be safe with Will.

I just have to let Jake go and stay with him. It's the right thing to do.

Life will always be simple, easy with Will.

I reach up on my tiptoes and kiss him firmly on the lips. He wraps his arms around me, holding me tight to his body.

He tastes of beer, and his kiss feels exactly the same as always.

He's nothing like Jake. Which is good—I think.

Will is sweet and lovely, but…no, something's missing. And it's been missing since Jake came back into my life, I now realise.

I wind my fingers around his neck, up into his hair, kissing him harder, pushing myself into him, into this kiss, trying to ignite the fire I feel in my belly whenever Jake kisses me. Whenever Jake looks at me.

But it doesn't come.

Was it always missing? Or is it because of Jake? Am I done for life now? Will I never again feel with anyone how I feel when I'm with him? When he's touching me, kissing me, making love to me?

Am I ruined to him?

I break off breathing heavy. Will's eyes are hooded, alive with love for me.

But all I feel is lost and confused and lonely.

In this exact moment, I realise that I don't want simple. I want Jake in all his crazy complicatedness.

I do love Will, but I love Jake more.

It's always been him my whole life. And I don't want to lose him. He's my best friend. My everything.

I have to talk to him. I need to tell him that I don't care about the redhead. I don't care about any of it. All the mistakes we've both made. We can start fresh from now.

I'll tell Will everything, right now, if that's what he wants. I'll do whatever he wants me to do. Because I love him.

Totally and completely love him. I always have. And I can't imagine another moment in my life with him not in it.

I glance to where Jake was at the bar, but he's nowhere to be seen.

Where is he?

"I'm tired," I say to Will. "You mind if we sit?"

I need to find Jake.

"No, come on." Will puts his arm around my shoulder and steers me back to our table. "We can leave soon if you'd like."

"Yes, that would be good."

Where has Jake disappeared to?

Will smiles at me and plants a kiss on my hair.

I know I should feel terrible right now for Will, but I can't seem to muster up any guilt at all.

All I want is to see Jake.

I sit down in the chair next to Stuart, the others now filled with Simone and Denny.

She looks so totally smitten with him. It warms my heart. I want to be sitting here like that with Jake. The world knowing we belong to one another.

"I'm just going to use the bathroom," Will says. "Then we can head back if you like."

"Sure," I say, distracted. I'm just relieved he's going so I can find Jake.

When Will is gone, I take a surreptitious glance around the room, looking for Jake.

"He's gone, honey," Stuart leans across and whispers in my ear. "Dave's taken him back to the hotel."

I get this terrible, awful, sick feeling deep in my stomach.

"Did he…go alone?"

Stuart slowly shakes his head no.

My heart starts to compress in on itself.

I swallow down, my throat tight. "The redhead?" I have to ask, even though I'm pretty sure of the answer.

"Yes." He gives me a sad look, pats my leg with his hand, and picks up a shot off the table, handing it to me.

"Drink this, sweetheart. It won't fix things, but after a few of these, things sure do start to seem a lot easier."

Holding back tears that are burning my throat raw, I take the shot. I put it down in front of me, pick up the salt shaker, pour it on my hand, lick it off, and then throw the tequila back without hesitation.

It washes the burning of my tears away, leaving me instead with the welcome burn of alcohol.

I don't bother with the lime or beer. Instead I chase it down with my margarita, downing it in one.

"You okay, honey?" Simone asks me, giving me a sympathetic smile.

She must know Jake's gone back to the hotel with Zzhuliette too.

I plaster a bright smile to my face and nod, "Sure I am."

But I know she knows better. She knows me.

And the alcohol, well, that's just a soother for my heart, which is currently broken and lying shattered in pieces under the heel of a leggy redhead, who is more than likely right now in bed with my best friend and only true love of my life.

And really, I have only myself to blame.

I hesitated. You can't hesitate with a man like Jake.

CHAPTER TWENTY

Oh God. I'm so hungover. I actually think I'm dying.

After I found out Jake had left with Zzhuliette the redhead, I set out on a mission to erase the knowledge from my mind—with the obvious help of alcohol. Basically I wanted to get slaughtered and I achieved just that.

By the time Will had got back from the toilet, I was three shots in and back on the dance floor with Stuart.

I know he knew something was wrong with me. Honestly I think he probably thinks I'm overworked or have developed a drinking problem from spending too much time with the guys.

Will finally brought me back to the hotel around 3:00 a.m., as I was wasted. I remember him carrying me back to the suite. I think I was singing "Mr. Brightside" at the top of my lungs, and then I spent a long time in the toilet, throwing up.

Poor Will. He doesn't deserve any of this. He's kind and sweet. And I'm the devil.

I stretch my stiff body out, groaning, I blink my eyes open.

Will's sitting in a chair by the bed, eyes on me.

"I got you a coffee." He hands me over a Starbucks container as I sit up in bed.

"Thank you," I say gratefully. I lean up against the headboard and take a welcome drink.

"You went out?"

"Just to the Starbucks out by the hotel. I needed the air."

"Oh. Sorry I got so drunk. Simone? Did she get back okay? Is she on the sofa?"

"She stayed in Denny's room."

"Oh," I say.

Good for Simone. One day here and she pulls herself a fit drummer.

"Look, Tru." Will rubs his head, pushing his fingers into his hair. "Is there something going on with you? You just haven't seemed yourself at all since I arrived yesterday."

This is it. I can either tell him the truth or coward out.

Jake and I aren't going to be together. Not now.

The thought causes me actual physical pain.

And then I just know what I have to do—I have my answer. Even if I'm not going to be with Jake, I can't just stay with Will because it's easier.

Yes, I love him. But obviously not enough or I would never have slept with Jake.

Will deserves to be with someone who loves him and him alone.

I put my coffee down on the nightstand and, sitting up, crossing my legs in front of me, I face him.

"I have to tell you something." My body starts to shake. I take the deepest breath I've ever taken, trying to control my fears over what I'm about to do.

"I've been sleeping with Jake."

I see the shock, slowly morphing into horror and absolute pain echo across his features.

It is a look that will haunt me for a very long time.

"What?" he says slowly.

"I'm so sorry, Will."

He stares blankly at me. His face now washed of any emotion.

"What? Are you being fucking serious?" His tone is low and heartbreaking.

"I'm sorry. I didn't mean for this to happen."

He puts his head into his hands. "You didn't mean for it to happen! You've been having sex with Jake Wethers and you didn't mean for it to happen!"

"I never meant to hurt you."

I'm trying to keep it together and not break. It's not fair to him if I cry.

"Do you love him?"

The air seems to freeze all around us.

"Yes."

He puts his fist to his mouth, stifling a sob.

"Do you still love me?" His words are all broken.

I look up at him. Will, my lovely Will, who I've just broken into pieces. I can't help the tear that runs from my eye. I brush it away.

"Yes," I answer.

His face hardens. I barely recognise him for a moment. He's out of the chair now, pacing around.

"So you love me and him! How is that even possible? We're polar fucking opposites!"

"I don't know. I'm so sorry."

Pausing, he grabs the back of the chair. "When did it start?"

"Five days ago. The night before the article came out was the first time anything happened."

"So it was the fucking truth! You sat on the phone and lied to me, and all along it was the fucking truth! I actually felt sorry for you. I believed you! I fucking trusted you!"

"I'm so sorry, Will. I'm so, so sorry," I cry.

"It just all makes so much fucking sense now! The way you've been acting since I arrived, and the way he has been with you, and how you reacted to him when he was with that girl last night! I'm so fucking stupid!" he roars.

Then he turns from me, covering his face with his hands.

He starts to cry.

Oh fuck.

I climb off the bed, standing behind him. I put my hand tentatively on his back, tears streaming from my own eyes, but he moves away. "Don't touch me," he says, low and gruff. "Don't you ever fucking touch me again."

Leaving him, I sit on the edge of the bed, trapped in the mess I've made.

"Do you want to be with him?" he says suddenly, voice rough. He turns to face me.

I bind my hands in my lap. "I don't know. I don't know what I want." I put my head into my hands.

"How could you have been with someone like him? He's a fucking whore! All he does is sleep with women—it's what sells his shit music! Jesus Christ, Tru, he was all over another woman last night! That's how highly he thinks of you—he was off screwing someone else the moment you couldn't give him what he wanted!"

I don't know if it's the look on my face that makes him ask it, but whatever it is, I just feel sick, knowing I'm going to have to tell him the truth when he says, "Please tell me you haven't had sex with him while I've been here."

I can't lie to him. I want to. But I can't.

Closing my eyes briefly, I press my lips together and nod my head, slowly. "I'm sorry." Tears are still running freely from my eyes.

"I don't fucking believe this!" he yells. Holding himself steady on the back of the chair, he fixes his eyes on my face. "When?"

Oh God.

I rub the tears from my face. "Last night."

I hear his sharp intake of breath. "When last night?" I can see his jaw working angrily under his skin.

I wet my dry lips and gulp down. "At the party."

He looks puzzled momentarily.

"When I went to use the bathroom."

"You fucked him in a public toilet?" he yells like I've never heard before. I actually physically shake from the force of it.

"I just…I can't fucking believe this!"

He pauses for a moment. Then slowly, he lifts his eyes to my face.

"How could you do this to me? To us?"

I rub the fresh tears from off my face. "I'm so sorry. It just happened. I didn't mean for this to happen, but it's… *Jake*." I say this like it will explain everything away to him. "I've loved him since I was young."

"You haven't seen him for the last fucking decade!"

I don't even make the attempt to try to explain to him. He would never understand the connection I have with Jake.

"I've loved you for two years of my life, Tru! Two years! I gave you everything! Trusted you! Would have given you anything! I gave you my heart, for Christ's sake! I wanted to marry you!"

His words blindside me. He wanted to marry me? We'd never even talked about it.

"All of it gone, because you're some cheap whore who can't say no to a fucking rock star! I never had you down as some slut groupie."

He's looking at me with utter disgust and contempt. And I deserve it.

"I'm sorry," I cry. "I didn't mean for this to happen. I've loved Jake since I was young—" I repeat lamely.

"Spare me any more of the goddamn details!"

Nervous, I look down at my hands, my eyes fixing on the bracelets. Jake's and Will's.

And then I just know I want Jake. He's all I've ever wanted.

I unclip Will's bracelet from my wrist.

Getting to my feet, I hold it out in my hand to him. "You should have this back," I say quietly.

He looks down at my hand. Then he grabs the bracelet and throws it across the room.

His face becomes a blind rage. I've never seen him look this way before. Then he's striding across the room, purposefully, angrily.

"Where are you going?" I ask, panicked.

"To kick your fucking boyfriend's arse!"

I'm moving quickly behind, but Will is already through the door, practically sprinting down the hall, looking for Jake's room. He's like a man possessed.

I'm screaming after him.

Then I see Jake's door open, and he's standing there, scanning the hall, looking worried. He must have heard my screams.

Jake registers Will, then me, and it all just happens so quickly.

Will is on him, and he punches Jake in the face.

"No!" I cry out as I hear the crack from the impact.

I stop in my tracks, watching in horror as Jake momentarily loses his footing, staggering slightly, his hand going straight to his mouth.

"Did you think you could fuck my girlfriend and I wouldn't find out? That I would do jack shit about it?" Will yells at him. "I don't give a fuck who you are! I'm gonna beat the shit out of you!"

Jake moves his hand away and I see the blood. He looks down at his hand, then runs his tongue over his lip, licking the blood, and smirks.

"I'll let you have that first one, motherfucker, but not the next." Jake sounds unnervingly calm.

Then he punches Will hard in his face. It's so quick and unexpected.

"No!" I scream out again. "STOP, PLEASE!"

Will staggers back from the force, and I try to help him, but he pushes me away, hard.

I lose my footing and fall against the wall, hitting my shoulder, and fall onto my ass.

Jake's face flames with rage. And then he's on Will, punching him to the floor, hard, repeatedly, over and over.

I scramble up to my knees, finding my voice to scream, "No! STOP!" begging Jake to stop, and then Dave is there, pulling Jake off Will.

Denny appears in the hall from behind me, and he's straight in there, telling Dave to get Will out of here and taking hold of Jake, pushing him back because he looks crazy right now, like he's ready to kill Will.

I've never seen Jake look so wild.

Then Simone is beside me, helping me up off the floor, putting her arm around me, holding me close.

Dave pulls Will up off the floor. He's covered in blood, his lip looks cut, and his eye is swelling already.

I can't help the sob that escapes me. This is all my fault. He doesn't deserve any of this.

Will shakes off Dave's grip.

"So you need your fucking bodyguard and your pussy band member to help you fight your battles for you?" Will yells at Jake.

I've never seen Will like this before. He's like a different person. And I've done this to him.

I see Jake's eyes narrow, and he steps forward, malevolence clear on his face, but Denny pushes him back. "No, man. Leave it."

Dave pulls Will farther back down the hall. Turning, he releases him, pushing him backwards. "You need to leave. Get your stuff and go," Dave says firmly. "If you don't, I'll remove you myself."

Simone moves me out of the way, backing me up against the wall, as Will steps back.

He turns to me.

I see complete hatred on his face, which is meant solely for me. Tears are running freely from my eyes.

"I loved you, Tru. I would have done anything for you. But how wrong was I? You're just some cheap fucking whore, like he is. You deserve each other."

Then he turns and storms away. Dave walks past me, following Will as he goes back into my suite.

My whole body is shaking.

Everyone has just been witness to the fact that I've been sleeping with Jake behind Will's back. Even though they probably already knew, I still have never felt trashier than I do in this moment.

I should go after Will, I know, but what can I say that will make this better?

I knew what I was doing by telling him. Yes, it was the right thing to do. But I was also making my decision. I was choosing Jake.

He may not want me now after all this. And I don't know how I feel about him sleeping with Zzhuliette.

But I love him. I'll always love him. It's always been him.

The door opposite me opens and Tom stumbles out, looking half-asleep.

"What the fuck's going on out here?" He yawns, stretching his arms over his head, as he glances around, taking in the scene.

Me in my pyjamas in Simone's arms, crying. Jake bleeding from the mouth. Denny in his boxer shorts.

"Oh, right," he says, putting two and two together, dropping his arms down. "Guess I'll leave you guys to it then." Stepping back, he closes his door.

Jake hasn't taken his eyes off me, but I can't bring myself to meet his stare.

"Come on," Simone says to me. "You can't stay out here." *Because Will could come back out soon, she leaves off.*

My legs feel like lead as she moves me forward, steering me into Jake's suite. He steps back, making room for me to pass.

Denny closes the door behind us all, as Simone eases me down on the sofa, sitting beside me.

It's utter silence in the room. The most uncomfortable silence I've ever been in.

"Come on, man, let's clean you up." Denny jerks his head in the direction of the bathroom at Jake, breaking the unnerving silence.

Jake looks at me. He seems hesitant to go, but after a long, lingering moment, he wordlessly follows Denny through the bedroom to the bathroom.

"I'll get you some water." Simone gets up and quickly returns with a bottle of water and a wad of tissues, handing me them both.

I wipe my face dry with the tissues, putting the bottle beside me on the sofa.

"How did he find out?" she asks in a quiet voice.

"I told him." I glance at her, a fresh tear leaking from my eye. I wipe it away. "He knew something wasn't right from my behaviour last night, and I couldn't keep lying to him."

"You did the right thing."

"Yes, but I did the wrong thing in the beginning. I've fucked everything up, Simone." Leaning forward, I put my head in my hands as tears form in my eyes again.

Simone rubs my back. "You made a few errors in judgement, granted, but you're only human, Tru. And you're clearly in love with Jake."

I turn my head, glancing at her. "I know, but I still shouldn't have done what I did."

"No, you shouldn't have, but there's no changing it now, I'm afraid." She tucks my hair behind my ear. "So now you have to figure out what you're going to do from here." She nods her head in the direction of the bathroom.

She means what am I going to do about Jake.

"I don't know."

"Well, I'm taking it you and Will have broken up."

"But that doesn't mean I should jump straight into something with Jake, and...well, Jake spent the night with another woman." My lips turn down at the corners.

To be honest, I was half expecting Zzhuliette to be here in his room.

She shakes her head. "No he didn't."

I look at her surprised. "He did. Stuart told me Dave had brought him and her back here."

"I was leaving the party with Denny last night, not long after you left, and Tom said he was coming back with us, that he'd just got off the phone with Jake—said Jake had called him and he was wrecked and was in a real mess over you. He said he'd never known Jake to be like that over a girl, and it was freaking him the fuck out. I said I thought he'd left with that girl too, but Tom said there was definitely no girl with him because no girl would have put up with his whining over you."

"And from what I know, Tom spent most of the night in Jake's room talking him down. I know for definite there was no girl in here because Denny was so worried about him that he left me to go check on him too. When he came back, he said that maybe I should talk to you, because Jake was really screwed up over the whole Will being here thing."

"I've messed up so badly," I whisper, the tears starting again.

I'm relieved that Jake hadn't slept with her, but I'm all cut up over Will and how much I've hurt him. I just don't know what to do.

The bathroom door in the bedroom opens, and Jake comes out with Denny behind him.

My whole body tenses.

The blood's gone from his lip, but it's all swollen and readying for a bruise.

He comes over and sits on the edge of the sofa, opposite me, resting his elbows on his knees, clasping his hands together. He looks over at me with wary eyes.

I dry my tearstained face again and set the damp tissues on the sofa beside me.

"We're gonna go get some breakfast," Simone says, rising to her feet. "I'll come and see you later." She rubs my shoulder.

Then she and Denny are gone, and it's just me and Jake and a whole lot of silence.

"You told him," he says quietly, like he can barely believe it.

"Yes."

"Why?"

I look at him surprised. "He knew there was something different about me, and because I couldn't go on lying to him...and because of you, Jake...because I hated what this was doing to you—had done to you."

He stares at me with such intensity, it's momentarily almost too much to handle. My insides are quaking.

"Did he hurt you?"

I look confused.

"When he pushed you and you hit the wall, did he hurt you?"

I touch my shoulder. "No. I'm fine. I should be the one asking if you're okay."

I'm lying, it hurt, it still does, but I don't want to anger him any more than he already has been.

He puts his finger to his lip. "It looks worse than it is."

"Even so, I'm sorry."

"Because he hit me or because you told him?"

"Because he hit you. Because of everything I've done. I've fucked everything up so badly."

"Not with me you haven't."

I can't help but look at his face, searching, hoping he really means it.

"I'm glad he hit me, Tru, if it means he finally knows. I'm sorry he's hurt, but I'm not sorry he knows about us."

"Is there an us?" I hold my breath.

"You tell me."

I exhale. "Why didn't you sleep with Juliette?"

"I never intended to. I left because I wanted out of that party. I couldn't stand to see you with Will, and I took her with me because I wanted you to know I'd left with her…I wanted you to think I had slept with her—to hurt you. Not very mature, I know, but…" He shrugs. "So, I got Dave to drop her off at her place first, then he brought me back here, and I spent the night with a bottle of Jack, and Tom came later on." He stares straight into my eyes. "Do you really think I could have had sex with her, when I'd just had sex with you?"

"You kissed her."

304

"I was acting like a dumb-ass. Like I said, I wanted to hurt you, because you'd hurt me." He brushes his thumb over the scar on his chin. "I don't do rejection well. But I'd never go that far. And you kissed Will, remember?"

I knot my fingers together in my lap, nodding gently.

"It did hurt me," I whisper, "seeing you with her, knowing you'd left there with her. The pain I felt was unbearable. So I got drunk to try and kill it, and spent the rest of the night throwing up, before passing out."

That's my subtle way of telling him I didn't have sex with Will. I know it was weighing on his mind; he didn't have to say it.

I see his face relax, and he lifts his eyebrow. "You're such a lightweight."

"I am."

"I love you," he says.

I love you, just as simple as that.

I stare at him, wide-eyed. It's like time has frozen all around me.

Jake gets up, his eyes never leaving mine, and walks over to me. He kneels on the floor at my feet and takes hold of my hands.

"I love you," he repeats. "I've only ever loved one girl, Tru—and that's you. It's *always* been you. I loved you from the moment I knew how to love."

My eyes fill with tears again, quickly spilling over, down my cheeks.

Jake takes my face in his hands, caressing my tears away with his thumbs. "You're it for me. I want to be with you forever. I want you to be mine."

I stare deep into his eyes. "I've always been yours, and I always will be. I love you too…so much."

I don't think I've ever seen Jake look as happy as he does in this moment.

He leans over and gently kisses my lips. I press harder against them, wanting more from him.

He hisses, and I quickly pull back. "Shit, sorry, baby," I murmur, smoothing my finger over his cut, swollen lip.

"You're worth the pain."

"You hit him," I say, regretfully. "A lot."

"No one hurts my girl. Because you are, Tru…my girl."

"I know…and you're my guy." I trace my finger across his cheek.

"Forever." His eyes close under my touch.

"Forever."

"Are you really sure he didn't hurt you?" He opens his eyes after a moment and runs his hand gently over my shoulder.

"I'm fine, really. It didn't hurt."

"Come on," he says, getting to his feet, pulling me to my own. He leads me through to the bedroom, pulling the duvet back; he climbs into bed, making space for me.

I'm hesitant.

I've only just broken up with Will. Somehow it doesn't seem right climbing into bed with Jake.

"Please," he says softly, seeing my hesitation. "I just want to hold you."

I climb into bed beside him and he wraps his arms around me, holding me to him, and pulls the duvet over us.

He kisses my hair. "I love you so much," he murmurs. "This is it now. Just you and me."

I tilt my head back, kissing a place on his neck. "Just you and me," I echo.

I nestle my head into his neck, breathing him in, feeling suddenly exhausted as I try to work through the conflicting emotions still raging through me.

When I wake I'm in Jake's arms, the sky coming in through the window looks dusky. We've slept the whole day away.

I'm supposed to be going home. Jake too. Our flights out of Paris are tonight.

Suddenly the thought of leaving him crushes my chest.

Then I think of Will, and pure sadness engulfs me. Tears instantly prick my eyes.

I wonder if he got an early flight. I hope he got home okay.

Will. Lovely, sweet Will. What have I done to him?

I hope he's okay. I didn't want it to end the way it did. Maybe I should call him? Try to explain?

No, what good would that do, and anyway, he hates me. He's right to.

I cheated on him. I broke his trust and his heart. I've scarred him; he won't trust another woman for a long time to come because of me. And he's so gentle and caring; he didn't deserve any of what I've done to him.

But I love Jake. I know it's a poor excuse but I couldn't help myself.

The way I feel about him is indescribable. It's overwhelming. Sometimes so much so that I feel like I'm gasping for air with the intensity of the feelings I have for him.

But then, is this the right way for Jake and me to start our life together, off the back of a broken relationship?

I don't think it is. But I suppose my and Jake's relationship started a long time ago. It spans our lifetime.

I hurt for Will and how I treated him, I always will, but Jake is where I want to be.

He's my home.

Jake stirs in his sleep, his eyes opening slowly. And when he looks at me, all I see in them is complete love for me.

"Hey." His voice is all sleepy and sexy.

"Hi," I say quietly.

I look at the bruising on his lip; the swelling has gone down a little. A reminder of what happened only this morning.

I trace my fingertip over it. Jake takes hold of my hand, kissing my fingertips. Then puts his hand on my face, tucking my hair behind my ear.

"I love waking up with you. I want to wake up every morning looking at your face," he murmurs.

Shivers run over my skin.

"Me too. But we have to go home tonight." My lips turn down at the corners.

"Do we?"

"I've got work to do at the magazine." I sigh. "And you've got PR to do for the US leg of the tour."

"I don't care about any of that. It can wait. Stay with me here in Paris for a few more days. I'm not ready to be away from you, not when I've only just got you."

I stare at his face. "I guess I could call, Vicky…"

"So you'll stay?"

"Yes."

He smiles, a beautiful smile that reaches all the way to his eyes. Then he moves his face closer to mine and kisses me gently on the lips, tracing his fingers over my skin, moving them into my hair. It feels gentle, tender.

"How's your lip?" I murmur.

"It doesn't hurt anymore." He rolls me onto my back, keeping me in his arms. His kiss deepens and I know what he wants.

This is it.

This is the first time Jake and I will be together properly. The first time we'll make love as an official couple.

The thought makes me feel heady. No more guilt, no more sneaking around. Just him and me.

I wind my fingers into his hair, letting his tongue roam mine, kissing, nipping, licking.

I lift, allowing Jake to pull my vest off. His mouth goes straight to my nipple.

My hips lift with the feeling and he puts his hand there, touching me through the fabric of my pyjama bottom and panties.

"Oh God, Jake," I groan.

I put my hand between cotton and skin, taking him in my hand. I don't know if I'll ever get used to his size. It surprises me even now.

I start to work my hand up and down.

Jake hisses between his teeth, then sucks harder on my nipple.

"God, Tru, you drive me crazy. I just want to be inside you all the time."

"Sounds good to me," I breathe, pushing myself into his hand.

He yanks my pyjama bottoms and panties down in one, and I kick them off my legs.

"What no panty ripping today?" I tease. "What is it with you and panties anyway? What's your beef with them?"

He lifts his head, grinning at me. "It's a love/hate relationship, baby. I love how they look on you. Hate that they're blocking my access."

I giggle.

"Do you like it when I do it?" He trails his finger down my stomach.

"I love it," I murmur, kissing his lips.

"I never ripped anyone's panties off before, you know," he says, under my still-moving mouth.

I stop kissing him. "You haven't?" I just figured this was a Jake thing.

He shakes his head.

"So why do you tear mine off?"

He stares down at me with his beautiful blue eyes. "Because that's how crazy you make me feel. I've never wanted *anyone* the way I want you, Tru. I just can't wait to be inside you."

His words are so intense, so fixed with meaning, that the muscles in my tummy clench, leaving me feeling doubly delicious.

It amazes me how easily his words can unravel me.

"I love that it's our thing…so do you want me to put them back on so you can rip them off?" I bite down on my lip.

"Fuck no! I'm not covering you back up now, and anyway, I've got my whole life to spend ripping your panties off."

His whole life. I love the sound of that.

He slides his finger inside me.

My hips buck, and I grind myself into his hand, and all thoughts of ripped underwear slip from my mind. I start to work his still-growing erection quickly in my hand.

He moans, and kissing my shoulder, he bites gently on my skin.

"I want to make love to you," he groans, rubbing his thumb over my hot spot.

"Ahh," I moan. "Yes, and now, because if you keep doing that then I'm going to come any second."

Jake pushes his boxer shorts off, then lies between my legs, framing me.

"Are you on birth control?"

"Yes, why?"

"Because I don't want to use a condom. I want our first proper time together as a couple to be special. I want to *feel* you, Tru."

"But…" I trail off. I know I shouldn't think it, but all those women he's had sex with.

And as if reading my thoughts, he says, "I've never had sex without a condom before in my life."

"Never?"

"Never," he reaffirms. "STDs and unwanted pregnancies are not something I ever aspired to have, Tru. And I get regular checkups. My last was a week before we met back up, and I haven't had sex with anyone since then but you."

He wants me to be his first.

"So it's kind of like I'm taking your virginity." I grin.

"I guess it kind of is." He chuckles lightly, then his eyes turn serious. "I've never made love with anyone but you, because I've only ever loved you."

I lift my hips up, pushing against him, my feelings for him driving through me. "I want to feel you, Jake. I want you to make love to me."

His eyes turn lustful, laced thick with desire. And without taking his from mine, he very slowly eases himself inside me.

"Fuuuck," he groans slowly.

I watch him with contentment and love, my own desire fuelling me. I reach my hand up to his face.

"You felt amazing before, Tru, but, Jesus Christ. You feel fuckin' insane."

He leans down, putting his mouth on mine, slowly pulling out of me, he eases himself back in, groaning once again into my mouth.

"I love you," I whisper.

I wrap my legs around him, holding him deep inside me, not letting him go.

He traps my face between both his hands. "I love you, and I always will." He kisses me deeply, passionately, as he starts to pick up pace, losing himself to the moment, to me, the sensation, as he moves me all over the bed, making desperate love to me.

I have never felt happier, or more loved, than I do now here with Jake.

Chapter Twenty-One

Jake and I spent the rest of yesterday in his suite. We got room service and watched a movie and did other things, of course.

I called Vicky at home and explained everything that had been happening with Jake and Will. I thought it was going to be a really awkward conversation, but Vicky's not stupid; she knew.

She told me to take as long as I need off work, the bio's the focus anyway, and as I'm now getting up close and personal with our intended, she didn't mind.

But I do. I don't want to take liberties.

After I came off the phone with Vicky, I did start thinking about the bio and how it is kind of weird that Jake and I are a couple and I'm still going to be writing it.

I started to think maybe I shouldn't be.

When I tried to broach the subject with Jake, he just brushed me off. He said it doesn't matter, as most of the European tour was noted before we started anything together, so it's not a big deal.

But I don't know; a part of me feels like it's a conflict of interest, then on the flip side I don't want to lose this great opportunity for my career, so I'm trying not to overthink it at the moment.

I called my dad too. He wasn't surprised about Jake and me either. He must have sensed it when they visited.

And whereas my dad was absolutely delighted about Jake and me, my mum was, as I expected, a little more reserved about it.

She knows what it's like to live with a musician, and with one as famous as Jake and his past tendencies, she said to me, as she had before, that she's worried for my heart.

I love her so much for her concern, but I know Jake will never break my heart. I'm not just any other girl to him. We've known each other a lifetime.

Yes, I know life with Jake will be bumpy, crazy, and a little difficult at times, but I don't think he would ever truly hurt me.

I know because I can see his love for me in his eyes every time he looks at me, and I wonder how I never saw it there before.

Maybe I couldn't see it because he was afraid to truly show it to me. But now all those doors are open, and I couldn't be happier.

"Baby, can you pass me the jam?"

Jake and I are eating breakfast out on the balcony of his suite, with Paris as our backdrop.

Stuart is inside working in the living room, rearranging Jake's cancelled appearances back in the United States. The ones he's cancelled to stay here with me.

Stuart could work out of his own suite I suppose, but he does need to ask Jake things from time to time, and I think he gets a little lonely in his suite. I know I would. And I think he's just used to being around Jake. I love the friendship they have, and I like having Stuart around; he's fun and cool.

Jake passes over the jam, and as I'm taking hold of it, he catches hold of my wrist and pulls me forward across the table. Meeting me halfway, he plants a long, delicious kiss on my lips.

"You taste yummy," I murmur. He's been eating *pain au chocolat.*

"So did you." He winks, and my face instantly flushes.

He's referring to what he was doing to me in bed first thing this morning.

Shivers run from my head to my toes at the memory, heat rising fast in me.

I sit back in my seat. Picking up a knife, I spread jam on my croissant.

"So what do you want to do today?" Jake asks. "We could go sightseeing, do the whole touristy thing, Eiffel Tower and that, and go out to lunch. We could go to the delicatessen that makes the minicakes you love…or I can take you shopping and buy you lots of pretty things. I'm sure Denny would be up for it if you wanted Simone along for the shopping?"

Simone decided to stay on as well. She took a few days off work to spend with Denny, as they are getting on *really* well. I'm so happy for her.

Tom and Smith took the jet back to LA. So there's just the four of us, and Stuart, and of course Dave and Ben are still here in Paris also.

And Paris is beautiful. I've barely seen any of it while I've been here, and I really want to go out with Jake today, but I don't think I should.

I scrunch my face up in anticipation of what I'm going to say.

"What?" He sighs, running his fingers through his hair. "Is this the me-spending-money-on-you thing again? Because seriously, Tru, we're together now and I have a lot of money and I want to spoil you rotten."

"No, it's not that. I mean, I don't want you spending ridiculous amounts of money on me, but I get that you're rich and things are different when you're rich, so I'll have to get used to that. It's just..."

"What?" His brow furrows.

"I just thought maybe we could stay in."

"We stayed in all day yesterday."

"I know, and it was so awesome that I want to do it all over again."

His frown deepens, causing a line to form between his brows, so I know he's not buying it.

"Yesterday was awesome, no doubting that, and last night and this morning too, but that's not it, Tru. There's something you're not telling me. Why don't you want to go out with me?"

"I do...it's just..."

"It's just what?" His tone is so forceful that I give him a sharp look.

"Well, it's just, I um..." I drag my fingers nervously through my hair. "I just know that if we go out together, it's highly likely that we'll be photographed together, because you're, well—you. And because you're you, and you're out with a woman...those photos will undoubtedly end up in the tabloids at some point."

"You don't want people to know we're together?" He's still frowning at me. "Are you ashamed of me or something?"

Ashamed of him? Where did that come from?

"No! How could you think that?"

"Um." He rubs his forehead with his fingers, giving me a hard stare. "Because you don't want to be seen in public with me."

"It's not that. I do want to be seen in public with you. I'm so happy to be with you. I love you. It's just…" How do I say this without causing a row? "Will and I only broke up yesterday."

His face darkens at the mention of Will, just like I knew it would.

"And I just think it would be really insensitive of me to go out in public with you and for those pictures to end up in the press for him to see. It'd be like rubbing salt in his already raw wound, and I don't want to hurt him any more than I already have done."

"So this is about Will. What a fuckin' surprise!" He throws his hands up in the air. "All you seem to care about is his feelings. What about my feelings, Tru? Or are they still irrelevant to you?"

I look at him shocked. "Your feelings were never irrelevant to me. I care about you, Jake—so much. I couldn't bear the thought of you hurting. I love you—I'm *in* love with you."

"Well, you've got a funny way of showing it." He folds his arms over his chest.

"You're being irrational."

"Me?"

"Yes, you!" I'm starting to get really annoyed now. "We had an affair behind Will's back! I broke his heart only yesterday morning! I'm trying to spare causing him any more pain than I've already done!"

"And you don't think I wasn't in pain? All the time you were still with him, stuck between me and him, and then having to see you with him at *my* show and then the after-party. I sat here that night driving myself fuckin' crazy thinking about you in that room with him! Sleeping in that bed with him! Jesus Christ!" He picks his cigarettes up off the table and angrily gets one out.

"I didn't sleep with Will, I told you, and I haven't since *we* started sleeping together."

"You think I'm talking about sex here, Tru?" He slams the cigarette packet back on the table. "I'm talking about the fact that you were lying in bed, next to him, all night, when it should have been me. I should have been the one waking up beside you."

"You have me now!" I yell, frustrated. "And every single day from now! Why are we even talking about this?"

"Because you don't want to be seen in public with me!"

"I do!" I take a calming breath in through my nose. "I just want to wait a little while," I say in a calmer voice. "Let things settle down."

"So you're telling me you won't go out with me?" His gaze is fixed and determined.

I shake my head no.

"Fine." He pushes out his chair, the metal legs scraping loudly against the stony floor, and gets to his feet. "I'll see if Denny and Simone want to do something with me. Maybe I should take Stuart as my date." He tosses his unlit cigarette onto the table.

"Jake, please, let's not do this." I stand up, reaching for him. "I don't want to fight."

"Yeah, well I do."

He storms off into the living room.

I get out of my chair and follow him in.

"You're being unfair," I say from behind him.

Stuart looks up from the laptop.

"I'm being unfair?" Jake rounds on me.

"Yes. You're acting like a spoilt child who can't get his own way."

Stuart gets out of his seat and quietly slips across the room and out the main door. I don't blame him. I wish I could leave too.

"Yeah, and you're acting like someone who still has feelings for her ex! Are we really back there again, Tru? You stuck between me and Will again? Do you want to go back to him?"

"What? No! Where is this even coming from?" I grip my head in frustration. "I chose you! And I would choose you every single time! But I broke Will's heart in doing so. The very least I can do is try and make things a little easier for him."

"You didn't choose me." His tone is low and cold. "Will made the decision for you when you told him the truth. You never said to him, 'I'm ending this with you because I want to be with Jake.' I was just your fuckin' consolation prize."

I feel like he's just slapped me.

"Screw you, Jake."

I storm into his bedroom, get my room key off the nightstand, and head straight for the main door.

Jake's still standing where I left him.

"Where are you going? Running off back to Will?" he says bitterly from behind me.

I stop at the door.

"No, I'm just getting as far away as possible from you and your goddamn self-destruct button!"

I slam the door loudly behind me, then run to my room, tears streaming down my cheeks.

Look at us. Two minutes into our relationship and we're already fighting.

I just wish he could see things from my point of view. I'm not trying to hurt him, but I don't want to cause Will any more pain than I already have.

Is this going to be Jake and me? When it's good, it's great, and when it's bad, it's really awful.

We never used to fight like this when we were younger.

But I guess back then, sex and passion weren't part of our relationship, and those two things can go a long way to flaring up arguments. I don't know, maybe we've just moved too fast together.

I'm in my bed, where I've been for the last hour and a half, staring blankly at the TV, stewing and crying over my fight with Jake.

I wonder if he's gone out with Simone and Denny.

Part of me wants to go and see him and sort this out. But I'm still majorly pissed off with him, and my pride just won't let me.

I've done nothing wrong, so I'm definitely sitting this one out.

Adele suddenly starts to ring on my nightstand. I haven't checked my phone in days.

As I pick it up, I see there's a load of missed calls, voice mail messages, and texts.

Will, I'm guessing.

I'll deal with them later, because right now, Jake is calling me.

"You're calling me?" I say in still-angry-Tru mode.

I'm not ready to forgive him just yet, even if his calling me is just so ridiculously sweet considering he's only down the hall. At least, I hope he is.

"Well, you were massively pissed off at me for good reason," he adds quietly. "And I thought I'd try calling first, see how the land lies…see if you've calmed down yet. So have you?"

"What?"

"Calmed down."

"Maybe."

"Can I come and see you?"

"No." I grin.

"Why?"

"Because you're a dick, Jake Wethers."

"I know. But I'm a dick who's crazy in love with you…if I said I was sorry, would that make us okay?"

I sigh, keeping up the pretence of my anger, which disappeared the second he said "crazy in love."

"It'd be a start."

"What about some flowers?"

"They wouldn't hurt."

"How about me, on my knees outside your door, holding a bunch of flowers?"

"You're outside my door, aren't you?" My skin shivers in delight.

"Maybe," he murmurs. I can hear his smile down the line, and it touches me.

With butterflies swishing through my stomach, I climb out of bed and pad my way across the room, through the living room, and swing the door open to find Jake on his knees outside my door with a huge bouquet of flowers in his hand.

He looks up at me with his gorgeous blue puppy-dog eyes.

"You look beautiful," he says.

"And you look like an idiot, get up," I say, suppressing the huge smile I feel.

He gets to his feet and holds the flowers out for me to take.

Taking them, I hold them to my nose and inhale. They are absolutely beautiful. All pinks, purples, and creams. Roses, peonies, lilies, and gerberas, and some I don't even recognise. They look expensive.

"So you bought me flowers by way of an apology." I lift an eyebrow.

"I did." He smiles, a careful smile.

"Did you order them in?" I'm not ready to let him off the hook just yet.

His brow furrows. "No."

"Send Stuart out for them?"

"No," he says, clearly affronted. "I went out to the flower shop down the street and bought and picked them myself."

"I didn't hear any screaming from your fans when they spotted you in the street."

He grins. "I put a disguise on."

I squint at him, cocking my head to the side.

"Sunglasses and a hat."

"And no one recognised you?"

"Nope." He shakes his head.

"Thank you," I say softly. "They're beautiful."

He reaches for my hand. "I'm sorry I was being a jerk."

"You weren't being a jerk, you were being irrational."

"I was. It's just because I love you so much." He moves his hand from mine and strokes his fingers down my cheek.

"I love you too," I whisper.

He stares into my eyes, a serious look on his face. "I thought about it after you left, what you were saying, and I talked to Stuart…and I get where you're coming from." He sighs. "I understand what you're saying, and…I'm sorry for the way I acted and the things I said. I know you chose me, and that you want to be with me. I don't even know why I said any of it." He runs his hand through his hair.

He looks nervous, confused, and totally out of his comfort zone. And I guess he is. Jake's never had to consider anyone but himself before now.

"It's because you're irrational." I give him a small, teasing smile.

He nods gravely. "I am, and I deserve whatever punishment you see fit to give me."

Curling my fingers into his T-shirt, I pull him into the room, shutting the door behind him, and put the flowers down on the table by the door.

"I'm sure I can come up with a suitable punishment," I murmur, cocking my head to the side.

He grins his sly grin at me and my stomach free-falls.

Walking backwards, my fingers still firmly hooked into his T-shirt, I lead Jake towards the bedroom.

When we reach the bed, he grabs hold of my waist and yanks me firmly against his body and kisses me hard.

Easing me out of my vest, he drops it to the floor.

I pull his T-shirt off over his head and run my fingers over his bare chest, touching his tattoos, tracing my fingers lightly over them.

He shudders under my touch, and I love the feeling.

Jake lifts me up onto the bed, and I edge backwards as he climbs over me, then leans down and begins kissing my neck.

"I don't like fighting with you," he murmurs, tracing kisses over my skin.

"I don't either, but the making up is pretty good."

Jake lifts his head, looking at me. "I'd say it's awesome."

He sits up and yanks my pyjama bottoms off, and grinning over at me, he takes hold of my panties and tears them in two.

I start giggling.

Then he's cutting my laughter off when he dips his head low, using his mouth to turn my laughter into groans of his name, as he sets to work on our making-up session.

"We should go out today," I say, lifting my head up from his chest.

We're lying in bed after a very long making-up session, me draped across Jake, while he strokes his fingers over the skin on my back, his own skin rough and tickly on mine.

"We don't have to, beautiful. We'll just stay in here, and that means I can ravish you all day long."

"As good as that sounds, I think we should go out." I sit up. "We can't hide away forever," I say, thinking on it. "There's always going to be that day when our picture ends up in the paper, so let's just let that day be today. We're in one of the most beautiful and romantic cities in the world. We should make the most of it."

"You're sure?" he says, looking across at me hopefully.

"I am."

"So I can take my girl out on a proper first date?"

Ah, so that's what this has all been about. He wanted to take me out on a first date.

And now I just love him even more if that's at all possible.

"A first date sounds perfect to me."

"God, I love you, Trudy Bennett," he says, pulling me back down onto him, kissing me firmly on the lips.

"And I love you, my little storm."

He pulls a face at me, eyebrow raised, then flicks his gaze downwards, to his sizeable manhood.

"Okay, well maybe not small." I giggle.

"That's more like it. Now move your hot ass off this bed and get ready. I'm taking you out to show the world that you're mine." He smacks my ass with his hand.

"Oww!" I squeal. "Okay, I'm going!" I climb off the bed, leaving Jake lying there in all his beautiful glory, as I go to take a shower.

CHAPTER TWENTY-TWO

It took us a little while longer to get out, as Jake decided to join me in the shower, and we…um…well, you know.

We've decided to go to the Louvre, because neither of us has ever been and I've always wanted to go, and I love that it's something brand-new we can do together.

So we're in the back of the Merc with Dave driving us and Ben in the passenger seat.

Two lots of security are needed today apparently.

That fact makes me feel a little weird, but I'm trying to push it to the back of my mind, because I'm going to have to get used to this kind of thing being with Jake.

Stuart has also called ahead to let the staff at the Louvre know Jake is visiting today.

Apparently this is how it works in celeb world. You have to preannounce your arrival.

Good to know.

It's weird living like this. Pre-Jake, if I wanted to go somewhere I did, without having to plan everything or bring security along for the ride.

So basically, we're going on our first date with Dave and Ben.

Kind of kills the feel of it, but I don't want to say anything to Jake and upset him, because this is life with Jake. Everything has to be structured, security with us all the time, and the places we go have to be informed in advance of his arrival.

It's a lot crazy. And it's going to take some serious getting used to.

Jake is holding my hand, running his thumb over my skin. I think he knows I'm nervous about going on our first outing together as a couple.

Honestly, my stomach is popping over.

People are soon going to know I'm his girlfriend. And I'm going to become public enemy number one with his female fans.

My insides start to tremble, and not in a good way.

Dave drives the car down Avenue du Général Lemonnier and enters the underground parking garage of the Louvre. A space nearest the lifts has been reserved for us, and there is an attendant already waiting to meet us.

Okay, so let this begin.

Dave parks up, and he and Ben get out of the car.

Ben opens Jake's door.

"You ready?" Jake asks me.

I can't seem to answer. I'm frozen to my seat. In truth I'm scared and even more so now we're here.

I've been living in a bubble with Jake. Our relationship this last week has been just him and me cocooned, despite all the Will stuff. Now we're about to go out in public together, and everyone will know I'm Jake Wethers's girlfriend, and then it won't be just him and me anymore. His world will become a part of us.

And I'm worried that it might take over.

"Give us a minute," Jake says to Ben. Grabbing the door, he closes it.

"What's wrong?" he asks, turning to me, his gaze worried.

"I don't know." I shrug, finding my voice. "I guess it's all just got a little real now, and I don't mean us," I add at his worsening expression. "I just mean you, who you are, the world you live in. The one I'm about to become a part of."

He looks at me, puzzled. "Tru, you've known all along how my life is."

I take a deep breath. "I know, I guess…it's just this—us going on our first date, and we have to bring Dave and Ben along with us, and Stuart has to call ahead to prepare them for your arrival—at the Louvre for God's sake! That's how famous you are, and it just feels…a lot crazy. And a little un-date-like," I add quietly, wringing my hands together in my lap.

"It is crazy, baby." He takes hold of my hands, trying to soothe my tension. "And it's a part of my life, granted—but not all of it. I know this part isn't great, and I'm sorry if this doesn't feel like a date." His lips turn down at the corners. "But I've never been on one before, so I'm kind of new to all this. You're gonna have to help me out with this stuff, okay?"

"Of course I'll help…I'm just—I guess I'm just a little scared."

"What of?" He looks concerned again.

"The fact that my life is going to change, majorly, by being with you, and because of that, I might not be able to do things I used to."

"Don't be scared." He tucks my hair behind my ear. "Nothing will change for you—I promise. I'll make sure your life stays exactly the same, just with the added bonus of me in it." He grins. "And this here today is a small thing.

The people who come to the Louvre won't have a care or a clue about who I am."

"Yeah 'cause art fans never listen to music, Jake." I raise an eyebrow at him. "*Everyone* knows who you are."

"Not everyone. I bet there are millions of people who don't know me. And I bet every single one of them is in the Louvre today."

"You're an idiot," I say, laughing.

"Takes one to know one."

"It does." I put my hand against his warm cheek. "I love you."

"I love you too, and everyone else will love you when they get to know you."

"Except for your legions of female fans."

"Yeah, well, maybe not them." He smirks.

I roll my eyes at him.

"But they will love you when they see how happy you make me...and you do, Tru—make me happy—you always did. I don't know how I coped all those years without you."

"Jonny," I say gently.

He looks down.

"Hey, I didn't mean to upset you." I put my fingers under his chin, touching his scar, as I lift his head.

"You didn't." He meets my eyes. "It just makes me sad that Jonny's never going to get the chance to feel about a girl like I do you."

"Then we're just gonna have to live it twice as large for him." I lean in and kiss his lips gently. "Come on, superstar. Let's get this show on the road."

Jake holds my hand tightly as we walk towards the lift, us being led by the attendant and Dave, with Ben walking behind us.

I feel like I'm under armed guard because I'm carrying a precious cargo into the Louvre.

It's so surreal.

We all ride up in the lift in silence. It's making me a little fidgety.

We get out on the first floor, and standing outside the lift is a smartly dressed man, tall, dark wavy hair, and obviously waiting for us.

"Mr. Wethers," he says, stepping forward as we exit the lift. "I'm Alexander Baudin. It is very good to meet you. We are absolutely delighted to have you visit us here at the Louvre today."

His English is excellent, although heavily accented and very sexy sounding.

Jake shakes his outstretched hand. "Call me Jake, please, and this is my girlfriend, Trudy Bennett."

"Lovely to meet you, Ms. Bennett," Alexander Baudin says, taking hold of my hand to shake.

"So what were you looking to see today?" Alexander Baudin asks, walking forward. We follow.

"This wing of the Louvre we are currently in is home to some of our many prints, drawings, and paintings. The likes of *The Young Beggar* and of course our resident lady, the *Mona Lisa*." He turns, smiling at us. "I am happy to accompany you today, give you a guided tour."

"Thank you for the offer, but we'll be fine," Jake says, coming to a stop. "I'm sure you're a busy man and I don't want to interrupt your day."

"It is no problem." Alexander Baudin smiles.

"I appreciate the offer," Jake says kindly, leaning closer to him. "But I'm here on a date with my girl, and we have enough company as it is." Jake tilts his head in the direction of Dave and Ben, who are loitering nearby.

"Ah, I understand," Alexander Baudin says in a lowered voice, nodding. "Here is a guide of the Louvre." He pulls a leaflet from the inside of his jacket pocket and hands it to Jake.

"I hope the both of you enjoy your day here, and if you need anything at all, please let me know."

"We will, thanks," Jake says.

Alexander Baudin smiles at us both once more and departs.

"Okay, baby, so where to first?" Jake says, opening out the guide for the Louvre.

We've been in the Louvre for just over an hour looking at paintings. We haven't got very far because there are so many, and I keep getting stuck, because some of them are truly amazing, so very beautiful, and I've been feeling quite emotional just looking at them.

It makes me wish I could create something so wonderful.

I don't think Jake's as taken with them as I am though. If the wall was covered with guitars, he'd probably be more interested, but I love that he's showing a keen interest for me.

And he's being so lovely, so attentive, constantly touching me, holding my hand, and I'm having the best time with him.

I'm just ignoring the fact that Dave and Ben are following us, and that we are getting stares from people who either recognise Jake immediately or recognise him but are not sure where from.

It's not too horrendous; weird, but bearable.

I hear a phone ringing, and turning, I see Dave pulling his phone from his pocket.

He turns away from us to take the call.

I focus back on the painting in front of me, *Woman with a Mirror*.

"This painting is so beautiful," I say to Jake. "I think it's my favourite so far."

"It's not as beautiful as you," he whispers in my ear from behind, sliding his arms around my waist.

"You're such a charmer." I rest my head back against his chest.

"Jake." Dave comes over. "That was Stuart on the phone. There's some pictures of you and Tru, here in the Louvre, that have just hit the networking sites, and they're doing the rounds, making it to the paps' sites. I just wanted to let you know things could get a little busy when we're leaving."

"Okay," Jake says, sighing.

"What does he mean—*busy*?" I turn to face Jake.

"It means there's a high probability there will be paparazzi waiting for us outside when we leave."

My stomach knots.

"How did they get pictures of us?"

"Camera phones, baby."

"Gotta love technology." There goes our lovely date.

I start to chew on my bottom lip.

"Should we leave now?" I ask.

"No." Jake shakes his head. "Just forget about it, I want to keep enjoying my day with you."

"But what if we get mobbed?" My voice has gone a little shrill. In all honesty, I'm starting to freak out.

"We won't get mobbed." He chuckles, tucking my hair behind my ear. "And if we did, that's what Dave and Ben are here for. They're very good at their job, Tru. The best in the business, and that's why I have them working for me. You're completely safe, don't worry."

I don't feel safe. I suddenly feel exposed and vulnerable.

Is this how it's always going to feel? The thought haunts me a little.

"Come on," Jake says, taking me by the hand. "We've got a lot more of this place to see."

I let him lead me along, but I'm not interested in the paintings anymore. I just feel tense and have visions of getting mobbed by hordes of screaming girls and the paparazzi, and I can't let go of the feeling.

After another fifteen minutes and a little farther into the Louvre, I'm starting to notice the volume of people near us increasing.

Dave and Ben obviously notice too, as they have moved in closer to us.

Where we had space before, now we have very little.

I can feel Jake getting tense.

I don't think it's because the gathering attention is bothering him; I think he's frustrated because he knows it's bothering me, and he just wanted us to have today together.

Our first date together, we are now sharing with not only Dave and Ben but about fifty other people.

A member of the security staff from the Louvre comes over and speaks quietly to Dave.

The security guy stands back, staying with us, and that only causes me to feel even more edgy than I already do.

Dave makes a quick call, then comes over and speaks into Jake's ear.

Jake moves back away from me to listen to what Dave has to say.

I'm trying to focus on the painting before me, but I can't. I don't even know what this one is called. I've barely taken it in.

I'm trying to ignore the eyes around me, but my whole body feels like it's on fire, burning under their scrutiny.

I don't think I'm cut out for this.

I hear Jake sigh loudly, then see him nod to Dave.

He comes over to me. Standing in front of me, he takes my hands and says in a quiet voice, "Baby, the paps are here, outside…they've somehow found out which car is ours in the parking garage, and…there's a load of them waiting out there for us."

"How many?"

"Enough. And the loitering has obviously brought some attention, and well…now the crowd has grown because people know it's me in here." He sounds really uncomfortable and embarrassed saying this to me.

"Oh," I say.

"The staff here are trying to clear the parking lot, but Dave has called Stuart, and he's on his way to come collect us now in the other car."

"Okay."

"I'm so sorry about this, Tru." He puts his hand on my face, but I can't even enjoy the feel of his skin on mine because I'm so conscious of the fact that people are staring.

I feel like I'm in a zoo and I'm truly on the wrong side of the fence.

"It's okay," I say, trying to keep my voice even. "It's not your fault. This is just how things are. I understand. Come on, let's go."

I take hold of Jake's hand, and we start to walk through the Louvre, following Dave. Ben is behind us, and the museum's security staff is with us too.

People are following us and stopping to stare as we pass by.

Honestly, it makes me want to break out into a sprint.

All these beautiful things here in the Louvre and all people seem to want to do is stare at Jake.

I get he's beautiful. I want to stare at him all day long too, but it's just plain rude to stare so blatantly and to follow him…us…when we are clearly out together for the day, without any recrimination whatsoever.

I hold on a little tighter to Jake's hand. He squeezes it, giving me a small, uneasy smile.

He's feeling bad that we're having to leave, and I know he's worried as to how I feel about it, especially after what we talked about in the car just before we arrived.

How do I feel?

Stressed, a bit panicky, annoyed that we can't even go on a simple day out together without attracting the crazy.

Is this how it's always going to be?

I don't know if I'm cut out for this. It's scary as to the level of attention Jake receives.

We reach the main door and Dave pushes it open, then I'm hit with some camera flashes. There are paparazzi out here.

I thought they were in the parking garage. How the hell did they know we'd be coming out this way?

"So you two are together then? Are you finally settling down Jake? Is Trudy the one?"

The voices are coming from left, right, and centre.

Jesus Christ, this is insane.

I keep my head down. Jake's arm is around me now, tight, holding me to him. Dave is on Jake's right, arm on him, guiding us over to Stuart's waiting car. Ben is at my side, staying close to me.

"Trudy! Look this way, gorgeous, let us see your face!"

I need to get out of here. I don't think I've ever felt as uneasy in all my life as I do right now.

I tilt my head farther down, practically tucking my chin into my chest.

The next thing I know, we're at the car. Dave has the door open and Jake is guiding me in. I shuffle along, sitting behind the passenger seat, and then Jake quickly climbs in behind me.

Dave shuts the door, pushing some paps out of the way in the process. Ben climbs in the passenger seat, and then Stuart's driving us away, pretty quickly.

My heart is bumping around my chest.

I turn in my seat, looking out the back window, worrying the paparazzi might be following.

I can't see any suspicious-looking cars, but then there's plenty around. And I'm thankful in this moment that the windows are so heavily tinted in this car.

Jake takes hold of my hand, pulling my attention to him, and it's only then I realise my hand is shaking.

"Hey, are you okay?" His voice is soft and soothing. He takes hold of my chin, forcing my eyes to his.

"I'm fine." My mouth's dry. I moisten my lips with my tongue. "That was just…um…a little crazy." I take a deep breath. "Is it always like that when you go out?"

"Not always, no." He shakes his head. "That was a little more hectic than normal, but I'm guessing it's because you're with me, and the press will be after a picture of us together."

"And the ones on Twitter weren't enough?"

"Apparently not."

"I don't get it though, Jake. You've been out with women before, that's not exactly a rarity."

That sounded a little shittier than I intended.

He gives me a look. "No, Tru. I've fallen out of clubs with women before. I've never taken anyone out on a date."

"How did they even know we were on a date?" My voice is shrill again.

"Well, baby." He strokes my cheek with the back of his hand and I'm relieved at his touch. "Anyone who took one look at us together could have easily worked that out—figured out that I'm crazy about you."

"But we only started seeing each other properly yesterday!"

Okay, so I'm freaking out a little. A lot.

"It doesn't take them long, Tru. You're in this business, you know how it works."

"I might be a journo, but I am nothing like them!" I say with indignation.

"That's not what I meant, and you know it." He gives me a look. "I'm just saying, you work at a magazine, you see how things are with celebrities. My life is not private in a lot of ways, no matter how much I try to keep it as such. And this is their job, the paps. They make their living off the shit going on in my life and the lives of other celebs. It's just how things are. Not all the time, but a lot of it, and if something happens in my life—like me being out on a date…the possibility of me having a girlfriend—well, then, the media becomes interested…interested in you."

"But I'm no one special."

"You are to me." His voice is intense. "You're everything to me," he adds in a lower tone. "And I'm sorry this hasn't been a first date, like a first date should be." He cups my cheek with his hand. "I will make it up to you, I promise."

Then looking at Jake here, before me, him staring back at me in earnest, filled with love for me, I feel suddenly overwhelmed by my feelings for him, and at the depth of those feelings. And momentarily forgetting that Stuart and Ben are in the front of the car, only a few feet away, I lean forward and kiss him, hard.

Parting my lips under his, I let his tongue move into my mouth, and then I feel it pass between us. The energy, the desire, and I start to feel that stirring in my body that only he can create.

I want him, right here and now.

I know he feels it too as he groans a little sound in my mouth. Jake grabs a firm hold of my hair, kissing me even harder.

It takes a long moment, but I do eventually become very aware of the fact that Stuart and Ben are in the front of the car, especially when Jake's hand goes to my leg and starts to move higher.

Knowing for sure they don't want a Jake and Tru porn show, I pull back from him.

Jake looks at me, disappointed. I flick my eyes in the direction of the front of the car. I'm really glad the radio is on fairly loud, which will have drowned out the sound of our kissing. But even so, my cheeks have flamed with embarrassment at my loss of control.

He smiles and leans close again, running his nose up the sensitive skin on my neck. He reaches my ear and whispers, "I can't wait to get you back to the hotel…I am going to undress you, slowly…and I'm going to kiss you, *everywhere.*"

I can feel his words, down there, and that heat rises again in my belly. I love how he makes me feel.

"*Te quiero,*" I whisper back to him.

"Jesus Christ, Tru," he groans quietly in my ear, his breath hot on my skin. "You know what that does to me. If you keep talking like that, I don't give a shit who is in this car with us, I'll take you right here and now, on the backseat."

His words do crazy things to me and I'm feeling turned on and suddenly reckless.

Maybe it's because I'm still pumped up with adrenaline after what just happened at the Louvre, or because of how much I do love him, but I suddenly have the urge to turn him on, to challenge him.

"*Joder,* Jake…that's what I want to do with you now," I whisper.

He knows exactly what I'm saying to him. That is one Spanish word he does know.

I feel him stiffen beside me.

I flicker a glance in Stuart's direction, seeing his eyes are on the road. Ben is talking on his phone, speaking to Dave, presumably.

So shifting back in my seat, I move closer to the door, turning my body towards him, and run my fingers up my thigh, lifting my skirt up. Ever so slightly, I part my legs.

Jake sharps in a breath. His eyes are on me and they're glowing.

I love this sense of power I have over him right now. It's exhilarating.

I stare at him, meeting his hot gaze, and moisten my lips with my tongue.

Smiling seductively at Jake, I lower my skirt back down, pressing my legs together, feeling proud of my wanton little moment, thinking, *My work here is done, until the hotel, that is,* but Jake shakes his head no.

My legs start to tremble.

He moves closer, positioning himself beside me, and puts his foot up on the rest between the front seats, covering any possible view of my legs with his. Jake rests his hand on my lap, then very gently pushes my legs apart with his hand, and I let him.

My heart is thudding in my chest, and my mouth is suddenly dry.

Jake slides his hand under my skirt. Reaching my panties, he hooks his fingers into them, and moving them aside, giving him the access he wants, he starts to touch me. Then very gently, he slips his finger inside me.

My whole body nearly explodes. I have to bite my lip, hard, to stop myself from making a noise.

I turn my face to his. He stares back at me. His eyes daring and heated.

I have never in all my life done anything like this. And I know I should care there are other people in the car with us, but it's hard to right now. All I care about is Jake and the way he's making me feel.

He starts to move his finger, in and out, in a rhythmic motion, his thumb rubbing over me, and my heart is beating so hard, my legs shaking uncontrollably, and I know what's going to happen if he doesn't stop.

"Jake, stop, or I'm going to come," I mouth to him.

He grins and rubs his thumb a little firmer over my hot spot.

My body shudders.

"Please," I mouth again, pressing my legs together, onto his hand.

He grins again, seemingly satisfied with himself and the effect he's had on me, and slips his hand out from under my skirt, then rearranges his very noticeable erection in his pants.

I'm relieved and disappointed at the same time.

And I have a good mind to do the same to him—work him up to the point of near combustion.

Stuart pulls up out front of the hotel a few minutes later, and I'm still struggling to gather my cloudy, but very horny, thoughts.

I'm so worked up and desperate to relieve the ache Jake has left me with, that I'm just about ready to do it anywhere with him.

Once we're out of the car, Jake grabs hold of my hand, leading me straight into the hotel, practically dragging me through the lobby and into a waiting lift.

Once the doors are closed, he pushes me up against the wall, his mouth on mine, hard and fast, his hands everywhere.

Then, before I know it, the lift doors are pinging open on our floor, and Jake's pulling me down the hall, unlocking the door to his suite, and then we are finally alone.

Jake starts to walk towards me but I back off.

Payback time, mister.

He cocks his head to the side, staring at me perplexed.

"Stay there," I breathe.

I've never really been this confident sexually. I'm more of a straight-to-the-basics kind of girl. And I've most definitely never been confident about my body.

So I have no idea where that little skirt lifting show came from in the car or why I let him do what he did to me or even why I want to carry on the show in here. But I do. I want to do it for him, because of him.

Jake makes me feel confident…and so very sexy.

I'm feeling pretty glad right now that I'm wearing my good underwear, as I start to unbutton my shirt, slowly, one button at a time.

I watch Jake's eyes as they follow my hands down.

I slide my shirt off, down my arms, letting it fall to the floor.

Then I kick off my heels and unbutton my skirt at the back, slowly easing the zip down. I shimmy it over my hips, then let it fall to the floor and step out of it.

Now I'm just standing here in just my black lacy underwear.

Jake's eyes are on fire, devouring me, and he looks like he's about to pounce any second now.

I run my hand down my stomach and hook a thumb into the elastic of my panties, slowly inching them down over my hips.

Jake's breathing is shallow. His eyes are fixed on my hand, watching, waiting.

He puts his hand on the stretch in his jeans, adjusting himself, obviously feeling the discomfort in his pants.

I stop pulling my panties down, changing my mind, and bring them back up to rest on my hips.

He cocks his head to the side.

Slowly, I walk over to him.

My heart is pumping hard in my chest. I've got heat in my belly, and I'm flushed all over.

Jake grabs hold of my hips, pulling me hard against him the instant I'm within his reach.

Shaking my head at him, I remove his hands off my hips and step back a little.

"Not yet," I whisper.

"I want you now." His tone is urgent, intense. It travels through me, hitting me in just the right spot.

I lean close to his ear and whisper, *"Yo voy a chupar."*

He sharps out a breath. "Fuck, Tru," he growls. "If you want me to wait, you're not going about it the right way."

Moving back, I smile at him, snagging my lower lip with my teeth.

"Tell me what you just said. I need to know." His words are breathy, ragged.

I love that I can do this to him with just words.

"Let me show you," I say, dropping to my knees before him.

Then I'm undoing his jeans, freeing him, and showing him just exactly what I meant.

CHAPTER TWENTY-THREE

"Why won't you tell me where we're going?" I ask Jake again, turning in my seat to face him.

He flickers a glance at me. "Because it's a surprise."

"Why is everything always a surprise with you?"

He slows the car to a stop at the red traffic light.

"Because I like seeing the look on your face when you discover what the surprise is." He reaches over and strokes my cheek with his fingers.

"You would still get the surprised look even if you told me, you know—I'm great at surprised faces."

"Yeah, I'm sure you are," he laughs. "But still, it just doesn't equal the look of seeing it in your eyes as you see it for the first time."

Huh? Well now, I'm just confused.

"Okay, so what if I told you I don't like surprises." I fold my arms across my chest.

"You haven't seemed to mind them so far," he says confidently, shifting the car back into drive as the light changes to green. "And you definitely didn't seem to mind the one I gave you earlier."

My cheeks instantly flush.

Memories of Jake sneaking up behind me when I was in the bathroom, brushing my teeth, getting ready to come out tonight…and then I was coming, but in a whole different way.

"Well, yeah I did like that one." I grin across at him, unfurling my arms.

"See? Surprises can be good." He takes hold of my hand and kisses it, then rests it back down so he can signal his turn.

Earlier was amazing, but I think it was also Jake's way of cushioning the blow, pardon the pun, because after we made love, he'd had some of those amazing cakes delivered as we never did get to go to the delicatessen, and while we were sitting in bed, feeding each other cake, he told me that the pictures of me and him leaving the Louvre had hit the tabloids in full-colour glory, telling the world we're together. They also know Jake and I grew up together. That we used to live next door to one another and had been best friends growing up.

So now the whole world knows pretty much everything about Jake and me.

Except they don't know we had an affair.

They don't know I still had a boyfriend when we started seeing each other. They haven't locked on to that little piece of information, yet, and I hope they never do. For Will's sake as much as my own.

The word is that Jake has found "the one." His girl next door.

It's sweet, in an intrusive, weird kind of way.

Jake was worried how I'd feel because of my privacy concerns, and because of how I had wanted to spare Will's feelings as much as possible.

I reassured him I was fine with it all. It was bound to hit the press one day, so sooner rather than later.

So now it's out, Jake and I can get on with just enjoying one another.

I stare out through the heavily tinted window, looking at Paris all around me. I feel like I'm the luckiest girl in the world to be with Jake. To have him back in my life, and for us to finally be together.

And for him to love me back, like I've always loved him.

If only we'd told one another how we felt when we were younger, maybe we would never have lost touch. Maybe we would have always been together, and Jake would never have had the drug problem, and I would have been there for him when Jonny died.

It's sad to think we've missed out on so many years together, but we have each other now and that's what matters.

So, I have no idea where I'm going tonight, which is a tad frustrating, but the flip side is that it's just Jake and me tonight. He told Dave and Ben to stay at the hotel.

I know, I couldn't believe it either.

Dave was not comfortable with Jake's going out alone. But Jake is the boss and what he says goes. He can be pretty authoritative when he wants to be. And it's really very sexy to see in action. I might let him be all authoritative with me in bed later tonight.

I know why Jake wanted to go out alone with me. He's trying to give me a normal night out after today's escapade at the Louvre. Trying to prove to me that life can be normal with him at times.

So there's no Dave following us. Just Jake and me in his new hire car, a two-seater black BMW Z4.

It's a sexy car, just like its driver.

Jake had it delivered earlier for us to go out in tonight, and Stuart has also changed the Mercs, so now Jake's got Audis for the remainder of his stay.

However long that will be.

We haven't talked about going home yet. I know I have to go home soon, as I need to get back to the magazine and do some work before the US leg of the tour starts. But I'm reluctant to bring the subject up because I don't want to leave him yet, if ever.

Every time I think about being without Jake, I get this awful strangling, tightening sensation in my tummy.

So for now, I'm not thinking about it.

Jake takes the next turn, taking us down the Rue de la Paix.

He pulls the car over just outside Tiffany's and turns the engine off.

"What are we doing here?" I ask, a little frisson of energy bursting in my tummy.

Of course I have an idea, well, a hope, of what we're doing here, but I have to ask just to be sure.

"There's something I need to pick up," he answers.

"Oh, okay."

My little glimmer of sparkly hope vanishes.

Of course, I don't want Jake spending lots of money on me, but if he ever felt the need to buy me something pretty from Tiffany's, then I wouldn't take total offence to it.

I've always wanted jewellery from Tiffany's.

A: Because I love Audrey Hepburn and wanted to be her for a while when I was younger, and I still kind of do.

B: I love the song.

But mainly C: Because the jewellery is just so ridiculously beautiful, but it's also so very out of my price range.

Anyway, he's here to pick something up, and that's cool.

Maybe it's something for his mum. He did speak to her on the phone earlier.

He told her about him and me.

Apparently, she's really pleased and is looking forward to seeing me again.

Honestly, the thought makes me nervous. Maybe it's because after all these years, I'll be seeing Susie again as Jake's girlfriend and not just his friend.

I climb out of the car and Jake meets me around the other side.

Luckily, the streets are fairly quiet tonight, as I don't fancy another mobbing like we had earlier.

Jake takes hold of my hand and we walk towards Tiffany's.

I've been in a Tiffany's store before, of course. Looked around, then left before I either killed my Visa or cried.

The closed sign is up, but the place is all lit, and I can see a man walking towards the door.

They've kept the place open late for Jake.

Oh, the power of money and status.

We're greeted at the door by the man inside, who identifies himself as Devin.

Devin is well groomed and very attractive. He reminds me of Stuart in a way. I wonder if he's gay.

"Your piece is ready for you," Devin is saying to Jake as we follow him over to the brightly lit, glossy, sparkly counter.

But I'm barely listening. It's so damn pretty in here. My head is swivelling on my neck.

It looks even fancier than the one on Bond Street back home. It probably isn't; it's just because it's here in amazing Paris that I think so.

More than anything, I want to visit Tiffany & Co. in New York. The original and the best.

One day, Tru, one day.

I'm getting distracted, there's just so much to look at, and my fingers are itching to touch things.

A display of rings to my left catches my eye, so I drop Jake's hand and wander over to have a look, leaving him to get his "piece."

The thought makes me want to giggle. I'm so immature at times.

My eyes roam the gems in the glass case. White diamonds, sapphires, yellow diamonds, and, oh my god, a pink diamond. A freaking pink diamond! I didn't even know you could get pink diamonds!

I'm actually freaking out a little here. Because this has to be the most beautiful ring I have ever seen in my whole entire twenty-six years on this planet.

It's platinum with a pear-shaped pink diamond and a single row of round brilliant white diamonds hugging it.

I think I may have just died and gone to girlie heaven.

I'd sell my grandma to have this ring, that's how amazing it is. Of course I'd never tell her that; she'd have my hide if I did.

My eyes scan around for a price for the ring, but there isn't one, which means it's ridiculously expensive.

Like I could ever have afforded it anyway. I can't even afford moderately priced Tiffany's. Not even cheap Tiffany's, if there is such a thing.

That ring will be worth more than I can earn in a lifetime.

"See anything you like?" Jake says in a husky voice from behind me.

Without thinking, I say in my still-dreamy state, "Look at that ring, it's so beautiful," pointing to it.

Then I realise, smack bang, how it will look to Jake that I'm standing here, gazing dreamy-eyed at a pink diamond ring, which actually looks a lot like an engagement ring, and I'm pointing said ring out to him in a dreamy voice.

I'm such a girl at times.

"Um…I mean it's nice, you know, as rings go. So did you get what you came for?" I ask, abruptly changing the subject.

I turn away from the dream ring to face him.

"I did." He pats his jacket pocket, looking pretty happy with himself.

Jake looks absolutely delicious tonight. And very smart. He's dressed in blue jeans, but he's wearing a shirt and a suit jacket with them. It shouldn't work but it does on him, and he looks so very hot.

I'm wearing my sleeveless floral print dress. It's fitted at the waist and has a cut-out back. It's pretty, with a real sexiness about it. I've teamed it with my cream heels. And my hair is down and curly, just as Jake likes it.

He takes hold of my hand, and opening the door for me, I exit first, leaving Tiffany's.

"Bye, sparkly," I murmur quietly to myself.

"What did you say?" Jake asks.

"Um…what? Nothing." My face flushes scarlet, and I quickly march to the car, leaving Jake to chuckle softly behind me.

I've just got in the car and put my seat belt on, when I turn to Jake, wondering why he hasn't started the car yet, and see a Tiffany's box sitting on the armrest separating me and him.

My heart does a little dance in my chest.

I look from the box to him.

"I got you a little something," he says, looking surprisingly nervous.

"Is that what you went in there to pick up?"

"Uh-huh." He nods.

"What is it?" My insides are doing cartwheels at the moment, but I'm keeping a poker face on. I don't want to come across as the girlie idiot I truly am.

He smiles. "Open it and find out."

I reach forward and pick up the box. Cracking it open, I find inside the most beautiful necklace I've ever seen. Ever.

It's a platinum heart locket pendant with a heart-shaped diamond set in the centre.

I can't believe he bought me this. I think I may actually cry.

"It's so beautiful, Jake," I breathe.

"Open it up." He points his chin at the locket.

I remove the locket from the box, putting it back down on the armrest. Then using my fingernail, I pop the locket open.

I gasp. The smile on my face has just reached maximum size.

"Your dad sent me the picture," he says, looking shy. I love shy Jake. "The other is from the after-show party in Sweden."

Printed inside the locket are two pictures of Jake and me. One is from when we were toddlers. We must be three years old, max. The other is from the after-show party in Sweden like he said.

Overcome with emotion, I launch myself at him. Kissing him hard and passionately on the mouth, knotting my fingers into his hair, holding him to me. Jake kisses me back with equal passion, his hand cupped around the back of my neck, holding me to him, his tongue roaming my mouth, moving with mine.

"So you like it then?" he whispers into my mouth as our kissing slows.

"I love it, and I love you."

"Birthday present number three," he murmurs, brushing my hair back off my face.

"I've still yet to get you anything."

"I got all my twelve the moment you agreed to be mine."

"Who knew you were such a hopeless romantic, Jake Wethers." Smiling, I trace my fingertip over his lips. The light bruise from his fight with Will is still evident there.

It's crazy to believe that was only yesterday morning. It feels like we've done so much together since then.

"Only with you I am. And I'm also horny twenty-four-seven." He runs his hand up my thigh, pushing the hem of my dress up with his fingers.

"Again?" I say.

"Always."

"Well, we're not doing it here, in the car on the street, Pervy Perverson."

"Pervy Perverson?" Jake splutters out a laugh.

"*Friends.* You never watched?" I say at his puzzled expression.

"No, dork, I was too busy touring and earning a living, while you were bumming around at uni watching soaps."

"Shut your face, and put my necklace on, PP." I grin at him.

Jake holds his hand out for the necklace, so I place it in his palm.

I turn away from him, moving my long hair away from my neck.

Jake places the cool metal around my neck and catches the fastener at the back. His hands linger on my shoulders, and then I feel the touch of his warm lips on the nape of my neck.

It sends shivers running down my spine.

I reach my hand back, touching his thigh, and lean myself into him.

He smells and feels amazing, and a heat starts to rise in my body, pooling in my belly. And now I'm turned on.

I start to inch my fingers up his thigh.

Jake catches hold of my hand. "We're not doing it here, MP."

"MP?" I turn, looking at him, puzzled.

"Mrs. Perverson." He smirks, then leaving me cold, he starts the car, puts his belt on, and pulls out into the road.

Mrs.? Hmm…I'm liking the sound of that.

Mrs. Trudy Wethers.

Has quite a ring to it if you ask me. Not now of course. But then Jake's not exactly the marrying kind, is he.

The thought makes me feel a little sad.

"Where to now?" I ask, ignoring my own crashing wedding bells, and instead trying to poker some info out of him.

"Now it's time for birthday present number four."

Jake pulls the car up on the main road, a stretch away from the Eiffel Tower. It is a little busier around here of course. Tourists are all around.

Out my window, I see a young guy waiting by the road-side, and I instantly know he's here waiting for us.

"Come on, baby," Jake says, climbing out of the car.

By the time I'm out of the car, the star-struck young guy is taking the car keys from Jake and is walking around to the driver's side with a huge smile on his face.

"You didn't just give the car to a random stranger, did you?" I ask, smirking.

"No," he laughs, gently swatting my behind with his hand. "He works for the place we're going to. He's going to go park the car for us. He'll probably joyride it first—can't say I blame him, because I would if I was him. But as long as it's back for when we need it, I'm cool."

"Aww, you're so sweet, baby, letting the teenager go for a joyride in the hire car." I nudge him with my hip. "And you're also silly, romantic, and looking *very* hot tonight."

"Yeah?" He turns to me, that lusty Jake fire in his eyes again. "And you're beautiful and insanely sexy, and right now I want to peel that dress off you and do dirty things to you right here and now in the street, but I think we might get arrested if I do."

I press my legs together, trying to control the tremble in them he's just created with his words.

"Later?"

"Oh, most definitely." He nods. "Now come on, beautiful, let's get moving before I start getting stopped for autographs." He does a quick, comical glance around, then holds out his arm for me to take.

I link my arm through his, boxing up my sudden urges for later, and we start to walk down the Parisian street together just like any other normal couple, heading in the direction of the Eiffel Tower.

I feel relaxed and happy and not at all worried that we're going to get mobbed by TMS fans.

If people are looking at us, I don't even notice, because I'm too busy staring at Jake, drinking him in.

"What?" he asks, staring down at me.

"Nothing. I'm just happy." I rest my head against his shoulder as we walk.

"Me too," he murmurs, kissing the top of my head.

As we near the Eiffel Tower, I look up and get a feeling of vertigo from the sheer height of it.

"Wow, it's so amazing," I murmur.

"Yeah, it's pretty cool, isn't it," Jake says, following my gaze skywards.

"Have you ever been here before?" I ask.

"No."

"But you've been to Paris?" I haven't. It's my first time here. I've always been more of an Ibiza girl.

"Yeah, I've been quite a few times," he replies.

"So why have you never visited here, or the Louvre, come to think of it?"

"Because I was saving them for you."

"What?" I stop walking. We're just under the tower now.

Jake turns to face me, sliding his arms around my waist, pulling me close.

"I knew one day I would eventually see you again, and I knew when that day came, I wasn't letting you go for anything. And these were the things I wanted to do with you when I had you back. No one else, just you."

"So you were waiting for me?"

"Yes."

Holy fuck.

"And what if fate had decided we were never to be?"

"Then there would never have been anyone else. There is no one else for me. Only you."

Just when I think he can't get any sweeter, he goes and says something to top his last heavenly saccharin.

I reach up on my tiptoes and kiss his cheek.

"I'm never letting you go," he whispers as my lips touch his skin.

"I don't want you to. Ever."

I spy over Jake's shoulder a guy, an older guy, loitering by a doorway at the bottom of the tower.

"I think one of your staff is waiting for you."

Jake glances over his shoulder and signals two minutes to the guy.

He nods and steps back just inside the door.

"He's not my staff, smart-ass," he says, slapping my behind. "Just hired for the night."

"I hope I'm not just a hire for the night." I press my lips together, holding back my smile.

"Depends on what you have to offer." He raises an eyebrow, giving me his fuck-me-now stare.

"J-Jake Wethers—are you Jake Wethers?" comes a young-sounding voice to our right.

Ah crap.

I turn to see a young lad, maybe thirteen—fourteen max—staring at Jake, agape and wide-eyed, like all his Christmases have just come at once.

Jake nods to the kid and puts his finger to his lips, glancing around.

The kid, obviously in some state of shock, just nods his head slowly at Jake.

He looks quite comical, bless his soul.

Leaving me, Jake steps closer to the kid, and says, "I'm out on a date with my girl and I don't want a crowd, you know."

"Uh-huh." The kid nods.

"So just don't tell anyone I'm here—okay?"

"O-okay." The kid nods again. He sounds like he's slipping off into a coma.

"You got a camera phone, kid?"

"J-Johnny," he says, coming to life a little, scrabbling to dig his phone out of his pocket. "My name's Johnny." He hands Jake his phone without a second thought.

"Great name." Jake smiles.

"Tru, would you mind?" Jake turns to me, holding the phone out for me to take.

"Sure, no prob." I smile.

I take the phone from Jake and set the camera on. I take a photo of Jake and Johnny the kid, and then hand the camera back to him.

"Th-thanks," Johnny says to me.

He turns and stares at Jake again. He looks like he has a million things he wants to say to Jake, but they're all stuck in his head. Poor kid.

I know the feeling all too well.

"Th-thanks for the p-picture," he stammers out.

"Anytime…and remember, not a word." Jake winks at him, then takes my hand and leads me inside the door.

"I think that poor kid was in a state of shock." I laugh as we walk into the lift together.

Jake's hired hand is here to accompany us for the ride up.

"I think you might be right."

"That was a nice thing you did back there, baby." I squeeze his hand.

"Just doing my bit for mankind."

I look at him, puzzled.

"Tru, that picture of him with me will help that kid get laid, or if not, at least get a girl to play with his dick, and that's all that counts when you're a teenager."

"Is that right?"

"Yup." He leans in close and whispers in my ear, "That's what I was hoping for at Lumb Falls all those years ago."

"Oh," I say, my pulse quickening as the memories flood my brain, but this time in a whole new light.

Letting go of my hand, Jake reaches behind me, resting his hand against my ass. He cups it with his fingers. "We'll have to go back there one day and you can do all the things to me I missed out on back then."

I gulp down. Sex with Jake under a waterfall.

Holy hell.

Before I get a chance to respond, the lift doors ping open, and on seriously wobbly legs, I follow Jake out and find myself in the foyer of a restaurant.

There is a waiter here to greet us.

"Mr. Wethers, Ms. Bennett. My name is Adrien and I will be your server for the evening. Please follow me to your table."

Jake takes hold of my hand again, and we follow Adrien into a large dining space.

I gasp audibly in shock.

The place is clear. I mean clear. Nothing except for a table for two positioned by the window, and when I say window, I mean the place is wall-to-wall glass all the way around, so wherever I look all I can see is Paris at night.

And draped around the whole place are white, twinkly fairy lights, and Jeff Buckley is midway through singing "Lilac Wine" softly in the background.

I feel like I've just stepped into heaven, and it stops me in my tracks.

Stopping too, Jake turns to me.

"You hired the Eiffel Tower?" I breathe.

"I don't have that much pull, Tru—well, I don't think I do." He gives me a cheeky smile, pushing his hand through his hair. "I just hired the restaurant for the night—you know." He shrugs like this is an everyday thing, downplaying himself like always.

My heart is bumping clumsily around my chest.

"Jake, this is…" I'm struggling for words. "How did you manage to pull this off?" I ask, feeling breathless.

"Stuart. He can be pretty persuasive when he wants to be. Especially with my money in his corner." He rests his hands on my shoulders, running his fingers into my hair. "Do you like?"

"Mmm, just a bit." I bite down on my smile.

"Lilac Wine" ends and "Hallelujah" begins to softly lilt into the air.

"You ready to sit down?" Jake tilts his head in the direction of our table, which Adrien is waiting by.

I shake my head no. "Dance with me."

He smiles and it lights his whole face. Jake turns to Adrien. "Give us five."

"Seven," I say, knowing the song hits just about that length of time.

"Seven," Jake corrects.

Adrien nods and disappears off through the door to his right.

Jake takes my hand in his, puts his arm around my waist, and pulls me close. I lay my hand against his chest as he starts to move us, dancing together.

"You are so getting laid tonight," I say, looking into his blue eyes.

"I'm holding you to that." There's this intensity in his gaze that makes me shiver from my head to my toes.

"Do," I whisper as I rest my head against his shoulder.

I can hear his heart beating up through his chest, his heat caressing me, his special Jake scent soothing me.

And I know unequivocally this is my happiest moment with him so far, and I just know there's going to be so many more to come.

"*Te amo*," I murmur quietly.

"You too, baby, and I will, forever," he whispers, kissing my hair.

And we stay here dancing for much longer than our seven minutes, with Jeff Buckley and the lights of Paris as our only other company.

CHAPTER TWENTY-FOUR

I let myself in my flat, lugging my heavy suitcase in behind me.

Simone's at work. She came home a few days before I did. Her work is a little stricter on holidays than mine; I guess that's the awesome part of having a boss who is also one of my best friends.

I just couldn't bear to leave Jake, and he wasn't so keen on letting me go either.

Pulling my phone out of my pocket, I stare down at his last text; the one I received the moment I was settled in my first-class seat on the plane to bring me home:

Just think about it please. I love you so much. I want you in my life, permanently. I want to wake up every day with you beside me.

...

"Don't go," Jake whispered, holding my face in his hands.

"I have to. I've got work to do at the magazine, and you've got promo for the tour to do... and I'm sure you need to go into the office to check up on the label... baby, it's only for a week and then we'll be back together," I added, staring up at his sad eyes.

"It's one hundred and sixty-eight hours without you." Jake sighed.

"Did you just work that out in your head?"

He nodded.

"Smarty-pants."

"Stop changing the subject."

I hooked my fingers into his T-shirt. "It's not a long time and then we'll be back together."

I don't mean that. It feels like it's going to be forever, especially when he just broke it down into hours like that.

But we've been in each other's pockets far too much recently, and I don't want Jake to get bored with me. The distance will make him miss me, make him want me more.

Or get lonely and go looking in search of comfort elsewhere.

I quickly shut out that thought, and my stupid irrational side.

The time apart will be good for us.

Jake stared into my eyes, his blue ones caressing my soul, and I could feel myself faltering, weakening to his plea.

No. Be strong, Tru. It's only a week.

No, it's one hundred and sixty-eight hours…

"I'll miss you, baby," I said, forcing my strength. "So much. But we both have to work." I reached up on my tiptoes and kissed his lips.

"Move in with me."

What?

"What?" I leaned back away from his face, resting down onto my unsteady, high-heeled feet, searching his expression.

"I've spent long enough without you in my life, Tru, and I won't do it again. Come and live with me in LA. Move in with me."

I run my finger over the screen on my phone, staring at his message again.

…

"Jake, this is crazy! We can't move in together!"

"No, what's crazy is that I'm standing in an airport saying good-bye to you again."

"This isn't the same as back then. We're not fourteen anymore. We're not going to lose each other. I'm yours and you're mine, and that's never going to change." I held my friendship bracelet up to him as proof of this. *"I'm just going to work for a little while, and then we'll be back together when I fly out in a week. You're only asking me to move in with you as a knee jerk, because of how you feel right now about being away from me."*

He took hold of my arm and kissed my friendship bracelet.

"No, I'm not. I want to live with you because I'm in love with you. I want to share my life with you. Just tell me you'll at least think about it?"

I closed my eyes briefly. *"I'll think about it."*

His hands moved around my neck, and then he was kissing my deeply.

"You won't regret it," he murmured.

"I haven't said yes, yet." I lifted my eyebrow at him.

"No. But I'm just hoping on the fact you seem to have a hard time saying no to me."

Dragging my suitcase through to my bedroom, I dump it down on the floor, then sit on the edge of my bed in the silence for a moment.

The last time I was here, I was here with Will. Everything has changed so much since then.

I feel a sudden, unexpected tear trickle from my eye. I hurt Will so badly, and I'm never going to be able to take that back or fix it for him.

It's hard, feeling happiness to the level I do with Jake, when I know it came at the price of Will's pain.

It was easier to block it all out when I was still in Paris with Jake, but sitting here now, surrounded by memories of Will and the time we spent together, just makes it all so real. And it hurts that I hurt him so terribly.

I loved Will. I still do. Feelings like that don't just disappear overnight.

I just wish there was some way to tell him how truly sorry I am.

Never would I change choosing to be with Jake; I just wish I'd had the foresight to do it the right way.

But is there ever an easy way to break the heart of the person you're in a relationship with, to leave them for your soul mate?

With a sigh, I start to unpack my suitcase and set to work on doing my laundry.

I hate washing clothes, but it helps to keep my mind occupied from sad thoughts of Will and scary thoughts of moving in with Jake, until Simone gets home from work.

She's late getting in, as work was busy, but she brings pizza home with her, and we sit in the living room eating and drinking wine.

Simone tells me all about Denny and what's been happening with them since she got back home from Paris.

By the sounds of things, absence is definitely making the heart grow fonder in their case.

She is totally smitten. And I'm so happy for her.

But it's making me miss Jake even more, hearing her talk about missing Denny.

I've been away from Jake for just over half a day, and it's already hurting like a bitch. So lasting a week just doesn't feel like a physical possibility at the moment. I feel like I'm missing one of my limbs.

But I'm going to do my very best to hold out for as long as I can, because it's healthy for us to have time apart.

"So how was it leaving Jake?" Simone asks, picking her wine up and taking a sip.

"Horrible. Hard. Teary."

"You're seeing him in a week though?"

"Yes." I nod. I take a sip of my own wine, then put down my glass and take a deep breath. "Jake has asked me to move in with him."

She splutters on her wine. "Seriously?"

"Seriously. He's asked me to move to LA to live with him."

"Wow," she says. "So are you going to?"

"I don't know." I shrug. "It's a lot to think about. I love living here with you. I love working at the magazine. I love Vicky. My folks are here in the UK. I just don't know."

"You love him?"

I meet her eyes. "Like no one before. I always have."

"Then you have your answer," she says softly.

I drag my hands through my hair, trying to compile a coherent sentence, but nothing's coming, except for that she's right.

Adele starts singing on the coffee table. One quick glance at my phone tells me it's Jake.

I haven't heard from him all day, as he's been on his flight back to LA. He must have just landed.

"I was gonna go call Denny anyway." Simone smiles, getting to her feet. "Say hi to Jake for me."

"Hey, baby," I murmur, answering.

"Come to LA. Now. Please. I'll send the jet for you."

"A simple, 'I miss you, Tru,' would have done." I start to chew on my thumbnail.

"I miss you, Tru. Too much. Now will you please come to LA? I'm going nuts here without you."

"It's only been, what, thirteen hours?"

I'm not going to admit to him I'm going nuts without him too.

"Twelve, and you're not missing me?" His voice is laced with hurt.

"I am. Like you'll never know. Worse than I did when we were kids."

"So why are we even doing this?"

"Because it's healthy to spend time apart."

"That's just *Cosmo* bullshit. Tru…baby, please, I miss you so much, I can't even begin to explain. I hate that I'm not with you right now." He sighs. "Okay, that's it." He sounds suddenly alert. "I'm cancelling the PR stuff for the tour. If you won't come to me then I'm coming to you."

"You can't do that!" I exclaim. But I love that he wants to.

"I'm the boss. I can do whatever I want."

"Jake, the tour, it's important to you and the guys."

"Tom and Denny can do the PR rounds, which means I can be with my girl until the tour starts back up."

"You're talking crazy." I giggle.

"The only crazy thing I've done was let you go earlier, at the airport. I spent twelve years away from you, Tru. No more. You won't come to LA, then I'm coming to you."

I trace my fingertip over a groove in the coffee table. "I never said I wouldn't come to LA."

There's silence down the line. I can hear his shallow breathing. "You'll move in with me?" His voice is soft, tentative.

I take a deep breath. "Yes."

"Baby, you have no idea how happy you've just made me, or how happy I'm going to make you." I can practically feel his smile.

"Jake, you already make me happy. All I need is you. I have you, I'm the happiest girl in the world."

"When will you come?"

"Give me this week to sort things out here, and then I'm all yours for good. I just need to figure out work stuff with Vicky. Figure out the flat stuff with Simone, and tell my folks, of course."

"Your dad is going to kick my ass for taking you away from him, isn't he?"

"I'd say it's quite likely." I laugh.

"I'll take his ass-kicking if it means I get you here with me...so I just have to spend this week away from you, then you're mine, for good?"

"Yes."

"Okay. I can live with that...just," he adds.

We spend the next few hours on the phone making plans, talking nonsense like Jake and I do, and I love it.

Eventually I hang up the phone with him, with much reluctance, but I need to sleep, as the jet lag finally catches up with me.

I go to bed, thinking about how I'm going to be quitting my job and moving to LA, and also that I'm going to have to find a job once I'm out there. I'm not sponging off Jake.

I've got some savings, so that should tide me over until I can get sorted with a job. I wonder if Vicky has any magazine contacts out there. Jake will have, but I'm not having his influence getting me a job. I want to do this on my own.

And I fall asleep thinking of Jake and all the amazing things we have to look forward to together.

Life doesn't get any better than this, as it is right now.

I wake to the sound of Adele singing. It takes me a minute to grasp my bearings.

I'm in my flat. In my own bed.

I squint at the clock—4:00 a.m.

Grabbing my phone off my nightstand, I see it's Jake.

"Baby, I miss you too, but it's four a.m."

"Tru."

I know instantly something is wrong by the broken sound in his voice.

"Jake, what's wrong?" I sit up in bed, concerned, my stomach tying into a thousand knots.

"Tru, it's—it's my dad…he's dead."

My heart stops in my chest.

"Paul?" I ask, clarifying he doesn't mean his stepdad, Dale.

"Yes."

Jake hasn't seen his dad since he was nine that I know of. And their history…it's complicated, difficult, and right now I'm unsure which way he's going to go with this.

Sadness or relief?

"Baby, I'm so sorry," I say tentatively.

"It's fine. I mean, he's dead, and I hadn't seen him since…so, you know…"

"I know," I breathe. "I'll come to you now. I'm getting the next flight to LA." I start to climb up out of bed.

"No. It's fine. I'm fine. I have to come to the UK, for his funeral."

"You're going?"

"He was my dad, Tru." His tone is sharp.

"I know. I'm sorry. I didn't mean…"

"No, I'm sorry," he backtracks. "My head's just a little fucked up right now." He sighs. "I just need you, Tru."

"I wish I was with you. I'm so sorry I'm not." I chastise myself for this whole time-apart thing.

"When are you coming to the UK?" I ask.

"I've chartered the jet for a midnight flight. I'll be there early evening your time."

"Where is the funeral being held?"

I have no clue where Jake's dad has been for the last seventeen years.

"Manchester. In two days. I'm arranging it. There's no one else to do it."

"Leave it to me. You don't want to be doing it, baby."

"It's okay. I mean, Stuart's helping."

"I want to help."

"Okay…um…speak to Stuart, see what he needs."

"I will…so should I meet you in Manchester?"

"No, I'm coming to London first. I need to see you… and the funeral's not 'til Friday. Is it okay if I stay with you at your place? I just—"

"Jake, you don't even have to ask. I want you here. And the funeral, do you want me to come with you?"

I don't want to presume he'll want me there. I don't want to presume anything at the moment.

"I can't do it without you."

"Then I'm there. It's you and me now, Jake. And what about your mum? Is she coming to the funeral?"

"No." His tone is curt.

It's understandable why Susie wouldn't want to go, but I thought she would to support Jake.

"Okay," I say, unsure what to say right now.

There's a pause between us before Jake speaks again.

"I need you, Tru." I can hear his ragged breathing down the line.

"I'm here. I'm always here for you."

"I know it's late there, but will you stay on the phone with me?"

"Of course I will. So what do you want to talk about?"

"You and me. Our future. What we're going to do together."

"You mean you want me to talk about that house we're going to build on an island in the Maldives that belongs just to us, and we're going to live off the land like a pair of castaways."

"I love you, Trudy Bennett."

"And I love you, Jake Wethers."

"So tell me more about this island?"

And I do. I stay on the phone with Jake until the sun rises and it's time for him to catch his flight to London.

I shower, dress, force a little bit of breakfast down, and then head in to work, taking the Tube.

I'm tired. I've had little sleep, but I couldn't sleep at the moment if I tried. I'm too worried about Jake.

Vicky beams brightly at me when I knock on her open door, then I watch as her face drops when she sees mine.

"What's the matter, my darling?" she asks, worried, getting out of her chair and coming over to me.

"Jake's dad died." My voice wobbles and I know I'm set to cry any minute now.

I'm not upset about Paul dying—not at all. I'm upset because Jake is.

I can feel his pain like it's my own even though there's an ocean between us.

He hurts. I hurt.

"Oh, sweetness." She puts her hands on my arms, searching my face. "How is Jake doing?"

I shrug. "He hadn't seen his dad in a long time. They had a...difficult relationship...but honestly, I think it's hit him pretty hard."

"Come, let's sit." She guides me over to the little sofa in her office.

"I'm really sorry to do this to you again, Vicky...but I need to take some time off to be with Jake. He's flying in today, and the funeral is in Manchester on Friday. Of course I'll work from home, and I'll catch up on whatever I miss before I go to the US for the rest of the tour."

"It's fine, Tru." She takes my hand, patting it with her other. "Everything is in hand here with your column. The important thing at the moment is Jake and making sure he's okay. We can worry about the bio and everything else later."

I feel the weight lift off my shoulders.

"Have I told you lately how wonderful you are?" I can feel tears forming in my eyes.

"It's been a while." She winks at me.

"Well you are, and I love you lots and lots." I wrap my arms around her, hugging her.

Then the tears start to run from my eyes.

How am I going to cope without her and Simone when I move to LA? And my mum and dad, for that matter?

I can't even tell Vicky about the move at the moment. I will soon, but dropping this on her is enough for now, I think.

"Oh, my darling girl, don't cry," she says, hearing my sniffling. She hugs me tighter.

Thank God I wore waterproof mascara today. Subconsciously, I must have known I would be crying a lot today.

Releasing myself, I get a tissue from my bag and dry my eyes.

"Sorry," I mumble.

"Don't be sorry. You've had an emotional time of late, a lot of changes in your life. I'd be worried if you weren't crying. Now, do you want something to drink?" she asks, getting to her feet, moving towards her desk.

"Coffee?"

"I was thinking something a little stronger." Her tone is conspiratorial. Then she pulls a bottle of Jim Beam from out of her desk drawer.

"Perfect," I say, a little smile forming on my lips as Vicky grabs two cups off her shelf.

I leave work a little over an hour later, having spent that time in Vicky's office talking and drinking whiskey.

I feel a little lighter after the chat, and a lot lighter after the whiskey, and now I'm more than ready to see Jake.

Eight hours to go.

As I push out of the glass doors of my building, the cool air hits my skin, and the lightness, kindly provided by Jim Beam, unfortunately, starts to lift.

Taking a right, I turn to head towards the Tube station for home.

"Tru?"

Pausing, I turn around to see Will standing about twenty yards away from me.

He's dressed in blue jeans, a plain white T-shirt, and a black leather jacket. He looks like he hasn't shaved in a while, and I can see the bruising left from his fight with Jake around his eye. I hate that they fought because of me.

He looks different but still handsome. Just Will. The Will I loved—love.

I feel a sudden pang for him. The intensity of it surprises me.

"Will? What—what are you doing here?" I try to recover myself from the shock of just seeing him here in the street.

"Sorry, I just…" He takes a step forward.

"Have you followed me?" I ask.

That sounded really conceited. I wish I could take it back.

"No," he answers softly. "I'd just popped into work to drop something off, and I saw you go into your building. I just…I wanted to talk to you, so I hung around and waited." He pushes his hands deep in his pockets. "I called you…left messages…but you never called me back."

"I'm sorry." I hug my bag to my side. "I just didn't think it was a good idea to talk then, you were angry…rightly so… and I didn't want to make things worse for you."

"How are you?" He takes another step closer.

"I'm okay." I tuck my hair nervously behind my ear. "How are you?"

"Oh, you know." He shrugs and runs his hand through his lovely blond hair. It looks all mussed up. Very un-Will. It suits him.

His eyes meet with mine.

He looks nervous and sad. My heart is aching seeing him here looking this way.

This is what I've done to him.

"Do you have time to have a coffee?" he asks.

"Um…"

"I mean if you're too busy, I understand."

"I'm not too busy. Of course I'll have coffee with you." I smile.

He smiles too. It's nice to see. I've missed his lovely smile.

I've missed him. I just didn't realise how much until now.

"Shall we go to Callo's?" he asks.

"Yes, let's."

We walk side by side in relative silence for the five-minute walk to Callo's.

When we arrive, Will holds the door open for me. I walk into the café, the aroma of coffee, and memories, so many memories, hitting me straightaway.

This was our place. We always had lunch together here.

It's sad being here with him now, like this, apart. I guess I never thought there would be a day that I would ever be without Will.

As it's early, Callo's is empty; only Will and I here, so we get a small table by the window and order two lattes.

"Are you not in work today?" I ask in a vain attempt at small talk while we wait for our drinks.

"No," he shakes his head. "I took a little time off after I got back from Paris—you know."

I bite my lip. I can feel tears forming in my eyes, but I don't want to cry in front of him. I don't deserve the right to cry.

I knot my fingers on the table in front of me. Taking a deep breath, I say, "I'm so sorry, Will. For everything. For the pain I've caused you."

He meets my eyes, and all I can see in them is hurt. And I can't help the tear that escapes from my eye.

I quickly catch it falling.

"Tru, that day...when I pushed you away in the hall and you fell...I didn't hurt you, did I?" He sounds tormented.

After everything I have done to him, he still cares whether he hurt me or not.

It makes my heart hurt more.

Another tear drops. "No, of course you didn't." I shake my head.

"I saw the papers," he utters quietly. "You...and *Jake.*"

I close my eyes briefly.

"Are you happy?" he asks.

"Yes...and no. I'm not happy for what I've done to you. I'm so sorry, Will." Tears are running freely from my eyes now, and I don't care who sees.

I can see Will's eyes shining, but he's holding himself together.

"I hate myself for what I did to you." I wipe the dripping tears from my chin with the back of my hand.

"I don't hate you, Tru. I wanted to, but I can't...I love you too much."

I bite my trembling lip.

I never deserved this wonderful man here, before me, in the first place. And I most certainly don't deserve him now.

He takes a deep breath. "If I said to you that none of it mattered, what happened with Jake—that I still want you irrespective of it all." He pauses, pressing his lips together, before finishing. "Would you...come back to me?"

I'm so torn in this moment. Being away from Will, it was easy to forget how much I loved him...still love him.

A part of me wants to say yes, a big part, to take his and my pain away.

But I can't.

Jake is my soul mate. My best friend. And I would always go back to him, every time.

I slowly shake my head. "I love you, Will. Very much. But...I love Jake more. He's my best friend. I'm so sorry."

A tear runs from his eye, which he quickly brushes away. "I just don't know how to live my life without you in it, Tru. Nothing's making sense right now."

I want to touch him. Hold him. I want to fix this, but I don't know how to.

"You deserve better than me." I blink out more tears. "You always did. You were always too good for me, Will. You deserve someone who would never, ever hurt you."

"But I want you," he says. A tear runs down his cheek. He doesn't wipe this one away.

My lip wobbles again, tears streaming. "And a part of me wants you too, but I belong to Jake. I always have. I love you very much and I always will, but...I love Jake more." I rub my runny nose on my sleeve.

At that, the waiter comes over with our lattes. I grab some napkins, quickly drying my tears.

The waiter has the good grace to pretend he doesn't see me crying.

Once he departs, Will reaches across the table and takes hold of my hand, squeezing it.

I start crying again.

And we sit here like this for a long while, not talking, leaving our lattes to go cold, holding hands, watching the world pass by through the window, just having this time together.

I know this is the last time I'll see Will, and for now, I just want to hold on to him for as long as I can.

After what seems like forever in only a short time, I reluctantly realise we can't sit here all day together. Will does too.

He pays for our drinks, refusing my offer to pay.

We stand just outside of Callo's, lingering. I don't know how to say good-bye to him.

I'm so confused. I don't want to let him go. But I know I have to.

I thought that telling Will about Jake and me was the hardest thing I'd ever had to do, but it's not. This here, letting him go, is the hardest thing I will ever do.

"Are you taking the Tube home?" he asks.

"Yes."

"Do you want me to walk you to the station?"

I shake my head no. "Thank you, but I think I should go alone."

We need to say good-bye outside of here. Our place.

Will looks up at the sign for Callo's. "I don't think I'll be able to come here again." He sighs.

"Me either."

He looks back and meets my eyes. And I can't help but cry again.

I bite my lip, trying to force the tears away, but looking at him here, knowing this is the last time I'm ever going to see him, it's breaking my heart.

"I'm so sorry." My lip quivers.

Without another thought, Will wraps his arms around me, enveloping me in a tight hug.

He smells of everything Will. Of warmth, comfort, and safety. Of the last two years of my life. I breathe him in, trying to hold on to it—him—for as long as I can.

I know I'm the one doing this, but knowing that doesn't make it any easier.

I never knew it was possible to love two men at the same time.

But I do. I love Will and Jake.

I just love Jake more, and that means I have to let Will go.

"I'll always love you, Tru," he whispers into my hair. I hear his voice break. "Jake will never be good enough for you. You deserve so much more than he can ever give."

Then he releases me and strides away, shoving his hands deep into his pockets as he walks, and I stand here outside Callo's watching him go.

Watching the biggest part of the last two years of my life walking away from me, at my behest.

CHAPTER TWENTY-FIVE

I'm really worried about Jake. He's been so distant, so closed off these last few days in the lead-up to his dad's funeral.

It's affected him so much more than I ever anticipated it would.

I guess I just thought because he hadn't seen his dad in so long, and what happened the last time he did see him, well...not that I thought he would be happy he's dead, I suppose I just didn't realise it would hit him so hard.

It's like he's here, but he's not. And I'm worried that he's slipped back into a time he's tried so hard to forget.

It's a hot August day here in Manchester, and I'm thankful for the sleeveless black linen dress I'm wearing and for the air-con in the BMW X5 that Dave is driving, taking us to Paul's funeral. Stuart's in the front next to him, and I'm in the back with Jake, who's been staring out the window since we left the hotel to make the journey to the crematorium. He's wearing a black Armani suit, crisp white shirt and black tie, and dress shoes. It's strange to see Jake in a suit, and even though he looks absolutely amazing, breathtaking, I want him out of these clothes and back in his Jake threads. I want my Jake back.

I just hope the surprise, if you can call it that on a day like today, will help lift his spirit and bring him back to me.

I called Susie, Jake's mum. I got her number from Jake's phone when he was in the shower yesterday morning.

She wasn't going to come to the funeral. Understandable of course after what Paul did to her and Jake. But she needs to, for Jake's sake.

I'm doing everything I can for him, but for this, I think she's the only person who can help him.

They lived it together; now they need to lay it to rest together.

It was weird speaking to her after all these years.

Once we got past the initial awkwardness, it was actually really nice to talk to Susie again. She told me that she's really happy Jake and I have found each other again, and more so that we're together. She said she always knew we were meant for one other.

I actually felt really teary hearing that.

Then I told her my reason for calling.

She took the first flight out of New York to Manchester. Stuart booked her into our hotel, but her flight was landing at lunchtime, so she's coming straight to the funeral from the airport. Dale couldn't come with her, as he's currently in China on business.

Susie and I are keeping our phone conversation between us.

That was my decision.

I don't want Jake to know I called her. I want him to think she turned up because she wanted to be here for him.

Not that she didn't want to help her son. Of course she does. She was just blinded by her own anger for Paul, understandably, and she just needed a nudge in the right direction.

Dave pulls the car down the long road to the crematorium. I feel Jake's hand tighten around mine.

I lean close to him and rest my cheek against his. "Are
you okay?" I whisper in his ear.

He moves back from me, staring into my eyes. He looks
so different, so little boy lost. It makes me ache for him.

I'm praying that Susie is already here waiting for us.

Jake lifts his hand to my face, tucking my hair behind my
ear, he kisses me gently on the lips and murmurs, "You're
everything to me, Tru. You know that, right?"

I nod, confused as to where he's going with this.

He takes my chin between his thumb and forefinger.
"Just...don't ever leave me. No matter what—just don't ever
leave."

I swallow down. He's worrying me with these words.

"I'm not going anywhere. I'm yours, Jake. You have my
heart. I belong to you."

Nervous and unsure, I lean in and kiss him lightly on the
lips. But he grabs hold of my hair, kissing me harder, desperately, his tongue invading my mouth, claiming me. And it
reminds me of the time he kissed me in bed when we were
still having an affair. The first time he talked to me about
Jonny. The desperation and intensity I felt then, I feel now,
and more.

It's almost like he's trying to tell me something with this
kiss. Something he can't say with words.

When Dave pulls the car up outside the building, Jake's
already released me from his hold, and I see Susie is here,
waiting with my mum and dad outside the building. I almost
sigh with relief.

As Jake registers her, I see it on his face, the surprise, the relief; I don't miss that, it almost breaks me.

Susie comes over to the car as Jake climbs out, me behind him.

She looks so different from how I remember her. I guess that's what happiness and a lot of money can do for you.

"What are you doing here?" He sounds confused, angry...happy.

Susie looks up at him, shading her eyes from the sun with her hand. "I thought you might need me," she says quietly. Reaching out, she takes hold of his hand.

I slip quietly away, leaving them both, and go over to my mum and dad.

"Hey, Daddy." I smile up at him as he puts his arm around me, kissing the top of my hair. "Hey, Mama," I say, leaning forward to kiss her. "Thank you so much for coming, I know it will mean the world to Jake."

"The only reason we are here is for you and Jake, baby girl," my dad says to me.

I squeeze him tighter, hugging him. I'm so lucky to have a dad as wonderful as mine is.

Jake comes over to us with Susie a few moments later. She looks like she's been crying; her eyes are a little bloodshot.

"Hello, Trudy," she says. "It's so wonderful to see you again." She puts her arm out for me, and I step out of my dad's embrace and into hers.

She kisses my cheek and whispers, "Thank you."

I give her an understanding smile as she releases me. Then she takes hold of Jake's hand, and they start to walk into the crematorium together. I follow behind with my mum and dad.

Then Jake stops, pausing. He turns and waits for me, holding his free hand out for me to take.

I slip my hand into his, and we all go into the service together.

After the funeral we all have an early dinner together at our hotel—Jake, me, Susie, my mum and dad, Stuart, and Dave.

Jake seems a little more relaxed at dinner. He's currently talking guitars with my dad, and he looks happier than I've seen him in days.

The funeral was difficult and over quickly, thankfully. We were the only ones there. Paul had no one. No family left except for Jake. No real friends. No one who really cared about him.

I know I should feel sad at the thought, but I don't. I hate him for what he did to Jake. And I never thought I would be happy that someone was dead, but I am, because now, maybe Jake can finally let him go for good. Let his past go once and for all.

There was no wake after the funeral, and this dinner most certainly isn't one.

This dinner is for Jake, to help lift his spirits. I've also got a little something planned for later, which I'm hoping will put a smile back on his face, one that I hope will stay there for a long time to come.

Not long after dinner is finished, Susie, tired from her flight, tells us she's going to retire early, which works perfectly for my plans for Jake.

My mum and dad decide to go home too, and Stuart goes for a drink in the hotel bar with Dave.

"You want to join Stuart and Dave for a drink? Or just have an early night?" Jake asks, threading his fingers with mine, pulling me to his side as we walk back through the lobby after seeing my mum and dad out of the hotel.

"Neither. We're doing something else tonight," I say.

Stopping, I turn to face him.

"We are?" His hands go to my hips, his head tilting to the side, assessing my face.

"Ahum." I nod, smiling.

"What?"

"That, my gorgeous boyfriend, is a surprise." I take hold of his hand, leaving him wondering, and lead him to the lifts to take us to the car park and to the waiting car, which contains everything I need for tonight.

As it's my surprise, and Jake has no idea where we're going, I'm driving...and tonight I'm driving James Bond's car.

Aston Martins are Jake's favourite car, hence the hire for our stay. And I'm so totally flooring it on the motorway.

I honestly didn't know it was possible to feel sexy driving a car. But I do right now. I feel like I'm a model in an advert or something.

It's so cool. And I keep wanting to let out little squeals of excitement, but of course I won't, because that would be weird, and also a little inappropriate considering Jake just buried his dad a few hours ago, or cremated him or whatever.

"So you won't tell me where we're going?" Jake asks as I push the car up to eighty-five.

I don't get to drive very often, and I have never driven a car as amazing as this one, so I'm totally making the most of it.

"Nope, it's a surprise."

"I thought you didn't like surprises?"

Keeping my eyes on the dark road ahead, I say, "I don't like receiving them. I never said anything about giving them."

"Touché." He laughs.

There's only so long I can keep it a surprise before he guesses where it is we're going, as he keeps looking at the bloody road signs. I should have had the foresight to bring a blindfold with me.

Jake, in a blindfold, totally at my mercy. Hmm, I'm liking the sound of that. Maybe later.

As I see the signpost signalling my turn to the place we're going, I slide a glance at him, checking out the look on his face, and he looks happy.

He turns to me, smiling widely. "You're taking me to Lumb Falls?"

"I am." I give him another quick glance, a little smile of my own forming.

Jake reaches his hand over and puts it on my thigh. "Are you going to let me do dirty things to you while we're there?"

"Well, I was planning on doing dirty things to you, actually." I bite down on my lip, giving him another quick glance.

"Have I told you just how much I love you?" He slides his hand a little higher up my thigh, fingers inching my dress up.

Heat pools in my tummy.

"You have." I swat his hand away, grinning. "But behave yourself, pervy, or you'll get no dirty tonight at all. I'm trying to drive James Bond's car here, if you don't mind." I put my best prim and proper teasing voice on.

"Yes, ma'am," he says, resting his hands back on his lap, grinning back at me.

He looks so free in this moment, and it makes my heart swell.

Tonight is going to be so much fun, I just know it. I knew bringing him here was the right thing to do.

I park the car up near the falls. Climbing out, I go straight to the boot and open it up.

I get out the picnic box and cooler that Stuart helped me get ready earlier on.

I hand the cooler to Jake, as he meets me around the back of the car.

Keeping hold of the picnic box, I grab the blanket, shut the boot, and lock up the car.

Jake follows behind me, taking the picnic box from my hand, leaving me with just my bag and the blanket to carry as I navigate our way to the shore of the falls in the darkness.

When we reach our destination, I set the blanket down and retrieve the lantern that I packed into the picnic box.

"Can I borrow your lighter, baby?"

Jake crouches beside me, handing me his lighter.

I light the candle in the lantern and set it down beside the blanket, then hand his lighter back to him.

Taking it from me, Jake pulls me to him and starts to kiss me.

He eases me back onto the blanket, his tongue roaming my mouth, meeting with mine, stroking it.

Being back here with him, kissing me in the dark like this, with only the sound of the rushing falls around us, feels amazing.

"Thank you," he murmurs.

"What for?" I push my fingers into his lovely thick hair.

"For this, bringing me here...for being you."

"You like?" I check.

"I love. We should come back here once a year. Make it our thing. It is our place, after all."

"Once a year it is."

He takes my face in his hands. "Just like this, Tru, late at night, just you and me, alone. No one around for miles."

I nod my agreement. Jake kisses me once more, lightly on the lips, then moves off me and lies down beside me, flat on his back.

Feeling content, I stare up at the night sky with its gentle smattering of stars and bright glowing moon.

Jake lets out a light sigh.

Instantly, I know his mind and mood have shifted elsewhere, and I think I know where to.

Maybe bringing him here to Lumb Falls hasn't been as effective as I had hoped.

I can almost feel his thoughts pouring out of his mind. I want to ask him what's wrong, but I know with Jake it's best to wait until he's ready to talk.

"You called my mom and asked her to come, didn't you?" He turns his head to the side, looking at me.

Truth or denial.

Denial.

I want him to believe she came off her own back.

"No." I shake my head, blinking.

"Tru…" He gives me the I-know-you-did look.

Biting my bottom lip, I release my sigh out through my nose. "How did you know?" I concede. "Did your mum tell you?"

He shakes his head no. "I just know you."

"Are you angry with me?" I screw my face up.

"No, of course not." He looks surprised.

"Are you angry with your mum?"

He presses his lips together and shakes his head.

No, he's not angry, he's disappointed, and that's worse. Way worse.

"She didn't realise how much it was affecting you, Jake. The instant I told her, she came off the phone and booked the next available flight to Manchester."

Turning away from me, he looks up at the sky. I hear him exhale.

"He tried to rape her that night." His voice is so quiet in the night air.

I turn on my side, facing him. "Your dad?"

He nods.

"He was drunk and high. He'd been out gambling, fuckin' around like normal...he'd been gone for weeks."

"I remember," I breathe.

"I liked it when he wasn't there. I always liked it best when he was off on one of his benders."

"I know." I put my hand on his chest over his heart.

"And that night he rolled home, broke, wanting money off Mom like usual. It was late, but I was still awake. We'd been watching a movie together—I can't even remember which one now, but she sent me to my room the second she heard his key go in the lock. She told me to lock myself in my bedroom and to not come out no matter what. I mean—what kid has to have a lock on their bedroom door, you know?" He laughs, but there's no humour there.

"I didn't want to leave her with him, but I did as I was told. I could hear them fighting downstairs. He wanted money, and she didn't have any to give him. Then he started beating her, like he'd done so many times before, and I could hear it and I just wanted it to stop, Tru. And I just knew this time was worse—I don't know how, I just knew." He drags his hands through his hair.

"Then I heard Mom running up the stairs, trying to get away from him. He was yelling, and I could hear her screaming out on the landing, and I just couldn't take it anymore—I just wanted to help her, I wanted him to stop hurting her. So I came out of my bedroom, and he had her there on the floor, and...she was covered in blood—her face was a mess, I barely recognised her and—" He pauses.

My heart is aching as I look at him, seeing him reliving that moment in his mind.

He turns his head and meets my eyes. "I saw the fear in her eyes, Tru. I'll never forget that look—she was terrified for me and for her. Horrified that I'd seen it—seen what he was trying to do to her. I was only nine, but I knew enough to understand what was happening. Then I just started yelling at him to stop. I tried to grab him and pull him off her. But I was nine, and he was stronger than me. He just grabbed hold of me and tossed me aside like I was a fuckin' toy—a fuckin' inconvenience. We were near the top of the stairs, and I went down the full flight."

I briefly close my eyes and feel a tear run down the side of my face, soaking into my hair.

"I don't remember much after that. I just remember hearing my mom screaming for help. Then the next thing I knew, your dad was beside me, and I could hear the sirens coming, and your dad just kept saying, over and over, 'I'm so sorry, Jake. I'm so sorry I didn't stop this from happening to you.'"

Tears are streaming down my face now.

"Afterwards at the hospital they told me I had hit my head hard from the fall. I had a concussion, had broken my arm and my jaw, and had cut my chin open, and I'd had to have stitches." His hand goes to his chin, touching his scar.

He looks so young in this moment, and I wish I knew how to fix things for him. To somehow take his pain away forever.

Jake puts his palms to his eyes for a moment. I know he's pushing back whatever emotion is in there.

I wipe my face dry with my hands.

That's the first time Jake has ever spoken to me properly about what happened that night. I knew bits and pieces, but I didn't know Paul had tried to rape Susie. That part was kept from me by my folks for obvious reasons.

Paul went to prison for what he did to Jake and Susie. Eight years he got. Eight measly years. I know, ridiculous, huh? Throw your kid down a flight of stairs and nearly kill him, beat and almost rape your wife, and here you go, we'll give you eight years in HMS's finest, with the chance of early parole.

"What did Paul die of?" I ask quietly.

I hadn't plucked up the courage to ask Jake what Paul died of in these last few days. He's been so closed off, and I didn't want to push things for him.

Whatever it was he died of, I hope he somehow suffered after what he did to Jake and Susie.

"A heart attack," Jake answers quietly. "He'd been dead for five days before anyone found him. It was a neighbour who alerted the police when they hadn't seen him for a while."

"Had you heard anything from him over the years?"

Sighing, he takes my hand in his and brings it to his mouth, kissing my knuckles.

"After he went to jail, he was clean for a while, and he was writing me, asking me to forgive him, but I never replied. Then we moved to the States with Dale, and I didn't hear anything until I was twenty-two and the band was flying high. He got in touch with me through Stuart. I don't how he got hold of his number, but he did. It took me a week before I called him back. I had all these things ready that I was going to say to him. I was going to tear him a shred—and you know what?" he snorts. "The second I heard his voice, I felt like that nine-year-old kid again. I felt so fuckin' weak in that moment, and I fuckin' blew it."

I rest up on my elbow. Looking down into his eyes, I brush his hair off his forehead. "It doesn't make you weak, baby, it makes you human."

He shakes his head. "I was weak, Tru. I didn't say a god-damn thing to him about what he'd done to me and Mom. And the worst thing was, he hadn't got in touch because he wanted to apologise for what he'd done, or to even see me—he called because he needed money."

In this moment, I hate Paul. I can feel the anger bubbling under my skin.

"Did you give him it?" I ask, chewing on the inside of my mouth.

I already know the answer, because I know Jake.

He sighs. "My lawyer sent him a nondisclosure saying that he could never talk about me or my past and what had happened. That he could never make claim to be my dad in the press or to anyone ever. If he signed he could have the money."

"Did he sign?"

He looks at me. "There was a two-hundred-thousand-dollar check sitting at the bottom of it, so yeah, he signed."

"You gave him two hundred thousand dollars?" I gasp.

"It's nothing to me, Tru. And if it meant keeping him and that part of my life away from me, then it was more than worth it. I knew the money wouldn't last him long though. He always could burn through money quick. He liked drugs...just like I do. I guess it's true what they say—the apple doesn't fall far from the tree." He rolls his eyes in on himself.

I grab his face, turning him to look at me. "You are nothing like him, Jake—*nothing*. And you never could be."

He doesn't look so sure.

"I am, Tru. I know you won't want to see it—I know you want to see the good in me, and I love you for that, more than you could ever know...but I am like him—a lot like him. I would never hurt you—I could never hurt you." He touches my face. "But the drugs and the booze...and the women." He sighs. "I'm exactly like him. My mom knows it too."

"She said that?" I gasp.

He shakes his head no. "She doesn't have to. I can see it in her eyes every time she looks at me—the disappointment, just how much I remind her of him."

"No, I don't believe that. Susie loves you. Yes, you've struggled in your past, understandably so because of what he did to you. But you're not that person anymore. You took control and you're stronger now."

His gaze softens on me. He brushes his knuckles across my cheekbone. "Because I have you back in my life."

I take hold of his hand, kissing it.

"Did you ever hear from him again?" I ask, lying back down beside him, keeping hold of his hand.

"Just before Jonny died. He'd gone through the money, like I knew he would. So I sent him four hundred grand. Thought it might keep him away for double the length of time. Then the next time I hear anything, it's from the authorities. I was listed as his next of kin. He had no one else. So it was left to me to bury him."

"Well, he's gone now, so we can leave all of that in the past where it belongs and move forward—start our life together properly."

"In LA."

"In LA." I smile. "Do you want a beer?" I ask, sitting up, letting go of his hand.

"Thought you'd never ask," he jibes, and I feel a little of my Jake returning to me.

I grab a couple of beers out of the cooler, pop the caps off, and hand him his as he sits up, facing me.

"To Lumb Falls, hot summers, and missing bikini tops." I lift my bottle and chink it against his.

"And more missing bikini tops to come." He grins at me, naughty Jake in his eyes, before taking a swig of his beer.

Resting his bottle against his thigh, he looks back over his shoulder, out at the darkened water of the falls for a long moment.

I wonder what's on his mind.

I'm just about to ask when he speaks. "I almost died last year because of the drugs." His face is still turned away from me.

My heart freezes solid in my chest. I guess tonight is the night for confessions from him.

"I drowned, and Stuart saved me," he adds.

"What? When? How?" I'm up on my knees now, putting my bottle down.

Jake turns and looks at me. His gaze is dark and torn. It's painful to see.

"It was after Japan. I know everyone thinks I went into rehab because of what happened there, but it wasn't. When I got back to LA, I was worse than ever...I was using—a lot. A few nights after I was back, I was out partying and was absolutely high off my ass. Dave took me home. He had to carry me out of the club and to the car, I was in that much of a state. He wanted to stay with me, but I told him I wanted to be alone—basically, I told him to fuck off. I shouted him out of the house. I treated him like a piece of shit that night, and he didn't deserve it. I'm lucky he stayed working for me."

I'm glad he did too, because I think Jake would struggle without him, but I don't say that.

"Stuart was out; I was alone. I passed out for a while on the sofa. When I woke, the drugs had worn off, so I took another hit of coke and sat out by the pool, drinking tequila. Then in my blind wisdom, I decided to get in the pool." He sighs. "The next thing I know, I'm puking up water, and Stuart is over me, holding me up."

"He saved my life that day, Tru. I owe him everything. He called 911, kept it out of the papers." He takes a drink of his beer. "Stuart went absolutely fuckin' nuts on me at the hospital afterwards though. I'd never seen him like that before."

"It's understandable, baby," I say softly, desperately trying to hold myself together. "If he hadn't gotten there in time…then…" I can't even say the words. I can't even bear to think how close he came, it's scaring the hell out of me.

I gulp back my threatening tears. "And that's when you went to rehab?" I ask.

He nods. "Stuart threatened to quit unless I sorted myself out. Said he'd watched me destroying myself for far too long…that losing Jonny had been hard on all of us, and he wasn't going to stay around to watch me die too."

"What did you say?"

"He's the best in the business, that's why he works for me and I couldn't afford to lose him." He shrugs. "So I agreed to go to rehab."

He's downplaying it. He loves Stuart like a brother, and he knew he was right about rehab.

"No one knows what happened that night, Tru. Not my mom or Tom, not even Denny. There's only you, Stuart, and the doctors at the hospital who know."

In this moment I despise Paul. More than I ever knew it possible to hate a dead person.

Jake struggles like he does because of him.

"You can always trust me with anything, baby." I touch his face. "I'll never judge you and I'll never break your trust, I promise you that. Just please…don't ever go back there again. Promise me that you'll never take drugs again."

He kisses the friendship bracelet on my wrist. "I promise you…so, that missing bikini top," he says, gently pushing me down to the blanket. Lying on top of me, he holds my hands above my head.

It's an obvious attempt at a subject change, and I allow it. Jake sometimes needs sex as a way to rid his mind of his demons. And if that's what he needs right now, then I'm more than happy to oblige.

"Mmm?" I reply, smiling.

"Well, if I remember right, I'm owed a reenactment and a few other things too."

"Well, it just so happens, Pervy Perverson, I have a bikini with me."

"And that's why I love you Mrs. P., 'cause you're just as pervy as I am." He smirks. "Now get your hot ass into that bikini so I can slowly take it back off you."

He climbs up off me. Taking my hands, he pulls me to my feet.

Moving away from him, with butterflies doing diving swoops in my tummy, I go to get my bikini out of my bag.

As I turn back around, I find a very naked Jake standing before me.

"Wow, that was quick." I laugh, eyes roaming his hot body.

"Well, when we're talking sex and you, baby, my clothes just disintegrate." He shrugs, grinning.

My stomach plummets off to a very happy place.

Unzipping my dress, I step out of it. Watching Jake watch me, I kick off my ballet pumps, and very slowly remove my underwear.

I'm just about to put the bikini on when Jake says in a gruff voice, "On second thought, if I remember right, you were topless that day, and you know how I hate panties on you…"

Coming close, he takes them from my hand and tosses them to the ground. He kisses me hard on the mouth. Then sliding his hand into mine, he breaks our kiss, leaving me breathless and wanting, and starts to pull me in the direction of the water.

"We're going in?" I tread carefully over the flat rocks.

"Absolutely."

"You want us to go skinny dipping?"

"Oh, most definitely." He gives me a cheeky look.

"Oh no, Jake. No way. It'll be freezing." This so was not part of my plan.

"It's a warm night," he coaxes. "The water won't be that cold."

"It will," I press.

Jake stops, turning to me. "The last time we were here, we were in the water…and tonight I want to see you…wet." His voice has gone all dark and sultry and is completely laced with inclination.

Honestly, I'm wet just listening to him, and my stomach has turned to molten lava, heating my insides.

But it's still not enough to want me to freeze to death in that cold-ass water.

"As awesome as that sounds, there is no way in hell that I'm getting in that ass-freezing water."

I step back, dropping his hand. "Let's just have sex on the nice warm blanket," I encourage.

Jake tilts his head to the side. His look is challenging, and I know exactly what's he's thinking.

"No way! Don't you dare, Jake Wethers!" I point my finger at him in warning, taking a step back.

"Noooo! Argghh!" I scream as he runs at me, grabbing hold of me.

Picking me up, he hoists me over his shoulder and carries me, kicking and screaming, into the water.

"Put me down!" I yell, laughing, wriggling in his strong arms.

Jake is laughing. Deep and loud. And I love the sound. It's been way too long since I last heard him laugh. So I keep wriggling in his arms, readying myself to take the hit of the cold water for him, to make him laugh, to make him feel happiness.

Jake's happy; so am I.

Once he's waded in to his hips, he slides me down his body, dropping me in the cold water.

"Arghhh! It's bloody freezing!" I screech as the water chills through me. "You're such an arsehole!"

"Don't be a girl." He laughs deep and throaty.

"I am a girl," I point out.

"Yeah? Well you feel like a woman to me," he says low, his hands going around my waist, pulling me close.

I can feel he's hard already. How, in this cold water? I have no clue. But I love that he is for me. Wrapping myself around his body, I hold on tight as Jake wades us farther into the water.

Once we're chest deep, I decide to take the plunge. Freeing myself from Jake, I swim out a little and immerse myself into the water, wetting my hair.

It's not too bad now I'm acclimatised to it.

As I surface, I see Jake treading water a few feet before me, staring across at me in the moonlit dark.

He's looks so beautiful, all wet, with the moon shining down on him. He looks like the star he is.

"What are you thinking about?" I ask.

"You. Then and now. How beautiful you were back then, and how even more beautiful you are now. How I wish I'd seen you through all those years, and how I'm counting myself as one lucky bastard that I got a second chance to have you in my life...and that you're crazy enough to be mine."

My heart swells in my chest, replete with love for him. I never knew it possible to love someone as much as I do Jake.

I can't ever imagine my life again without him in it, and I don't ever want to.

Jake is my everything.

I swim to him and wrap my arms around his neck. His arms go around me, holding me tight.

"I'll always be yours." I kiss his cheek, licking the cool water drops off his skin with my tongue, trailing a lead of gentle, sucking kisses to his mouth. "Back then, on that day, I wanted you to make love to me under the waterfall," I whisper against his lips, casting my glance in the falls' direction.

And without another word, I take off swimming for the falls.

Jake is hot behind me.

When we hit the cascading water, Jake takes me in his arms, kissing me like it's the first time, and he makes love to me here under the falls, like those two teenagers wanted to all those years ago.

CHAPTER TWENTY-SIX

"He's using again, isn't he?"

Stuart looks sadly across the table in the coffee shop we're in and nods his head once. "Yes, I think he is."

"You think or you're sure?"

"I'm sure," he says without hesitation.

Stuart should know. He lived with Jake, the addict, before.

"Me too." I sigh, stirring my coffee. I look down into my cup.

We're in Boston and it's two weeks into the US leg of the tour. And Jake's using drugs again.

It's become increasingly apparent over the last week.

I've never lived with an addict before, but the signs are pretty clear.

He's not sleeping. His moods are all over the place. His temper is short. He's drinking more than usual. Fidgety. I could go on.

After Lumb Falls, we went back to the hotel, happy together, and when we woke in the morning, everything was perfect.

Jake was Jake again. We spent time with his mum and my folks. We all had a wonderful few days together in Manchester.

Then one night everything changed. One phone call changed it all.

Stuart received a heads-up call from the press about a story that was going to be run the following morning. The press had found out about Paul's death. They dug a little deeper and found out he'd been in prison, and just what he went to prison for.

There was no way to stop the story, although Jake and Stuart tried.

So we left Manchester that night and flew to LA, to Jake's house.

My first stay at his place, my new home to be, wasn't exactly how I had imagined it would be.

Jake was tense and stressed. I was alone for most of the time.

When the story hit the news, I lost him. He became introverted.

I hoped things would get better once the tour started. Once he had work to focus on.

They haven't. They've got worse.

He keeps disappearing off on his own, sometimes even without Dave.

When I question him as to where he's been, he says he's just been having time out to clear his head.

Basically, he's out scoring drugs.

Jake's distanced himself from me. From everyone. He only talks to bark out orders to staff on the tour. And the only time I see him resembling something near to the Jake I know is when he's onstage performing at the shows. But the minute he's offstage, he's back to the same.

He's pushing everyone around him away, and I haven't got a clue what to do. How to help him. I feel completely out of my depth. And so very helpless.

Helpless to the fact that the man I love is slowly slipping away before my eyes.

I've considered calling his sponsor, even his drug counsellor, but I feel like I'd be crossing some arbitrary line if I do.

I just feel at a loss.

You have no idea how hard it is to try to hold on to someone when they don't want you to.

I've tried talking to him. He won't talk to me. He brushes me off, telling me there is nothing wrong.

There clearly is.

The story coming out about what he suffered at the hands of his dad that night was the final nail in the coffin for him.

He could just about cope with Paul's dying and the old memories and feelings that resurfaced for him, but this story coming out was too much.

I know he feels like he's been exposed to the world as the weak man he truly believes himself to be. It's crippled him, and the only way he knows how to deal with that emotion is to conceal it with drugs so he no longer has to feel.

The flip side of that, which he doesn't see, is that he stops loving too.

He's stopped loving me on some fundamental level.

It's still there, buried somewhere deep within him. But for now, this Jake I've got here with me doesn't love me. Not really. And it's not because he doesn't want to but because he can't.

So now it's up to me to try to find a way to bring him back.

I think he started using again around the time the tour began here in the United States. On some level I think I knew; I just didn't want to believe it.

But now it's become too hard to ignore.

He went to take a shower this morning and when he came out of the bathroom, I looked up at him and there was blood running from his nose.

That's when I knew what he'd been doing in there.

He downplayed the nosebleed. Said it was just because he was tired and stressed.

After I'd cleaned up his bleed, I went in the bathroom looking for evidence of drugs, but I couldn't find any.

He's adept at hiding his addiction. Now I just need to figure a way to out it.

"What do I do?" I ask Stuart, dropping my spoon onto the table.

"Confront him."

"Will he deny it?"

"Absolutely."

"Then what?"

"Keep trying. But, Tru, he won't recognise the problem until he's ready to—you need to know that, and be ready for the backlash that will undoubtedly come with it when you do confront him."

I put my head in my hands. "I just can't believe he's back there again." I lift my head. "This must be terrible for you, seeing him doing this to himself again...he told me what happened in LA...when you found him." I allude to the rest with my expression.

"I'm glad he told you. It shows how much he trusts you."

"Will you leave him now?"

Stuart looks at me, surprised. "No. Why do you say that?"

I knot my fingers together around the coffee cup. "Because Jake said you told him at that time if he carried on using, you would leave, and I just thought as he is again... then maybe you would leave."

I don't think Jake would cope without Stuart. Honestly, I don't think I could cope without him. I've come to rely on his friendship so much in these last few weeks.

He shakes his head, smiling. "I'd never leave him. I like the perks too much." He rolls his eyes, ironic. "Jake's like my family, just like you are now, chica." He reaches over and squeezes my hand. My eyes fill with tears. "It was just an empty threat."

"That worked," I say, blotting my eyes with a napkin.

"Yeah, but he was also ready by that point. He knew it, as much as I did."

"Is that what I should do? Threaten to leave him?"

He shrugs. Leaning back in his chair, he pushes hair off his forehead. "Anything is worth a shot, but Jake will only get clean if he truly wants to...he loves you like no one before. I see the bond you guys have, so the threat of you leaving might shock him into it. I know getting you back in his life meant everything to him. Maybe the thought of losing you again might just push him in the right direction."

"But what if..." I pause, swallowing against my own words, eyes down. I tap my fingernails on the table. "What if I threaten to leave him, and he still won't stop using?"

Stuart leans forward, closer to me. "Well, honey, before you do anything, you have to decide if that's the chance you want to take. The possibility of losing him. I don't think you would ever lose Jake permanently, but temporarily? Maybe, yes, it could happen, if he's not ready to face his problem yet."

I don't want to lose Jake. Not at all. Not even for a moment. But I don't want this version of him either.

"I already lost my Jake the moment he took his first hit." I sigh, lifting my eyes to meet Stuart's. "And if I have any hope of trying to get him back, then I'm going to have to confront this version of him, and simply go from there, no matter what happens."

The second I get back to our suite at the Ritz, I know instantly something is wrong. I can practically feel Jake's tension radiating through the air as I push open the door.

"Where the fuck have you been?" He's on me the instant I'm through the door. "Don't you answer your goddamn cell anymore?"

I sigh inwardly. Here we go again.

"Hello to you too," I bite out.

"I'm not fuckin' kidding, Tru."

"Neither am I." I give him a hard stare as I walk past him.

Getting my phone from my bag I see I have ten missed calls and five voice mails.

"I was out having coffee with Stuart," I say, putting my phone back in my bag and dropping it onto the table.

"I called him too and he didn't answer—why not?"

"I don't know, I'm not a mind reader. Maybe because he was out with me? Maybe because it's his day off? Why don't you ask him?"

I turn around to see Jake pacing the floor, anger clear on his face.

I don't know what's wrong with him right now, but it seems we are going to have to get past whatever this is before I can have the drugs talk with him.

"Baby, what's wrong?" I ask, walking towards him, hands out.

I'm trying the soft, tactical approach; it's the only way with him at the moment.

Jake can be irrational at times. Drug-taking Jake—always irrational.

"This is what's wrong." He marches away from me, leaving me dead in my tracks, and goes over to the desk. He grabs an envelope off it and marches back, shoving it in my hand.

"What's this?" I look down at it, confused.

"Open it the fuck up, and then you can answer me the very same question."

I stare across at him puzzled, then back down at the envelope.

Okay, so whatever it is has got him majorly pissed off.

Apprehensively, I peel the seal back on the envelope, reach in, and put my fingers around what feels to be photos.

Yep, it's photos.

Photos of me and Will from Callo's that last day I saw him.

One is of Will and me sitting across the table from one another; the next, Will holding my hand across the table; and the last, a photo of Will and me hugging outside of Callo's.

I look up at Jake. "Where did you get these?"

"Are you fucking him?"

I feel like he's just slapped me.

"No."

"I don't believe you."

"Believe what you want, it's the truth." I drop the photos onto the coffee table, along with the envelope. "Did you have me followed?"

"No. Do I need to?"

I glare at him.

"The press sent them," he fires at me. "They're running a story that you're having an affair with him."

I snort at the ridiculousness of it.

"You find something funny about this?" He stares at me with glassy eyes.

He's high right now. And he's also not amused.

Well guess what, Jake, neither am I.

"I'd say so, yeah." I drag my hands through my hair. "The press are about to accuse me of having an affair with Will—the man who was the one wronged because I had an affair with you. It's beyond ludicrous! We can't let this happen. We have to tell the press the truth—and I need to call Will and warn him about this."

I get my phone out of my bag, ready to make the call, but Jake lunges forward and grabs it from my hand.

"You're screwing around with him, and you're going to call him here in front of me!" he yells.

"Jake, I'm not cheating on you with Will. Barring the fact that I would never do that to you, when exactly would I do so? I'm with you all the time. And I'm also here in the US, and Will is in the UK. Seriously, please just see sense here and give me my phone back." I hold my hand out to him.

"You're not calling him, Tru."

"Give. Me. My. Phone. Back."

"No!" he yells, and throws my phone clear across the room, and all I can do is watch as it smashes to pieces against the wall.

"Have you lost your mind?" I cry, hands clutching my head. "Jesus Christ, Jake! Who is this version of you? I feel like I don't even know you anymore!"

I go over to where my broken phone lies. Crouching down, I pick up the pieces and hold them together like I can somehow repair it.

Staying there for a few moments, I take some deep breaths before speaking again.

"Whatever issue you have with Will," I state calmly, standing, putting down the remnants of my shattered phone onto the table—poor Adele. "He's done nothing wrong and it's only fair to warn him if he's about to get screwed over in the press. He's got a career to think about. Surely you can understand that."

Jake stares at me for a long moment, his chest rising and falling heavily. "I'll get my lawyers to bury the story."

"You can do that?" I feel a huge sense of relief. I don't want Will getting any more hurt than he has been, and if Jake can stop it, then all the better.

"I can do anything I want."

I hate it when he's arrogant like this.

I love sexy arrogant Jake. Not I'm-king-of-the-world-drug-taking arrogant Jake.

"So why all of this…hang on—was this some sort of damn test? The story's already buried, isn't it?" I ball my hands into fists at my sides.

Jake says nothing, just stares steadily back at me.

"Why couldn't you just talk to me properly about this instead of all the theatrics?"

His face laces with anger again. "How the hell do you think I felt seeing these photos, Tru?" He jabs a finger in the direction of them. "And then you side with him just like I knew you would!"

"Side with him? We're not in school here!" Then I pause, collecting myself, realising the yelling is getting us nowhere.

"Jake, I'm not siding with Will," I say in a calmer voice. "I know it must have been a shock for you seeing them like that, but please just try to see reason here. Those photos are not what you thought they were. And I get it, this issue you have with Will, I do, but you have to let it go now and trust me. He was the one wronged here, not us." I take a step closer to him. "I'm with you. I'll always be with you. I'm not a cheater, as ironic as that sounds. I only did what I did to Will with you because it was *you*, Jake. Because of how I feel about you. How I've always felt about you. I have loved you my whole life. You must know that. Yes, I handled it all so very badly, but I promise you, I will never hurt you like I did Will."

His eyes scan my face. "I just need to know if anything happened with Will when you saw him?"

Am I talking to myself?

"No." I'm trying to stay calm, I really am, but I'm struggling at the moment.

"Just the thought of you with him." He drags his hands through his hair, looking agonised. "When were you going to tell me that you were sleeping with him again? Were you ever going to tell me?"

Apparently, I am talking to myself.

"Argghh! Never!" I snap, my head finally popping. "Because there is nothing to tell! I saw Will on the day you flew over to London after your dad died. I'd gone into work in the morning to see Vicky before you were due to arrive. When I left the building, I bumped into Will outside. He'd seen me go in work and waited for me to leave. He just wanted to talk to me. I thought it was the least I could do after what I'd done to him. We went to Callo's for a coffee. We talked. I cried. He held my hand because I was sad that I'd hurt him. It was good of him after what I'd done. We left Callo's. He hugged me good-bye outside. And then we went our separate ways and I haven't seen or heard from him since."

Jake is staring at me, but it's like he's seeing through me. His pupils are wide and dilated, and I'm wondering if he heard a word I said.

"So why didn't you just tell me you'd seen him that day?" His voice sounds a little calmer.

I almost exhale with relief that my words are finally sinking in and this conversation is seemingly nearly over with. The downside—next I have to broach the subject of his very apparent drug use.

"Because your dad had just died, and I knew it would upset and stress you out. You don't see straight when it comes to Will, baby. I was going to tell you when things had calmed down, but then the story hit the news about your dad…what happened that night, and there's just never been a right time since."

Because you're using drugs again.

His face darkens. "So you just thought you'd keep lying to me instead?"

Here we go again. He's up and down like a goddamn yo-yo, and I am so absolutely done with his crap.

"Are you fucking kidding me? Don't you dare, Jake, don't you bloody dare." I point an angry finger at him.

"What? I've never lied to you."

"Um, no? Sorry, just when exactly was it you told me that you'd started using drugs again?"

He stares evenly at me. "I'm not using." He frowns. Then he rubs his nose.

"Sure you're not. So let me get this straight." I press my fingertips to my forehead. "It's not okay for me to hold something back—like having a coffee with Will—to try and spare your feelings at a terrible point in your life, but it is okay for you to break promises and lie to me about using drugs. Good to know how we roll, Jake," I add sarcastically.

"I'm not using drugs." He frowns again, and a little crease forms between his brows.

I lean back against the table and fold my arms across my chest. "Please don't insult me. I know."

"You don't know anything because I'm not using."

"Don't lie to me!" I cry, staring him down as I straighten up. "I want to know when it started and exactly what it is you're using."

"I'm not—"

"Don't fucking lie to me!" I yell. "I'm not stupid!"

"Yeah like I'm not stupid about what's been going on behind my back with you and Will."

I laugh. I actually laugh at his audacity. "Don't try turning this back on me, because it's not going to wash. Tell me what you're using. If you don't, I'm walking out that door and I'm never coming back." I ensure to keep my voice steady to let him know I mean it.

He lets out a light sigh. Stepping back, he leans up against the wall and pushes his hands through his hair.

"Just a bit of coke," he says evenly, shrugging.

Even though I knew, it still pains me to hear. And I feel a corner of my heart chip away.

"Oh no, Jake." I shake my head, despairing. "What were you thinking?"

"I've got it under control."

"You know, for a smart, successful guy, you are a complete bloody idiot at times!"

"Tru…"

"No, Jake, seriously, this isn't right. Where are they?" My eyes are scanning the room.

"What?"

"The drugs, Jake! Where are they?"

"There aren't any here."

"Don't lie to me!"

I start moving around the room, tossing cushions, pulling drawers out, searching the room like a woman possessed.

Where would an addict keep his drugs? Think, Tru. Think.

Then I remember him being in the bathroom this morning, and it clicks with something I saw in a film once.

I rush into the bedroom and head straight towards the ensuite bathroom. Jake is fast on his feet behind me, and that's when I know I'm heading to the right place.

I beat him there and pull the lid off the cistern. And there it is, sitting on top of a pipe.

A small bag of white powder.

Cocaine, I'm guessing.

Picking it up, holding it between my fingers, I turn to him.

His face is ashen.

My whole body is shaking with anger and fear. Fear mostly.

I hold the bag of cocaine up in front of me. "How long?"

He looks down, away from me.

"How long have you been back using? Or did you never stop? Have you been on this crap the whole time we've been back in each other's lives?"

His eyes snap up to mine. "No. When I said I was clean, I was telling you the truth."

"So when?"

"I took my first hit in Chicago."

I gasp. "The first show of the tour?" My words come out tinny and small.

Even though I had thought this to be the case, it's still just so hard to hear.

"Why?" My voice wobbles. My throat is thick with tears.

He shakes his head. "I was just on edge and…I needed something to take it off to get me through the show. It's not a big deal, Tru."

"Not a big deal? Are you being bloody serious?"

"I'm not addicted." He shakes his head.

"How many times have you used since Chicago?"

He shifts on his feet. Not meeting my eyes, he says, "Once, twice—max."

He's lying. Fear starts to spread through me like weaving spiderwebs.

"How. Many. Times?"

He sighs and leans back against the tiled wall. "Does it matter?"

"I'll take that to be every day then."

He doesn't argue the fact, so I get my answer. And my blood runs cold.

He's been high for the last two weeks straight. High when we've eaten dinner together. Watched TV together. Every time he's kissed me. Made love to me. He's had this crap in his body.

It tarnishes it all.

I feel lied to and cheated, and so very angry, and it just all suddenly bursts right out of me.

"I can't believe this, Jake! You promised me you would never get back on this crap! Back at Lumb Falls, you promised!"

"Yeah, well, things change." His voice is low and cold, and he doesn't sound like the Jake I know.

The Jake I love.

Tears are squeezing at my eyes. Feeling suddenly lost and adrift, I lower my hand, which is still holding the little bag of cocaine.

I see Jake's eyes follow it down like his life depends on it.

Disappointment, and an ache so raw, courses through me, and I fear it will tear me right open.

I'm losing the man I love to this trash in my hand, and I have no clue how to stop it from happening.

"Look, it's not a big deal," he says. His voice has changed again. It's gentle, his expression softened. "I just take a little bit to get me through the day, that's all. It's nothing for you to worry about, baby."

"You shouldn't need this crap to get you through the day at all," I whisper, my voice breaking over the words. "It's not right, Jake. You know this. You've been here before."

"I'm not addicted. I've got it under control this time."

"And that's exactly what an addict would say." I bite the inside of my cheek to stop myself from bursting into tears. "Just like the addict who pissed onstage in front of thousands of people…like the addict who nearly drowned."

His eyes narrow. His jaw is clenched. I can see it working under his skin.

I know he's trying to hold his anger in. For now.

"That was different." His voice is measured, even. "I wasn't in control then. I'm in control now—and I didn't have you then, baby." He tries to step near me, but I hold my hand up, stopping him.

"You have me now, but you're still using this crap. That doesn't stick, Jake. That's not a well-formed reason you have there. I don't think this is different from the last time at all. I think you'll end up right back where you were, floating facedown, dead, in a goddamn swimming pool, if you keep up with this!"

His gaze practically tears through me. I know that was harsh, but I need to shock some sense into him.

"I know things are hard for you at the moment. I know you've been struggling since your dad died, and the story getting out about that night—what he did to you, and I know you're under pressure with the tour and—"

"*Do you?*" he hollers at me. The level of his anger actually makes me jump out of my suddenly cold skin. "Because honestly, I don't think you have a fuckin' clue! What do you do, Tru? You write a stupid little column in a crappy fuckin' magazine! Me? I run a fuckin' music label and a band, taking care of everyone else, while simultaneously touring, so you know what? I don't think you know shit-all about the kind of pressure I'm under!"

I feel winded. I know that's not him talking, but it doesn't make it hurt any less.

"Thanks, Jake. It's good to know how I sit in your eyes."

I push past him, heading back into the living room.

He follows me.

Stopping, I turn around. I've only got my one card left to play.

"I know you're struggling, that's clear, and I know your life is pressured at the moment, but I can't put up with the drug taking." I hold the bag of crap up again, for the last time. "It's me or this."

"What?" His eyes widen with disbelief.

"You heard. You either go back to rehab and get clean, or I'm gone. I won't stick around and watch you screw your life up again." My whole body is trembling under the weight of my words.

All emotion disappears from his face, and he takes a deep breath in through his nose. "Again? Sorry, were you here the last time?"

I close my eyes tight, taking a deep breath in myself. Then I open them. "No. And why was that, Jake?" I stare hard at him. "It's me or this," I repeat, lifting the bag higher.

His jaw tenses, his eyes slip out of focus, then narrow back onto mine with a new determinedness in them. "I don't do ultimatums."

A pain hits me hard in the chest. He's made his decision. He's way more gone than I had realised.

As I blink through the agony, a tear runs from my eye. I wipe it away with my sleeve. Then I toss the bag of coke to him.

It hits his chest and drops to the floor.

"Have a wonderful life with your drugs, Jake."

I swivel on my heel, feeling more tears coming, and make to leave.

Jake grabs me from behind, pulling me back to him. "Tru, no, I don't want you to go."

"You can't have both!" I cry in his face.

"Stop acting like a child!" A sudden callous anger bleeds through his voice, and he leans his face close to mine, his fingers gripping my arm to the point of almost pain.

"Me? I'm not the one acting like a child!" I remonstrate. "I think you need to take a good long look in the mirror!"

His face contorts, and for a moment I don't recognise him.

He releases me, pushing me away. "Fuck you. I can do what the fuck I want, and if I want to shovel coke up my nose all day long, then I will—because it's my life. I got by just fine before you turned back up, interfering with your holier-than-thou attitude. I didn't need you then, and I certainly don't need you now."

I sharp in a breath, his words chilling me to my bones.

And in this moment, all I want to do is hurt him, just like he's hurting me.

"You know what, Jake? You were right—you are just exactly like your dad."

He looks like I've hit him, hard.

Then his face smoothes, his eyes fixing onto mine. "If that's the way you feel, then you know where the door is." His voice is cold, emotionless, and terrifyingly calm.

It's his ultimatum.

And I'm so hurt and angry that I can't see straight.

"It is. I can't do this with you anymore. I'm done." Lifting my chin, I turn on my heel, grab my bag, and slam my way out of the hotel room.

CHAPTER TWENTY-SEVEN

My heart is hurting deep inside my chest. I'm confused. My thoughts are all in a muddle.

And all I can see every time I close my eyes is the look on Jake's face when I said to him that he was just exactly like his Dad.

I didn't mean it.

Of course I didn't. I regretted the words the instant they left my mouth. But my pride wouldn't let me take them back.

Jake could never be like Paul. He's warm and loving, tender, and so very kind.

He's just lost at the moment, and he needs help.

But I'm not sure how to help him, or if I'm even the one who can.

Still, though, I walked out and left him at the point when he needs me most. What kind of person does that?

I know he said some shitty things, but so did I.

Honestly, my behaviour of late has left me questioning myself and my morals.

Not long ago I told Jake that I would never leave him, no matter what.

Last night I did just that. I broke my promise to him.

I kicked his ass about broken promises, and then I go and do exactly the same.

Rolling over, I look at the clock for the hundredth time in the last hour.

It's 5:30 a.m. and I'm in a cold, empty bed in a Best Western Hotel here in Boston.

I haven't slept all night. I've just lain here in the dark, watching it through to light. Running things over and over in my mind, trying to figure out what to do for best.

After I left the Ritz, I walked around the city for hours.

Knowing I couldn't go back to our hotel and having nowhere else to go and no phone to call anyone on, I checked into the first hotel in my price range I happened upon.

Once in the room, I took a shower, washing my hair with the hotel-provided shampoo. Then I dried it using the hotel hairdryer. It was small and smelt of singed hair and it took me forever to dry my hair, but I did it because I need something to focus on. Something to keep me busy.

Then I watched mindless TV for hours until I could no longer stand it.

And now, for the last four or so hours, I've had nothing to keep my mind busy, so I'm forced to think about my and Jake's fight.

What am I going to do?

I was so angry with him last night. Angry that he'd let himself get back there. Angry he'd lied about using drugs and that he'd kept it from me.

But I'm not angry anymore. Now I'm worried, and so very afraid. For him. For us.

If there is still an us left.

I just don't know what to do, what's best for him.

I wish I could talk to my dad about this, get his advice. But I don't want him to know what state Jake is in. And God, if I told my mum, she'd fly out here and carry me home kicking and screaming, I know that for sure.

I don't have Stuart's number to call him. It was in my phone, the phone that Jake broke in his little fit of rage.

And I don't want to call Simone and put all this on her. Not while she's all loved up in Denny world. Also I don't want to put her in a position where she has to lie to Denny about Jake's drug taking, if he doesn't already know himself.

I'm on my own in this one and will have to figure it out for myself.

One thing I do know is I can't stay here forever, hiding from Jake and his—our—problem.

All my things are at the Ritz, and right now I'm still in yesterday's clothes and panties. I need clean underwear if anything.

I know I have to go back, it's just…my pride is digging its pretty little heels in at the moment.

No, come on, Tru. You've been gone all night. You've left him stewing for long enough; you've made your point.

He has the show to do tonight at TD Garden. Go now and talk to him. Spend today sorting through this. Jake is too important to leave hanging for any longer.

I climb out of bed. I'm already in my clothes, so I just make a quick trip to the bathroom, and then, grabbing my bag, I leave the room.

I drop my key card in at the reception and step out onto the early morning Boston street.

There are no cabs to be seen.

Feeling frustrated, I start to walk in the direction of where I think the Ritz is.

As I walk, I see posters up for Jake's show tonight. Funny how I didn't notice them yesterday when I was still majorly pissed at him.

I stop and look up at the huge billboard, with Jake, Tom, and Denny on it, staring back down at me.

I can see it in Jake's eyes. The lost look. The one no one else sees. The look that only I can take away for him.

Suddenly, I feel such an overwhelming sense of love for him that it takes me over completely.

He's screwed up, but he's my screwed up. And I can't be without him, no matter what.

I'm so desperate to see him in this moment. I just need to get to him and right things between us.

We can get through his problem together. I can be strong enough for the both of us.

Catching sight of a cab with its light on heading towards me, I run out into the street and flag it down.

Jumping in the back, I say, panting, "The Ritz-Carlton."

The cab pulls away and I fall back against the seat, filled with nervous anxiety at seeing Jake.

When the cab pulls up outside the Ritz, I pay the fare and climb out on seriously wobbly legs.

I'm so nervous about facing him after what we said to each other.

No, this is Jake. I can do this.

Kicking my shaky legs into action, I make my way through the empty early morning lobby and straight into the waiting lift to take me up to Jake.

He'll probably be sleeping still, so I'll have to wake him because I don't want to wait any longer for us to talk this through.

I put the key card in and press the button for the twelfth floor, to take me up to the Presidential Suite, where we're staying.

The lift starts to ascend, and I stand here, hands knotted in front of me, stomach turning over, as I jig my leg on the spot. And I'm reminded of the time I was riding the lift going to do his interview, those few short months ago.

So much has happened since then.

The lift stops and the doors ping open.

I know something is wrong the second I step out onto the landing.

There are bottles of alcohol lying discarded on the floor, cigarette butts trodden into the carpet, and what looks to be a woman's top there too.

Going over to it, I bend down and pick it up. It's red, with the word "Hussy" in black on the front.

My stomach drops hollow.

I don't want to go in there. I don't want to see what's behind the door.

But I have to, I know.

Taking a deep breath in through my nose, I carefully push my key card in. I hear the little beep and the click of the lock opening, and very quietly, I push the door open.

The place is a mess, littered with bottles of booze and sleeping bodies, some clothed, some not.

The whole place absolutely reeks of sweat, booze, and cigarettes.

Jake had a party.

We had a fight. I spent the whole night worrying over him. And he had a party.

The knowledge makes me feel sick.

Obviously, my leaving him meant nothing to him at all.

Maybe he's been waiting for me to go all along. Maybe this is what he's wanted for a while now.

I guess this was the wake for the funeral of our relationship. Or celebration, depending on which way you look at it.

This is Jake. He's a rock star who parties, takes drugs, and sleeps with groupies.

He's not a relationship kind of guy. I was just foolish enough to make myself believe for a little while he was because I wanted him so badly.

Irrespective, I still need to talk to him. If just to get my stuff and get the hell out of here.

My heart is pumping hard as I dance quiet steps around the male and female sleeping bodies, no one so far that I recognise, as I look for Jake.

But he's nowhere to be seen in this huge mass of space called a living room.

I knew he wouldn't be. I was just delaying the inevitable.

He'll be in the bedroom. I'm just afraid of what I'm going to find when I go in there.

As I pass by the marble coffee table, I see the remnants of white powder on it and rolled up notes.

Anger flexes through me. That's a sure sign, as if the party wasn't enough, that Jake doesn't give a shit about me anymore.

I thought his love for me was just buried. But now I'm starting to think maybe it was never there in the first place.

Walking slowly to the bedroom, my heart beats a steady pain in my chest.

The bedroom door is closed.

Reaching out my trembling hand, I lace my fingers over the handle and take a deep breath in.

Please let him be alone in there. Please. I can just about forgive the partying and the drugs. But anything else, no.

I push down on the handle and slowly open the door.

My heart bangs hard, once, against my chest, then sinks down into my stomach.

And I look on, feeling like my world has come crashing down all around me, as I stare at the sight of Jake in bed with another woman.

He's faced away from me, but I know it's him. I'd know that tattooed body anywhere.

For a moment, I literally don't know what to do.

I'm paralysed.

The life I envisaged with Jake flashes before my eyes, then very slowly, and very painfully, slides from out of my vision.

My bag slips off my shoulder and drops to the floor with a thud.

The girl stirs, opening her heavily made-up eyes, rubbing them to panda, she focuses in on me standing here in the doorway.

She's wearing only a bra and, I'm hoping, panties under the sheets.

I feel physically sick. Sicker than I have ever felt before in my whole life.

She frowns at me, and I feel like an intruder.

Then I see what I think is a flicker of recognition in her eyes, almost like she knows me.

But I for sure as hell don't know her.

"What are you doing in here?" she asks in a not-so-nice voice.

I open my mouth, ready to ask her the very same fucking question, but nothing happens. I'm like a goddamn goldfish. The one time I need my mouth to work, and it fails on me.

Giving me a dark look, she reaches her hand over and shakes Jake.

He groans. Rolling over onto his back, he reaches his hand out and mumbles, "Tru."

I open my mouth again, but it still won't work.

I know I should be screaming, shouting, doing something, but I just can't seem to get my brain and body to function. I haven't even blinked yet.

Jake's eyes open slowly, garnering focus.

He sees the girl first. I see confusion gather on his face, then his head turns, almost as if in slow motion, and he sees me standing here in the doorway.

His expression freezes. Then he jumps up out of bed.

I don't know why, but I feel relief that he's still wearing his boxer shorts. Like that somehow makes it better, even though I've just found him in bed with another woman.

"Oh no! Nononono!" He holds his hands up, advancing around the bed, coming towards me.

The very bed we made love in two nights ago. The bed he told me he loved me in. The bed that he's just slept in, with her. Done…whatever, with her.

"No, Tru! This is not what you think!" He stops a few feet away from me.

I stare blankly across at him. I can't do anything else.

And right here and now, I know exactly how Will felt when I told him about Jake and me. At least I saved him from the actual image of it in his mind, like this is now burned into mine.

"What the fuck are you doing in here?" Jake roars at the girl, turning in her direction.

She visibly flinches. Then she scurries up out of bed, retrieving her dress from the floor, pulling it on quickly, and putting her feet in her tacky black heels.

"Tru…" Jake takes a step forward, moving closer to me.

I step back, bumping with the open door.

"I didn't have sex with her. I swear to you—tell her!" he turns on the girl again. "Tell her I didn't have sex with you!"

She looks at me, defiant. And in this moment, I see how young she actually is. Nineteen, twenty, max.

Walking towards us, passing between Jake and me, she simply smiles sweetly at me, shrugs, and walks through the open doorway.

"*No!*" Jake roars. "Tru, she's lying! I didn't have sex with her! TELL THE FUCKIN' TRUTH! TELL HER I NEVER TOUCHED YOU!"

But the girl is well out of the room, moving quickly out of the suite, avoiding Jake's wrath.

The whole place is waking from Jake's anger, and I see the place start to empty of people, leaving just me and him.

But they don't matter to me. The girl doesn't matter to me. Nothing matters anymore. Because I've just lost the one thing that did truly ever matter.

Everything now is inconsequential.

Jake's hands are in his hair, he's pacing the floor. He looks like he's in physical pain.

"I didn't even know she was in here. I swear." I'm not sure if he's talking to me or to himself right now.

I still can't seem to feel anything. It's as if the agony of seeing him in bed with her was so severe, the instant it hit my vision, my body instinctively shut down.

"I didn't sleep with her, Tru." He's standing before me again. "I swear to you. On everything I love, I swear I did not sleep with her. You have to believe me." His voice is desperate.

I drag my eyes to his, my mind still frozen, suspended in this horrific time zone he's trapped me in.

"Say something, *please*." His voice begs me.

My eyes move from him over to the messed-up sheets on the bed.

I feel a tear trickle out of the corner of my eye.

"No, Tru, no! You have to listen to me—I didn't have sex with her. I swear to you. After we fought and you left, I was so angry, but then I calmed down, and I missed you so much, and I wanted to tell you how sorry I was—that I love you—that I would do whatever you wanted me to—I'd go to rehab if it meant keeping you in my life. But I didn't know where you were—no one did, and I couldn't call you on your cell because I was a dumb fuck and I broke it. So I took the car and drove around the city for hours, looking everywhere trying to find you—but you were nowhere—and I was getting so worried, so I came back here to the hotel, and I sat in the bar facing the lobby, waiting for you to come back.

"But you didn't come. And I sat there for hours, drinking, and watching the door, waiting, and I was going out of my mind over you, and then before I knew it I was drunk, and these people had joined me in the bar. And I was hurting because you'd left, so I drank more and more, and then I took some coke, and the next thing I know, they're all back up here drinking and partying, and you still weren't back Tru...and I took more coke...and"—he rubs his swollen, glassy eyes—"I just remember coming in here, and then I must have passed out. But I wasn't with any girl—I promise you. I would never do that to you. She—she must have come in here after I'd passed out and—"

"Why?" My voice comes out broken, so I try again. "Why would she come in here?"

"I don't know!" His hands go to his head. "I don't understand any of it, but I'm telling you, I didn't have sex with her."

I hear his words, but I don't believe them. I don't believe him.

It's over.

Everything I envisioned with him, our life together, gone.

Tears start to trickle down my cheeks in quick succession, one after the other. I feel like I can't breathe, like someone is compressing my chest, taking the life right out of me.

Then Jake's grabbing hold of me, pulling me to him, crushing me to his chest, his arms tight around me, his face buried to my hair.

"I'm so sorry, baby. I'm so, so sorry," he repeats, his voice broken, as I sob silently into his chest, my tears slick against his skin. "I love you so much. I'll make this right, I promise you. I'm so sorry."

His heat is all over me. I breathe in through my nose. He smells of Jake, everything Jake.

Everything I love.

There's no trace of perfume on him, or any womanly scent of any kind, but then what does that account for anyway? I saw it clearly with my own two eyes.

Jake in bed with her.

And then that's all I can see. I can see his hands on her, just like they were on that redhead's in Paris. Touching her, kissing her, being with her like he is with me. Saying the things to her that were once reserved only for me.

And that's when the real pain hits in all its excruciating glory.

I never knew a pain like this existed. All consuming, and it's crushing me to nothing.

I need him to stop touching me. I need him to stop talking. I just want him away from me. Far, far away from me. I can't have his tainted body anywhere near me.

He's wrecked everything, forever.

I start to move in his arms, trying to free myself, but he keeps his hold tight on me.

"No!" I push myself free from him, staggering backwards.

He looks pained and afraid.

"Tru...please..." He holds his hand out to me.

And standing here, looking at him, disgusted by him, by what he's done to me—to us—I know what I have to do.

I can't live this life with him, no matter what I may have thought earlier.

I could have handled the drugs. I would have done anything to help him through it.

But not cheating. I can't work through that.

Maybe it makes me a hypocrite; I don't really care. But I just know I can't live a life tainted with his betrayal and the perpetual fear that would always be in the back of my mind that he's going to do this to me again one day soon.

And without another word, I turn from him and go to get my suitcase from the walk-in closet.

I lay it out open on the floor.

"What are you doing?" He's behind me.

"What does it look like?" I reply bitterly as I start to pull my clothes off their hangers, dropping them into my case.

"You're leaving me? You're not even going to talk to me about this—you're just going to walk away? Throw us away?"

I round on him, one of my skirts still in my hand. "I'm not the one who threw us away! We had a fight—about your goddamn drug taking! I go out to clear my head, I stay in a crappy hotel for the night, thinking things through—what the best thing to do for you is—for us—and then I come back here to talk things through with you, and I find you in bed with a...Fucking Girl! So Yes, Jake—I'm Leaving You!"

"I didn't touch her, Tru—I swear I didn't touch her!"

"I Don't Believe You!" I scream.

He steps back, looking like I've just slapped him.

I wish I had.

"You have to believe me," he says, quieter, his voice breaking. "Please, Tru. You have to."

I'm panting for breath so hard I feel like my lungs are going to explode. I clutch my hand, the one still holding the skirt, to my chest, trying to steady my breathing.

"I don't have to do a goddamn thing," I say low, wiping the still-running tears from my face with the palm of my hand.

"I can't lose you, Tru. *Please*."

He reaches for me again, but I step out of his reach.

"Get away from me!" I cry. "I don't want you near me ever again! And you don't want to lose me? Well you should have thought of that before you went on your bender with your tramp!"

I drop the skirt in the case. Then I go to the drawers and get my underwear out.

"But you said you'd move to LA. We're supposed to be living together. You promised me you would never leave me."

I laugh bitterly, finally bringing myself to look at him. And when my eyes meet with him, all I feel is anger and pain lancing straight through me.

"Yeah, well, things change," I say calmly, using his own words from last night against him. "You changed everything forever the second you let her into our bed." It hurts so very badly to say the words out loud.

"I didn't—"

"I Don't Believe You!" I scream at him again.

Pausing for a moment, with my hands on either side of the open drawer, I cling to it for support.

Then after a few silent seconds, I carry on packing my things into my case.

Jake stands here, his hands in his hair, eyes fixed on my every movement.

I just wish he'd go. I don't want him anywhere near me.

When I've got most of my clothes and can no longer stand to have him here watching me, I drag my suitcase past him and into the bedroom.

Jake follows me.

I leave my suitcase on the bedroom floor and go into the bathroom. I quickly gather my toiletries up and come back into the bedroom to find Jake standing beside my case.

Ignoring him, I dump my things in and zip it up. I don't think I've ever packed so quickly in my life.

I stand my case upright, ready to leave.

Jake moves before me. I drag my tearstained eyes up to his.

He's crying.

I watch as he rubs his tears roughly from his face with his hand. I've never seen Jake cry before. It hurts my heart so much.

"Please don't go. Just stay, talk to me, we can work this out. I know we can. I would *never* cheat on you—I swear to you. Just believe me, please. I love you so much. You're the only person I've ever loved. And I know I've screwed up with the drugs, but I would never cheat on you. You're my best friend. You're my everything." His voice is broken, just like my heart.

For a tiny moment, I feel a wobble.

I could stay, we could work this out. Maybe this pain will stop, if I stay with him. Maybe he can fix this.

No. He's had sex with another woman. It's too late.

Wordlessly, I walk away from him and go back into the closet, to get my passport from the safe.

Jake is in front of my case, blocking it when I get back.

He sees the passport in my hand, and his face breaks.

"Please don't leave me," he begs.

"Move, Jake."

"No."

"MOVE!" I try to push him out of the way, but he won't budge; it's like trying to move a wall.

He grabs hold of my arms, trying to stop me, to keep me with him.

Fighting against him, I push him away from me, hitting him in the chest as I do.

"Fine. I don't need my stuff—keep it." I walk to the bedroom door. Picking up my bag off the floor, I shove my passport into it.

"Tru, please!" Jake comes after me, grabbing my arm, pulling me back to him.

"Don't go. I can fix this—just give me a chance to make it right." His voice is desperate, broken, just like his expression.

All I can do is stare at him. There are so many words streaming through my mind, but I can't seem to grab hold of a single one to say to him.

He drops to his knees before me, holding my hands like his life depends on it.

"I'm begging you." He's crying again. "Please don't leave me. I can't live without you."

I weaken again, then I look up and see the bed, the messed-up sheets.

Jake asked that girl to tell me the truth—to tell me that they hadn't had sex.

She had nothing to lose by telling me they hadn't, and she said nothing but alluded to a lot.

And irrespective of her, I don't believe him. I know who and what Jake is. I've always known; I just wanted to see something else for a time.

Now, I believe what my eyes saw.

My trust in him is broken—gone forever—and without that, we have nothing.

I look down at his beautiful face for a long moment, taking him in one last time.

Then I let him go.

"We started on a mistake, Jake, so it makes sense that we end on one."

I yank my hands free from his, leaving him kneeling on the floor. I turn away and walk out of the room.

And out of his life.

CHAPTER TWENTY-EIGHT

I don't want you to feel forced into doing anything, my darling…it's just the publishing house is being very insistent that the last show is covered as part of the biography. They're saying they won't run the book without it."

Vicky's soft voice is relentless down the phone.

I lie back on my mum and dad's sofa, curling my legs up, tucking my feet under my bum, and stare up at the ceiling.

There's a crack in the far corner. I wonder if my dad knows it's there. I should tell him so he can fix it.

"…and I know this must be so hard for you, and honestly, I'll go with whatever you want."

There's a long pause.

Oh, she's stopped talking. That means I have to.

"It's fine, Vicky." I exhale. "When I said to you I would do it, I meant it. You don't have to worry about me."

"But I do, my darling."

"I know, and I love you for it. And for letting me work from home this last week—well, from my folks' anyway."

"You didn't have to work at all."

"I did. You've given me far too much time off as it is."

"Tru, you've just had your lovely heart broken in the worst kind of way. You need time to get yourself together."

She means publically.

It's bad enough having your heart broken by the love of your life, but when the rest of the world is feeding off that heartbreak, it makes it hurt just that bit more.

I squeeze my eyes shut, forcing back the tears I can feel threatening. "Thank you, but honestly I just need to keep busy. Working keeps me busy."

"I get that, honey. But this work we're talking about you doing now—the bio—involves...*Jake.*" She says his name like it's a swearword.

Which it kind of is to me right now. It makes me wince just hearing it out loud.

"It means you're going to have to see him again. Spend time around him."

I let out a light sigh. "I know."

And this is why you never mix business with pleasure, as I'm learning fast.

I knew getting involved with Jake while working for him was a little risky, but I ignored that small voice in my head because I figured it was Jake.

Jake, whom I've known and loved forever.

I never foresaw anything like this happening. That I would ever lose him again. So back then it didn't matter.

Now it does.

Because not only do I have to go and spend time around him again, but I have to write this damn book about him.

I really have no clue how I'm going to manage to do it after everything that has happened between us.

I'm trying to look on the cleansing side of it. Thinking that writing about Jake will be therapeutic. A way of getting him out of my system and letting him go for good.

Well that's what I'm trying to tell myself.

The publishing house is pushing for the book because I'm the one who has been cheated on by Jake, and they're relishing the thought of a book written about Jake Wethers by the woman he betrayed.

Hence the push to get me back to the show and back to him.

I'm also not stupid. I know Jake is ultimately behind this; this is his way of trying to force me to talk to him, to see him.

The publishing house has been onto Vicky, saying the last show of the tour, which is in New York in two days, has to be covered for the book. And if I don't attend and cover it, they will pull the exclusive from the magazine, and the book will be dropped.

That's all Jake.

He's got the publishing house doing his dirty work for him, pulling the strings, making it appear it's them forcing this, not him. But I know it's him.

Jake's very adept at getting people to do want he wants. I know that all too well.

And, it appears, he's once again going to get me to do what he wants.

I hate that I can't fight him on this. I want to. More than I can explain. I want to dig my heels in and say I won't do it, but I can't risk this for Vicky. The magazine is everything to her. And she means so much to me. She's one of my closest friends, and I won't let her down.

I haven't seen or spoken to Jake since I left five days ago.

When I left the hotel room and him, I got the next available flight out to Manchester and came straight home to my mum and dad's instead of going to London. I just wanted to hide.

Jake found me anyway.

I was being stupid. Of course Jake would know if I wasn't in London, there would be only one other place I'd go.

In hindsight, I should have checked into a hotel, but I was hurting and I just wanted my daddy and mama.

Jake was calling my folks' house pretty much on the hour, every hour, for the first day. My dad spoke to him. I refused to. I don't know what was said.

I don't want to know.

Oh, actually that's a lie, I know one thing. I overheard my dad telling my mum that Jake was going to walk out on the tour. That he was going to fly here to see me. Like he thinks he can just turn up here and I'd see him—not bloody likely—but my dad talked him down.

He said he would work on getting me to speak to Jake.

He's had no luck so far.

Jake sends flowers every day. I bin them. He sends letters. I tear them up without reading.

I don't want to know a thing from him or about him.

But then it's pretty hard going, being who Jake is, and the fact that our relationship, or once-was relationship, is current tabloid fodder for the dailies, thanks to his trampy little slut.

So now I can't even go online or watch the TV for fear of seeing something new about us in the news.

The girl I found in Jake's bed, Kaitlyn Poole is her name—I hate her, just getting that in there—sold her story to a US tabloid, and now it is worldwide news.

She's claiming that she and Jake have been having an affair the whole time he's been with me, and the press are lapping it right up.

Do I believe that?

Right now I'm struggling to consider anything about the situation as a whole, because I can't get my mind past the image of him in bed with her.

Kaitlyn "Bitch," as I refer to her, has pictures of Jake in bed from that night. They weren't clear pictures, kind of dark, taken with a camera phone I'm guessing. And he looked sort of asleep in them. Well, his eyes were closed. But that doesn't mean anything. My eyes are closed in tons of pictures because I always blink when the flash goes off.

But the point is, she was lying next to him in bed. Her face beside his—in bed.

Her in bed with Jake. That's all I need to know, to tell me everything I already knew.

Also there is one of her sitting on Jake's lap in what is apparently the hotel bar. You know the one he sat pining over me in, waiting for me in after our fight; yeah, that bar.

So details of my life, the life I shared with Jake, and his betrayal have been splashed all over the news for the world to see.

My pain is up for public consumption. And it's the worst kind of torture.

I'm not a public person. Of course I knew what being with Jake entailed, I just never foresaw this. And now I know, with absolute certainty, I'm not cut out for the type of life he leads. His life belongs to the whole world. I don't want that for myself.

Maybe Kaitlyn Bitch did me a favour. Because at least I now know what life with Jake really consists of. It's best I get out now, early on, before I got in too deep.

That's what I'm telling myself, anyway. My heart is telling me I was already in way too deep to begin with.

So for five days I've been hiding at my folks', letting my dad deal with the press at the door and on the phone, and the paps hanging around outside waiting to get a picture of me.

I hate to bring it to their doorstep, but I just couldn't go back to my flat—that would have meant dealing with it alone. I know I have Simone there, but it wouldn't have been fair to pull her into this, especially not when she's with Denny. That already ties her up in it enough as it is.

So I'm letting my dad kick paparazzi butt while I hide in the house, working on my column to keep busy.

My mum and dad have been great these last five days. I couldn't have coped without them, well not that I'm actually coping in any way…more coasting.

My mum has even managed to refrain from an "I told you so" about Jake, and my dad…well, he hasn't said it outright to me, but I think he believes Jake is telling the truth about Kaitlyn Bitch. And my dad thinking that Jake is telling the truth makes me wobble a little, if I'm being totally honest.

But what's making me falter just that little bit more is the whole "they've been having an affair" story. Because honestly, a story is what I believe that to be.

She's lied for sure about some of the times she said she was with Jake. They just aren't possible, because he was with me.

One of them was when everyone still thought Jake was in LA, but he wasn't, he was in London with me. It was straight after his dad died, and he got the jet over here to be with me. Because he needed me.

Kaitlyn Bitch is claiming to the press they spent the night together in a hotel in LA, that he flew her in. She even has her friend backing her up, saying she was with Kaitlyn Bitch when he called.

I could go public and out it as a lie, but I don't want to be pulled into the press any more than I am being, and really, what's the point? Ultimately it doesn't erase the fact that I caught him in bed with her. So whether they were having a full-blown affair or it was just a one-nighter that she's embellishing for the press, it's irrelevant.

He betrayed me.

Apparently, Jake is suing the paper that ran the story, the one that bought the rights to it.

Simone told me. Denny told her.

Really I don't care what Jake does.

I'm done with it all. I'm done with him.

I just want to get his little game called New York over and done with, so I can move on with my life.

"I can do this, Vicky," I assure her, not really sure if I'm trying to convince her or myself. "I'll be fine. I'm done with Jake. I'll go to New York, cover the show, then come straight home, and I'll finally be free of it all."

Free of him. Well, once the bio's done that is.

"Do you want me to come with you? Moral support, and also I can kick his ass for you if you want."

I smile at the sentiment. "Thanks for the offer, but if anyone were to be kicking Jake's ass, it'd be me. You've got enough on at the magazine at the moment. I'll be fine. Just in and out for the show. I'll arrange my flights so I'm there for a day, max. Do my job, and then straight back home."

I hear her exhale down the line. "I don't think it's going to be that easy, sweetheart. This is Jake we're talking about."

"I know. But I've had time away from him, and I'm feeling stronger now. I'm not going back to him, no matter what games he plays. I'll do my job, and then he's out of my life for good."

"As long as you know what you're doing."

"I do."

"Tru…look, this is just me playing devil's advocate here, as your friend…but have you considered the possibility that maybe Jake is telling the truth? I know you found him in bed with that trampy girl, but he's been so adamant about it, and her selling her story to the press about the whole torrid affair thing, and him suing them all, big guns, it just makes you think a little, you know?"

"I've considered it," I concede.

Minutes ago, in fact. And every other single minute of the day before that.

"But I just…" I sigh, rubbing my face. "I just don't know anything anymore, Vicky, except for the fact that I found him in bed with her."

I can't shut my eyes without fear of seeing it on playback.

"But sometimes the picture doesn't show the true facts, you know." I can mentally feel her nudging me. "Maybe you should talk to him. Listen to what he has to say. He's obviously desperate to see you, my darling, and he's struggling, that's plain for everyone to see."

Jake wasn't going to do the show at TD Garden after I left him, but somehow the guys got him onstage.

I haven't seen the show, this is all what I'm hearing from Simone when I've talked to her on the phone, not that I asked for any details, but she felt the need to share, and she's getting her feed direct from Denny, so I'm taking it as read.

But from what Simone said, Jake literally went onstage, sang straight through, number after number, no Jake banter, no nothing. He finished the set, walked offstage, giving no encore, and got Dave to take him straight back to the hotel. That's pretty much how the last few shows since have been as well.

And the worst thing about it is some of his fans are blaming his behaviour on me for leaving him. Can you fucking believe it! Some are blaming the skank I found in his bed too. But even so, it's just more crap to add to the pile. Another sharp prod to remind me of why I could never be with Jake again.

Also, Simone told me Jake's clean.

She said he hasn't used since I left. Apparently he got in touch with his sponsor. He isn't going back to rehab; he's doing it with the support of his sponsor and drug counsellors, so at least one good thing has come out of this whole continuing nightmare.

I'm glad he's clean. More than glad, I'm relieved. I might be pissed at Jake, but I don't want him hurting himself on that rubbish.

"Honestly, talking to Jake about any of it is the last thing I want to do right now," I say to Vicky. "The extent of my vocab with him will be about the tour and nothing more. I just want to go to New York, cover the show, and then come back to London and get straight back to work. I just need to get back to normal, you know?"

"I do, and I'll support you however I can."

"Thank you."

"Okay, so let's get this New York ball rolling. The quicker it's done, the quicker you're out—right? So do you want me to call Stuart and let him know you're going, or do you want to call him?"

"I'll call him," I reply without hesitation.

I haven't spoken to Stuart since I left. I miss him tons.

"Do you have his number there, Vicky?" I don't have anyone's numbers. They were all stored on my phone. The phone Jake broke.

I haven't got a replacement yet. There hasn't been an opportunity to do so, and there's no real point in having one at the moment. I'd only get calls I don't want to receive. I do miss hearing Adele though.

Vicky gives me Stuart's number, and I hang up from her.

I feel nervous calling Stuart. Calling him is the closest thing to calling Jake.

"Stuart Benson." His lovely, warm voice comes down the line and I feel my lip instantly wobble.

"Stuart, hi, it's Tru."

"Oh…um…hi."

Okay, so that's not the response I was hoping for. I guess he hasn't missed me like I've missed him. And there was me thinking we were good friends. I'm so crap at judging people.

"I was just calling to, uh…let you know that I'll be coming to cover the show in New York."

Silence.

Is he mad at me or something?

"That's great," he finally says.

445

He doesn't sound like he thinks it's great.

"Stuart, is everything okay? Are you angry with me or something?"

"No, of course not, gorgeous." Well that sounded the most Stuart-like sentence I've heard this whole phone conversation.

"It's just *something*," he adds, emphasising the "something," and my brain clicks in.

"Jake's there with you, isn't he?"

"Yes, I'm in the car, with—something—and I figured, you wouldn't want—you know."

"Who the fuck are you being so cryptic with?" I hear Jake's voice loud and clear in the background.

My heart starts to hurt just hearing his voice.

Oh God. I miss him so much.

No I don't. I hate him.

I think.

I don't know.

Crap.

Look at me. I hear his voice, and my head turns to mush. How the hell am I going to manage going to New York and seeing him for a whole day?

No, I'll be fine. I can do it for Vicky and the magazine. That's all that matters.

"I'm talking with my boyfriend," Stuart says to him. "Mind your own fuckin' business."

"Since when have you got a boyfriend?" I can almost hear the pause and Jake's mind working, and I just know what's coming next. "Is that Tru on the phone?"

My heart stops dead in my chest.

"No," Stuart says to him. "I'm gonna have to go, lover," he says down the line to me, "my ass of a boss won't let me—Jesus Christ, Jake! What the hell do you think you're doing?" I hear the tussle, and Stuart's voice fading away, as Jake wrestles the phone from off him.

Any second now I'm going to hear his voice.

I want to hang up. No, I don't.

My hand is clamped around the phone, suddenly slick with sweat.

"Tru, is that you?" Jake's deep voice comes breathy down the line.

My chest tightens. I can't speak.

"It is you, isn't it? That's why you're not saying anything."

I take a deep breath and exhale. "Yes."

"Tru, oh God, baby, I miss you so much." His words come out in a flurry, and I can hear the relief in his voice. "Please let me see you. I need to talk to you. I'm so sorry for everything. Please just let me see you." His voice starts to break down the line.

Tears fill my eyes.

I force them back with blinks, and then I steel myself to speak. "I'm coming to New York in a few days to cover the show."

"You are? Oh, thank God. Thank you, baby. You won't regret this, we can talk and sort all of this out and—"

"No, Jake. We're not sorting anything out, because there's nothing to sort out. I'm coming to cover the show because you're forcing me to. Anything else, you and I, we're done. For good. There's nothing to discuss."

"Tru, no, please."

My heart feels so heavy in my chest, it's practically labouring into my stomach.

I force a strength which I don't own right now, and maybe never will again, and taking a deep breath, I say,

"You think I don't know what you're doing, forcing me to come to New York like this so you can try and feed me your bullshit lies? Using Vicky and the magazine to get to me. It's low, Jake, even for you. And if you thought for one moment this would give you the chance to fix things, somehow make me care for you again, then you're sadly mistaken. All you are doing is making it easier for me to hate you more than I already do." Another deep breath. "Please ask Stuart to e-mail the flight and accommodation details to me. Good-bye, Jake."

"Tru, no! Wait! You've got it all wrong! Just talk to me, hear me out on this, *please.*"

I still for a minute.

I'm wobbling again. I close my eyes and see the image of him in bed with her.

"No."

I hang the phone up on him.

Dropping it to the floor, I start sobbing into my hands.

We land at JFK at 10:00 p.m. Simone is with me. I was going to come alone, as I'm only doing a short stopover. But Simone didn't want me to come alone. She was insistent. And she said she was going to come and see Denny soon anyway, so she was killing two birds.

Dave's in the airport waiting for us.

"Hey, Tru." He smiles down at me.

"Hi, Dave." I reach up on my tiptoes and kiss his cheek.

He looks at me surprised, and I see a little flush rise in his cheeks.

"I've missed you," I say to him. It's true, I have. I've missed all of them.

"Well, we've all missed you here too." I get the distinct impression he's referring to Jake in that sentiment.

"Hi, Simone," he says, taking both our cases from us. "The car's just up front."

Threading my arm through Simone's, we follow Dave out to the car.

Denny is in the car waiting for us—well Simone, not me, obviously. And she's a little more than overjoyed to see him.

It makes me hurt.

I'm happy for her of course, but it just reminds me of the time I landed in Stockholm and Jake was waiting in the car for me. The day we swapped our friendship bracelets.

I touch it on my wrist. I haven't been able to take it off yet. I'm still wearing the Tiffany necklace too.

I will take them both off, soon, I'm just not ready to yet.

A little part of me wondered if Jake would be waiting in the car for me, and I hate that I felt such a strong smart of disappointment that he wasn't.

He hasn't tried to make any form of contact with me in the last few days. No flowers. No letters. He's been completely quiet.

Maybe he's finally got the message after I told him on the phone.

Good, I'm glad.

I think.

Crap.

I sit up front with Dave on the ride to the hotel, to give the lovebirds a little time to themselves in the back, and I chat with him about everything from the weather to sports, making sure to avoid any conversation that could lead to Jake.

We're staying at the Mandarin Oriental. Dave parks up in the hotel car park and insists on taking my case up to my suite for me. Denny's all set with Simone's. He's so sweet to her.

Denny and Simone are staying on the fifty-second floor, so they get out of the lift first. I'm on the fifty-third.

Simone hugs me good-bye as she's getting out of the lift.

"Will you be okay?" she says into my ear. "I can stay with you if you want."

"Don't be silly, I'll be fine," I say, releasing myself from her embrace. "Go have fun with Denny and I'll see you tomorrow."

"You're sure?"

"I'm sure."

She reluctantly backs out of the lift. "You know where I am if you need me."

"I do, now go…'night, Denny." I smile at him.

"See you later, Tru."

Dave lets go of the hold button, and I wave to Simone as the doors close.

We go up one more floor, and then we're at mine.

Dave wheels my case along the hall for me.

"This is you," he says, stopping outside the double door marked Presidential Suite.

What the hell?

He puts the key card in and pushes open one of the doors for me.

"I'm staying in here?" I give him a confused look.

Dave nods and hands me the key card.

"Alone?"

"Yes, Tru." He chuckles.

I know I've stayed in these kinds of suites before, but the Presidential Suite is generally the best suite the hotel has to offer. It's always the one Jake stays in.

"But...this is too much for just me," I mumble, poking my head in through the door.

I gasp.

It's bloody massive. Bigger than any I've ever stayed in with Jake before.

I look back at Dave, wide-eyed.

He shrugs, smiling. "Stuart books the rooms."

On Jake's orders.

"I'll have to thank him, a lot," I mutter, taking my case from Dave. "Thanks for picking me up from the airport." I smile up at him.

"My pleasure."

"So I guess I'll see you tomorrow."

"You will." He smiles. "Good night, Tru."

"'Night," I reply.

Dave backs up and starts to walk down the hall, then he stops a few feet away and turns to look at me.

"I know it's not my place, and I don't mean to speak out of turn, but for what it's worth, I don't believe what that girl's claiming. I've worked for Jake for a long time and I've seen a lot, and I also have a knack for knowing when people are lying—something I learned in my years as a marine. And in my opinion, Jake's telling the truth." He presses his lips together, giving me one last small smile, then turns and walks away.

I close the door behind me and lean up against it.

Everyone believes Jake. I think even Simone does, to be quite honest, but she hasn't said. So it seems it is only me who doesn't believe him. But then I was the one who found him in bed with her.

And Dave was a marine? How did I not know that?

But still, don't digress and don't waver, Tru. Trust your own judgement. You know what you saw.

Jake's a womaniser. Everyone knows that. It's who he is, so why in the world would he ever change for you?

Pulling my case through the suite, I park it up in the humongous bedroom, and that's when I see a light blue gift box sitting on the equally humongous bed.

Jake.

I go over and sit on the edge of the bed beside it. Tentatively I lift the lid off the box.

Inside is a brand new iPhone. There's also a little card in the box. I open it and read:

This is to replace the one I broke. It's registered to your old number. I set it up for you with your ringtone.
J. x

With trembling fingers I pick up the phone, dropping the card back into the box.

I can't believe he bought me a brand-new iPhone—no, actually I can, this is Jake we're talking about.

Well, I'm not keeping it. He can't buy me back with fancy gadgets.

It is pretty though.

I might just turn it on, see what it's like, you know, in case I decide to buy myself one after I've given him this one back.

I switch it on and the screen lights up. I wait while it loads.

The screen saver comes into focus behind the icons. It's a picture of Lumb Falls.

Tears instantly fill my eyes from the barrage of memories it brings.

Is he trying to hurt me?

I press the music icon, ridding the picture from the screen, and see just one song sitting in there. Adele. My ringtone.

Selecting the song to play, I sit and listen as Adele starts to sing, a capella, from my phone.

I've never heard this version before. I wonder where he got it?

Over Adele's singing, I hear a light knock on the main door.

It's probably Simone coming to check on me. She's such a worrier.

I wander from the bedroom, phone in hand with Adele still singing, through the living room, and I swing the door open.

Jake.

My heart stops.

He looks beautiful, so very beautiful. He's unshaven, his eyes dark, tired, but he is still so absolutely, breathtakingly beautiful.

It makes my chest hurt.

His scent permeates the air. His special Jake scent. My insides start to ache, and my fingers itch with absolute desperation to touch him.

All of my anger towards him dissipates. All the things I wanted to say, thought I would say, to him—gone.

I'm rendered powerless by his presence.

I clutch my hand around the still-singing phone.

"You got it." He looks down at the phone in my hand.

My eyes follow his. "I—I did. Yes, thank you—you didn't have to buy me this though."

"Yes, I did." He looks up, straight into my eyes.

My legs start to tremble.

"You like the song?" he asks, blinking me free.

"Yes, thank you. It's amazing. I love it."

"She'll be happy to hear that."

I'm confused and a little suspicious. "Where did you get the song?"

He pushes his hand through his hair and hangs it off the back of his neck; I see the muscles in his arms tense. It makes me want to touch him even more.

"It's yours. She recorded it to the phone as a favour for me."

"She did?"

"Yes."

"Oh."

Holy fuck. He got me my very own a capella recorded ringtone. I am the only person in the world to have this version.

I have my very own special ringtone because of him.

What was left of my heart has just been crushed to smithereens. I can feel tears thickening my throat.

He makes it so hard for me to hate him when he does ridiculously lovely shit like this for me.

No, don't weaken. It's just all part of his plan to trick his way back into my life.

He had sex with another woman.

I think.

I don't know.

Fuck.

"Thank you," I mumble.

We stare at one another for a long moment. Adele stops singing in my hand, breaking it.

"Did you want something or…?" I pull nervously on the hem of my T-shirt, looking down away from his heavy stare.

"Oh yeah, I, uh…I brought your things." He pulls a suitcase out just from behind the wall.

My suitcase. The one I left in Boston. He's kept it with him this whole time.

To be honest I hadn't really thought about what he'd done with it.

"Thank you," I say, taking it from him. My fingers graze his in the exchange.

Heat sears painfully up my arm, coursing through my body, careening straight for my heart.

I wheel the case in, parking it up by the side of the door, desperately trying to control my feelings.

"So…um." He brushes his hand through his hair again. "Do you need anything or…?"

"No, I'm fine. Thank you."

This is so hard. There's no witty Jake banter. The ease that has always been between us is gone. It's almost like we're strangers. He's not my Jake anymore, and it hurts beyond words.

"Okay." He steps back. "So…I guess I'll see you—tomorrow."

He's leaving. A sinking feeling encompasses me. I don't want him to go.

Yes, I do.

Composing myself, I say, "Good night, Jake."

"Good night, Trudy Bennett." He smiles at me ruefully.

As I start to close the door, he speaks again. "Tru?"

I open the door back up.

"It's really good to see you again. You look...well."

"Thanks." I force a painful smile. "You too."

I close the door, shutting him out.

Leaning up against it, catching the breath I didn't know I was holding, I slide down, sinking to the floor, under the weight of the grief that is crushing me.

This is so much harder than I could have ever thought.

Taking a deep breath, I attempt to steady my emotions.

It's just one day, Tru, that's all. Get through tomorrow and the show, then your flight is booked for straight afterwards, and you're home free.

Or am I? Will I ever truly be free of Jake when he's already worked so deeply into my heart?

Adele starts to sing in my hand. Lifting it up, I see I have a text.

Jake:

When I said you looked well, what I really should have said was that you look beautiful. x

And there's my Jake.

Unstoppable tears trickle from my eyes as I start to drown in memories of him. The feel of his skin against mine, his kiss, the way he made love to me.

I don't think I can do this. It's too hard being around him.

No, I can, it's just twenty-four hours. Twenty-four tiny hours to get through.

But even as I think it, fighting my internal battle, I don't feel so sure anymore. And then my tears turn into full-on sobs, and I keep crying until all I'm left with is dry heaves racking my body senseless.

CHAPTER TWENTY-NINE

After Jake left last night, and I'd cried myself into a dried-out, puffy-eyed state, I immersed myself in the humongous bathtub, staying in until the water went cold, thinking about Jake and what I was going to do.

After coming to no conclusion, leaving me exactly where I was before, I raided the minibar. I had a couple of glasses of wine in the hope they would help me sleep, and I climbed into the ginormous bed.

The wine didn't help me sleep as I had hoped, because sleeping in a bed like this without Jake just felt wrong. Empty and so very lonely.

It just made me miss him even more than I already do.

All I could think was that he was here in the hotel somewhere. Somewhere close. And knowing I could pick up my phone and call him and I would be lying in his arms within minutes made it all the more hard.

The anger I'd been so desperately clinging to skipped out on me, leaving me with raw emotion.

I knew seeing Jake again would be hard, but I underestimated just how hard.

Seeing him there exposed me to my feelings in a blast, the ones I've been so desperately trying to hide from this last week. I was forced to feel the complete and utter intensity of them, and it's been bleeding the hell out of me ever since.

So after spending the night listening to Cyndi Lauper's "Time After Time" on loop on my new iPhone, crying along with the lyrics, I finally cried myself to sleep for a few hours. And now I find myself at 6:00 a.m. sitting at a table in the hotel restaurant, drinking coffee just for the want of something to do.

I look a puffy-eyed, tired mess, but I don't care.

As it's so early, breakfast has only just started to be served, so I'm alone in here with only the waiting staff for company. Exactly as I want it.

I nabbed a newspaper on the way in to read to keep my mind occupied. It's the *New York Times*, and I'm reading the business pages avoiding anything remotely entertainment-wise in case there is something about Jake in here.

Scanning my eyes over the text about the ever-rising price of gasoline, I feel a presence beside me. Looking up I expect to see the waiter, but it's Jake.

My heart jumps up in my chest, straight out of my mouth, and bolts for the door.

"Hi," he says. His voice sounds rough and smooth like only his can. "You mind if I join you?"

He smells strongly of cigarettes. He must have literally just had a smoke.

Swallowing my heart back down, I utter, "Um, no, of course not."

Jake takes the seat opposite me at the table, and I'm struggling to keep my eyes off him.

He looks like he hasn't had much sleep. His normally light eyes look dark, and his hair has that ruffled up look it gets when he's worried about something and has been driving his fingers repeatedly through it.

It makes me want to reach my hand out and smooth it down and soothe him.

I press my palms flat to the table.

"Have you already ordered?" he indicates my half-drunk coffee.

"Only the coffee."

"Are you eating?"

I shake my head no in response, resting my eyes back on the newspaper.

"You look like you've lost weight."

My eyes snap up to his. "Are you saying I was fat before?"

Here she is, Tru who wants to pick a fight with Jake. I was wondering when she'd show up. Apparently, at 6:00 a.m. in a hotel restaurant.

"No, of course not." He shakes his head, looking helpless. "I was just…trying to make conversation, I guess…" He trails off.

"Well, don't."

"You don't want to talk?"

"No."

My eyes go back to the paper, desperately trying to focus on the text, but now all I can feel is my anger and rage heating in my blood, bubbling up, and I just want to yell at him.

"Do you want me to leave?" he asks in a soft voice, tracing his fingertip over the tablecloth.

And that's all he has to say and I'm over the edge.

"Does it matter what I want?" I hurl at him.

His brow furrows. "Of course it does."

"No it doesn't! If it did, then I wouldn't be here right now having this conversation with you. I'd be home, getting on with my life."

"Tru…" He reaches his hand across the table, trying to take mine, but I snatch it away before he gets the chance.

"Why are you here?" I give him the coldest look I can muster up. "Did you just come down here to torture me some more—more than you already have?"

"Torture you?" He looks seriously pissed off at that statement.

"Yes!" I bang my hands on the table. "Torturing me, forcing me to be around you after what you did!"

"I didn't—"

"I don't want to hear it!" I cry, getting to my feet.

My heart is pumping so fast, so hard, and blood is roaring in my ears. I start to walk away from the table, and him.

"WILL YOU JUST STOP AND FUCKIN' LISTEN TO ME!" he roars, standing so abruptly that his chair falls out behind him, banging to the floor.

I blanch.

His voice is so all-consuming that everything in the room stops moving.

Me. Time. Air. Everything.

Jake's chest is pumping up and down angrily, his T-shirt rising and falling with each breath.

I don't think I've ever seen him so angry.

Momentarily stunned, I falter, but then I very quickly come back to life.

Turning on the spot, I state, "No, I won't bloody stop and listen to you because I'm not interested in a damn thing you have to say!" I curse the betrayal my voice does when it quivers slightly.

"Jesus fuckin' Christ, woman!" he growls. "You're so stubborn! And you will listen to me if I have to tie you to that fuckin' chair to do so!" He jabs a finger in the direction of the seat my ass just graced moments ago. "And I will keep on saying this until you hear me—I *did not* have sex with that girl, and I most certainly did not have an affair with her! I fuckin' love you, Tru! More than life itself! I would never do that to you! Now are you hearing any of this yet?!" He lifts his hands to his head in frustration. "Is any of this getting through to your stubborn-ass brain?"

He looks so angry and frustrated and lost.

But then so am I.

I fold my arms across my chest. "Words, Jake. That's all they are. I believe in facts, statistics, and logic." I'm throwing words at him, trying to confuse him, or maybe me, I'm not sure. All I do know is right now I sound like Vicky.

"What?" he seethes, jaw clenched, brow furrowed.

"I believe what I saw!"

"No, you believe what you think you saw!"

"Are you telling me I didn't walk in on you in bed with her?"

"No, I just—"

"So then I saw right."

"No!"

"Yes!" I wrap my hand around my ponytail, tugging on it hard, like the ache of that will take all of my anger and frustrations away.

"Nothing you can say or do will change my mind on this," I continue in a low, firm tone. "I believe what I saw. Now if you're quite done, I'm going back to my room."

I step back, but he stops me with his words.

"I'm not done." He sounds so authoritative, so angry, that I pale, and I literally can't move.

He stalks around the table, coming close to me. His anger is radiating, and it makes me want to step back, but I fight the urge.

"I won't give up until you believe me, Tru," he says low, leaning into my face. "I won't stop fighting for you—for us. I want you back and I will keep on trying, with whatever methods I can, until you believe that I'm telling you the truth—that you forgive me for letting you down with the drugs, and that I have you back in my life again."

Giving me one last determined stare, he turns abruptly and stalks out of the restaurant, leaving me trembling to the core and alone with the stares of the waiting staff who were just witness to our fight.

Wrapping my arms around my chest, my face burning, I bite back tears, and on unsteady feet I quickly leave the restaurant, heading straight for my room.

I'm shopping in Macy's with Simone. Well, Simone's shopping, and I'm just trailing around behind her.

She found out about my fight with Jake and ordered that we were going out shopping this afternoon.

Even though I wasn't in the mood, and would have been quite happy to hide in my suite until I had to show my face at the show tonight, I could tell Simone meant business. I'd pretty much lost any fight I had in me earlier from my fight with Jake, so I yielded.

I'm still reeling from it, to be honest.

He's not going to let me go. He's never going to give up on us.

Yeah, well good luck with that, buddy, because the more you push, the further I'm going to pull away.

I think.

I don't know.

Crap.

Jake has this innate way of being able to pull and tie up my strings like no one before, and when I'm around him I just seem to lose all sense and focus. And maybe a teeny, tiny part of me wants to go back. But a bigger part of me—the humiliated, betrayed part of me—doesn't.

And for now, humiliated Tru is in control.

Simone is loaded up with clothes she potentially wants to buy. I'm so far gone into my own wallowing I can't even begin to appreciate the pretty things surrounding me.

"I'm going to try this stuff on. Keep me company?" Simone asks.

"Sure." It's not like I've got anything better to do.

I follow Simone into the empty changing rooms and take a seat while she goes into the cubical to try clothes on.

"What do you think?" she asks, coming out of the cubicle in a beautiful fuchsia pink Miss Sixty dress a few minutes later.

My pretty-dress-spidey-sense finally shows up, and I'm instantly in love.

It's sleeveless, has a high, studded belt, a low hem, and a scoop neck, with a raw-edged detail across the chest.

"It's gorgeous," I murmur, wishing I'd been paying attention before now, as I would have picked it up for myself. At least I know Simone will lend it to me if I want to wear it. Not that I feel like going out much nowadays.

"I'd team it with those patent blue heels you've got there." I nod in the direction of the pretty high-heeled shoes sitting on the floor.

"You think?" She pushes her brows together. "I brought them in to try on with the black dress."

"Trust me," I say. "Put them on and you'll see."

Shrugging, she slips her feet into the insanely high heels and looks at herself in the mirror.

"Wow! You're right." She grins. "They do work together. Only problem is this outfit is on the wrong girl. No way could I pull this off, I'm too pale. This has you written all over it."

"Nah, it suits you just right."

"Try it on," she encourages.

Even though I love the outfit, I'm just not in the mood to play dress up. I can't get my mood past Jake.

"I'm not in the mood to try clothes on." I start to chew on my thumbnail.

"So don't try, just buy. We're about the same size," she says, assessing herself in the mirror again.

I snort. It's not the most attractive sound.

"We are!" She sounds defensive.

"Yeah, except for that my ass is about ten times as big as yours is."

"No it's not." She gives me a disapproving look. "I guarantee this dress will fit you, so I'm telling you that you are getting this dress and shoes if I have to pay for them myself. And you're wearing them to the show tonight as well."

"Like hell I am!" I say, my head snapping up. "I'm going to the show in my jeans and a T-shirt, comfortable flight clothes. I'm catching my flight straight after, remember?"

"You can change at the airport. You are going to that show looking your best, Tru."

"I'm not going to party, I'm working."

"And don't people generally dress nice for work?"

"Trash collectors don't."

"Knock it off, Tru." She comes over and sits beside me, in my soon-to-be-owned outfit.

"You're hurting right now." Her voice is soft, careful. "As to be expected. And the best way to help that hurt is to try to feel good about yourself. Put on a beautiful dress and a pair of killer heels, and yes, you may still feel crap on the inside, but on the outside you'll look knockout, and that will be the one thing that will keep the smile plastered on your face for the night." She nudges me with her shoulder, smiling.

"Fine," I huff. "I'll wear the stupid dress."

"Good. And while I'm in an advice-giving mood, can I give you another piece of advice?"

I turn my head, looking straight at her. "If it's about Jake, then no."

She gives me a no-nonsense look. "Talk to him, Tru. I've kept my opinion to myself on this, and I've done the supportive best friend bit, but now I'm telling you how it is—blanking Jake like this is no good for either of you." She puts her hand on my forearm. "And you can blast me for it all you want, but...I believe him. I think he's telling the truth. I don't believe he had sex with that tramp. I think she's just a gold-digging opportunistic little whore. And honestly, I can't even begin to imagine how painful it was walking in and seeing him in bed with her like that...and yes, he absolutely let you down with the drugs," she quickly adds, when I open my mouth to speak. "But you can't go on like this. You need to talk to him. And honestly." She sighs. "I think you know all of this too, but for some reason I can't fathom, you won't let him in to fix things. And it's just not like you to be so unforgiving, Tru."

I scuff the toe of my boot against the carpet. She's skirting so close to the truth right now. Closer than I want.

"Jake loves you; that is more than clear to see," she goes on, "and I know you love him too. So you just need to talk to him and figure out a fix for the both of you."

And because she's so close to the truth I get angry.

I get to my feet, feeling a little more than vexed. "You're supposed to be on my side here, Simone."

"I am on your side." She stands too, facing me. "And that's why I'm saying this. I hate seeing you hurting so badly when it can be so easily fixed. If you just talk to him, listen to what he has to say…" She puts her hands on my upper arms. "Honestly, babe, if I thought for one minute that he'd done the deed with that little tramp, then I'd be winging your corner and kicking his ass to hell and back. But I honestly don't think he has." She's shaking her head. "He's made mistakes, some big whooping ones, but not that *one*."

Tears are welling in my eyes.

"I'm not trying to upset you, honey." She takes me into her arms, hugging me. "It just really needed saying."

I squeeze my eyes shut, fighting back the tears. "I just can't get that image of him in bed with her out of my head." I bang my palm against my forehead. "And honestly…" I bite my lip, cursing myself for finally saying this. "I just…well I just don't think I'm cut out for all of this. I'm not cut out for his lifestyle—everything that comes with him."

Leaning back, she looks at my face. "That's what this is all about, isn't it? Why you've shut down on him completely."

I brush a stray tear away. "At first, I honestly believed he had cheated with her after catching them like that. But as time's gone on…" I sigh. "No, I don't think he has cheated, but her selling her story and all the attention it's brought to me…well, it just made me realise what my fears were all along about being with Jake."

I've known this for a while, but I've just been covering it with the whole cheating thing. It went way beyond Kaitlyn Bitch the instant the press set up camp on my parents' door-step.

"Which are?" she pushes.

"Who he is. Everything that comes with him. There's just no privacy, Simone. We can barely even go out on a date without someone there taking his picture, wanting his autograph, wanting a piece of him. It doesn't feel like there is just ever me and him—that he'll ever fully be mine—and yes, I know how selfish that sounds. But I just want a normal life. A private life. I don't want a life where every time I have a fight with my boyfriend, or we go on a date together, that it will be splashed all over the Internet the very next day for people's breakfast reading."

The truth is there's only ever been one time where I've felt like our relationship truly belonged to just me and Jake, and that was our night at Lumb Falls.

"So talk to him, tell him this," Simone urges gently.

I shake my head no.

"You're a stubborn ass, Trudy Bennett. Give the guy a fighting chance, seriously, because currently he's all broken up and hurting over something he didn't do, desperate to reach you and let you know that. But currently he's fighting out of the wrong corner. It's not fair to him, Tru, and you know it."

I've been mulling over what Simone said for hours.

She's right, and I know it. I should tell Jake that I believe him over the girl, and what my real fears are about being with him.

But I can't.

Because if I do he'll talk me back into his life, and right now that just isn't what I want.

Well, I think it isn't.

I'm standing backstage at Madison Square Garden with Simone. The support band is playing. They're pretty good. Really good, in fact.

They're a local band who won a competition through a radio station to support TMS here at their show in New York.

It was Jake's idea to put the contest out. No one knows that except for me and Stuart. Jake credited it as the band's idea.

He has such a good heart. I wish he would show it to more people than just me.

Ben drove Simone and me here from the hotel. I've got my luggage in the car. Ben is going to take me straight to the airport after the show. All I have to do is let him know when I'm ready to leave. Simone is staying on in New York to spend a few days with Denny.

I haven't seen or spoken to Jake since this morning, which is a good thing. I think.

I don't know.

I don't know anything anymore.

Spotting us, Denny comes over, eyes firmly pinned on Simone. I'm so happy they found each other. One good thing to come out of me and Jake, I guess.

I drift off to the side, giving them some space. I hate being the third wheel at the best of times. At the worst of times, even more so.

Just knowing Jake is around here somewhere is driving me nuts. I'm on constant high-alert for any sign of him.

So far, nothing yet. I'm wondering if he's avoiding me after our fight this morning.

I'm wearing the pink dress and ridiculously pretty blue heels that Simone forced me to buy earlier, and I'm already regretting the shoes—my feet are bloody killing me. Why don't I ever learn that pretty does not equal comfy?

I prop my butt up against the wall and bend over. Slipping my foot out of the shoe, I rub my sore instep with my hand.

When I glance up I see a pair of black Converses approaching me.

Eyes up to the black jeans, reaching the sleeveless, vintage '94 Nine Inch Nails *Downward Spiral* T-shirt, with a guitar strapped tight across it, the instantly recognisable tattoos on full show, to finally meet with Jake's face.

He looks amazing. Beautiful. Just like the rock star he is. And was always meant to be.

I slip my foot back into my shoe. Nerves instantly encompass me, encapsulating me.

"You should learn to wear sensible shoes." He nods down at my feet.

"I should."

"Then again, if you did, I'd never have got to carry you into the hotel that night." His tone is low, intimate, and his eyes meet mine intensely.

Nerve endings fire sparks out into my body, causing an intense rush of want and need for him.

Looking down, I break our stare.

"So...uh...Denny said you're leaving straight after the show." He takes another step closer to me.

We're only a foot apart now. I want to reach out and touch him more than anything. But I can't.

"Yes." I tuck my hair behind my ear. "Sorry I can't make the after-show party. I have to get back home—work, you know—and my flight's booked, so..."

"Sure, yeah, of course, I understand." He pushes his hand through this hair.

I meet his eyes, and I can see the blatant disharmony in them.

"So will I see you after the show? Before you leave?" he asks.

"Yes."

That's a lie. I won't be here when he comes offstage. I'm going to leave during the encore. Everyone's at their highest at that point, so I'll be able to slip away without being noticed.

I said good-bye to Jake once. Twice is just too much.

"Okay, so I'll see you after the show then." He smiles, his mood seemingly picking up.

"Yeah...looks like you're up." I nod in the direction of the roadie who is waiting to hook up his guitar.

Jake gives me a rueful smile. It almost breaks me on the spot.

Reluctantly, he turns to go.

"Jake?"

Stopping, he turns back, slipping his guitar around to the front.

"Have a great show." I smile.

"I will…and, Tru…" He takes a step forward, back to me. "You look beautiful in those shoes…and that dress, but then you look beautiful in anything."

Then he's gone, readying himself to perform to his adoring New York fans, unknowingly taking my heart with him.

Chapter Thirty

J ake is performing better than his last few shows; maybe that's because I'm here, or maybe it's because New York was his home for a time. I'm not sure. But because he's better, the guys are better, and the band as a whole is on fire, and the crowd sure is feeling it.

I'm happy for him, for all of them, that this tour is going out on a high, and I'm so glad I'm here to see it.

It's nearly two hours into the show and I know it's soon coming to an end. Which means it's almost time for me to go.

A part of me is struggling with the decision. A big part.

Simone and I are standing offstage in the left wing with Stuart so we have a clear view of the guys, but all I'm looking at is Jake.

It's all I've done for the whole show. It's impossible not to.

But he hasn't once looked, or even glanced, in my direction.

Whether that's a deliberate thing or he's just so caught up in the show, I'm not sure.

Beside me, Stuart puts his hand to his jacket pocket, feeling for his phone. He pulls it out, glances at the screen, and taking the call, puts his finger in his ear and disappears offstage.

With Stuart gone, I move closer to Simone, linking my arm through hers, to continue watching the show.

I glance at her face. She's all bright-eyed watching Denny onstage.

I feel a pang of pure envy. I wish Jake and I were still like they are.

A minute later I feel a hand tap me on the shoulder. I turn and see it's Stuart. He jerks his head to the side, signalling for me to follow him.

I slip my arm from Simone's and follow him offstage and down the steps.

Stuart leads me down a corridor where it's quiet. He does a quick look around, making sure we're alone. "I just got a call advising me that the girl, Kaitlyn, will be officially withdrawing her story about Jake."

"What?" I'm surprised. No, scrap that, I'm stunned.

"She's admitting she lied about sleeping with Jake."

"And why would she all of a sudden do that?" I give him a suspicious look.

Stuart shrugs.

My spidey sense kicks in. "Stuart, do you have something to do with this?"

He purses his lips. I can see considering in his eyes, which immediately tells me he did.

"Maybe," he utters.

I smile at him, shaking my head, relief filling me. Even though I figured Jake was telling the truth, to hear it from Stuart, from the horse's mouth, is such a weight off my mind, knowing Jake has been telling the truth all along.

"How did you get her to fess up?" I question him.

He grins. "Let's just say I can be very persuasive when I want to be."

"Stuart…?" I press.

Letting out a breath, he says, "I went to see Kaitlyn at her home. Jake doesn't know this, and don't you tell him either."

"And she agreed to see you?"

"Well, I turned up on her doorstep under the guise of being a reporter. Once I was in her house, I told her who I really was, and there wasn't much she could do about it then. She wasn't happy, but I wasn't going anywhere until she listened to what I had to say. She needed to hear what this was doing to Jake…to both of you."

My chest starts to feel tight at the memory of this last week. Of Jake being in pain.

"And she listened?"

"Yes. She might be money hungry, Tru, but she's not a bad person. And that's what it was all about—money. She's desperate for cash. The reason…well, she has asked me to keep private, and I can't break that promise. But that night with Jake, she saw an opportunity and she took it. Knowing what I do, I figure I'd have done the same. So I offered her what she needs in return for her to tell the truth. The deal was that she'd retract her story, publically clearing Jake of any wrongdoing. She said she needed time to think it over. I gave her my number and told her if she decided to do the right thing, to call me. That was her on the phone just then. She's going to issue a statement tomorrow telling the truth."

"That's brave of her, knowing the shit she's going to get from the public."

"It's surprising what people will do for their children."
I can tell the instant he says it, he knew he shouldn't have.

My eyebrows go up. "She has a kid? She only looked like
a kid herself."

He sighs in on himself. "She's twenty. And an old twenty
at that. Her kid is sick, really sick. The dad's not around.
She has no family, and she needs money to pay the hospital bills." He glances around. "I'm telling you this because I
know I can trust you."

I touch his arm. "You can."

And then it's suddenly very hard to hate her when I
know she was only doing this for her sick kid.

"Is there anything I can do to help her?"

He looks at me, surprised. "She's made your life hell this
last week, and you're asking if you can help her? You will
never cease to amaze me, chica."

I shrug. "My mum and dad raised me to care for others
in need, no matter the cost."

"That's some good folks you have there. And thinking
on that, there's someone out there who could do with a
touch of your caring nature right now." He tilts his head in
the direction of the hidden stage.

"I know," I sigh.

I want to help Jake, I really do. I want him to feel better, but I can't help him the way he wants. I can't live this
lifestyle with him.

Swallowing back threatening tears, I say, "I think Jake
should know what you've done to clear this up for him."

Stuart shakes his head no. "Right now Jake needs to
believe there is good in people, and him finding out it was

me sorting out another mess for him won't do that. Just leave him to believe she changed her mind and came clean."

Nodding, I see his reasoning.

"How are you going to pay Kaitlyn though? I'm guessing she'll need a lot of money…I have some I can give to help."

He chuckles. "Don't worry, gorgeous. I might be keeping it from Jake, but it doesn't mean he's not paying. He still fucked up big-time with the drugs, and it was because of that he landed himself in this situation. The money's coming from him. I'm just going to pass it off as a charity donation."

"Can you do that?" I laugh.

"Sure I can…because technically it is a charity donation." He winks.

"Well, Jake might not be able to thank you for what you did, but I can." I wrap my arms around him, kissing his cheek. "I don't know what Jake would do without you, or me, for that matter." Leaning back I look into his face. "We'll always be friends, right?"

"Of course, chica." His brow furrows as he lets out a light sigh. "You're not getting back together with him, are you?"

I step back, needing breathing space. Looking to the floor, I shake my head.

Knowing Jake hasn't cheated doesn't fix my real concerns about being with him.

"Whatever reason you have, gorgeous, just know Jake loves you—*a lot*. So whatever it is—whatever the real problem is—talk to him about it, see if you can't work through it. The way I see it is you guys are meant to be together, and when it's a love like yours, then there shouldn't be anything you can't work through."

Looking up, I meet his eyes. "Okay." I nod. "Come on, let's go back, catch the last part of the show."

Stuart stares at me for a long moment, lips pressed together, assessing me.

He knows I'm fobbing him off, but thankfully he leaves it there and holds out his arm for me to take.

Linking my arm in through his, I walk back with Stuart to the stage.

I know my heart should feel light now, knowing the truth, but it doesn't. If anything it feels heavier.

We get back to the side of the stage, joining Simone, just as the guys are finishing up. I look over at Jake onstage and all I feel is conflicted.

Suddenly the whole place darkens as the song comes to an end.

The encore is about to start in a few minutes. This is when I promised myself I would leave.

I hear movement behind me. Turning, I see a roadie carrying a huge keyboard fixed to a stand, looking impatient for me to move. I nudge Stuart and Simone, and we all back out of his way, letting him pass by.

Denny and Smith come bounding offstage and over to us. They are pumped up and covered in sweat.

I'm guessing Jake went offstage with Tom to the right wing.

I see Simone beaming at Denny as he talks to her. I wish I was with Jake right now.

No, I don't.

The crowd's cheering and the guys' enthusiasm is infectious as I listen to their quick talk, but my heart is dying a slow death in my chest, because even though I said to Stuart I would stay and talk to Jake, I know I can't.

If I do, he'll just talk me round, and I know I'm not cut out for all of this.

The encore is readying to start, and the chants are growing louder and louder. The place is practically vibrating under my feet as the fans demand TMS back onto the stage.

The place is insane, electric.

You can literally feel the energy from the crowd; it's like a physical presence touching my skin.

Denny and Smith are called for and they disappear back onstage to take their places.

Then the spotlight hits, illuminating Jake.

He's sitting on a stool, at the keyboard the roadie just carried on, facing left stage, straight in my direction.

The crowd goes insane, clapping and cheering.

Jake never plays the keyboard onstage. He knows how to play, but he's more of a guitar man. I was always the piano player out of the two of us.

A sudden nervous energy sweeps over me, spreading from my head down to my toes.

Speaking into the mike, Jake addresses the fans. "This tour has been amazing for us in so many ways. It was always going to be a hard one for us, but you guys—our fans—have helped us make it a real tribute for Jonny. So we thank you for that."

The crowd picks up with cheers again.

"Another amazing thing about this tour," Jakes says over the cheers, "was that it brought someone back to me whom I made the mistake of once letting go many years ago—someone important."

He looks straight at me in the muted darkness. My whole body trembles under the weight of his stare.

His eyes drift down from mine as he starts speaking again. "She once asked me, if I had to pick one song out of every song ever written to best describe me, which it would be. I said the song I'm about to sing."

My skin starts to prickle as I remember our conversation that night in bed…

"If you, Jake Wethers, had to pick one song as your title song to describe yourself, what would it be?"

"'Hurt.'"

"Why?"

"Some people said Reznor was writing a lyrical suicide note, others said he was writing about finding a reason to live. But I think it's both…it just depends on which side you're looking at it from."

"And which side are you looking at it from?"

"Now…a reason to live."

"Reznor's version or Johnny Cash's?"

"Johnny Cash…I have a few things in common with him."

"Like?"

"The drugs…the women…hanging out for the girl of my dreams…you're my June, Tru."

I hear his deep inhalation of breath echo around the stadium before he says, "So tonight, I'm singing this for her, my June."

That will mean nothing to anyone else, but everything to me.

Jake looks across at me, his fingers hovering above the keys. He looks lost, afraid, and desperate.

I can't move. I'm pinioned to the spot.

He closes his eyes, concealing his pain, then presses his fingers down on the keys and begins to play "Hurt."

Leaning his mouth close to the mike, he starts to sing, and I feel a stabbing pain in my chest so hard that I can barely breathe.

Jake's voice is deep and powerful and is echoing raw around the stadium.

And I know in this moment what he's doing.

He's not playing Cash's version, he's playing Reznor's. He's telling me he's back there. He's telling me he's lost his reason to live.

Me.

I see it in his eyes when he opens them again, looking straight at me, singing so hauntingly.

And I can't help the tears that start to run down my face.

My heart is breaking as we stare at one another. Jake is singing his body dry to me, and for this moment it's only him and me in this crowded stadium, in the whole world, the entire universe.

I can't believe he's baring himself to the world like this.

Exposing us.

This isn't Jake. He's private. And I don't want this. This is exactly what I don't want.

Then it's all too much, and I'm moving before I realise. Turning, I push past Stuart and Simone, and run offstage.

I have no idea where I'm going, I just have to get away.

Away from his pain, from my pain. Just far away from this complete agony that he's inflicting upon me.

I hear my name being called from behind, but I can't stop.

I'm running past people, God knows how in these heels, tears blurring my vision.

The next thing I know Jake is grabbing hold of me from behind, pulling me around to face him.

"I'm sorry. I'm so sorry," he says, panting, breathless. There are tears in his eyes. Mine are dripping off my chin, down onto my lovely dress.

There are people everywhere, watching us.

"You shouldn't have done that." I pull myself free from his hold and step back down a corridor out of everyone's view.

Jake follows me.

I wipe my face dry with my hands. "You shouldn't have sung that song."

"What am I supposed to do? You won't talk to me. You won't listen. You've just cut me off dry." His face crumples. "I knew the only way I could get you to finally hear me was through music. And that song, what we talked about that night..." He steps close to me, cupping my cheek with his hand.

I almost break at the feel of his skin on mine after being so long without him, so bereft without him.

"You're my life, Tru. My everything. And you always will be. I need you to know that, and I need you to believe me when I tell you I didn't have sex with that girl."

I swallow past my salty tears. "I know, Jake. Stuart just got a call saying the girl is withdrawing her story. She's admitted it was all a lie."

"She has?" His words come out in a breath. I see myriad emotions pass over his face—shock, but mainly relief. Complete and utter relief. "So you know it's the truth."

I gulp down hard against the words I know I have to say.

"Jake, I believed that you've been telling the truth for a while now. I didn't at first...seeing you there with her, it was so horrific..." I wince at the memory. "But I do now. I believed you long before she decided to tell the truth. Hearing her admit it is of course a relief, but it doesn't change anything. We still can't be together."

I watch as a dozen emotions scroll across his face.

"Why not?" he asks, hurt.

"Because I'm not cut out for this life with you. I'm not strong enough to handle the stuff that comes with it—with you. Deep down I already knew, but this past week with what happened, and the constant press attention it brought, details of our private life becoming reading material for people, has just proven to me what I already knew. I thought I could live with it—live my life so publicly if it meant having you, but...I can't."

I leave his stare, casting my eyes down, the pain in his face almost too much to bear. Fresh tears break free down my cheeks.

"I'll give it all up." His tone is suddenly fixed, serious.

I've only heard him sound like this once before—when he was going to cancel the PR for the tour and come to me in London.

"I'll leave it all behind—the band, the label, everything," he adds resolutely.

My eyes flick back up to his. "No, Jake, you can't do that for me."

"I can, and I will," he says steadily. "I'll give everything up without a second thought if it means being with you. We can move away from everyone just like we talked about that time. You remember on the phone? When we talked about building a house on an island. It doesn't just have to be a pipe dream, we can really do that. Just me and you. We can have a house built wherever you want, away from all of this."

"Jake…" I shake my head. "It wouldn't work because it's not who you are. This is what you live for—the music, the performing. It's who you are, and if you gave it up for me, after a time you'd start to resent me."

"I wouldn't."

"Yes, you would. And even if by some miracle you didn't, it still wouldn't make a difference…because they're not ready to let you go." I gesture in the direction of the chanting crowd out beyond in the stadium, the ones calling out his name. "The world, your fans, they love you too. And they're not ready to let go of Jake Wethers—not yet… maybe not ever."

His eyebrows pull in. "And I'm not ready to let go of you, and I never will be."

Briefly closing my eyes, I say, "I'm not enough for you, Jake. That's why you turned back to the drugs after the news story broke about your dad. I don't know what is enough for you, but it's not me. I'm not enough to keep you straight like you once said I was."

"You can't honestly believe that. Jesus Christ, Tru!" His tone is so forceful, it yanks my eyes back to him.

His eyes are as fiercely determined as his voice.

"I was just being a weak fuckin' idiot! It was about me and him—my demons that I never exorcised, *never* about you or us. And I promise you I will never go back there again. Losing you because of what I did—because of the drugs—was the single worst thing that has ever happened to me. If I was ever going to need to keep using, it was this last week losing you. But I stopped, Tru. I haven't touched a thing since that night, and I won't ever again.

"When I drowned that night in LA, nearly dying like that, I thought it was enough to stop me, but it wasn't… because I didn't know the meaning of the word 'dying' until you left me. This last week without you…" He pulls in a sharp breath, briefly closing his eyes. "I'm nothing without you, Tru, *nothing*."

His words on some fundamental level are reaching me, touching me, because I know exactly how he feels. I've felt so lost, so adrift…so dead inside without him.

But how can we be together with all these problems we have sitting between us? I know I can't deal with the life that accompanies him.

I shake my head. "I just don't know, Jake."

"I do." He tightens his hold on me, clinging to my face desperately with his hand, tangling his fingers into my hair.

My emotions are rising to epic proportions, so I clench my teeth, forbidding any more tears to fall.

"When we're good, we're great, Jake. But when we're bad, we're fucking horrendous. From the moment we came back into each other's lives, all we've managed to do is hurt one another, badly—and too many times to think of." I exhale. "I once used to think we were meant to be together, but now…now I'm not so sure. Maybe we just wanted to be together so badly when we were younger that we tried to force it so desperately now. Maybe our time just passed long ago."

"No." He shakes his head vehemently. "We're meant to be."

He puts his other hand on my face, forcing my eyes to his.

"I'll never be good enough for you, I know that. But I'm no good without you, and if that makes me a selfish bastard for wanting you as badly as I do, then so be it because I can't live a life that doesn't have you in it."

He stares deep into my eyes, breathing deeply. I can feel his hands trembling against my skin.

"Marry me," he says without hesitation.

Every ounce of air in my lungs whooshes straight out of me, a thousand thoughts scattering across my mind.

Freeing a hand from my face, Jake reaches into his jeans pocket and pulls out a ring.

The ring.

I stare at him, my eyes wide.

"I got it before we left Paris."

It's the pink diamond ring I was looking at in Tiffany's the night he bought me the necklace.

"I—I can't believe you bought it." I'm gasping for air.

He holds the ring up between us. "I knew I'd be asking you to be my wife from the very second you walked into that hotel room and back into my life. And when I saw your face that night, looking at this ring, I just knew—I knew it belonged on your finger, and I've been waiting for the right moment ever since to ask you. I know now is not the most romantic or perfect time to propose." He glances around at our dim concrete surroundings. "But now is the only time I have before I lose you for good. So I'll ask you again…" He pulls in a deep breath. "Trudy Bennett, I love you beyond any lyrics I could ever write, or any words I could ever say. I always have, and I always will. Marry me?"

I stare at him, speechless.

My best friend. My lover. My life.

And he is my life. He always has been, even through our years apart.

Jake is all I think of, all I see when I look into my future. And try as I might to fight being with him for fear of his lifestyle, of getting hurt by it, it simply hurts more to be without him. I see that now.

Eventually, I would have followed my heart back to him, because he is my everything.

Jake once said onstage that Jonny was the mighty in their storm, and now I see that Jake is *my* mighty storm. He's broken and complex, and no one knows him like I do, or ever will. He needs me.

He's my storm to calm. And I'm going to spend the rest of my life doing just that.

"Say something, Tru, please, you're killing me here." His voice is painted with nerves, his chest rising and falling heavily. "Just say anything but no—don't say no—just tell me what I need to do for you to say yes and I'll do it. Because I can't spend another second without you."

I reach my hand up and touch his face, smoothing my fingers over his skin, trying to erase his fears and the lost look in his eyes, the one that only I can see.

Then I smile.

"You don't need to do anything. Yes, I'll marry you."

His face breaks into the biggest smile I've ever seen, mirroring my own. Complete adoration in his eyes, reserved only for me.

"You will?"

"I will."

I hold my left hand up to him, and halting my breath, I watch as he takes my hand and slides the ring over my knuckle, setting it to rest on my finger.

The diamond is huge against my hand.

Keeping my hand in his, Jake lifts it to his mouth and kisses the ring on my finger. Then I can't contain my bubbling happiness any longer, and it bursts out of me in full Technicolor glory, and I'm grabbing his face, kissing him hard, smothering him with the absolute pure love I feel for him.

"I love you so much," he says against my lips. "I'll never let you down again, baby. I swear. I'll make you so happy."

"I know," I breathe. "I know."

"Um…?" I hear a voice from behind Jake, and moving my mouth from his, I glance past him to see Tom grinning at us both.

Jakes turns, taking me with him, unwilling to let me go just yet.

"What?" he says irritably to Tom.

"Well, Romeo, we were just wondering if there's any chance of you making an appearance back onstage at any point tonight. Because there are twenty thousand seriously pissed-off fans out there"—he thumbs over his shoulder—"who can't figure why the fuck you just bolted offstage like a crazy person midway through a song…and apparently my singing just isn't cutting, so I'm envisioning a fuckin' riot any minute if you don't get your sorry ass back out onstage."

Laughing at Tom, I slide my hands into Jake's back pockets. "You better go finish your show." I smile up at him.

He looks down at me, reluctant.

"They paid good money to hear you sing, baby. You owe them that encore. I'll be here waiting when you're done. I'm not going anywhere. Remember, I promised. I'm yours now, forever." I slide my hand out of his pocket, lifting my ring up to him.

"Forever," he echoes. Brushing my hair off my face, he kisses my lips again. "Come on, then, let's go give these people what they paid to see."

He's about to move when I ask him, "Are you still going to sing 'Hurt'?"

I don't want him to. I want him to leave that song behind now. I want us both to start afresh.

Jake rests his hands on either side of my neck. Touching my face with his thumbs, he tilts his head to the side. I see the flicker of memory and humour in his eyes as he shakes his head no. "I'm thinking maybe I need a new title song, and I was thinking...I dunno." He pushes his lips together in thought, his brow creasing. "What about...'I Can't Get No Satisfaction'?"

I grin, feeling that familiar pull and heat in my belly, remembering just exactly what we did that night after all our talking was done.

"Hmm." I scrunch my face up in thought. "Well, I'll have to see what I can do about that."

Spying a room that looks very much like a dressing room, I take Jake by the hand and start to lead him towards it.

Turning to Tom, I say, "Tell them he'll back out onstage in five minutes."

"Ten," Jake adds from behind me.

I stop, turning, and meet his shining eyes.

"Technically the song lasts just short of four minutes," I state, smiling.

"Oh, this is the unreleased extended version, Mrs. Wethers."

"Mrs. Wethers-to-be," I correct.

"Technicality." He smiles. "And one that I'll be rectifying very soon."

Then he sweeps me up off my feet, and squealing with laughter, I let him carry me into the dressing room, closing and locking the door behind us, leaving Tom and the rest of the world outside to wait.

Bonus Scene: Jake and Tru's first meeting from Jake's point of view

THE HOTEL

I can't fucking sit still.

Ever since Stuart told me the name of the interviewer coming this morning, I've been pacing around like a dickhead. My head is flipping about all over the place.

What if it's her?

What do I say?

She might be pissed at me. I was the one who stopped contact when I moved to the States. And when I hit the big time with the band, she never attempted to get in touch with me.

That'd be just like Tru to hold a twelve-year grudge. She was always a feisty one.

Tru Bennett.

It might not be her.

How many Trudy Bennetts could there be in the UK who are music journalists?

She was music first, a writer second. It has to be her.

What time is it?

I'm driving myself nuts here. I just wish she'd hurry the fuck up and get here so I can put myself out of my misery.

I know I'm acting like a crazy motherfucker right now, but it's Tru.

There was only ever her for me, and that never changed in the whole time I've been apart from her.

She was the only one who knew me back then, and only she could tie me up like this.

She was my best friend, the only girl I ever loved, and I've missed the shit out of her.

It's times like this when I wish I wasn't clean. I could really do with a hit right now.

Fuck. I need a smoke.

I get them out of my pocket and light one up.

"Do you want a drink?" Stuart asks, walking into the living room. "Maybe a whiskey?"

"No. Yes. No." I pull on my smoke and blow it out.

"Any conclusion on that drink yet?" Stuart says, cocking his head to the side.

"Yeah."

"Yeah, you want one? Or yeah, you don't?"

"Don't."

"It might calm you down." He crosses the room, heading towards the minibar.

"Yeah, but if I have one, then I might not stop."

He gets one of those mini Diet Coke cans out and cracks it open.

Coke, that's what I need right now, and not of the diet variety.

"This girl sure has got you freaked out." Stuart has another drink, and, draining the can, he tosses it in the trash.

I turn to him, taking a long drag of my smoke. "Because she's not just any girl."

"No?" Stuart raises his eyebrow.

"No." I take another long drag, then stub it out in the ashtray. "She's the only girl I've ever loved."

"I didn't think you did love?"

"Only the once."

Grinning, Stuart comes over and picks up the ashtray.

I know he's going to clean it out. He hates my smoking. I think he's worried it will prematurely age him or something.

Gay guys. I'll never understand them. Stuart's cool though, he's been with me from the start, and he's great at his job. He's also saved my ass more times than I care to remember.

Women are my thing. I've never had a girlfriend. I just like to fuck. Hard. And often. Then move on to the next.

There has only ever been one girl I loved, one girl I wanted to be mine, and she might be walking through that door any minute now.

What if she looks completely different?

She used to be really beautiful. She had this amazing ass and a smoking-hot body, even as a teenager. And she had the best pair of tits I had ever seen, not that I'd seen many back then, well only hers to be honest, and I only got to see them by accident when she lost her bikini one time when we were swimming. Even at thirteen she had a sizeable pair. Tru was an early developer, all for my luck.

Fuck. What if she's married now and has kids or something?

Whatever. Either way it's Tru, and I need to see her.

"What if it's not her coming?" Stuart asks, walking back through, with my, yep, clean ashtray.

"Then your next job is to find her for me."

At his expression, I give him an And-no-I'm-not-fucking-kidding look.

"Do you have OCD or something? You know there's treatment for that kind of thing, right?" I grin at him.

"OCD is better than STD, Jake." He raises his eyebrow.

I've never had an STD in my life, cheeky bastard. Sheeted and ready to go. I never leave the house without a condom. Well, I never know when I might need one. Trust me, I've had sex at the most inappropriate of times, with the wrong kinds of women.

Aside from making music, fucking is the only other thing I am good at.

Jesus Christ, what time is it? She should be here by now.

It's got to be her because she's late. Tru was always late for everything.

I wonder if she still plays the piano. I'll have to ask her. If it is her, that is.

Fuck, is she ever going to turn up!

The suite phone starts to ring and I instantly tense up.

Stuart answers. "Send her straight up, someone will meet her."

"She's here," he says, turning to me. "I'll send Dave to meet her at the elevator."

I sit down on the sofa.

Okay, I've gotta knock this off, I'm acting like a fucking woman.

It's just Tru. And if it's not, then it's just another lame-ass interview to get through. Then afterwards I can finally stop being a pussy and find her.

I grab one of the hotel-provided mints off the coffee table, unwrap it, and put it in my mouth. I don't want to stink of cigarettes if it is her.

It's another five minutes before I hear a knock at the main door.

It's definitely got to be her because it's a clear two minutes up here from reception, and Tru was always good at taking her time.

I stand up. Nervous energy is rushing through me.

I can hear Stuart talking. I strain to hear the other voice, but I can't hear a thing.

Would I recognise her voice anyway? It's been so long since I last heard it.

It seems ages before Stuart walks into the living room, and there she is behind him.

Tru.

It's her.

And fuck me, she looks beautiful, stunning, and I know in this moment I am never letting go of her again.

She walks a little farther into the room.

I can't take my eyes off her. She looks amazing.

She's wearing a loose grey T-shirt, belted, showing her tiny waist off, and her tits look amazing in it, perfect. And she's got this cute little skirt on. It's short and is showing plenty of leg. Fuck, those legs got long, and she's wearing this pair of come-fuck-me-now boots that would look amazing wrapped around my waist.

"Tru?" My voice comes out a little hoarse. I take a deep breath. "Trudy Bennett? My Trudy Bennett?" I repeat like a fucking moron.

Of course it's her, you fuckwit.

I take a step forward. "Shit, it really is you."

What the hell is wrong with me? Why can't I stop talking like a dumb-ass?

"Yes. It's really me," she says.

She sounds like a fucking angel. My dick twitches and starts to harden in response.

Aw, fuck no! Don't get a hard-on, Wethers, for fuck's sake. What are you, fifteen?

Distraction quick.

I think of that time I walked in on Stuart kissing a dude.

Yep, that'll do it.

Down you go, boy.

Okay, game face on now, Wethers.

"Holy shit," I say, smiling at her, moving a bit closer. "When Stuart said the name of the interviewer was Trudy Bennett, I just thought—there can't be that many Trudy Bennetts here in the UK, can there? I mean, there probably is, but…" I laugh. "But then I just thought it would be too much of a coincidence for it to be you…and shit…here you are."

What the fuck was that, dickwad? If that's what you call your game face nowadays, then you are so totally screwed.

I haven't felt this lame around a woman since I was last around her, and at least I had the excuse of being a teenager back then. What's my excuse now?

It can't be because I'm clean because I fucked every hot chick there was in rehab, including the hot married counsellor and a few other skirts since I've been out.

It's because it's her.

"Here I am," she says.

She sounds nervous. I like that she is. It gives me a rise.

I walk over to her, just needing to be closer to her.

And the nearer I get, I see a blush colour her cheeks.

She just looks so fucking beautiful.

Tru is the most beautiful, perfect person I have ever seen in my life.

More than anything I just want to touch her, but I'm almost afraid to.

And fuck, she smells amazing.

It's not just the perfume, it's her. The scent takes me back years. And I suddenly feel an overwhelming sense of love and protectiveness over her.

I haven't ever wanted a woman in the way I want her now. I don't only want to screw her; I want to hold her in my arms.

"It's been, what—eleven years?" I ask her, trying to get my head straight.

"Twelve," she corrects.

"Twelve. Christ, yeah, right." I push my hand through my hair. "You look different...but the same—you know?" I shrug.

"I know." She smiles. "You look different too." She gestures to the tattoos on my arms.

I grin down at them.

"But still the same," she says, pointing her pretty little finger at my nose.

She means my freckles. I fucking hate them.

I rub my hand over my nose. "Yeah, no getting rid of them."

"I always liked them."

She did?

"Yeah, but you liked the Care Bears, Tru," I tease.

She blushes again.

"You remember that, huh?" she murmurs, looking down.

I have the urge to reach out and run my fingers over her pink cheeks.

Actually, I have the urge to do a lot more with her right now.

Kiss her, peel off her clothes…

"I remember a lot." I give her my best smile, the one that has woman dropping their panties for me.

"Come on, let's sit down." I grab hold of her left hand, for two reasons.

One—I'm feeling for a wedding ring. Two—I just really need to touch her.

No ring. Thank fuck. But my skin heats at the contact with her, and my cock twitches in my pants again.

Fuck! Not again.

Stuart and a dude. Stuart and a dude.

While I focus on getting my dick to tame the fuck down, I lead her over to the sofa and sit down.

She sits next to me but leaves a huge gap, I notice.

I turn towards her, crossing my legs. I look at hers while she puts her bag on the floor.

That cute little skirt of hers has ridden up and is showing plenty of those sexy stems.

I suppress a moan as an image of me touching her leg, running my hand over her smooth, olive skin, up and under that sexy little skirt, flashes through my mind.

"Do you want something to drink?" I ask her, chasing the mental picture away.

She turns her legs towards me.

Fuck! Is she teasing me or something? I'm itching to put my hands on her and see if her skin is as soft as it looks. If she were any other woman, I'd have done that and more by now.

She'd be shirtless and skirtless, and I'd be well on my way to fucking her to the finish line, if she was anyone else.

But she's not just anyone.

She's Tru.

She was my best friend, and is, and always will be way more than a quick fuck, irrespective of what my cock is saying right now.

It's the most fucking confusing feeling I've ever had in my life. And I don't do confused. I want something, I take it, or I make it happen.

But I just can't do that with her.

I fix my eyes on her face, avoiding the temptation to look at her legs again or her tits, for that matter, and give her the respect she deserves.

"Water would be great, thanks," she says. Her cheeks redden again.

Did she used to blush this much when we were kids?

"Water?" I query. "You sure you don't want orange juice or something?"

She shakes her head. "Water's fine."

"Stuart!" I yell.

He shows his face a few seconds later. That was quick. I bet the nosey bastard has been standing by the door listening in.

"Can you get Tru a glass of water, and I'll have an orange juice, please."

Stuart nods, smiling at me, then goes off to get our drinks.

Nosy fucker has been listening in.

I'm feeling restless. I need a smoke but I don't want to light up in front of her for some unexplained reason.

"So, this is a little crazy, huh?" I say.

"Hmm. A little." She casts a glance at me, pressing her gorgeous pouty lips together.

I want to kiss them, see them around my dick...

"So how have you been?" I ask her.

"Good. Great. I'm music journalist now, obviously..." she mumbles.

She seems really uncomfortable around me. Maybe she's not as happy to see me as I am her.

"You always were a good writer," I encourage.

"I was?" She looks surprised.

"Yeah, those stories you used to make up when we were little, and then you used to make me sit and listen to you while you read them back to me." I chuckle.

She was such a cute thing when she was younger.

Her face goes bright red. "Oh God," she groans. "I was so lame."

I laugh. "You were five, Tru. I think we can forgive the lame." I drag my fingers through my hair. "And of course you always loved music, so it makes sense the two went together. You still play the piano?" I ask her.

She was amazing on the keys. I could sit and listen to her play for hours when we were younger.

"No. I stopped..." She pauses. It makes me curious. "I just, um, haven't played in a long time. I fell out of it, you know," she adds, sounding really uncomfortable now. "Well obviously you don't know." She gestures to my guitar.

I smile at her, but I'm not feeling it.

Why is she so uncomfortable around me? I thought she might be pissed at me for stopping contact but not uncomfortable.

It's not the whole me being famous shit, is it? She was the one person I would never have expected that from.

I sigh inwardly.

Stuart reappears with our drinks.

Tru thanks him for her drink.

"Anything else?" Stuart asks me.

Apart from her?

I look at Tru in question. She shakes her head.

"No, we're good, thanks," I say, dismissing him.

I have a drink of my juice.

"So I'd ask how you're doing, but…" She gestures around at our surroundings.

"Yeah. I'm great." I force a laugh and rub my hand over my chin. Leaning forward, I put my drink down on the table and rest my forearms on my legs.

The girl I loved, still love, doesn't appear to have missed me like I've missed her. The one girl that has meant so much to me for so long, the one I had to let go of, but never forgot, and have been too afraid to find, looks like she'd rather be anywhere but here with me.

So yeah, I'm absolutely fan-fucking-tastic.

I wonder why she came. Probably forced to by her editor.

I feel like such a dumb-ass. I've been here freaking out like a fucking idiot over her, and she's just indifferent to me.

"I've followed your music career," she says out of the blue.

"You have?"

Now I am surprised. I wouldn't have thought she cared to.

"Of course I have. Music is my job."

Of course it is. So it's not because it was me, but because of who I am.

"But that's not just why," she adds. "I wanted to see how you were doing. And you've just achieved so much. I was really proud watching you on TV and reading the articles about your music, and when you set up your own label—I was like, 'Wow'…and I've got all your albums, of course, and they're really brilliant."

What?

I don't get her. One minute she's acting like she couldn't give a shit about seeing me. The next she's tripping over her words, trying to give me the impression she does.

Easiest way to find out—ask her. I've always been in the mind-set that you should say what you think. What's the point in sitting on shit, trying to figure it out for yourself when the answer to your question is sitting right in front of you?

"Why didn't you get in touch with me, Tru?"

She stares at me for a long moment. I see what I think is confusion flicker over her face.

"Um…you're not exactly easy to get in touch with, Mr. Famous Rock Star."

I hear the hard edge clear in her voice.

Yep, she's pissed that I cut contact with her. That I can work with.

Indifferent, no. But angry, yes.

And angry makes her so very fucking hot right now. Even hotter if that's possible.

"Yeah, that's me—one of the most accessibly inaccessible people on the planet," I say, staring at her.

I'm totally giving her edge, because right now all I want to do is piss her off further.

I want her to get her issue off her hot chest, so we can get to the good stuff. And I can imagine an angry Tru is a very hot Tru.

I keep my eyes on her, but she's not saying anything. What the fuck! Why isn't she kicking my ass right now?

The Tru I knew would have torn a strip off me.

Maybe she's not the same girl she used to be.

She seems the same, but maybe not.

I need a smoke. Fuck waiting.

I get them out of my pocket and perch one between my lips. "Do you smoke?" I ask.

"No."

"Good." *Nothing worse than a woman who smokes, if you ask me.* "You mind if I do?" I don't normally ask anyone ever. I wanna smoke, I smoke, but for her it just seems appropriate to ask.

"No," she says firmly.

So she does mind.

But I need a smoke, so I'm taking advantage of her inbuilt politeness and am having one anyway.

Lighting up, I take a long drag, pulling back hard, enjoying the momentary relief the nicotine gives me.

I drop my smokes and lighter onto the table, and then I suddenly hear music.

Is that Adele? Where the fuck is that coming from? It better not be Stuart listening to his crap music again.

Tru scrabbles for her bag.

It's coming from her cell. I'm surprised she's got Adele as her ringtone. Doesn't fit with the Tru I remember. But then a lot isn't fitting with her right now.

"Sorry," she mumbles, pulling her cell out, silencing it. "It might be my boss."

I watch her face as she quickly reads the text. A small smile forms on her lips.

Boyfriend, maybe? I fucking hope not. But look at her. No, she'll have a boyfriend, there is no way she'll be single looking like she does.

I bet he's a stuck-up asshole.

I'll find out who he is from her and get Stuart to do some digging on him later.

I need to know what my competition is.

Anyone else, I'd just be able to take without an ounce of work, but not her.

If there's anything of the Tru I remember still in there, and I'm pretty sure there is, then I know for sure that I have my work cut out for me to get her to be mine.

"Adele?" I grin, referring to her cell. I like to tease her. I always did.

"I like her." She sounds defensive.

"Oh, me too." I nod, holding back the smile I can feel rising. "She's a nice girl. I just figured from what I remember of you, I'd have been hearing the Stones playing on your cell."

"Yeah, well I've changed a lot since you knew me."

I'll take that as the dig it was meant as. Wow, she really is harbouring a grudge against me.

Which means she still cares. I'm so totally in the game.

I watch her with interest as she puts her cell away. Oh, she's pulling out her notebook. She wants to start the interview.

We haven't seen each other for twelve fucking years, and she wants to interview me. It stings more than I expected.

"So, I should get started with the interview—I'm sure you're really busy, and I don't want to keep you for longer than necessary."

I'm really in the mood to play now.

"You're not keeping me." I take a long drag of my cigarette. "And I'm not busy today. My schedule is clear."

"Oh. You haven't got any other interviews after mine?" She looks surprised.

Stage one of getting her commences…now. Flattery.

"Well I did have…consider them cancelled."

"No! Don't do that on my account." She practically squeals it at me.

Okay. So flattery isn't going to swing it with her.

Fuck, this is hard work already. Am I sure I'm cut out for this?

For her, Wethers, yes.

"I don't mean I'm not happy to see you," she starts babbling. "Of course I am, and would love to talk old times with you, but I don't want others to miss out on a great opportunity because of me."

She's nervous again. Good sign.

"A great opportunity?" I give her another one of my panty-dropping smiles.

She shrugs, looking abashed. Her cheeks redden. "Oh, you know what I mean," she says quietly.

Okay, Wethers, now is the time for sensitive. Hit her with our history. Get her remembering the good old days. You've got thirty minutes to win her over before she walks out that door and you lose her again. Don't fuck this up like you did the last time.

507

"Look, Tru." I move towards her, putting all my focus on her. Women love that. "I haven't seen you for twelve years. The last thing I want to do right now is talk business with you, or anyone else for that matter. I want to know all about you—what you've been doing since I last saw you."

She shrugs and looks down. "Not much."

"I'm sure you've done a lot more than 'not much,'" I urge with a little force. I need to get her talking. Come on, Tru.

She looks up at me with those beautiful brown eyes. I see a flicker of hurt in them.

It makes me feel like shit to know I once hurt her so bad that she still feels it even now.

"What did I do after you left Manchester?" She shrugs. "I lived my life, I finished school." She sounds bitter.

Fuck.

"How was it?" I keep my eyes on hers. I'm not letting her go anywhere.

"School? It was school. A little lonely after you left, but I got through it."

"You still see anyone from school?"

She tucks her hair behind her ear. I have the urge to do just the same.

"No, I'm friends with a couple of people on Facebook, but that's about it. What about you?" she asks.

I laugh. Not fucking likely. The only person I ever wanted to keep in touch with was her, but I just couldn't.

"No," I reply. "Then what did you do after school?"

"Moved here to go to uni. I got my degree in journalism. Then I landed a job at *Etiquette*, the magazine I work for, and I've worked there ever since."

"Cool." I take another drag of my cigarette.

Let's move this on now.

I'm itching to know if she has a boyfriend or not. I know she's not married, but I also don't want her knowing I checked for that already.

Play it cool.

"You're not married?" I let my eyes go to her left hand, giving her the impression it's the first time I'm checking for sign of a ring.

"No," she says.

"Boyfriend?" I take one last drag on my smoke and stub it out.

There's a long pause. I'm not sure if it's a good or a bad thing.

"Yes," she finally replies.

Bad thing.

Even though I figured she'd have one, it still drives a jealousy nail through me I didn't know existed.

Holding my calm, I ask, "Live together?"

"No. I live with my flatmate, Simone, in Camden."

She sounds a bit pissed that I've asked. I wonder why. Maybe she wants to live with him and he doesn't.

What fucking idiot wouldn't want to wake up to that beautiful face every single day?

One thing on my side is that it can't be serious if they don't live together. But then it also depends on how long they've been together.

"How long have you been with the boyfriend?"

"His name is Will, and we've been together for two years."

Two years and not living together. Very good sign.

"And what does Will do for a living?"

"He's an investment banker."

Yep. He's a prick. "Smart guy."

"He is. He's very smart—top of his class at uni, and he's climbing the ladder at work very quickly." She sounds defensive over him, and it pisses me off.

I grab my smokes and light another one up.

Tru unclips her pen from her notebook and opens it up. "It's been really nice catching up with you Jake, but I really should get to the interview—especially if I want to keep my job."

Oh, she's back to that again. For fuck's sake. What do I have to do to keep her interest in me and off this fucking interview?

I hate interviews at the best of times. Even more so when all I want to do is figure out how to get her back into my life and into my bed.

"You won't get fired," I state.

I'd ruin the fucking magazine if they ever even considered firing her.

"You sound pretty confident of that." She laughs, and it sounds forced.

Does she not think I have that kind of pull? I'll show her just exactly what kind of pull I have, and also just what I have to offer her.

"I am." Staring at her, I take another drag of my smoke.

She shifts in her seat. I like that I make her nervous. And I'm so going to use it to my advantage right now.

"You okay?" I probe. "You seem a little uncomfortable."

"Of course I'm not uncomfortable," she bites out.

She so fucking is. And it's so fucking hot.

"I just need to—"

"Do your job," I finish for her. "Okay, go ahead, ask me anything. I'm all yours, Tru, for the next thirty minutes."

She wants to interview me, fine, interview me. But I'm going to have some fun while she does.

When I said I was good at two things, making music and fucking, that was a lie. I'm good at something else—very good, in fact—and that's talking.

I glance at my watch, giving an air of indifference and confidence, as I lean against the sofa, putting one arm to rest on the back. I give her another one of my trademark smiles.

It disarms her again. I can see it in her eyes. Good, because that was the intention.

She puts the end of the pen in her mouth, and I lose focus.

My dick starts to harden again as I watch that pen in her mouth, watching her chew it.

Fuck.

I've actually turned into a horny teenager. I can't stop getting hard-ons around her, just like I couldn't back when I was young.

And because my dick is big, it shows a lot when it gets hard, and no, that's not me being a cocky bastard, it is big. Huge, in fact.

I surreptitiously shift it about in my pants while she's not looking, having a drink of her water, begging the eager fucker to go back down.

At least I'm sitting, so it shouldn't be noticeable while it tames itself.

"It's been said in the past that you're a perfectionist when it comes to your work," she says out of the blue.

"—your music, and because of that you can be...at times, difficult to work with. Do you agree with that? Do you consider yourself a perfectionist?"

Now that's got my attention. I resist my urge to laugh.

This is the Tru I know.

Let the games begin.

"People don't work *with* me, Tru, they work *for* me. And the guys in my band, the ones who matter, don't seem to have a problem with the way I run things. But to answer your question, I want my music and my label to be the best they can be. Currently they are, and I intend to keep it that way, so if I have to bust a few balls and have myself labelled as a complete shit to work for, or a 'perfectionist,' to keep me, my band, and my label at the top of their game, then yeah, call me a perfectionist. I've been called worse."

She's staring at me, mouth wide open.

Good.

I watch as she scribbles down my answer, feeling pretty pleased with myself.

"The general feeling and what people are saying is that *Creed* is your most chart-friendly album to date. Do you agree with that?"

"Do you?"

"Me?"

"Yes. I'm assuming you've listened to the album?"

I'm testing her.

"Of course I have..." She starts to stumble.

She's so sexy when she's nervous.

"...and...yes, I agree with the general consensus. I think that a lot of the songs are holding a softer tone than your previous albums. Especially 'Damned' and 'Sooner.'"

She's garnering focus. Disarm her again.

"Good. Then the point of the album is being received." I give her another smile, enjoying the feeling I get watching her thrown expression.

"So tell me—what would you be doing right now if you weren't talking to me?"

"I'd be catching up with an old friend."

"Um…" She stumbles once again.

I'm enjoying throwing her off balance. It's fun. And seriously hot to watch.

"Okay…it's been a while since you toured, are you looking forward to getting back on the road and playing live again?"

I lean forward, closer to her.

She crosses her legs in front of me.

I can't help but look at them. Fuck, her skin looks so soft. I bet she tastes amazing.

Focus, Wethers. Eyes up. You might be playing, having a little fun here with her, but respect her, remember. Treat her like the serious journalist and writer she is.

I look at her face as an idea starts to form in my mind.

"Playing live is what I love to do, it's what I live to do…and I have a feeling this tour is going to be a very interesting one—probably my most interesting to date," I add, as that forming idea turns into a sudden flash of inspiration.

Oh yes, this is a good idea. A very good idea. It relaxes me for sure.

Tru Bennett isn't going anywhere. Well, not without me, anyway, especially with what I have in mind for her.

"Oh yeah, and why's that?" she asks, interested.

Enjoying my newfound relaxed state, I run my hand through my hair. "I've just had a recent addition to my team, and I know for sure she'll make things different, interesting...better."

I see a hint of what I think is jealousy in her eyes.

Nothing to be jealous of, Tru. But I like that you are.

"And this new addition," she questions. "I'm taking it she's not new a band member?"

Lips pressed together, I shake my head.

"So she's part of the team putting the tour together?"

Yep, she's definitely jealous. "I put the tour together," I assert.

"Right. So she's...?"

"Let's say she does...PR." I hold back the smug grin I feel.

"So tell me about your personal favorites on the album and where the inspiration for them came from?"

Ah this is more like it. Talking music with Tru—I can get on board with this.

We go through the next half hour talking music. It feels like old times, and it passes far too quickly.

I like the fact that she doesn't ask me a single question about Jonny, as I know for sure the next bunch of idiot interviewers will try to do just that.

And it's for reasons like this I love her. Because she has compassion, she cares about people.

She cared about me once. I want that back.

I watch her as she finishes scribbling down my answer to her last question.

Then she closes up her notebook and puts it in her bag.

Fuck, she's done. Time's up.

I don't want her to go.

Even though I'm sure my little plan will work, I have this odd sense of loss creeping up on me.

I need to know when I'm going to see her again.

"Thank you," she says.

"It's been really good to see you, Tru."

"You too." She smiles at me, and it almost cracks me wide open.

She picks up her bag and gets to her feet. I stand too.

"Did you bring a coat?" I ask.

"It's in my bag." She turns to me, looking up at me with those beautiful brown eyes of hers, and my heart starts to fucking hurt. "Thank you again for the interview," she says. "It was great."

"You don't have to thank me; I'd do an interview for you anytime." *I'll give you my whole world if you'll let me.*

"I might hold you to that." She laughs.

"Do."

"Thanks again for your time." She's making for the door.

"So you're heading back to work now?" I ask, following behind her like a lost fucking puppy dog.

I want her to stay. More than anything, I want her to stay, but I can't think up one reason to make that happen.

"Yes," she answers.

"Do you need a ride? I can get Stuart to drive you," I offer.

I see a flicker of disappointment cross her face.

Stupid fucker, why didn't you offer to drive her? It would have given you more time with her, you dickwad.

"It's okay, thank you," she says softly. "I'll walk, it's not far."

Maybe I could offer to drive her now? No, it'll sound too lame and desperate, dumb-ass.

"You're sure?" I ask, just for the sake of something to say. Anything to keep her here for a second longer.

"I'm sure." She smiles and glances at the door.

She wants to leave. Fuck.

I reach for the door handle, then stop.

Dinner. Ask her out for dinner.

"Do you have plans tonight…because I was wondering if you would have dinner with me?"

She looks a little stunned. Good thing or not?

It seems like forever before she answers. "No, I don't have plans, I'm free. Completely free."

A good thing.

I nearly sigh with relief.

"Great. Cool. So we can catch up properly without the threat of an interview hanging over us." I give her a cheeky smile.

"Yes," she says. Her voice has gone all pitchy. She clears her throat and adds, "Sounds like a plan."

"Eight o'clock okay?" I ask, smiling again. It's hard not to around her.

"Eight o'clock is great."

"Write me down your address and I'll come pick you up."

She pulls out her notebook and writes down her address for me.

She hands it over. We touch in the exchange. Heat fills my body again, heading straight to my groin.

I notice her hand is trembling slightly and her skin flushes.

Do I have the same effect on her as she has on me? Maybe, just maybe.

I hold in the huge smile I feel.

A quick glance at her address, then I fold this piece of gold up and put it in my pocket.

I open the door for her, letting her through first. I'm a gentleman for no one but her.

When we reach the main door, I stop and face her.

This is it. Now or never. I need her to leave here thinking of me.

Taking the plunge, I lift my hand to her face, skimming her soft skin. I tuck her beautiful, thick hair behind her ear; I would love to get my fingers tangled up in it.

Leaning down, I press my lips to her cheek, kissing her.

She feels amazing.

Her breathing hitches.

Good sign, Wethers.

I literally have to stop myself from punching the air like the jerk-off I am.

Letting the kiss linger for as long as I can without it getting weird, I resist the urge to pull a move that will fuck everything up, and I move back away from her.

I need to take things slow with Tru if I'm going to get her to be mine.

I want her, but I want her in the right way.

I give her a warm smile. "So I'll see you tonight then." I open the door.

"Yes, tonight. At eight."

She walks through the door, stumbling slightly.

I hold in the laugh I feel. She's so goddam cute.

"Bye, Jake."

She's lingering. A great sign.

"Bye, Trudy Bennett."

She turns and walks down the hall. Yep, she still has an amazing ass.

I watch her walking away down the hall.

The phone in the suite rings, so I reluctantly close the door.

Hearing Stuart talking, I figure the next interviewer is here. I groan inwardly.

The last thing I want to do is sit and talk to some fuck-tard.

What I really want to do is go rub one out and get this Tru hard-on out of my system so I don't try and jump her when I see her tonight.

Actually, that might take a few dates with my hand for that not to happen.

With a sigh, I walk back in to the living room, heading for my cigarettes, hating that she's not here anymore and wondering just what the fuck I can pull out of my sleeve to impress her tonight.

I don't do romance. I do fucking.

Stuart appears in the living room.

Gay guys do romance. They're the closest thing to women.

Stuart will know what romance-type shit will turn her head in my direction and away from her prick of a boyfriend.

"Stuart..." I say, raising my eyebrow. "I need your gay-pertise."

ACKNOWLEDGEMENTS

I want to say my biggest thanks to Jenny Aspinall. I can't say enough about how much you've helped me. We hit the ground running at chapter one, and you saw me through to the end. You held my hand when I went into meltdown (which was often!), you laughed with me, talked Jake and Tru every single day, and I just had an absolute blast doing this with you. You're my rock star, chica!

My next big thanks go to Sali Benbow-Powers and Lori Francis. You both came into TMS at its final stages and rounded off what had already been an awesome experience. Sali, you just absolutely crack me up! I adore your shouty caps—I know I've hit the mark when I get them. And Lori, your Americanising for Jake gave me the biggest laugh I have had in ages! I can't thank you both enough. I truly heart you girls.

Thank you to Gitte Doherty and Totally Booked for all the support you have given me. You will always be my first go-to for my next read. And thanks to Sarah Hansen and Samantha Baer (my Sam squared!) for those last bouts of edits.

As always, humongous thanks to my amazing hubby, Craig, and my two beautiful children, Riley and Isabella. Writing TMS was intense, and you let me be MIA in the urge to get it finished, with no complaint whatsoever. I'm all yours now.

Thank you to Poppet for my beautiful cover design, and to Tattoos by Fabio for use of his amazing artwork on Jake.

Also, a huge thank-you to Renae Porter for the amazingly beautiful book trailer (I still can't watch it without crying!) and for the added touch of Jake's chest tattoo—I love it!

Lastly, my heartfelt thanks go out to you guys—my readers. Without you I'd have no one to share my imagination with. Thank you for taking a chance on me.

About the Author

Samantha Towle began her first novel in 2008 while on maternity leave. She completed the manuscript five months later and hasn't stopped writing since. In addition to *The Mighty Storm*, she is the author of *The Bringer* and the Alexandra Jones series, all penned to tunes of the Killers, Kings of Leon, Adele, the Doors, Oasis, Fleetwood Mac, and more of her favorite musicians. A native of Hull and a graduate of Salford University, she lives with her husband, Craig, in East Yorkshire with their son and daughter.